I0585388

About the Author

Donna Maree Hanson is a traditionally and independently published author of fantasy, science fiction and horror. She also writes paranormal romance under the pseudonym of Dani Kristoff. Her dark fantasy series (which some reviewers have called "grim dark"), Dragon Wine, was first published by Momentum Books (Pan Macmillan digital imprint) in 2014. *Shatterwing: Part One*, and *Skywatcher: Part Two*, are now re-published independently in digital and print-on-demand formats. *Deathwings* and *Bloodstorm* were published in 2017. The final installments in the Dragon Wine series, *Skyfire* and *Moonfall*, were published in 2018.

In April 2015, Donna was awarded the A. Bertram Chandler Award for "Outstanding Achievement in Australian Science Fiction" for her work in running science fiction conventions, publishing and broader SF community contributions. Donna also writes science fiction romance, with *Rayessa and the Space Pirates* and Rae and *Essa's Space Adventures* out with Escape Publishing. *Opi Battles the Space Pirates* was published independently in 2017. In 2016, Donna commenced her PhD candidature researching feminism in popular romance at the University of Canberra. Also available is her epic fantasy series The Silverlands: *Argenterra, Oathbound* and *Ungiven Land*. Donna lives in Canberra with her partner and fellow writer, Matthew Farrer.

You can contact Donna at her website http://donnamareehanson.com
Or sign up to her newsletter, Wing Dust, on her website
Or on Twitter @DonnaMHanson
And Facebook www.facebook.com/donnamareehanson

Also by Donna Maree Hanson

The Silverlands (Epic Fantasy)

Argenterra: The Silverlands Book One

Oathbound: The Silverlands Book Two

Ungiven Land: The Silverlands Book Three

Dragon Wine Series (Dark Fantasy)

Shatterwing: Dragon Wine Part One

Skywatcher: Dragon Wine Part Two

Deathwings: Dragon Wine Part Three

Bloodstorm: Dragon Wine Part Four

Skyfire: Dragon Wine Part Five

Moonfall: Dragon Wine Part Six

Love and Space Pirates (Science Fiction Romance)

Rayessa and the Space Pirates

Rae and Essa's Space Adventures

Opi Battles the Space Pirates

Short story collections

Beneath the Floating City: Short science fiction stories

Through These Eyes: Tales of Magic Realism and Fantasy.

MOONFALL
Dragon Wine: Part Six

By

Donna Maree Hanson

Copyright information

Moonfall first published by Donna Maree Hanson 2018

Copyright © Donna Maree Hanson 2018

The moral right of the author has been asserted.

All rights reserved. This publication (or any part of it) may not be reproduced or transmitted, copied, stored, distributed or otherwise made available by any person or entity (including Google, Amazon or similar organizations) in any form (electronic, digital, optical, mechanical, audio) or by any means (photocopying, recording, scanning or otherwise) without the prior written permission of the author.

National Library of Australia Cataloguing-in-Publication Entry

ISBN   978-0-6482795-4-9 (ebook)

ISBN   978-0-6482795-5-6 (print on demand)

Cover design by www.crocodesigns.com

Edited by Stephanie Smith

Proofread by Jason Nahrung

Map by Russell Kirkpatrick

To report a typographical error or errors, please email donnamareehanson@gmail.com

Dedication

To my circle of family and friends with love

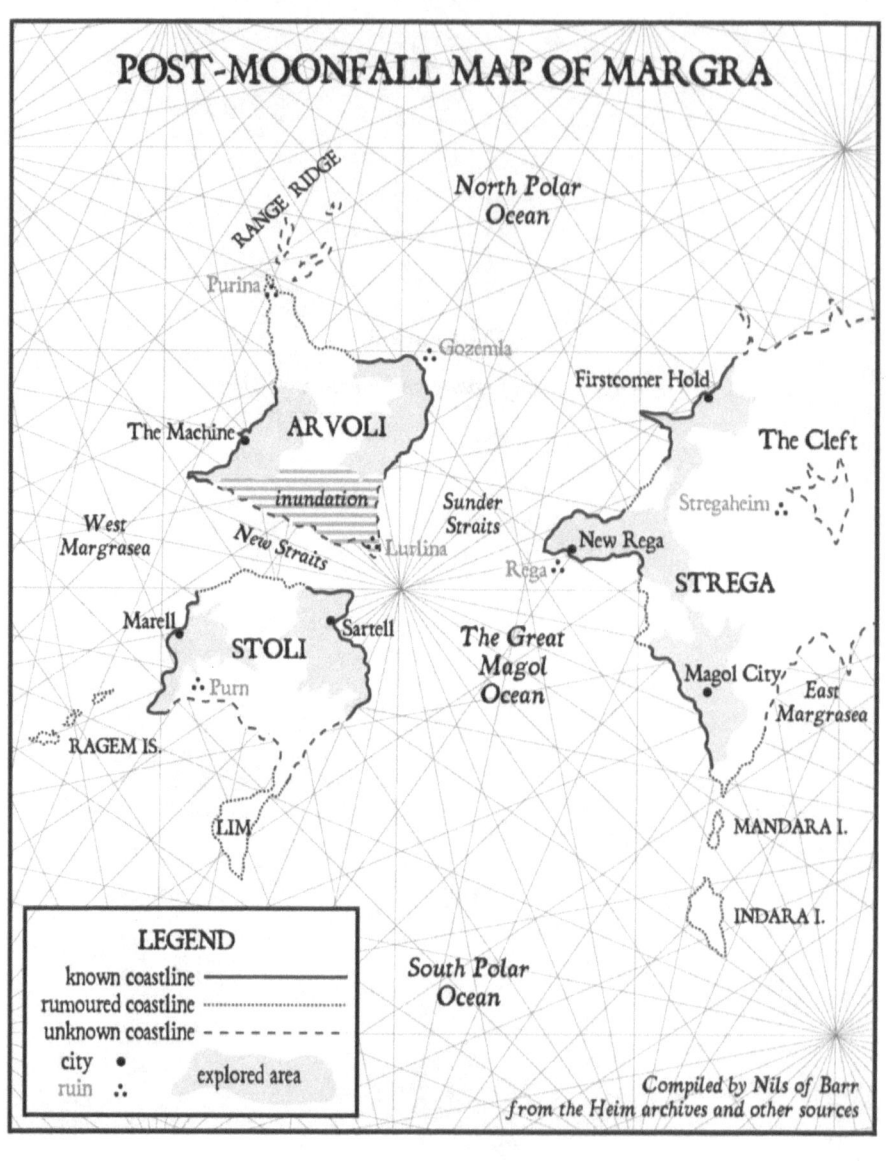

POST-MOONFALL MAP OF MARGRA

RANGE RIDGE

North Polar
Ocean

Purina

Gozenila

Firstcomer Hold

The Cleft

The Machine

ARVOLI

inundation

Sunder
Straits

Stregaheim

West
Margrasea

New Straits

Lurlina

New Rega

Rega

STREGA

Marell

Sartell

STOLI

Purn

The Great
Magol
Ocean

Magol City

East
Margrasea

RAGEM IS.

LIM

MANDARA I.

INDARA I.

LEGEND

known coastline ———————

rumoured coastline ··············

unknown coastline – – – – –

city •

ruin ∴   explored area

South Polar
Ocean

*Compiled by Nils of Barr
from the Heim archives and other sources*

Prologue

Magic and dust swirl and twirl, building momentum as the remains of a dead moon hurtle toward the surface of Margra. Ancient bindings undone, fractured magic and tortured gravity will combine for the final assault. Moonfall has come.

Part 1

Dry cup, dry hearth—a house without dragon wine is not a home.

Chapter One
THE QUEST BEGINS

Salinda surveyed the group heading into the Ways for the trip to the Arvoli continent, noting it was larger than she had anticipated. She had wanted to leave the younger ones behind, but there was no point in trying to keep them safe. If they didn't succeed, there would be no safe.

She shuffled beside Nils, holding the underside of her distended abdomen to relieve the pressure, even though the glide was there for her use. For the moment, she needed the exercise, needed to work off some excess energy and ease the strain in her lower back. Otherwise, she would sit on that glide and fret and nag and nobody would benefit from that.

Her mind was busy with "what ifs?"—What if they didn't find the machine? What if they didn't know how to use it? What if they were too late?

The glow of the cadre in her mind brought comfort and she sensed that it had a keen edge as if its purpose was on the verge of being fulfilled. At the very least, the cadre was not saying she was going the wrong way.

She glanced sideways at Garan. His cadre was quiet, had been since the Ufak Monta had taken possession of him. Even though the Moon Binder spirit had stepped back to allow Garan control over his body, he was subdued, and that worried her. Was it the Moon Binder spirit that was brooding and making plans? Or was the change in Garan's behavior just a side effect, of little consequence? Either way, there was nothing she could do about it right now. They needed Garan and it appeared they needed the Ufak Monta. Unfortunately, they also needed the cadre, and resolving that dilemma would take place in the future.

There were a few more stairs to go before reaching the Way Gate. "Garan, can I lean on your arm?" she asked. She patted Nils on his forearm to signal the change in walking partner, thus giving Nils the freedom to chat to Karol, who had come alongside.

"Of course," Garan said, transferring the tether of the long glide that held most of their supplies to his other hand. He eased his elbow out so she could place her hand there.

"How are you feeling?" she asked him, surreptitiously studying his face.

"Well. Perfectly well," he responded, keeping his eyes ahead. He slowed his pace and put his arm around her to ease her way up the next riser. "You should use the glide," he said with a grunt, as if she weighed as much as a boulder.

Giving him a narrow-eyed glare, she said, "I will when I get to the top." She let out a sigh and looked at him. "Garan, tell me how you really feel...you know...inside."

His violet-colored eyes met hers and he looked away, his cheeks turning pink. "Scared," he said, barely audible. Then he faced her, eyebrows lifting. "Affronted. Curious." Finally, he shrugged. "And more besides."

Salinda nodded as she listened. If it had been her, she'd feel that way. Maybe enraged and angry, too. Garan, though, was a gentle soul, so it was no surprise that he didn't use those terms to describe his inner state. "Curious? Why?"

Garan chuckled, a low sound in his throat. "I have the essence of an alien being inside me." He grimaced, and then shrugged helplessly. "What can I say?"

"You do, but you had a cadre inside you, too. Didn't that prepare you? You know, for another presence inside your mind?"

Garan's eyes widened and he looked ahead, ready to assist her up the next riser. Nils was several steps ahead of them, leading the way, with Karol chatting away excitedly. Garan turned and tugged on the glide tether. "'Tis not the same. The cadre is mostly inert. Its sense of personality is muted. There is power there, but it generally waits for you to touch it and wield it. The Moon Binder spirit has a strong will and sense of identity. It takes over without asking. It dominates. It is so big it makes me cringe. I cannot fathom the depth and breadth of it. I am lost when it comes forward."

Salinda brushed her fingers across his chin. "That is why, Garan, you have to fight it. You have to find a way to touch and hold your own strength of purpose and identity when the Moon Binder tries to take over."

"That is easy for you to say."

"You sensed this being, this spirit, when none of us could. It called to you and summoned you through the Ways and the in-between. No one else can do this except you."

Garan wiped his mouth, rubbed his chin and shook his head. "I know. That is why I am scared. I am not sure I am strong enough. I do not want to fail."

She schooled her features into a mask of purpose. "You cannot fail. You must not fail!" she told him, before deciding she needed assistance after all. "I think I'll use my glide now."

Garan inclined his head. "I will fetch it." He untied it from the back of the supply glide and brought it to her, doing the necessary work to help her get seated.

Once she was on the glide, Salinda could not talk so intimately with Garan. By the look on his face, he was relieved. *Poor Garan*, she thought. *So much power in him and he is so young.* Life was unfair sometimes.

The cadre warmed within her. *What about his cadre?* it suggested.

Salinda frowned. *What about it?*

She knew the answer. The Moon Binder's presence in Garan's mind interfered with the cadre and, possibly, Garan's own inherent power. She would have to test that theory during the journey. They had to know where they stood before reaching the machine. Possibly well before, so that, whatever the results, they could plan.

Salinda usually found long journeys in the Ways tedious, so having a deep problem to think about would help pass the time. No time to be bored. She hoped no one tried to talk to her because she wasn't up for being sociable right now. There were complications to navigate…again.

Nils reached out and touched her hand as she was passing through the Way Gate. "Are you well?" he asked her.

"Yes, quite well," she responded automatically. Truth be told, her feet hurt and her ankles were swollen. She could hardly walk, let alone run. The baby was putting a lot of pressure on her bladder and her nether regions. *Yes, very well indeed*, she thought, mocking herself.

♋♋♋♋♋

Nils consulted his mental map when he reached the third junction. The Way looked to be intact and the in-between glowed healthily. That gave him confidence to continue on. This was a section of the Ways that he had not traveled since awakening from his prison of sleep, and before that he had

3

only come this way once. This was the section of the Ways that led to the continents of Strega and Arvoli. The great city of Stregahiem had been destroyed when Ruel split; Arvoli had been severely damaged, with many of its people fleeing to the Stoli continent.

"Is everything all right?" Danton asked him from behind his shoulder.

Nils turned. "Yes. I am assessing the health of the Way before we proceed."

Danton flashed a grin. "It looks fine to me."

"To an untrained human eye, perhaps. You have not been here before to blow it up." There was a thinness ahead, like the substance of the Ways was nearly dead. It appeared whole at this stage, though, so they might be able to get through.

Danton grunted. "Still sore about that, eh? Well, it kept the nasty folks out of your precious Ways and city. And didn't you do your share of blowing up? I thought Brill said…"

"That demolition cleared a dangerous section of the Ways that were discontinuous and—"

"In danger of being compromised by nasty humans."

Nils inclined his head. "I concede your point. I withdraw my adverse comment."

Danton slapped Nils on the back and it was all Nils could do to stop falling over. "No need. I understand. These Ways mean a lot to you." He cocked his head to study the walls. "I have to say they have been helpful. Saved our skins a number of times."

"Yes, they have. It is just that having humans use the Ways freely makes me uncomfortable. I worry that my elders would not like it, even though they do not exist anymore. Old habits are hard to break."

"Is there a problem?" Salinda yelled from the back of the line.

Danton waved a hand. "All good. We're moving."

Nils stepped ahead of Danton, his shoulder aching from the impact of the man's heavy hand. Danton may have lost weight, but he had lost none of his strength; surely the dragon wine they had plied the rebel with had not had this effect. He pondered Salinda's enthusiastic avowal of the wine's properties. Nils half-turned to regard the rebel, then heard Salinda repeat her question. "No, no problem," he replied, not needing to shout at her as sound carried farther in the Ways.

He took a step into the next section and nothing bad happened. The world did not stop turning or fall on his head. He kept walking, a smile lifting his lips at his fanciful thoughts. Examining the in-between around him, he detected weaknesses. His affinity with the Ways was not so acute here. Peering ahead, he could tell there was something not quite right, something to worry about.

"I like being in the Ways," Karol commented after not talking for a short time. Nils's mind had grown occupied with other concerns and was startled. He jumped, and then looked down at the Hiem child, too small to be called a youth. Karol had not left his side since they had left Barrahiem, only forced to move on when Nils opened the Way Gate and ushered the group through. "Indeed. Perhaps you can tell me what you know about the Ways and I can embellish your understanding. It will pass the time."

Karol peered up at him. "They are alive."

Nils's skin prickled, the boy's comment unnerving him. "Alive? In what sense?"

Karol kept walking and peering at the in-between, his hand reaching out to caress it lightly. His white fingers glowed faintly when they skimmed the surface of the wall and pale blue light spread out from where his fingers touched. "It lives and breathes, and perhaps it thinks and feels."

Jolted, Nils nearly cried out a "No" in denial. Quickly, he calmed himself. This was a child, an untaught child.

Theoretically, the Ways had a symbiotic relationship with the Hiem and the energy gleaned from those passing through kept them healthy and strong. Yet, in these latter days, he had begun to think that that "life" had been lost. However, since he had found Karol, the increase in the light emanating from the in-between had indicated otherwise. And the manner in which Karol spoke of the Ways showed that his views came from his own direct experiences and observations. Perhaps, Nils thought, he should not judge too quickly; the child could know more than he himself.

Nils licked his bottom lip before speaking again. "Do you know what it thinks?"

Karol blinked and gazed at the in-between. He shook his head. "It is trying to say something, only I can't grasp it. Maybe the longer I am here I will figure it out."

Nils shuddered, a sensation of death creeping over him. He decided to stop asking the boy questions and gave the in-between a hesitant and slightly resentful look. It had never spoken to him.

They walked along in companionable silence until the next junction. Here the Ways were less well preserved. There was moisture in the air. They were passing under the New Straits that separated Stoli from Arvoli, which had once been the shallow Arvlen Sea. The inundation caused by Moonfall had changed the landscape. There used to be an isthmus connecting the continents, but that had collapsed in the aftermath of Moonfall, or so the archives said. His work, to prepare a map for their present quest, had shown him the true extent of damage to the world.

Nils raised a hand, signaling those behind to halt. He grabbed Karol's shoulder to make him stop, too, because he had kept walking as if in a dream. Karol started, gasping and turning around to face Nils, his arms rising to clasp his upper arms as if warding off a chill. His face was a picture of misery. Tears gleamed on his upper cheeks.

"It hurts!" he said.

Nils stared and then shut his mouth. The child was obviously referring to the Ways. Nils glanced about him nervously. Could they feel pain?

Gathering his courage, Nils turned to Danton and Brill, Laidan and Eneit, who stood waiting close behind. "I need to inspect the Way. I suspect its condition is not good."

"Do you need help?" Brill asked.

Nils was about to reply in the negative when Garan came forward, passing the tether of the supply glide to Brill. "I will help you."

Nils let out a slow breath. He did not know who was speaking: the Ufak Monta or Garan. Garan had had an affinity with the Ways, even before his possession. Yet something in the tone suggested the Ufak Monta was in control. Nils damped down his nervousness. "Thank you."

Garan stood shoulder to shoulder with Nils. "Water is leaking through the roof."

Nils could not see water coming through, but could sense the dampness and faint sounds that suggested trickles of water. "I suspected as much. But we must pass this way, as we have no means of floating on the sea."

Garan's gaze glowed and Nils backed up a step. This was an effect of the cadre and not something he had seen in the Ufak Monta. The lad was truly unnerving.

The light faded from Garan's eyes. "'Tis sturdy enough for our passage. The return I cannot vouch for." The voice was dead flat, devoid of emotion, so it had to be the Ufak Monta talking. "We should move now before more seismic disturbances alter the structure of the Ways." Then, casually, he put his hand on the in-between. A bluish glow spread out from his hand. The walls of the Way, which had been duller than the previous section, brightened. Nils kept his wonder in check. He had no time to throw questions at Garan, whoever he may be, whatever he may be.

Garan turned and took the tether back from Brill with a nod of thanks and resumed his place next to Salinda in the line. With one last look at the in-between, which had now faded back to dull gray, Nils raised his hand and signaled to start moving. Karol clasped his hand and smiled up at him.

"Did you see that?" Karol asked in a rapt voice. "How did that human do that?"

Nils turned and brushed away the wet strand of long hair that was clinging to the boy's face. "A very special one. Let us move along quickly. The Way is stable now. Unfortunately, it may not remain so."

Nils had a fleeting desire to hold Salinda. Suddenly, he was overwhelmingly grateful that she had come into his life and enriched it with all these humans. If not for rescuing her for his own selfish reasons, he wouldn't be here now in this company. He wouldn't have kin around him. He wouldn't have a reason for living. Or a reason for dying.

Chapter Two
BENEATH AND BELOW

An oppressed mood hung over Garan. The weight of the Ways pushed down on his body, his mind. It was worse in this section where they walked under the sea, where the very fabric of the Ways seemed so thin, so ready to fracture. It was hungry too. Garan fed it, sending a small trickle of power through a finger trailing against the wall. That helped somewhat, and did not seem to deplete the store of power he had inside himself. He had not viewed his power in this way before. However, with the cadre and the Ufak Monta inside him, he could now sense the extent of it. While it awed him, he did not understand its origins, only that it was a part of him, like tissue and blood.

Feeding the Way gave him some comfort, some confidence. There was a whole lot of water up there. He could sense it, moving in tune to Belle Moon and Shatterwing as their mass tore at the fabric of the Ways. That movement, that ever-present tension, was bearing down on the Ways, and on them. The Way had little will to resist; it was easier to crumble, easier to die.

Garan told it otherwise. *You need to live.* It was not impressed with that proposition, but it accepted the energy he gave it. The Ufak Monta fed him information, broadened his understanding of the Ways. His alien possessor had turned respectful and had not taken him over completely. For that Garan was grateful, except there was a problem. The Ufak Monta's presence was affecting him. Garan knew he was changing as a result of the

9

possession and there seemed little chance of fighting it. Garan knew not where the Moon Binder spirit was leaking into the essence of him. It was like a low fever, an infection too invisible to fight.

"That was well done, Garan," Salinda commented as they traveled along.

He did not have to be walking with her, but he did. He wondered why that was so. Why not Laidan, who had started treating him better? He loved hearing her voice, watching her small movements as she walked and talked. Why not there? Why not with Danton, who he admired? No, it was Salinda he drew comfort from. He was drawn to her. Or was it the cadre that was drawn to her, to the other cadre she carried?

That gave him food for thought. "Thank you."

"Was that you or the other?" she asked.

Garan gave her a half-hearted grin. "A bit of both."

"I see," Salinda replied, eyelids lowered, lips drawn together in thought. "I couldn't see well from here. Did you make the in-between glow just now?"

Garan faced her as they walked. "Yes."

Salinda's mouth twitched into a smile. "I gather that is going to help us," she ventured. Her eyes glowed faintly in the gloom of the Ways. He detected a faint ripple of power from her. This made his eyes widen in surprise. He had not felt her use the cadre like that before. She seemed to be assessing the Ways too—or maybe she was assessing him.

"I hope so." Garan looked down and then back at Salinda. "We need to move quickly through this section. I do not wish to alarm you. There is a sea above us, hungry to get in."

The light was fading from her eyes as Salinda shifted to more mundane topics. "I've never been to Arvoli."

Garan nodded. "Me neither. It is said to be flooded. I wonder what that means. What that looks like."

"Me too. I think one of the owners of the cadre came from there. I have visions sometimes of floods."

"Are you sure 'tis not just anxiety? I hear 'tis a common thing when people have a lot on their minds. You are never free from worry, I suspect." Garan shot her a grin.

Salinda laughed out loud. "Oh, Garan, you have a gift for understatement. I thought it was Nils's gift, but you also have it."

Garan pouted as he thought about her comment. Was it him speaking, or the other, or the cadre? Source, it was crowded in his head. He liked it not. He was beginning to lose a sense of himself and his heartbeat quickened at the thought. Change did not come easy and not without pain. Unconsciously blinking a few times as he thought it through, he realized he had already changed. He was different. If he lived through this, would he know himself anymore?

Some hours later, they stopped for a meal. With help from Eneit and Laidan, Garan unpacked dried fungi jerky and flat bread. Nils made them tea over a small burner he had brought. They were safe beneath land now, perhaps under the coast of Arvoli. There was water above, only it wasn't as savage or as hungry. Garan sipped his tea as he chewed, which helped to moisten the dried fungi and made it easier to swallow. They couldn't cook a meal right there in the narrow Way, yet they had to eat something.

"What are you doing?" Garan asked Laidan, who was tugging at sacks on the supply glide.

"I'm looking for the dried fruit. I want something sweet."

Garan joined her and found the particular sack, untying it and handing it to her. Laidan's smile dazzled him, until the Ufak Monta pricked at him with a stab of disdain. Garan shook himself and went to finish his meal.

Laidan went back to Eneit and Brill and shared around the sweet fruit, a mix of lairn apples and melon that grew in the Barrahiem gardens. Salinda required a longer rest than her companions, and Garan was relieved when Danton spoke up, loudly. "I am really feeling my injuries. I need a nap. I hope nobody minds."

After getting a few encouraging replies, Danton stretched out with a blanket and fell instantly asleep. At least, he appeared to be sleeping.

Seeing the odds stacked against her, Salinda bit her lip, shook her head slightly and rested against the supply glide with various sacks supporting her back and knees. Garan fretted about the toll the trip was taking on her fragile health. Then he recalled Brill saying something similar and getting a sharp retort. Not fragile then, but certainly in need of more rest than she was allowing herself.

By the time Danton and Salinda were ready to travel, Garan and the others had the supply glide packed, except for the few items supporting Salinda. Once she seated herself on her personal glide, Garan quickly tied on the remaining packs and they headed off.

Garan sensed when they were fully under the Arvoli continent, the sea having faded from his mind. There was still water above him—a thinner layer. It sat in depressions in the land, filled valleys and swelled lakes. It was not going anywhere.

Nils had halted the group again and descended the junction point stairs. Garan grew agitated as Nils approached a Way Gate that loomed out of the darkness as Nils's light brushed against it. A sense of danger grew suddenly in his gut. Then the Ufak Monta pushed his mind aside, making him run forward, shoving the tether into Brill's hand as he passed by. With possession of his body out of his control, Garan could only be dismayed when he knocked Laidan out of the way, not taking the time to apologize.

"Stop!" his voice boomed. It was deeper and more powerful than his own. "Do not open that Way Gate!"

Nils turned suddenly, his robe swirling about his feet, his long silver-white hair flaring out with the speed of his movement. His silver irises flashed within widened eyes. "What?"

"'Tis flooded. You will drown us if you open that gate," Garan said, coming up alongside Nils.

"I was not going to open it. I was assessing it for that very thing." Nils's chin jutted out.

"My apologies. I can tell you 'tis flooded on the other side. This Way Gate opens in a low-lying area. We need to move on."

"How do you know that?" Nils asked, not quite able to disguise the indignation he was obviously feeling.

Garan sympathized. Nils was the master of the Ways, not Garan. Yet, the creature within Garan experienced the Ways as an extension of itself. As a spirit, untethered by flesh, it could see the Way Gate from inside and out. *A handy trick*, Garan thought sardonically. He envied such an ability and then sighed, realizing he had the ability for the moment.

"I can see it in my mind's eye. I can feel the water like a weight in my mind. We should continue on."

Nils inclined his head. "This we will do."

Garan gave him a salute, a flourish of the hand and fingers that seemed to come naturally, but it was a movement that Garan had never seen or done before.

Nils was momentarily taken aback, and then returned the salute. "How did you know that gesture?"

"Wing dust!" Garan exclaimed and looked at his hand. "I have no idea."

"Was it the Ufak Monta?" Nils asked, leaning in eagerly.

"Could be. Was it a Hiem gesture?" Garan asked.

"Yes," Nils replied, his expression suddenly thoughtful.

"But I thought the Moon Binders were dead and gone before the Hiem came to Margra."

"So did I," Nils replied, his eyes flashing silver as he turned away. "Curiouser and curiouser."

Garan followed him. "Nils, what do you mean?"

Nils kept walking in long strides up the risers to the junction, Garan following behind.

Nils scanned the Way. "I…I am not sure. I am truly surprised. It gives me an urge to scour the archives again. The really old sections that talk of the first years on Margra. I heard only a smattering from school as a child. I have not read them myself. Perhaps…"

"Perhaps the Moon Binders were still here then."

Nils's gaze was distant, his brow furrowed. "I do not know, perhaps…truth is not always truth, is it?"

Garan nodded. "I'm beginning to believe that myself."

Nils continued up the stairs to rejoin the waiting group.

"I think 'tis best we stay in the Ways as long as possible," Garan ventured before heading back to his position.

"Very well, I will do my best," Nils replied.

As Garan passed down the line, Danton caught his hand and shook it. "Thanks for the save."

Garan grinned. "Nils knows what he is doing. I should not have interfered."

"Two heads, they say, are better than one." Danton patted his forearm and let him go.

"Well, we have plenty of heads, so we will succeed."

Garan stopped to check on Laidan and Eneit. "I'm sorry for pushing past you before. Are you two doing all right? Not too tired?"

Eneit snorted. "We are not tired." She brandished her stave and gave Laidan a meaningful nod.

Laidan's hand tightened on her own stave. "Not tired. Just bored. I mean, it's not really interesting down here, is it?"

That was a matter of opinion, Garan thought. "'Tis a bit too interesting above though."

Laidan laughed lightly. "Good point. I'll remember that."

Salinda's eyelids lowered when he returned to her side. "In case you are interested, Garan, I'm very tired," she said and laughed.

Garan grinned, face burning. He gave the tether he retrieved from Brill a slight tug. "I'm sorry to hear you say so, Salinda."

Salinda's light laughter sounded behind him and, ordinarily, Garan would have enjoyed it, but there was something looming ahead. Something dangerous.

"Nils," Garan called.

Chapter Three
HOLDING THE FORT

Squab was happy to remain in the underground city of Barrahiem. The city was more amazing than anything she had ever seen or imagined. Her life on the surface had not prepared her for this. No histories or tales of such places and the people who made them had ever tickled her ears before: life had been too savage and hard. Her mind was befuddled to some degree by a kind of euphoria that claimed her after she had expected to die and hadn't.

Turning her gaze from those who had departed, she let it sweep across the surface of the dark lake below and then to the roof above. The vast cavern had huge rock columns that climbed upward from the lake and from the ground to clasp the roof above. White stone formed the buildings, the covered walkways, the balconies; alien designs decorated the columns and the walls partially glimpsed through archways lit by the ambient light. But if meeting Nils hadn't rocked her sense of reality, being alone with alien children in this wonderland of architecture and culture certainly wouldn't either.

The wonders she had seen vindicated her choice to make her death matter. Yes, the world was ending. She was probably going to be dust like her fellow creatures, who were huddled, like her, in the depths of Margra for protection. It was futile perhaps...but then, maybe not. Not if you listened to that woman, Salinda. She had power that could embolden one, that inspired hope in the despairing. The kernel of optimism inside Squab was planted by the words of that woman, and that kernel was growing, taking over her mental spaces, her heart. Now, she had a purpose. And that made her happy. Even though tears still tracked down her cheeks.

Saying goodbye had been hard. She wanted to fight with Danton one more time. It had been all she could do not to sob when Danton had thanked her for staying behind, saying he owed her. He'd relaxed his posture as he looked around him and flashed her "the grin". The grin that had soothed her soul-riven hurt when they first had met all those years ago. The grin she might never see again.

With the quest party no longer in sight, she realized one of the alien kids, Miraka, was standing at her side. The girl was always ready to run errands. "Do you think they will come back?" the young Hiem asked, breaking into Squab's thoughts.

"I hope so," Squab said, turning to the girl. "Now, are you and your friends up for leading the N'Barek people through the tunnel back to here for resettlement?"

Miraka gave her a weak smile. "It's called a Way and, yes. We just have to wait for the quest group to pass through."

Squab wanted to be alone with her thoughts and came up with a chore for Miraka so that the kid would take off. "Have you taken the children to the gardens to get their breakfast?"

Miraka turned silver eyes in her direction. "No, I didn't know you wanted me to."

"Well, I think it would be good to get them down there so you can teach them to fend for themselves. Take your buddies with you, too. Some know what they're doing and some still need supervision."

Miraka studied her a moment longer, then nodded before backing away. Squab guessed that Miraka knew what Squab was on about, wanting to be alone and all. Savvy, that one, never missed a thing. As the Hiem kid departed, gathering companions along the way, Squab grinned. They were going to get on famously.

As she looked around the once-dead city, she thought about the future, the immediate future. With refugees arriving, it would be bustling. Not like Sartell, which was a ghost town: nothing but the uneasy spirits of the dead and the overwhelming stench of their bodies. If those gathering here were all who remained on Margra, it was a poor beginning, but not entirely hopeless. No, not entirely hopeless. They just had to survive for a new beginning to happen.

And survive they would if Squab had anything to do with it. She sent her gaze back over the city, trying to ignore her turbulent thoughts. She decided to walk down to the lake, take her mind off everything. She was only staying behind because someone had to do it. And, well, it was purposeful. Not long ago she had been going to die pitifully, without meaning to her life or death.

The stairs were clear of dust and the lake's dark surface glittered in the reflected light. Signs indicated the sacred area where no one except Nils was to go. Danton had briefed her on the alien creature's rules. Farther along, she caught sight of the island. The sign said females were able to go there. It looked too far for a casual swim. A short distance later, she found the beach. A hand-painted sign said Rebel Beach and that made Squab chuckle. In the midst of all they had lost, Danton still had a sense of humor. Gazing out over the lake, she saw something floating in the water. "What in the…"

Her heart fluttered and the hairs on the back of her neck lifted as she squinted and puzzled over the object. She shuffled along the beach, leaping over the half-built raft that sat at the edge. There was nothing for it. She had to go in. No time to undress; she dived in and surfaced close by the object. Another stroke of her arms and she let out a startled cry. It was a body. A male, human body. Her gaze shot across the lake surface toward N'Barek, its lights flickering in the distance, looking so innocent. What was going on? How had someone ended up dead? Her mind leaped to murder, but they were meant to be the good people. Her knowledge of people was too tarnished by nasty experiences to consider what good actually meant.

Squab shook her head. There was no time to sink so low in her thoughts of people, but how had one of them ended up in the lake? There were other ways than murder, she supposed. An accident?

A flicker of movement made her turn her head. Another man's body floated nearby. She grabbed the one next to her by the shoulder of its tunic and took a few strokes to grab the other. There was no point in fouling up their water supply with rotting corpses.

Before she had dragged those two bodies to the shore, she spotted another body. A female, a look of surprised horror etched on her face.

How she wished she hadn't sent Miraka on an errand. Now she had to go looking for her. They had to get over to N'Barek before there were more corpses.

🦀🦀🦀🦀🦀

Laidan hated being in the Ways. She acknowledged that they had saved her on a number of occasions, yet they still made her nervous. The worst bit had been the dripping water from the sea above. She had had to use mind techniques to keep calm. *I'm going to die anyway*, she had told herself.

Eneit had taken her hand and squeezed it. Laidan appreciated that. Eneit didn't like it any better than her friend did, but she chose to comfort Laidan.

Nils put up his hand again. Brill paused and she came to a stop behind him. Anticipating that Garan would come racing past, she turned sideways, still holding onto Eneit.

Good guess…Garan was barreling up the path and almost made it past without mishap, then his elbow caught her in the gut. She grunted as the impact squeezed the air out of her.

Eneit grinned, shaking her head. "He did it again. He doesn't know how big he is, does he?" She removed her hand from Laidan's to run fingers through her spiky hair. Her gaze centered on Garan up ahead, her brows knotted in thought.

"Garan is ignorant of a lot of things…he's still nice. You have to consider the package as a whole." Laidan blinked in surprise. She had defended Garan.

"Really?" Eneit turned to her with a stunned expression. "He was my brother's best friend, you know."

"I do. He suffered a lot when Turnet died. It was a terrible accident."

Laidan's memories of that time were patchy, a few glimpses of trauma. She did remember enough to know she had acted badly, and the lectures she'd received from the Master Elder and Salinda were further proof. They kept walking. Laidan felt bored by the dull light and the need to put one foot in front of the other, until a rumble under her feet make her heart *thump*. Before she could say anything there was a yell.

"Hurry," Nils cried, "the Way is collapsing."

Eneit and Laidan shared a look, nodded, then tossed their staves onto the supply glide. It would make running easier, faster.

The vibration she had felt became a low sound in her ear. She touched the wall of the Way and it rippled under her fingers.

"This way," Brill shouted at them as he followed Garan and the others down the junction stairs toward a Way Gate.

Wind tossed her hair, and a damp, moldy smell came from the Way in front of them. The low rumble was growing louder, the wind in her face laced with damp.

Laidan ran just behind Eneit who had the tether to the supplies. Thank the source Eneit was practical like that.

Laidan had to fight the panic in her mind, the panic that wanted to push the girl out of the way so Laidan could get out. *Must get out.*

"Hurry," Nils cried again.

The angry noise coming from the Way grew louder, drowning out other sounds, and her feet found it difficult to find purchase as the ground began to pitch this way and that.

Eneit flagged. Whizzing through the air ahead of them, Salinda turned around on her glide. "Hurry, you two."

A crack opened above them. Water gushed down, nearly sweeping Laidan from the stairs.

Garan opened the door and water rushed in. Laidan was flat out trying keep a forward momentum as the floodwaters pushed against her thighs. The crack above them opened wider, bringing a deluge.

Eneit was nowhere to be seen. "Eneit?"

The girl *whooshed* up behind Laidan, breaking the surface of the water, tether in her hand. The water had swept her backward. Coughing and spluttering, Eneit tried to get to her. Mouth tight, she pushed forward against water that was waist high. Laidan went back and grabbed for her hand.

The supply glide had stayed above water, adjusting to the change automatically. At least their food was not wet.

A square of gloomy light signaled where the outside was. Eneit's hand kept slipping from hers until, finally, Laidan firmly gripped Eneit's wrist. The girl's face was tight with panic. Despite their swimming lessons, Eneit had little confidence in the water, especially in a strong current.

"Laidan?" It was Garan. She turned and saw him coming toward her. She was losing her footing as water and mud pushed against her feet.

"Reach for me," Garan commanded.

Holding tight to Eneit, Laidan stretched her arm, her hand slapping the water just short of Garan. She wanted to wail in despair, and then Garan reached to take her hand. "Do you have a strong hold on Eneit?" he yelled above the churning of the inundation.

"Yes," she assured him.

A tug on her arm, strong and sure, pulled her toward the Way Gate. Garan powered through the current as if there wasn't one. Before she could react, she was through to the outside.

A sound like a scream issued from the Ways as the roof gave way and a fist of wind punched them. Nils stepped forward to shut the Way Gate and it slid closed, cutting off the sounds of destruction from within.

Eneit was crying; hair normally spikey was flat against her head, her hand gripping the supply glide's tether so tightly her fingers were white.

Brill came up and embraced her, splashing water as he walked. "You're safe now, Eneit."

Eneit accepted his embrace and nodded, wiping away tears that rolled down her face.

They were knee deep in water, but safe. Salinda asked if they were all right, along with Danton, who said it had been a very close call.

Laidan looked around. They were in a narrow ravine with high walls around them. She could see a blush of red on the horizon and a black sky, although there was a growing light. She walked behind the others to the edge of the ravine, sloshing through the water, which now came to mid-calf. Ahead lay a flat plain, with scattered small mounds of earth, like miniature mountains. Water ranged as far as they could see. It was flooded still after all these years.

Eneit came alongside to slide her fingers through Laidan's and squeeze them. They were so lucky to be alive. They all congratulated themselves and thanked Garan and Nils for saving them.

"Here comes the sun," Garan said.

Their collective sigh filled the air as brilliant white, yellow, pink and red outlined the clouds. The black sky overhead was combed with light gray. Laidan had never seen anything like it. It was truly auspicious. She hugged her arms to her chest, suddenly chill. It really was a special day. Perhaps their last one. Laidan found that hard to process and didn't bother trying. One day at a time. That was the way it had to be.

Garan waved an arm. "Follow me. We need to walk to the next gate and hope that the collapse is isolated to that section only. Then we will know if we can return to the Ways."

Nils turned to them. "Be alert. We may not be alone."

Laidan nodded to herself, then watched Salinda's dark gaze lift to the sky. She could sense dragons, couldn't she? Did she feel them now?

Salinda caught her look and shook her head slightly. Her hand rubbed at a spot on the side of the bulge that passed for her middle.

Eneit retrieved their staves and handed Laidan's to her. Straight away, Laidan felt better.

Chapter Four
THE ARVOLI PLAIN

Danton swallowed a hard lump in his throat. He was standing on another continent. In a place that was once a home for millions of living, breathing people, but from where they stood there was scant evidence of prior occupation. If he believed Nils, then the Way Gate stood where there once had been a thriving city, or large town, and now it was an empty ravine, partially filled with green-colored water, with a skin of algae on top.

After taking a few moments to recover from their close scrape with the collapsing Way, they decided to walk, or wade, through the water. Garan had been ahead to assess another Way Gate that was nearby, but was shaking his head, letting them know in that silent way of his that they could not return to the Ways for this part of the journey.

"Which direction?" Danton asked, trying to smile at the lad. He had to admit it made his balls twitch just thinking that Garan had some ancient, alien spirit inside of him. Salinda, and Mez before her, had carried the cadre and, really, wasn't that kind of like the same thing? Was he being selective in his prejudice?

Garan pointed ahead without smiling, or even acknowledging him in the normal friendly way that he used to.

Brill caught his eye and Danton nodded. "Okay then," Danton said, "let's go." His gaze drifted to Salinda, who was talking quietly with Nils as he walked alongside her glide. Danton wished she wasn't there, wasn't risking herself and the unborn child. It wasn't his business, though, and besides, who was he to stop Salinda? He shook his head, annoyed at his own arrogance. This was her day. The day she'd been working toward since she was a teenager in the prison vineyard. They were going to use the cadre *she* had been carrying, all this time, to stop moonfall. Salinda had every right to be there and he should support her.

23

Nils looked up then and Danton lifted a hand to acknowledge him. "Do you mind walking with us, Danton?" His gaze shifted. "And you, Brill?"

Danton detected the disturbance in the air that indicated Brill had come along behind him.

In his hand, Nils had the tether to the glide with the supplies. Eneit had done an amazing job to keep hold of it after being swamped. She had needed to take a break.

Nils had been relegated to a quest follower, rather than leader. Garan and his invisible hitchhiker had assumed the leadership of the group, as far as traveling through the Ways went. Danton looked toward Garan who was now a good hundred strides ahead.

Eneit and Laidan followed behind the Skywatcher, their staves held at an angle, at the ready to bring them to bear on any attackers: they were very serious about this and rightly so. Eneit was particularly vicious with the stave and both of them had increased their fitness. Neither of them had complained during the long trek so far. That Laidan hadn't been complaining surprised Danton most of all. It was certainly a sign of her new maturity after healing from her injuries and recovering at least some of her memories.

Danton didn't let his guard down as they sloshed their way across the plain. Nils hadn't given any particular reason for having him and Brill walk with them, but then he noticed Nils often looked at Salinda and seemed very fidgety. When Danton studied Salinda from under lowered eyelids, he realized what was worrying his Hiem friend. He was nervous about Salinda; two spots of color adorned her cheeks and her face was moist with sweat. Danton was happy to lend Nils some comfort with his presence. He knew Salinda well enough not to directly enquire if she was all right. So he continued to make small observations on their surroundings, while his boots squelched and the legs of his trousers became wetter and wetter, if that was possible. It wasn't cold, so that was something. While they walked, the sky lightened to a shade of mottled ash and pale smoke, and the clouds sat there as if they didn't expect to be parted by a falling moon anytime soon.

The view ahead and to the side changed after they left the ravine. What had seemed to be earthen lumps in the distance now turned out to be the remains of buildings that had collapsed in on themselves through the passage of time and the never-ending flow of rain, wind and sun. Nils pointed out key features of the ruined city. Danton took it all in, unable to hide his amazement.

They tracked around the bottom of the first ruined building. A cry from Laidan had him running forward to find she'd been startled by thick metal prongs poking up from the earth, which had, at first, looked like a giant grasping hand. A play of light on the metal spikes had given the impression they were moving.

Danton eyed them warily. "Easy done," he said to Laidan. "Keep being alert."

Garan, Laidan, Eneit and young Karol kept moving ahead of them. Danton stood still waiting for Nils, Salinda and Brill to catch up. He gazed at a decayed gray, lifeless mound and thought about the people who once lived here. It was nothing like Sartell or the other towns. This was a piece of history sent to remind them of past glories, and how little they had advanced since Ruel split.

He moved on when the others reached him. The next mound was similar and they checked for signs of life before quickly moving on. Ahead were twin mounds, not as tall as the other single ones, and broader. Light glinted off something in these and Danton's nerves went on high alert.

"Danton," Salinda said, a hint of warning in her voice.

"What is it?" Danton asked out the side of his mouth, keeping his gaze locked on the twin mounds.

"Dragon," she said, awe in her voice.

"Shit," Danton said, reaching for a weapon. "Wing dust! How are we to fight that?"

"We don't," Salinda replied calmly. "I can feel its mind. It has a full belly. It's not interested in us."

"Sure it's not! Let's give it a wide berth, in any case." He jogged up to Garan and told him to give the twin mounds a miss. A glint in Garan's eyes disturbed Danton, yet Garan replied, "Very well."

Garan changed direction, moving off to the side, at a right angle to the twin mounds. Danton couldn't make out the dragon and wondered what was glinting silver.

There was a familiar sound of wings disturbing the air and Danton tensed, waiting to be swooped upon. A large dragon with brilliant silver scales now passed overhead. It was small and sleek, with wings that were almost transparent. Not like a Stoli dragon at all. It called out once, a musical sound that did not shred his eardrums. He cast a glance at Salinda who was regarding him with a smile on her face.

"What?" Danton said.

She shook her head. "Nothing bad. It's an Arvoli dragon. Something rare and unique. I feel that it has a story. There aren't many of them left. I sense its loneliness. Arvoli dragons live off food found in the water and the sea."

Danton allowed himself to admire the glorious beauty of the beast as it faded from view. The pearlescent scales had been reflecting the light and that was what he had been seeing before they disturbed it.

"May we resume our original path now?" Garan called.

"Yes, yes," Danton said and waved. He didn't care if they thought him overly cautious. His companions started forward. Salinda cried out then and Danton spun around, expecting an attack. Nils leaned over Salinda and Danton saw he was rubbing her lower back.

"Salinda is uncomfortable," the Hiem explained.

Danton blinked, paused, waiting for his brain to filter his response. Then he came right out with it. "Are you in labor, Salinda?"

Her pain-filled gaze met his. "No," she replied, staring at him and daring him to contradict her. Her gaze swept left to where Nils stood. Danton slowly lowered his head, interpreting her look and suspecting that she did not wish to alarm Nils.

"Well then, you will let us know if and when that happens."

"I will," Salinda replied and closed her eyes as Nils rubbed her back as he walked and she sat on her glide.

Danton squeezed his hands into fists. Things were about to get complicated. "Wing dust!" he said softly to the air in front of him. He increased his pace to join Brill up ahead. He might have to whisper in Brill's ear to make sure the lad was ready.

It took most of the day to reach the next Way Gate. Nils and Garan whispered together for ages before even approaching it. Like there was some kind of rivalry between them about who knew the Ways better. Personally, Danton liked that there was more than one opinion. It gave him another level of reassurance.

Nils opened the Way and Garan stepped through. Nils held the Way Gate open. Danton whistled under his breath as he studied the design on the exterior. Now that he knew what they were, their design was distinctive. They weren't all the same, just similar. He wasn't sure what this design translated to. He guessed it was the name of the place the Way accessed.

Garan came out. "'Tis not safe. We need to skip this one and head for the next."

"Damn," Salinda said behind him.

Danton walked up to Nils and Garan. "Just how unsafe is it?"

Garan's head shot up. "We are not far enough away from the collapsed section."

"We are past it though, right?" Danton asked.

Garan's eyes narrowed. "Yes," he said after a time, "but I do not—"

"I don't think we can afford to spend the night out here. And as we are all going to die if we don't get to the machine in time, maybe we should risk it."

Nils blanched at his remark. Garan just tilted his head slightly to one side. "Your point is well made. But if there is another collapsed section barring our passage we will have to double back to this Way Gate."

"Can you tell if this section is collapsed at any point?" Danton asked.

"The signal here is not strong, it could mean there is damage. We could aim for the next gate. It is not far. This land was densely populated and there are many gates."

"If there are many Way Gates then maybe we won't have to backtrack far. I say we go for it," Danton said.

"Very well, we will enter here." Garan looked around. "The water is less in this area so we will probably not have to worry about flooding."

Nils opened the Way Gate again and Garan stepped inside.

Following, Salinda slipped past him on her glide. "I didn't realize you were such a pessimist. I hope to die of old age. What about you?"

"I already am old."

Salinda laughed and disappeared inside. Brill gripped the supply glide tether and entered, followed closely by Karol, Laidan and Eneit. Nils waited to shut the Way Gate after himself.

It was instantly dark. Normally, it was possible to see a little in the Ways, the dull gray walls casting some light, but this was pitch-black. Danton could taste dust and damp.

"Lights," Danton called. "We need lights."

27

Compared to the Ways they had traveled previously, this Way was definitely dead. He asked Garan about it.

"Mostly dead," Garan said, deadpan.

"Oh. Good," Danton replied, accepting a light from Nils.

"Hand out some rations, will you, Brill? I think we can eat and walk for the moment."

"How much longer?" Danton asked Garan.

"If the Way is uncompromised we will arrive at our destination by sunrise."

"Wonderful. I want this done, over with."

"Arriving is the least of it," Garan replied. "There is much to be done and not all is clear. If the Way is not functional I fear our plans are..."

"Screwed," Danton said.

Garan looked at him. "Correct."

"Look, Garan," Danton began, stopping to take a bite of some bread Brill handed to him. "I'm pessimistic already. I don't need you to make me feel suicidal."

Garan's head tilted to the side again and his expression was quite un-Garan-like. "You are a strange man, Danton. I do not always understand you."

"Believe me, the feeling is mutual these days," Danton said, a shiver running down his spine. "Who am I talking to anyway? You or the beast within?"

Garan's expression soured. "You seek to amuse yourself at my expense. I am who I am, who I need to be. I have stopped complaining and fighting against it. I had hoped you would, too."

"Right, so it's both of you. I don't envy you, Garan."

Danton patted Garan on the shoulder and moved off to talk to Brill—he wanted the young rebel on his guard. Nothing was predictable in this situation. They could trust Garan, but with that being inside him, there was no telling when things would get a bit crazy. Danton wanted to be ready. He wanted to keep the damage low. He wanted Garan back whole, though he wasn't sure if that would be possible.

Karol came running up to him. "Nils wants to talk to you."

"Coming," Danton replied and gave Garan a departing salute. To his surprise, Garan returned a salute so intricate and patterned that Danton nearly fell over in surprise. What the hell was that? He felt more uncertain and afraid than ever. He didn't like not being able to weigh up the odds, not being able to plan.

"What's up?" Brill said as he came abreast of the young rebel.

"Nils wants to talk. Keep an eye out for trouble."

"I am," Brill said and looked meaningfully behind him to where Garan loomed in the shadows.

Good, Danton thought. He wasn't alone in his worries. A moan in the dark sounded loudly.

Salinda!

Donna Maree Hanson

Chapter Five
NEVER A GOOD TIME

Salinda finally had to admit that there was something wrong. She was in labor. That had been the fifth contraction. She'd been denying the fact to herself, as well as to her companions.

Nils huddled close to her, not quite sure what to do if his fidgeting was anything to go by.

Danton came at a run. "Salinda!"

"Yes," she said, meeting his gaze and willing him not to scold her. "It's coming. Early stages, I think."

"How long will it take?" Nils asked.

Salinda turned to glare at him. "Really? You are asking me that? I don't know."

Nils shook his head. "You do not know how long the birthing process takes?"

"I...er..." Salinda considered. "No. Not unless the cadre knows."

"And what does the cadre say?" Danton asked, a frown marring his forehead.

"Not much. I can't really communicate with it right now. Not until this pain eases."

Salinda cast her gaze around the group that was now drawing up near her. "Anyone know anything about birthing babies?"

Garan didn't even register the question. Laidan tilted her head as if she was trying to remember something. That didn't inspire confidence. Karol gaped as if he had just been slapped. That would be a no. Eneit clenched and unclenched her stave. "Eneit?" Salinda prompted.

Eneit shook her head. "I can't. I don't," she gulped, her shoulders sagging.

Salinda smiled, surprised by the relief she felt. "Eneit?"

The girl sighed long and loud before meeting Salinda's enquiring gaze. "I helped my mother deliver children a few times. I was learning, you see, but you can't rely on me. I've not done one by myself. I'm too little. I'm a child."

Salinda laughed at that. Most of the time Eneit pushed the fact that she was grown up.

Her gaze shifted to Brill who was carefully studying his boots.

That left Danton, who was finger-combing his hair. "Well then, I think we have a team of two: me and Eneit."

"You?" Salinda stared. "What do you know about giving birth?"

"A little. I grew up on a farm," Danton said, his eyes dark and serious.

"That's not the same thing."

"Similar concept," Danton said with a grin.

Salinda allowed herself to be reassured by Danton's casual confidence.

"Can I do anything?" Nils asked, although the shaking in his voice indicated that it was the last thing he wanted to do. "I don't know anything about birthing babies."

"Just moral support," Salinda replied.

Garan walked forward. "We must keep moving. 'Tis not too far."

Danton twisted his mouth, thinking. "As you aren't having it right now, that's good news. Do you need to lie down? We can put you on the larger glide with the supplies."

The contraction had eased off and her backache lessened. "I am all right for now. At the moment, it's not bad."

Garan strode ahead, not waiting any longer. The rest of them fell in behind him. Danton and Nils flanked Salinda as her glide skimmed over the ground.

Salinda refused to be abashed by being in labor. Birth was a natural process. If she had been thinking straight, she could have found a midwife among the refugees and brought them along. Too late now, she had to make do with what she had. When the child was born, she would still be ready to fight. It was all a matter of timing. She had no control over that. She shook her head and bit her bottom lip.

"What is it?" Danton asked.

"Nothing," she replied, but then spoke up. "I have to prepare for what's ahead. I need time to think."

"Well, then...let me know if anything changes. I think we can up the pace a bit. I'll go chat to Garan."

Danton sprinted away. Salinda watched him converse with Garan. Nils reached over and squeezed her hand. "I recall childbirth is painful. I hope it is not too bad for you."

A few smart comments came easily to her lips and she bit down on them. Nils meant well. "I do too." Her gaze narrowed. "How do the Hiem give birth...I mean, how did they?" she asked.

Nils looked forward, his expression distant as if he was remembering something. "In the lake was the tradition."

"A water birth. It makes sense. This child was conceived in water, in the lake."

A look of pain crossed his features. "That seems so long ago. I was so angry then. So consumed in my own misery. I fear I was not nice to you."

Salinda squeezed his hand companionably. "We have done all right."

Danton came back at a jog. "You okay to pick up the pace, Nils? We are going to run for a bit. You can hitch a ride on the glide if you need to."

Nils straightened his back, his chin up. "I can run. Thank you for your concern. I am quite well."

Salinda's eyebrows drew together at this. Nils did not cough as much as he used to. The sojourn in the healing tray may have effected a deeper healing. Of that she was glad. His ongoing cough and fatigue had always worried her. She'd never thought they would get this far. She smiled to herself. They had achieved a lot. Unfortunately, it wasn't over yet and there was no prize for second place. They either would win or lose. No second chances.

"Good," Danton replied. "I'm going to put a tether on your glide, Salinda. Just hold on and I'll tug you along."

"Thank you." Now that her body was quiescent, she sent a barb into the cadre. "You need to help me figure out what I am going to do."

She had to readjust her balance from tipping too far backward when Danton put on a burst of speed. They were all running now, following Garan.

"Well," she asked the cadre, "what are my options?"

The cadre warmed and she sank into it. Strangely, it replayed recent

33

moments in her life. It showed the room in which she'd found Garan possessed by the Moon Binder spirit; Nils was there and the creature in Garan was speaking: *You have part of the solution in you, as does this vessel. Divided, it won't work.* Salinda held tight to the glide as she considered this memory. She hadn't understood it at the time, had thought it meant the cadre. And, obviously, the cadre believed the words were important.

Lights flared in the dark, bobbing up and down with the movement of the runners. Distracted by her surroundings, she forced herself to reflect on the words and almost understood them, but then a contraction took over. Her abdomen tightened and she rested her hand on it as the pain peaked more powerfully than the previous ones.

"Was that another contraction?" Danton asked, the lamplight giving his tanned features a grayish cast.

She nodded, still experiencing the contraction, unable to talk. Danton kept running, putting on another burst of speed. Salinda gritted her teeth and held on, losing touch with the cadre.

After nearly an hour, the pace slowed to a jog. Danton huffed and puffed in front of her, and Nils's breathing had grown ragged, but she didn't have time to worry about him. She was concentrating on keeping her seat. The alternative—being strapped to the supply glide—did not appeal. She didn't think she'd like to have contractions while being in that position. In fact, she had a desperate need to walk, only waiting until they stopped for a break before doing so.

Danton looked around. "There is a gate here. We need to exit as the Way ahead is blocked."

Nils glanced at her sideways, his silver eyes picking up the light from the handheld lamps. "I will go forward and consult with Garan."

"Fine," Salinda said, giving his hand a squeeze.

Danton had been right to insist they travel as far as they could in the Way. Now they had to exit. It took them a few more minutes to reach the opened Way Gate. A smell tickled her nostrils, a reek of tainted water, and she was puzzling this out when she passed through the exit. Water sloshed around her as everyone trod through it. Garan held a light to illuminate their path.

Fatigue plagued her. Another contraction came and went. Salinda was tempted to sleep sitting up. It was very late at night, perhaps the early hours of the morning, and she just wanted to close her eyes, although she also wanted to be alert and awake. The short break they had had did not make up for a lack of sleep. She had not had a proper sleep for many weeks; the baby inside her did not allow such a luxury.

The glide traveled at a consistent pace, and Salinda found her eyelids drooping. Soon she was dreaming. She was aware she was dreaming. She dreamed that she was awake and riding on the glide. Then she lost awareness. She didn't know for how long. A deep roar jerked her awake as did the cries from her companions.

Her gaze shot to the sky. Meteorites were burning a path through the heavens. For one panicked moment, Salinda didn't know what to do.

"Take cover," Danton yelled. The water was everywhere, although it seemed shallow enough. Its dark surface reflected the flame trails of the meteorites, confusing the eye.

Dark shapes loomed nearby. *Rocks?* she wondered. She was about to find out, because that's where Danton was headed, the others doing the same and disappearing behind dark, irregular shapes.

"It's highly unlikely that they will land on us," she commented to Danton, who crouched next to her.

"With our luck, I'm sure the probabilities are high. Besides, it's the dust and heat resulting from each impact that I'm worried about." He glanced at the water. "And steam."

The meteorites hit the ground with such a roar that Salinda felt the pressure block her ears. Then the wind fluttered cool, before blasting hot. She clung to Danton's shoulder, bending her head close to his. The other hand she put over her mouth as dust swirled around them and filled their surroundings. The water peaked in waves that sloshed around the base of the rocks. She heard cries and realized that the rest of their group may not have gotten off as lightly as she and Danton. He had chosen their shelter well.

Salinda kept thinking the wind would lessen, except it grew stronger. Her exposed skin hurt and steam rose up from the ground. "Danton?"

He jumped on the rock to keep his feet out of the water. Salinda hoped the others were able to do the same. Danton hung there, the light now dangling from his belt, gripping the rock with fingers and toes, panting like crazy.

She edged the glide closer to Danton, using him to shelter from the wind and dust pummeling them. Gradually she felt the strength of the disturbance was lessening. It was still hot and windy, but the dust didn't bite as much as it had. The water beneath their feet was less agitated.

However, the hail of rocks from Shatterwing was only going to increase over time. The sooner they reentered the Travel Way, the better. There was no guarantee of safety in there, of course, but she would feel better mentally and emotionally.

Danton tentatively lowered his boot-clad foot into the water and drew it out again. "It's still too hot."

೧೧೧೧

Nils shivered and clung to the boulder he was sheltering behind. The water bubbled up beneath him. Never before had he experienced such a thing. His previous celestial encounters had been through a telescope, or read about in the archives. Even worse, these were small meteorites, nothing like Moonfall. Ashamed of himself and the fear he experienced, he almost wept.

"How are you holding up?" Brill asked, breaking into Nils's thoughts. The young rebel was lower down, to the right of him. Brill's light hung at his belt, casting erratic shadows on his face, his eyes and mouth becoming dark holes.

Nils just groaned, because he could not form words yet. The violent bubbling of the water began to lessen. Steam still rose off the surface and Nils sweated. He wished he had a glide like Salinda, then felt remorseful. He had not thought of her at the moment of crisis, when his instinct for survival had cut in. Reliving that moment of terror, he did not think he had ever moved so fast.

Dust tickled in the back of his throat and, as the cough fought to surface, the more desperate he became to suppress it. He recalled the hacking coughs that had formerly plagued him, knew how they possessed his whole body. He couldn't afford that now, knowing he would lose his grip and fall into the hot, watery soup below.

He tried a light clearing of his throat, which only made the urge to cough stronger. Tears dripped down his cheeks; he was a fearful, shivering wreck. He gently cleared his throat again, but he could not suppress it: he coughed and coughed again. The fingers on his right hand lost their grip and his foot slipped. Panic made breathing more difficult. The stench of boiling stagnant water made his throat spasm. He fought and fought to maintain his grip as he was possessed by a fit of coughing.

"Careful," Brill said, "the water is still hot."

36

Nils caught himself and established another hold. Then he coughed again and slipped a bit farther down. His fingertips bled as they clung to the boulder's rough surface.

A breeze sprang up, a cooling breeze that built the water into little waves. A blue glow issued from behind one of the boulders and cries sounded from Laidan and Eneit. Something was happening.

"Hello?" Brill called out. The cooling wind grew in strength, ruffling Nils's robe and Brill's hair. Frowning, Brill looked at Nils. "I'm going to test the water again. I think that's a cool current coming through."

Brill dipped his fingers in and waited. "It is still warm though no longer boiling. I think you can climb down now." Brill waded toward the boulder in front.

Nils slid, scraping his fingers and toes as he did. Once on the ground, standing in the water, he bent over and coughed the dust from his throat and lungs. For an interminable moment, he could not breathe and then the spasm eased.

"Source preserve me!" Brill blurted. Nils moved over to him and saw what the boulder had obscured from view. His jaw dropped.

Garan hung suspended in the air, a light blue glow surrounding him. Eyes closed and arms outstretched, Nils thought maybe Garan was praying, or doing some kind of worship. His feet hovered above the water, which swirled around him faster and faster. Nils looked to see the air stir the water, saw a funnel extend upward. Nils realized that Garan was calling forth water and air and cooling it. Laidan ran over, creating a foamy trail, and grabbed Brill by the arm, shouting excitedly, "Can you see? Can you see?"

Eneit stood behind her, eyes wide and head shaking as if denying what her eyes were seeing. Nils could sympathize. He had never seen or heard of anything like this.

Soon the water around Nils's feet was cool. Danton came splashing over to him and jerked to a stop. "By the great dragon's holy ass."

"What is it?" Salinda said, drawn along by the tether in Danton's hand. She was rubbing her back again. "Oh," she said and gaped along with the rest of them.

Karol came striding over, lifting his feet high and holding his robe out of the water. "It's the Ufak Monta. It said it didn't have time for this and, *boom*, there it was."

The funnel overhead slowed and dissipated. Rain fell around them, soon becoming a drizzle. Garan lowered to the ground, the water coming up to his ankles, and the glow faded. Garan opened his eyes and Nils shivered at what he saw in them. Garan's normally violet-colored eyes blazed blue with power.

"We must move now. The next Way Gate is close by," Garan's voice said. Nils knew it was the creature speaking. He wondered again why this Ufak Monta had been sequestered in a sealed room in the bowels of Barrahiem. That signified it was dangerous, yet this creature had just helped them without being asked.

Why did this creature exist? Previous attempts to elicit information from the beast had resulted in little. It had seemingly given control of Garan's body back to Garan, but it kept intervening, taking over with overt signs of its power. If they hadn't been trying to save the planet, maybe Nils could have indulged his curiosity. Right now, they had to trust. Nils usually found doing that difficult, but it came easier these days. His kind had survived, so now he must make sure everyone stayed safe.

"Come," Garan said, turning, expecting them all to follow.

Nils let out a sigh and starting sloshing after him. His robe was already wet so he didn't bother to lift it out of the water, although he did have to tug and pull at it when it clung to his legs. Ahead, backlit by the rising sun shooting bands of red across the horizon, loomed a cliff face. Not too high, it was enough to indicate that a Way Gate might be situated there and, as they trod closer, Nils detected the signs. The way the rock was shaped, its color and position.

Garan's course never wavered, seeming to know exactly where it was, as if the Travel Ways were part of him. Nils sucked in a sudden breath. What more proof did he need that there had been more interaction between the Moon Binders and his ancestors than was generally known? Then Garan climbed up to a raised area in front of the Way Gate. Nils drew closer and saw that it was a ledge. Garan leaned down with his hand outstretched. Nils grabbed hold and was lifted effortlessly up to join Garan.

Danton and Brill called to the others and they all helped each other up to the ledge.

Nils studied how Garan opened the Way Gate. There was no chant as a Hiem would use. Garan performed a ritualized bow, kissing the ground, and then he pressed the locks in sequence. The door opened and its dark maw beckoned.

Chapter Six
THE WAY IS
BLOCKED

Brill stepped into the Way warily. Laidan flanked him and Eneit was just ahead of him. The girls were quiet, despite whispering feverishly together after Garan had pulled his superhuman trick of levitating and calling forth cool air and water.

"The Way is intact," Garan said in a monotone that was uncharacteristic of him. Brill suppressed a shiver.

"That is good news," Nils replied.

"So we are only slightly behind schedule," Brill observed. Laidan flashed him a nervous smile and nodded.

A groan from behind brought Brill back to reality. He'd been dreaming of a short nap given that they had run and jogged through the Way for some time before the meteors struck.

He moved a little farther into the Way, making room so that Karol could edge past him and Brill could share a word with Danton.

Danton pushed Salinda's glide ahead of him through the gate gently as she seemed unable to control the glide herself. Her face was tight with pain.

Brill lifted a hand to catch Danton's attention. Danton was focused on the glide until they drew abreast of each other. "How is she?" Brill whispered.

Danton's shadowed, haggard face showed distinct signs of worry. "Ask her. She doesn't say much."

Brill grimaced and repositioned himself to catch Salinda's eye. She glared at him. She'd obviously overheard.

"Managing all right there?" Brill asked in an attempt to appear casual.

"I'm alive." Salinda looked up and Brill followed suit. The ceiling was alight with stars.

"What?" he exclaimed.

Danton joined them. "Glowworms have taken up residence."

"They do not harm the Way," Garan said, coming alongside them. "We need to move on. 'Tis not far now. This section of the Way is healthy and when the Way is healthy we can move faster."

"Oh, good," Brill said, and then put his hand out to stop Garan turning away. "That thing you did..."

Garan met Brill's gaze. "I did what had to be done. This body contains much untapped power. This vessel is ignorant of its abilities."

Brill's stomach clenched. He was talking to the daemon spirit of a being from another race. Chills broke out on his skin. "Right," he said, poking a finger into Garan's chest, "that vessel is my friend."

Cloaked in shadows, Garan's face looked haunted. "I do not intend to harm this vessel."

"Garan. His name is Garan. What is your name, anyhow?"

Garan's expression froze. "You want to know my true name?"

"Yes, I suppose so." He saw that Danton and Salinda were also interested.

"In your language, I am called Heavenly Light."

Brill met Garan's gaze. "Heavenly Light," he repeated, not quite sure he had heard right. If Nils was right, this being was a dangerous prisoner. Heavenly Light ran counter to that; it made him think of someone gifted with the source.

"Yes, that is what I said. Now, if you are ready, we shall move on." Garan turned to the gate. "Nils, you may close it now." Not waiting on Nils, Garan moved off up the Way.

Salinda groaned again. Did that mean her pains were closer together? Brill lifted an eyebrow at Danton.

"I need to walk," Salinda said and pressed a button on her glide to lower it to the ground. Danton pulled on her outstretched hands to help her to her feet. She stood doubled over and rubbed her lower back.

Brill scooped up Salinda's glide. "I'll carry this for you."

"Thank you," Salinda said.

Danton stroked her back and made soothing noises. "You will get through this," he said softly.

"I hope so," she replied.

Brill had never heard her sound so down.

"Thank you." Danton noticed Brill held the glide. "And we should stay alert. Could you warn Laidan and Eneit to do the same? If there are glowworms, who knows what else might be in here with us."

Brill's stomach tensed and knotted. He had not thought of that.

Garan led them on at a swift pace with Nils close on his heels. Brill couldn't hear what they were saying to each other, although it seemed animated, even argumentative, at times. Karol strode behind them, pulling on the tether to the supply glide, his thin frame not appearing to be daunted by the pace or the burden of the glide.

Eneit and Laidan walked together, their grips tight on their staves, their postures signaling alertness.

Salinda lagged behind. After about half an hour, Brill slowed until Salinda drew level. "Do you want the glide now?"

She shook her head. "Just a bit longer. Walking helps. Then when I'm back on the glide I can catch up."

"All right then."

Danton acknowledged the conversation with a nod from his position at the rear, his dark gaze constantly checking his surroundings. He kept Salinda company, too, as well as protecting the rear. Brill looked up at the dark gray roof, noting that all signs of the glowworms were gone. His stomach growled and he rubbed it in sympathy. His body knew it was time to eat breakfast. Not long after, Garan slowed as they neared a junction.

Nils turned to the group and when Salinda and Danton joined them he said, "We should take a rest and eat now, in preparation for our exit. We are nearly there."

Danton spoke up loudly in agreement. Brill was definitely grateful to have a break.

After a word from Danton, Karol started to distribute rations from the supply glide. Eneit and Laidan joined him. The sack of mushroom jerky went from hand to hand. Coming along behind, Laidan doled out water. Eneit took out the flat bread and handed one to each of them. Garan took his portion and Brill noticed there was no change to his expression when Garan ate. It was just so unlike Garan, whose enjoyment of food was well known.

41

As Brill took his food, he looked up and noticed Salinda, bending over and clutching her middle, Danton rubbing her back.

"Here, I'll take theirs," he said to Karol, Laidan and Eneit. "Eat yours, and rest."

"Thanks, Brill," they chorused. Karol closed and retied the sack before replacing it on the supply glide. The pale, young lad joined Laidan and Eneit and they huddled together to eat, talking quietly. The younger ones hung together lately, it seemed. It was a good thing, except it made Brill feel old.

When Salinda finally relaxed and Danton helped her to sit, she took the rations he handed her without speaking. Danton accepted his own parcel of food.

Brill had the sudden feeling that they couldn't continue on this way. How was Salinda going to use the cadre? Not until after the birth, surely. Brill bit into his rations and chewed mechanically, not liking the direction of his thoughts.

ლლლლლ

"Damn it to all hells," Squab cursed as she entered N'Barek with Miraka in tow to be greeted with chaotic scenes.

"Hello!" she shouted, to no effect. The ground trembled beneath her feet and screams erupted; people ran back and forth and some fell to the ground crying and weeping as if the end of the world had come. It was close, but it hadn't arrived yet. Waving her hands and yelling did nothing to attract attention either. Due to her hasty departure, Salinda hadn't given her any specific names. Squab recalled that the leaders had stayed behind in that observatory place.

She put her fingers in her mouth and whistled, a piercing, shrill sound that stopped people in their tracks.

"Hello," she began again. "Salinda sent me to relocate you to Barrahiem. Do you understand?"

An old woman rushed up with such speed and agility it belied her face, furrowed with age. "What do you want?" She flung a wrinkled hand out behind her. "Can't you see we have a crisis here?" She was dressed in layers of homespun cloth, the outer layer dark brown. The tip of the inner layer had no doubt once been cream colored, but was now edged with black grime.

"I can, but I've—"

"Don't waste our time. We've got to get to higher ground. We

42

shouldn't have come here in the first place. Not down here. It's not safe. The city is sinking."

The woman looked ready to dart off. Squab grabbed her shoulder and held her in place.

"I'm not here to waste time. I'm here to take you to Barrahiem." Squab pointed to where Barrahiem would be if they could see it. "It's safer there and there's food and accessible water."

"You want to move us to another city? One that rattles and shakes like this one, I suppose."

Squab put her hands on her hips and glared at the woman. "No, it doesn't shake. It's safer. It's better built. I agree it was a mistake to bring you here first. There were good reasons for it, though they no longer exist. Help me get the people together and I'll take you."

The ground juddered sideways and the old lady squealed. Squab's stomach did a flip-flop and Miraka grasped Squab's upper arm to steady herself.

Screams erupted around them. Squab caught the frightened old woman's eye. "Help me and we can get out of here."

Remembering the bodies, she asked, "Did you happen to lose some people in the lake?"

"Aye, we did. They chose a house down there, said they liked the water. That first night there was a tremor and the ground tipped them in, house and all. We couldn't save them."

"Ah, I'm sorry for your loss. Now, can you point out people who would be useful in organizing others? I understand there are two groups. The Vanden people and the observatory people. Is that right?"

"Yes. I'm from Vanden."

"Do you know any observatory people?" Squab asked hopefully.

"My son is a Skywatcher. He didn't come down to the city. I know his friend Mateiu. Perhaps he can help."

"Can you go find him and bring him here?" Squab asked in her best nice-voice, though to her ears it sounded like dry rocks grating together.

The woman straightened her spine and lifted her chin. "Of course I can, you dolt. Why don't you ask nicely?"

"I thought I did."

The woman stomped away, muttering to herself. Miraka grinned at her. "You probably need to talk slowly and simply, and say 'please' a lot."

43

Squab shot her an angry look. She was in no mood for cheek. "You keep your pert comments to yourself."

Miraka smiled broadly and her silver eyes glistened with merriment. Squab was tapping her foot and considering collaring someone else when she caught a glimpse of the woman coming back with a slightly younger man. This must be Mateiu. He looked tall and rangy, with gray hair and bright gray eyes in a red, seamed face. When he drew closer she saw he walked with a slight stoop.

Miraka leaned over to whisper, "You need to ask the lady's name." She giggled. "You should probably tell her your name, too."

Turning her head slowly to meet the young Hiem's gaze, she raised an eyebrow. "You could have reminded me earlier."

"I am not familiar with human ways," Miraka said with a smirk.

Squab appreciated the advice and the girl's humor. Source only knew, Squab was going to need to keep her temper.

The old lady wheezed as she came up. "This is Mateiu." His Skywatcher robe with a faded stars and moon pattern hung limply from his shoulders.

Squab kept her expression bland. She knew if she smiled, her scar would likely scare the man off. "Hello, thank you for coming. My name is Squab. Salinda sent me to help you all move to Barrahiem."

"Why isn't she here?" the old woman asked.

"Dear lady, pray tell me your name," Miraka said. "I am Miraka. I am afraid that Salinda, and the others you met, had to go on a quest."

"A quest?" the old lady snorted. "Nonsense. She doesn't want to face us after putting us here in this broken-down place."

Squab put her hands on her hips again. "She didn't know. The advice she got was that the city was sound. And it's entirely for another reason she invited you to Barrahiem—the gardens there should supplement your food, there's water, and lots more houses."

"If it's so great why didn't she take us there in the first place? Now we've gotta move again and we have lost a whole family."

"It's complicated. Barrahiem does not belong to us...humans. We had to wait for an invitation."

The woman harrumphed and folded her arms across her chest.

"Your name, good lady?" Miraka repeated with such sweetness that Squab blinked in surprise.

"My name is Ilowa. I lived outside Vanden and came in to help with the harvesting and stayed in town."

"Thank you, Ilowa. Now, can you go talk to people and ask them to get ready to come with us, please."

"I can do that," Ilowa said. She turned to Mateiu. "What do you think? Should we listen to this lot?"

Mateiu grinned, showing yellow teeth with a front one missing. "Yes, yes. Salinda wouldn't send someone who was no good. I'll go talk to the observatory folk. Where do you want them, miss?"

Squab's face twitched at the "miss" and then turned to point to the Way Gate. "If you get them to line up there, Miraka will take the first group through. She's going to light beacons along the path for the others to follow. I will bring up the rear when all is done here. If you can help with counting people, or letting me know when the city is clear, I'd appreciate it. Miraka has friends at the other end who will show where you can take up new residences."

"Okay then," Mateiu said, rubbing his hands together. "I'll head on up to where most of the observatory folk are. Ilowa, I suggest you do the same with Vanden folk."

"Don't be telling me what to do. I was wise to this before you, so don't start lording it over me now." Ilowa turned and stormed off, heading for the lower section of town while Mateiu headed up the hill.

Squab squinted at Miraka. "You'd better head over to the Way Gate. I can see people heading there already. They probably overheard us."

Miraka showed her fine white teeth as she smiled. "Well, you were sort of yelling at each other and the sound carries."

The ground shivered beneath her feet. Squab was keen to get out of there, yet she decided it was best to look at the subsidence and the lake first.

♋♋♋♋♋

Squab took her time assessing the damage. A whole section of shoreline had collapsed into the lake, taking two houses and part of another with it. There seemed to be some fundamental issue with the floor of the cave that supported the city. Peering into a gap, she saw that water was leaking through the cracks in the stone foundations. Another tremor nearly made her lose her footing.

It was a good thing the evacuation of the city was already under way. Looking out over the lake, she tried to think of what would happen if N'Barek sank. Would they lose some of the lake shore in Barrahiem? And if so, would it be bad enough to erode the foundations of Barrahiem also? Source forbid that they would have to flee their safe haven.

While Ilowa's attitude was annoying, Squab did have some sympathy with her. Being sent somewhere only to be quickly uprooted again could feel like carelessness. And Squab had to agree that losing a family from an already small population was hard on everyone. Squab wished Danton were here. He'd know how to placate these people and make them feel good as he'd done for her many times. She could be spitting mad, ready to physically attack someone, and he'd talk her down. She shook her head.

Another slight movement, detected through the soles of her boots...and she was out of there. She patted a wall on her way up the stairs. "You will stay put until we leave, won't you?" Not expecting an answer, she still felt better for articulating her deep fear that they wouldn't get out in time, that she would fail in a simple task. Admittedly, it was more complicated that Danton or Salinda had imagined. And Nils had an overly high opinion of his people's technology and artefacts, having said the city was safe when it wasn't. If she ever got to see the Hiem again, she would tell him so.

To her relief, a pile of supplies sat in a neat stack when she reached the place where she had talked to Ilowa and Mateiu. A queue of people lined the stairs to the Way Gate, the evacuation in progress.

Ilowa was waiting for her, sitting on a low wall with arms folded and feet tapping an impatient rhythm. Her eyes widened when she saw Squab. She pushed to her feet, her rustic dark brown skirt brushing her knees. "Where did you go? People had so many questions I couldn't answer."

There was no one around but themselves, so she figured Ilowa had given answers and was just here to prod Squab. That was all right, Squab could deal. She'd managed up to fifty rebels. What was one old woman to that?

"Where are all these people with their questions?" Squab asked, trying not to smile. Not that she didn't want to show amusement, but she knew how ugly she was. Ilowa didn't need to take fright at her face.

"I sent them on and told them to find you later. Don't be surprised if you don't have fifty people bugging you all night."

Squab nodded. "Are these your belongings? Do you need help?"

Ilowa sat back on the wall again. "I'm not going." The old woman glared at her belligerently and then lowered her gaze.

Squab was instantly furious and burst out with: "What?"

"I don't like you. Besides, I quite like the idea of having this place to myself."

A growl escaped Squab's lips before she could stop it. "Look here, old woman, soon your supplies will run out, and this city is likely to sink."

"I don't care," Ilowa said, waving a dismissive hand. "Go on without me."

Squab stood there with her hands on her hips, a low growl filling the air between them. It was time to take the gloves off. She smiled.

The old lady looked and blanched.

"Do I have to throw you over my shoulder and carry you all the way there?" Squab rolled up her sleeves and took a step.

Ilowa got off the low wall she was sitting on, picked up her pack and bags and quickly scampered up the stairs to the Way Gate. Squab shook her head. That woman was going to continue to give her grief. "Oh, well," she said with a sigh, quite liking the feisty old woman. At least life wouldn't be dull and boring.

Before taking her leave of the city, Squab did a check of all the houses, finding a few people who were being tardy or having trouble carrying their things. After she rounded them up and got them on their way, she stood alone in the ancient underground city. The air was still, not unpleasantly cool, and it was quiet. Not a cross word, not an argument and not a question being fired at her. Maybe she should stay here instead of looking after that lot in Barrahiem. She shook her head. That was idle fancy. She wasn't about to abandon her duty.

The city moved beneath her feet, just as she was about to take a step. The stress on the large stone slab under her feet caused a high-pitched whine that hurt her ears. That sound also had her running for the stairs to the Way Gate. She had no idea what was happening. Feeling the instability of the stone beneath one's feet was more terrifying than facing a dragon and, as she had seen one of them up close, she was a fair judge of that level of fear. An instinct for survival fueled her speed.

Once inside the Way, she slowed and bent over double to catch her breath. Her heart was beating double-time.

As she headed back to Barrahiem, she could still detect vibrations under her feet. Something terrible just happened to N'Barek. Or possibly aboveground, on the surface.

Now that she had caught her breath, she sped up and ran along the

Way at a brisk jog. She extinguished the beacon lights as she went, not bothering to collect them. With that last tremor, she had a terrible thought about Barrahiem and had to know that the place and everyone in it was safe. It was her watch, after all.

Chapter Seven

LIFE'S LABOR

Salinda didn't know whether to be happy or annoyed that her labor appeared to be going very slowly. Leaning against Danton, she managed to catch a nap, until the tightening in her abdomen woke her and she had to breathe slowly through the pain. That one had a bit of a kick to it.

Danton jerked awake, apparently knowing she was awake and uncomfortable. He helped her drink water. Nils was arguing with Garan at the base of the junction's stairs. Beyond them was the last Way Gate. Then, it was back to the surface for the group, to find the machine.

"Can you ask Garan and Nils to come here?" she said, patting Danton on the hand to get his attention. "I think we need to discuss a few things before we leave."

"I wish that you would go back to Barrahiem." Danton shook his head and studied her face. "I know you won't and it's probably too late, anyway. You should have turned back when your pains started."

Salinda bit back a retort. Danton had no right to talk to her that way, even if it came from solicitude. "I have to be there, Danton. I have the cadre...well, one of them."

Danton ground his teeth. "You can be so infuriating sometimes." He climbed to his feet and dusted off his trousers with sharp slaps down his thighs.

"I know," she replied, looking up at him. She knew he was referring back to when he had left the prison vineyard and she refused to go with him. He strode away briskly, anger radiating from his back.

Her mind wandered to how different life would have been if they had left the vineyard together. She would never have found Nils, for one, and

Nils was important. Not only did he know the location of the remaining machine, he understood what it was meant to do and, she believed, how to use it. She didn't understand machines. She barely understood the healing tray and had never dared change its settings in case she broke it. It wasn't that she was suspicious of machines, they were just not within her experience. What point were machines in a society that had barely progressed beyond the wheel? The world seemed to concentrate on technology that related to war and killing and, even then, a dragon harpoon was probably the most advanced. Explosives were technology, she supposed, and you didn't need a machine to make them.

Salinda hugged herself as she reflected and waited for Danton to return with the others.

Danton shook Brill awake as he passed the young rebel. Brill, in turn, woke the others. Salinda leaned out from the wall and saw Nils and Garan heading her way.

While they had had a plan, her labor changed things, and something the Ufak Monta had said needed clarification. Salinda couldn't shake the feeling that it was important to discuss it now, rather than later.

Nils loomed over her, appearing taller than ever now she was sitting on the ground. She looked at his pale face and looked lovingly into his silver eyes. She studied his beautiful silver-white hair. He really was beautiful. "Salinda, is there something wrong?"

Salinda held back a laugh. She rolled her eyes…what was wrong with her? But his question was funny, wasn't it? She was in labor, the rest of the moon was about to fall, the world was about to end. Was there something wrong? Of course there wasn't!

She pulled herself together. "We need to talk. I heard you speaking with Garan. Is there a problem between you two?"

Nils looked sideways, as if motioning to Garan who was now heading in their direction. "He is not to be trusted."

"Garan? Or the Ufak...thing?"

"Both. Garan is changed by the Ufak Monta."

"The change is permanent? If we found a way to make it leave the 'vessel', then Garan wouldn't go back to being his old self?"

"No, I—" Nils stopped talking as Garan stepped into the light of Danton's lamp.

"You want to talk?" Garan asked. "We should keep moving."

Salinda reached out with her hand so that Nils could help her to stand up. Nils stared at the hand until a prompt from Salinda jolted him to assist her to her feet. "I think I need to sit on the glide," she said.

Danton fetched it for her and once she was seated on it, she saw that everyone was there, waiting, watching.

"We do need to move. However, I think there are some things we should sort out first."

Garan looked to the others and then back at her. There was no sign of the blue glow in his eyes that indicated that the Ufak Monta was either in control or communicating to Garan.

"I'm in labor. That's a complication to our plans," Salinda began.

Garan chopped down with his hands, a gesture she had never seen from him. She blinked in surprise while he spoke. "It has been obvious for some time that you were in the process of birthing your child."

"All right then," she said, riled. "What did you mean when you said we couldn't fight divided?"

Garan blinked and cocked his head. "I do not recall."

"Actually, it was the Ufak Monta. Any chance you can get it to speak directly with us?"

Garan was silent, his expression giving away no emotion. Salinda didn't think she could cope if he showed resentment or anger. Then he rocked back and clenched his teeth. Within a breath, his eyes filled with blue light. "You wish to speak to me?"

"Yes, thank you for coming out to speak to us. In the chamber where we found you, you said something about being divided. I feel that perhaps we should understand more about what you meant."

A contraction came again, hard and painful. Salinda panted as pain took possession of her body. There didn't seem to be a way to block it. She realized they were all staring at her, then groaned and threw her head back. Danton stepped over and rubbed her back and for that she was grateful. He had also prevented her falling off the glide in the heat of the moment.

"Thank you," she said when the pain started to die off.

"I detect a presence in this vessel. I also detect it in you. From communicating with it, I understand that they were once one, part of the greater whole. If you wish to maximize this power you need to unite it in one being."

Salinda had understood that the cadre had been split. She hadn't

51

understood it needed to be reunited. Her first thought was that she should carry it and wield it. The cadre had been with her for so long it was part of her, and she didn't know how to exist without it. She had to face facts, though. She was incapacitated. Unless she could push this child out this minute without complications, she was useless. But, without the cadre, she would be superfluous, which scared her; how would she live without a purpose, without power? Her mouth opened and shut and nothing came out. Tears filled her eyes and she looked to Danton, who nodded slowly. Rebelling at Danton's tacit agreement with the Ufak Monta, she looked at Nils. He stood still, hands clasped in front of him, eyes downcast as if in prayer.

"Nils?"

He lifted his gaze to her. "I do not trust this Ufak Monta." Salinda, dumbstruck, gaped at him.

Garan seemed to have no reaction to this declaration of distrust. Salinda thought he was the obvious choice to take her cadre. He was a good man, with his own power. She stared into the blazing blue eyes and then she understood. Garan would have all the power concentrated in him. He had his own inherent power, the cadre, and the Ufak Monta, which had already put on a display of levitation.

Salinda closed her eyes, trying to hold back the despair building inside her. There was truth in what the Ufak Monta said, but Nils's distrust was very real, too. She didn't know how to proceed. If she was to join the cadres and transfer the whole of it, who would she pass it to, and how? In her current state, with her mind and body distracted by labor and the associated pain, it was not to be thought of.

Salinda forced herself to look at Garan. "When do we do this?"

Garan's gaze went up and around. "Not in here. The Way is too hungry for life and energy. I do not know how it will react. Outside, when we are closer to the machine, I think."

Salinda swallowed a lump of regret so intense she wanted to choke on it. "I don't think I can wait that long."

Brill put up his hand. "We can go ahead and see if the machine is there." He jerked his head at Laidan and Eneit.

Salinda bit her lip. Eneit was the only one who knew anything about childbirth. Eneit shook her head. "I will stay with Salinda."

Salinda balled her hands into fists as another pain came on, swift and hard. She didn't want to let on, but Danton could tell. He shook his head. "Let's get out of here. In the light of day we can look at things afresh."

Eneit came forward and squeezed Salinda's hands. "I will see how you are progressing when we get outside."

Salinda squinted at her. "What do you mean?"

"You will see," Eneit said, looking anything but enthusiastic.

"Can Nils help?" Salinda offered. The child was half his and why should he get off free and clear? Salinda blinked at the strength of her resentment. This labor was making her unhinged.

Eneit grinned. "I doubt it."

"Let's move, then."

Garan and Nils argued again at the door. Salinda wasn't sure what had got into both of them. Garan put both his hands on the Way Gate and leaned his forehead against it.

Nils paced in the small space behind him.

"The Way is clear," Garan intoned at last.

"I told you it was," Nils grumbled and walked forward. "I will open it."

Garan stepped back and inclined his head. "Very well, but you didn't know it was safe—you assumed. I can tell. My understanding of the Ways is superior to yours."

"It is not. You are using magic."

Garan blanched. "Magic? It is not magic. You know that. Why are you so threatened by me?"

Danton pushed to the front. "Do we have to do this now? Can't you wait until we get outside? Then you can throw rocks at each other if you like."

Nils pulled himself up to his full height. "We would not throw rocks. That is a ridiculous idea."

"There are too many rocks on this planet already," Garan quipped with something like his old humor.

"Well then, open the source-cursed door," Danton said, not bothering to hide his impatience. Salinda let out a moan, having failed to hold it in.

❧❧❧❧❧

This part of Arvoli consisted of marshland, mud, ferns and palms. There were no buildings, or the machine, as far as Salinda could see. The sun was up, its rays just tipping over the horizon. Dark gray clouds obscured the light and a haze in the air further blunted its edges. They had wasted a few hours in the Way, resting and eating and talking, and perhaps that had been their last meal together. Salinda scolded herself for such negative thoughts.

The skin of her abdomen was tight. She hoped the baby wasn't coming in the next five minutes because she didn't fancy squatting in the mud.

"How far and which direction, Nils?" Salinda asked.

Nils came forward and scanned the scene spread out before them. "Not far. A couple of hours ahead, we veer slightly left. If the machine still stands, we should see it well before then. According to the records, there will be a ridge. It should still be recognizable, even if the elements have altered it somewhat."

"Danton, do you think it a good idea to mark this spot so we can find our way back? In case we…"

"Good idea," Danton replied.

Hearing this, Brill started to make a pile of stones and branches, with Karol standing by and nodding at the progress.

Danton nodded to her and pushed in front. "I'll lead the way. Brill, take the rear."

Salinda turned the glide around three hundred and sixty degrees. Danton was worried about something. Could there be people here? A threat? The marsh spread out on both sides, covered in rust-colored bracken. A rocky mound topped with stunted shrubs and tough sprouts of grass housed the Way Gate. She guessed it would be hard to spot if you didn't know it was there. They had to make sure they knew where it was to get back. At least the marker would help, but Salinda still fretted. If they survived to return to Barrahiem, that was.

Garan came up to her. "See that?"

Salinda turned and looked behind the Way Gate, where the land rose up in a mound. "Yes." She turned back to him, puzzled.

"It is visible from a distance. The surrounding area is quite flat. You will find it again."

"Oh? Thank you." Salinda let that little worry slide away.

Shaking her head, she engaged the glide and followed along behind Nils. Eneit walked beside her.

"So what do you need to do to check my progress?" Salinda asked.

Eneit blushed a little when she turned to reply. "I remember my mother looking and saying she could see the baby's head."

Salinda processed this. Eneit needed to give her a checkup and examine the birth canal. "Is it important? I would spare you such a task."

"It might give us an idea of how long. If I can't see the baby's head, you have time. If I see the head, and depending how much of it, I can probably...well, maybe, say how close."

"How long does it take to give birth?" Salinda asked her.

"Some give birth a couple of hours after the first pains, some take days."

Salinda thought she'd been going for half a day a least, maybe longer.

"All right then. It is best we know. The pains are getting stronger and a bit closer together. Is that normal?"

"Yes," Eneit said. "You haven't started screaming yet, so it's not coming right now."

Salinda sat up straighter and gaped. "I...what?"

Eneit met her gaze and paled. Biting her lip, she shrugged. "Women scream...er, sometimes."

"Do all of the women scream when they give birth or only some?" Salinda asked hesitantly. She didn't think she would scream. She had suffered a lot of pain, particularly at Gercomo's hand. She was stoic.

Eneit nodded, her eyes sad. "I told you I've only been to a few births with my mother. She said that they all do, some louder and longer than others." Eneit paused, studying Salinda's face. "I don't think you're a screamer."

"Thank you for saying so. I hope I don't scream. I do not wish to distress anyone."

Eneit laughed. "My mother said that's the last thing you think of when you are giving birth."

"I'll keep that in mind."

They had traveled some distance into the marsh. Danton slashed the vegetation to make a path for them. Palms towered over them, the green and mauve of the foliage quite striking. Stoli didn't have such lushness. Salinda looked down, noting the ground was dryer, and the group seemed to find walking easier, their boots not sinking into mud. Then the vegetation thinned. Soft mounds of grass-covered earth ranged out to one side and the land inclined upward on the left-hand side. That was where they were heading.

"Danton?" Salinda called.

Danton, who had been at the front, came back at a run. "Is it time?"

"No. Eneit wants to check my progress." She pointed to one of the soft earth mounds. "I thought we could have some privacy there. What do you think?"

His eyelids narrowed. "I will check it first, but...yeah...looks good." He squeezed Eneit's shoulder and leaned down to speak into her ear. "Let me know if you need anything?"

Salinda heard him perfectly well and knew she shouldn't worry. Between Eneit and Danton, everything was covered. Nils and Salinda could sit back. She frowned as she looked for Nils. He was talking quietly with Garan. What was wrong with him? Why wasn't he being considerate like Danton? Nils was probably afraid, like she was. She shook her head. *I don't have the luxury of being afraid.*

Eneit took Salinda's hand and led her around to the other side of the mound. Eneit's hands shook and Salinda was close to saying, *Don't worry about it*, but couldn't.

"I'm sorry," she said instead. "I wish you didn't...need to help me."

Eneit looked up at her, her eyes shadowed. "I don't mind really. It's just that it is a big responsibility. What if something goes wrong? It would be my fault."

Salinda shook her head. "No. No one would blame you. We have to do the best we can. I'm sure it'll be fine. And with all that is going on right now...well, let's just say a new life might cheer people up."

Salinda chuckled to herself. A most inconvenient baby, yet a special child. It was Nils's offspring and hers. Her mind went back to where it was conceived, in the sacred part of the lake. The cadre warmed inside her, confirming for her that she was doing the right thing now, and had done the right thing then.

"Should I sit or lie down?" Salinda asked when Eneit let go of her hand.

"Whatever feels comfortable. It won't take long, just leave the bottom of your robe clear."

Eneit helped her lower herself down. Salinda didn't think she could climb back up if she lay down so she sat and followed Eneit's instructions.

Eneit got on the ground on her hands and knees and Salinda looked to the sky. There had been lots of babies born at the prison vineyard. She knew for a fact that Ange had fathered quite a few children. He'd dragged them away from their mothers to sell them as slaves, sending them downriver with the wine. Having been out on the rim with Mez, Salinda didn't see, didn't know and didn't gossip about childbirth. Consequently, she was completely ignorant of the process.

"That's good," Eneit said, wiping the dirt from her hands. "I can't see the head."

Salinda put out her hand so that Eneit could pull her up. "What does that mean?" Salinda asked, just as another contraction began.

"It means that the baby is not coming right away. If your pains gradually get stronger and more painful, it could be a couple of hours or more. I remember my mother said first babies can take longer. Days even."

Salinda stilled, rubbing at her distended belly and feeling its pressure on her bladder. She squatted to relieve herself. When she finished, she turned to Eneit. "Do you mean that there will be worse pain and more contractions...hours and hours of it?"

"Yes, as far as I know. You are off to a soft start. It will get more painful."

"Wing dust!" Salinda cursed. This changed a few things. They couldn't risk the cadre being out of action while she experienced pain over a long period. It was time. And if the Ufak Monta was to be believed, then the cadre had to be unified and then transferred to someone else right now. Her mind quailed, but she punched that sensation down. If she didn't surrender it, they would all die. Time was not on her side. They were close to the machine.

She watched as pinpricks of light brightened the dark clouds and formed into balls of fire—more meteorites, a broad band of debris coming down. Salinda didn't think she was nimble enough to dodge any that might fall on her. She huddled with Eneit in the shelter of the mound. Salinda detected tickles in her mind. *Dragons*. Their emotions strong with fear. Distant cries reached her ears. Dust was thrown up, creating a light haziness.

Salinda turned in the direction of the closest dragon. She could make it out in the distance, wings flailing. It appeared to be on fire. Then the dragon disintegrated, dissolved into a faint violet light falling to the ground. Standing there transfixed, she didn't hear Eneit until the girl shook her arm.

"What is it?" Eneit asked. "Is there something wrong with the baby?"

Salinda focused, trying to sense those dragon minds. They were gone, all of them. Salinda pointed. "I saw a dragon in the distance. The meteorites did something to it, to a lot of them."

"You mean struck and killed them? That's a good thing, isn't it?"

Salinda shook her head. "No, something in the rock destroys them. I thought..." Salinda decided to stop talking. Being pregnant had done strange things to her brain, so it didn't pay to theorize too much right now. "Let's find the others."

Danton and Nils were both on the lookout for her.

"The baby is not close yet. There's another problem," she said.

"With the baby?" both of them asked at the same time.

"No. With me. With the cadre. We have to unify and transfer the cadre now."

Danton called the group together while Eneit fetched the glide and Salinda sat on it. The others sat cross-legged on the ground, in a rough circle.

Garan walked over and said, "Give it to me." He loomed over them, but then lowered and inserted himself into the circle.

"No," Salinda said, and shook her head emphatically. "Garan must surrender his cadre as well. We have to join them together and then put it in someone else."

"I do not agree," Garan said. Salinda was suspicious. It sounded more like the Ufak Monta and she could not trust it to have so much power.

"Too bad," Danton said, "Salinda calls the shots."

Garan's mouth was tight and, judging by the flexing of his cheek and jaw muscles, was fighting not to answer back.

Salinda nodded to herself and sighed. It wasn't that she was undecided: this was going to be hard.

"Who then?" Danton asked. Salinda noted he wasn't volunteering. Physically, Danton was able—mentally too—but after being tortured he had lost some bravado and confidence. He also had a deep-seated fear of the cadre, which she knew from way back. It's why she had the cadre, as Mez had ended up giving it to her.

Salinda turned her gaze on Nils. "I think it should be you, Nils."

The circle was quiet. Nils turned his silver-eyed gaze on her and his expression was one of surprise. "Could you repeat that? I was not quite understanding you."

"I want you to be the holder of the unified cadre. It makes sense. All the information about that machine is in your head." She reached over to clasp his hand.

He snatched it away. "No!" He shot to his feet, looking down at her. "You ask too much of me."

"Oh, Nils. I know I do. I am so sorry. You are the best candidate."

Garan's eyes shone, blue-tinged. "It is a good choice. Besides me, the little Hiem creature is right for the task for the reasons you outlined."

"What about me?" Brill said. "I can do it."

Salinda smiled at him. "Brill, you are so brave and true. Thank you, no. I have thought about this for a while now. It has been in the back of my mind, although the circumstances were different. I decided that if anything happened to me, Nils should take my cadre."

Danton said in a soft voice. "Why did you think that something would happen to you?"

Salinda turned to him and put her hand on her rounded belly. He nodded, understanding her fear. Salinda might know little about childbirth, but she did know it was risky. She knew women died, and their babies too.

Her mind wouldn't allow her to contemplate happiness and a life without complications. She sent her gaze to the deadly sky. She had a will to live and a will to fight...but that was it. She wasn't all-powerful. She couldn't reach out her hand and sweep Shatterwing from the sky.

The cadre gave her a slight edge, knowledge and some power. It was not enough. Her head turned and she studied Nils. He had walked away from the circle, his feet kicking up the mud-splattered hem of his robe.

Sympathy for Nils welled in her heart. He had been through a lot and learned so much, and had moved forward emotionally since their first meeting. He no longer wished that the child she was going to give birth to didn't exist. He had hope in his heart for the first time. She needed to translate that hope into a will to sacrifice himself, his sanity even. The concept of the cadre frightened him, much in the same way that it frightened Danton and even Brill.

Yet, it made such perfect sense: knowledge and power united in Nils. That was why she had mated with him, that was why she loved and valued him: because he was the key, the key she'd been looking for. He had read Trell's book. He knew what those seven did, he knew the result—the cadre.

She hated to use his ties to the other Hiem he had discovered, but knew she must. "Nils," Salinda said, "we need you. Margra needs you. The people we have in Barrahiem, human and Hiem, need you."

Nils turned around and she saw the tears in his eyes, saw the fear in them. Fear of the future, fear of this unknown phenomenon that was the cadre. He drew near to her. "Don't ask this of me, Salinda."

Salinda lowered her head and regarded the dirt and tufts of purple-gray grass in front of her. "Trell is in the cadre," she told him. "He is in it. He was the original holder of the cadre."

Nils fell to his knees in front of her. "No! No," he said in a voice hoarse with emotion, "it is not possible."

"Yes, it is, Nils. You see, the seven you read about in Trell's book, they are the same seven in the cadre. Remember when I went deep into my cadre to find out how to transfer it? I found three of the names of the original holders. When I started to translate Trell's book while you were in the healing tray, I recognized those names." She lifted her head and saw the pain in Nils's expression. She turned to Garan. "The cadre you hold is the other four. One of them is Trell."

Garan cocked his head. "You told me that name. I looked, only I did not connect with him."

"Trell is one with the source, like the rest of my kin," Nils said, grasping at anything to avoid believing.

"No, Nils. His spirit lives on in the cadre. He tried to save the world from Moonfall and succeeded to some extent. We are here because of the seven's actions. Trell wants to finish the job. He needs your help."

Nils sobbed and shook his head. "No. No. It cannot be."

Salinda reached for Nils's hand and squeezed. "Do you want to take the risk that I am wrong? Do you want what is left of your beloved grandsire to go to another? To Brill or Danton?"

Laidan was not a candidate because of her previous injury. It wasn't right to put the cadre back in her, not after she had cut ties with it. Plus, whatever brain damage Laidan had suffered meant Salinda couldn't risk it. Brill was an option, but second choice. Karol she didn't know about. He was a bright soul, but it was Nils she needed. *They* needed.

Nils had his head lowered and his straight silver-white hair hung forward to mask his face.

"Think, Nils. You can help save us. You can meet with Trell again. You can vindicate your life."

He raised his head slowly. "You think I will die?"

"I don't think so. Not from carrying the cadre. Look, Nils, the cadre is a wondrous thing. It is light and knowledge and power. It will enhance you.

"Don't you understand? I don't want to give my cadre up, I have to. I can't risk the planet on my whim. I am in labor, I'm giving birth. I can't focus on the cadre. The pain undermines my control and—" she shrugged "—birth is messy. I can't get the cadre to do what needs to be done. You have to be in that machine anyway, because you know what Trell wrote in that book. You can take the cadre there, too. It can help you, fill in any gaps. I know it."

"You are guessing," he said with narrowed gaze. His emotions were in check now and there was a trace of anger in his voice. "You don't know. This cadre of yours is all hand waving and nonsense."

"You know that's not true. You are deflecting. The cadre is here for a reason. People have carried it in their minds and passed it on for more than a thousand years so it could be here for this moment. Over time, it has grown more than the original. You could use this power and knowledge to help you. Don't be afraid of it. I am not. I am afraid of being without it." Tears came into her eyes. "Indeed, I don't know how I will live without it, but what I feel is not important."

"Can I give it back to you after? I do not want to be changed from what I am."

"I believe so. It will not harm you. Indeed, you may not want to give it up afterward." She tried to keep her voice emotionless. The truth was, she didn't think she could transfer it back again, or whether it would be the right thing to do. The need to weep was strong and a contraction started up again. "I don't think the cadre suffered when I transferred it from Laidan to Garan. I don't think unifying it will either. It nearly did that itself when I was transferring it. They are two halves that need to be joined together."

Nils knelt in front of her, head lowered. She stroked his silky hair. "I love you, Nils. I wish I didn't have to ask…"

His head lifted and he met her gaze. "I will do it."

Salinda ignored the pain in her abdomen as best she could and leaned closer to him. She kissed his forehead. "Thank you, Nils. Thank you from all of us."

Nils's shoulders heaved as he wiped his eyes. Salinda's gaze moved around the circle. Brill's head was lowered and so was Laidan's. Danton's dark eyes met hers. He nodded, a silent show of support. Garan sat there stonily. Now she had more convincing to do.

61

Donna Maree Hanson

Chapter Eight
A UNIFIED FORCE

Persuading Garan to surrender the cadre wasn't as hard as Salinda had expected. He sat cross-legged opposite her, hands resting on his knees. Nils sat in stony silence watching them both, making them a triangular shape. The others stood behind, watching, waiting.

She had asked Nils not to go anywhere, as she had no time to chase after him. She had to do this now.

Her cadre was primed. It glowed in her mind. The tendrils of the cadre were disentangling themselves from her thoughts. Emotional pain disguised any physical discomfort. She didn't want to say goodbye, but knew she must.

"Garan, how are you going?" she asked, detecting nothing from him. "Have you started to—"

"I cannot feel it," Garan said, his voice choked. His face was screwed up, his jaw muscles bunching. His eyes snapped open. "I cannot do it."

Salinda paused in her own removal process, panting with effort. She wiped at the sweat on her forehead and lip. A fever appeared to be in possession of her body. "Try again," she hissed.

Garan closed his eyes, his forehead knotting with concentration. Sweat beaded on his upper lip and his curls grew damp. With a grunt, he surged to his feet. "It's no use. I cannot touch the cadre."

"Nonsense, Garan. You just need to concentrate."

"No, Salinda. It won't let me. The thing—" he slapped the side of his head "—is in the way."

Salinda put her head in her hands. She really didn't have time for this. No wonder the Ufak Monta hadn't protested. It knew. It was doing it deliberately. Her teeth clenched as she calmed herself. The cadre, half out of her mind, started to boil and she had to send soothing thoughts at it.

"Ufak Monta," Nils called in a commanding voice, "release the boy."

Garan turned to him, eyes flashing blue. "I cannot leave this vessel. I will die. It is not my time yet."

Danton scoffed. "You're already dead. You just won't accept it."

The glowing blue eyes focused on Danton. "I do accept my state. I was put in that statue for a reason."

"A reason?" Danton said, not quite able to suppress a nervous chuckle of disbelief. "Don't tell us you have a mission. We have enough of those around here already."

"I have a purpose. I cannot pass out of this vessel unless I have another who is willing to carry me."

Danton growled and Nils let out a moan. Salinda cursed. "Wing dust and shitballs."

Another contraction hit and its intensity was more than any previous one. She breathed through it, unable to continue arguing.

"Salinda?" Danton called in concern.

She waved him off. The contraction began to ease. "Right then," she said, panting as the last vestiges of the pain held her, "we need a volunteer to take on the Ufak Monta." She considered her companions. Nils was out of the question, of course, and she and Garan were out. She didn't know the risks, the potential harm. Who knew what the side effects would be for Garan? Eneit put up her hand, but after a glare from Salinda, she lowered it again.

Danton stood up, paced away, kicked at the ground. He came back and stared down at them, a scowl on his face. "I'll do it. I hate the thought of it, but I'll do it."

"I should be the one to do it," Brill said. "You have suffered enough."

Danton shook his head. "No, I will do it. I'm the least valuable—"

Both she and Brill protested.

"Shut up and sit down before I change my mind," Danton said to them, and then looked directly at Garan, at the creature inside him.

"Come here," the Ufak Monta commanded.

Danton swallowed hard, then dropped to his knees in front of Garan. "Be easy on me," Danton said and then sucked in a breath. His upright body jerked rigid. In the space of one indrawn breath, he fell backward, unconscious, his legs bent awkwardly beneath his torso.

Brill scrambled over to him, freed his legs and checked him over. "He looks okay...except—" Danton started to convulse, muscles contorting and his face twisting in agony.

Brill grabbed Danton by the shoulders; Laidan and Eneit ran around to his legs and grabbed one each. Together they lifted him clear.

Salinda drew her gaze away and focused on Garan's hand. "Is it gone? Are you free of it?"

Garan jerked his head down once, decisively. "Yes. 'Tis gone. I feel sick. Dizzy." His normally tanned skin was pale and clammy.

"Don't give in to it. We don't have time for you to be ill. Start disentangling the cadre. Soon I won't be able to do anything and we'll be stuck."

With a nod, Garan licked his lips, swallowed and closed his eyes.

A tickle in her mind let Salinda know the cadre was disentangling. She continued with her cadre. This was definitely going to be tricky. "Nils, I don't have time to explain things to you in detail. Just start freeing up your mind. Take a memory, a good one. Use that to anchor you to the cadre when it comes to you. It will look like an oval of light. Just look into it and draw it into you."

Salinda turned to the others. "You should give us some space. You don't have to leave. I don't think you should, because I'm not sure how I'll be after I surrender the cadre."

"Garan?" she queried urgently. Her cadre was hot and light now. She couldn't see too much else as the glowing cadre filled her vision.

"'Tis coming free. Give me a bit more time."

Salinda was beyond speech now. *By the source, I hope this works. Nils better be ready.* Their bond throbbed. That was a good thing. She could feel Nils, sense his fear, and sent comforting thoughts his way.

The cadre was almost free. Fear leaped into the space it occupied and her mind started to drift, to panic at the emptiness. A growl left her lips, startling her.

"Garan," she said, not sure she could hold the cadre any longer. It was leaving her.

"Ready," he said, and she stopped fighting the cadre and let it go. The ball of light was in front of her. She could see it with her own eyes. Tears tracked down her face, hot and wet. Suppressed sobs wracked her body. Garan's cadre floated free of him and they circled each other, drawing closer and closer. Then they merged and Salinda and Garan were thrown backward, landing on the ground.

Salinda perched on her elbow. "Nils, reach for it. Send in your memory."

The unified cadre was enormous. It swelled with light. Lightning bolts shot out of it, arcing over their heads to hit the ground. Its colors changed, turning mauve like Garan's own inherent power. Garan sucked in a pain-filled breath.

Salinda hurt everywhere and her mind mourned its loss.

"Nils," she gasped, "hurry!"

She watched the writhing mass of light hover as if undecided. She wanted to call out to Nils again. He couldn't back out. Not now.

His eyes were beams of light—silver streaks that linked to the cadre. After hovering for a few moments, the cadre surged forward, smashing into Nils's head.

A concussion threw Salinda back. She fought for consciousness and lost.

ᏨᏨᏨᏨᏨ

Brill ran forward, leaving Danton's inert form sprawled in the dirt with Eneit, Karol and Laidan to watch over him. Laidan sobbed and Eneit and Karol did their best to keep her calm and keep hold of Danton.

The inner circle formed by Nils, Garan and Salinda was flattened. All three of them were out cold. Nils's body jerked and twitched and his mouth struggled to fight a grimace, alternatively showing his teeth and then sticking out his pale pink tongue. He did not respond to Brill calling his name.

Shocked, Brill just stood there gaping, not knowing who to tend to first and not knowing who was most in need.

He stood in the center and spun around and around indecisively. A call from Karol jerked him to a halt. Danton's convulsions were worse. The younger ones were having trouble keeping his limbs from kicking out and as Brill ran up to him, Danton's jaw clenched so tightly, the skin of his neck went white. Brill felt sure Danton's teeth would break under such pressure.

Brill threw himself on the ground next to Danton's head. "Danton! Danton?"

There was no response, no sign of recognition. Brill wanted to weep. All of those he trusted and followed were incapacitated. He didn't know what to do. How to proceed. Salinda hadn't mentioned that this could happen. Perhaps she hadn't known.

One of Danton's hands flew up and slapped Brill in the cheek. Brill blinked back the pain and the surprise. "Eneit? Can you look after Salinda? I know she's not doing much, but is lying like that good for her or the baby?"

Eneit nodded once and launched to her feet. She ran over to Salinda. Calling her name, Eneit checked Salinda's limbs and then proceeded to roll her on her side. Brill let out a pent-up breath. Eneit knew what to do.

"Karol, can you see to Nils?" he asked.

Karol looked up from where he lay over Danton's legs. "Yes, I will try."

Karol trotted off and dropped to Nils's side. He stroked his fingers through the Hiem's hair and spoke quietly to him. Karol looked up. "His mind is like a white storm. I cannot see inside."

Brill frowned. Was Karol able to read minds, or was it obvious from Nils's unconscious state?

Laidan stood up. "I should check on Garan."

"Thank you," Brill said. He held Danton's right hand with his knee and leaned over to hold the left one. Danton's legs jerked spasmodically. Brill didn't think he was in danger of being kicked. Not unless Danton had developed some extraordinary flexibility.

A loud roar overhead signaled more trouble. *Could it get any worse?* Fine lines of light crisscrossed the sky. More Shatterwing falling down. If these unconscious people didn't pull themselves together, the mission would fail. Brill didn't know what to do with the machine; he didn't know how to find it, let alone how to operate it.

No, he thought. *I can try. That's all I can do. If I have to leave them behind, I will go on alone.* How hard could it be?

ତ୨ତ୨ତ୨ତ୨ତ୨

Chaos reigned in Barrahiem. Squab was almost pleased that Salinda, Danton, and especially Nils, were not there to witness it. While the observatory people and the Vanden people had accepted Nils, they weren't too happy to have a bunch of Hiem teenagers already in residence when they arrived.

Squab had to fight her way through the arguing mass of people and then shout and, finally, whistle piercingly to be heard. "There is plenty of room in the city for every one of you with lots to spare. Although I am ruling out the dwellings close to the lake."

"Why do they get the prime spot?" shouted a stout woman, her headscarf indicating she was from Vanden. "We want to be close to Salinda too."

Realization hit. It was a power thing. Some of these refugees were jockeying for position, and being close to Salinda, the person who by all accounts was some kind of source-preserved saint, was who they focused on.

"Salinda is no more important than anyone else," Squab pointed out. She didn't add that it was Danton she considered the leader. Then she reconsidered, recalling how Danton idolized the woman. Perhaps she was in charge, but that meant dragon shit to Squab. She had a job to do and all this fighting and arguing was getting in the way of things. She had to establish a calm, well-allocated city. She had to get these miscreants settled and show them how to harvest food in the gardens. At the same time, she had to make sure they didn't destroy the garden by going in too hard and stripping everything. Considering their behavior, they were probably entirely capable of it. They had lost their minds. They were a rabble.

Squab breathed in long through her nose and exhaled slowly through her mouth, then spoke. "Vanden folk, you will take up that section over there, from the top of the slope to the balcony rail."

Cries of indignation reached her. "You are saving the best spots for them observatory folks. They always have the best of everything. Our grain. Our children..."

Squab decided to ignore those comments. She didn't care. She just wanted peace and quiet.

"Observatory people. You will take up that section on the other side. None of you will be situated near the Barr family node. Understand? This central section is reserved."

"No, that's not fair," a man screamed into her face. By his clothing, she thought he was a Skywatcher.

"It's entirely fair. You are being offered sanctuary—take it. I will happily let you leave and go back to your home."

"When will Salinda be back? She will listen to me," he demanded. The man turned and pushed his way out of the mob.

Squab flashed a grin and the man recoiled. "I can't wait for that to happen, but as I'm currently in charge, *you-will-do-as-I-say!*"

That man backed away, only to be replaced by another person. Squab squeezed her hands into fists as the urge to hit out climbed into her mind. Soon she wouldn't be able to stop herself. Someone's face was going to get broken, maybe two faces...maybe ten...

A few of the outliers began to run for the stairs. Now they were competing for the best abodes in their allocated sections. People dropped bundles on the stairs and called to one another. Family members barred the entrance to a set of houses, waving their family to hurry after them to reinforce their claim. There was no need for this. There were plenty of houses. These people should have used their energy to clean these new accommodations and settle in. Now there was a frenetic energy in Barrahiem and Squab tried to fight against it, fight against the people milling around her, pressing close, calling out, yelling, crying. *Angry. I am so angry.* These people should have been grateful burden beasts happy to be fed and watered. They were just spoiled children, fighting and whining. The suffocating press of them didn't seem to diminish. She wanted to smack them all in the face.

"Step back," she commanded in a voice that was close to a savage howl, surprising herself, while those closest to her stepped back. A couple toppled as they tripped over those behind.

"I am going to count to one hundred. Those not inside their new abode will be escorted back to the surface to await moonfall."

People looked at each other with expressions of derision, disbelief, fear. Squab was beyond caring. "One. Two. Three," she began, in a low voice. If she saw another angry person demanding something, she wasn't going to be responsible for her actions. A stampede of footsteps indicated that people were peeling away from the group around her.

She heard another huddle break off, muttering to themselves, wending their way to various houses. Feeling the press around her lessen, she opened her eyes.

Two or three remained to challenge her. She lifted an eyebrow, and snarled, "Forty-five. Forty-six. Forty-seven."

Miraka came up beside her and nudged her with her hip. The remaining man and two women stepped away and glared meaningfully at each other, then ran for the stairs.

"That was well done. I had no idea humans could be so feral." Miraka's smile was slight, but her assessment was not.

"It's not just humans," Squab replied. "Any animal can act irrationally when it is afraid. They are scared, Miraka. Like I'm scared. I can't show them my fear and I can't let them ride roughshod over me. Chaos would result. They need rules."

"Why do you care? You don't even like them. I can tell."

Squab considered Miraka's pale skin and spiky hair, the narrow chin and smooth white forehead giving the girl an alien look. Squab shrugged pensively. "I don't hate them. People don't like me, generally." She lifted one of her hand's to her face. "I scare them. Hey, sometimes I scare me. These people, and you and your friends, well, you are the future. We need you if this world is to survive. The best thing I can do right now is manage the situation, keep Barrahiem running smoothly, so that if Salinda, Danton and Nils and the others achieve their goal, if they save us from moonfall, then we will have a functioning city here at least." She turned and waved her arm in the general direction of the scurrying refugees. "These people surviving, raising children, creating a community, give us hope and maybe one day, whether a hundred or a thousand years from now, Margra will flourish again. We will move beyond moonfall and Shatterwing and its curse. Maybe the world will be better than it ever was."

Miraka gnawed on one of her forefingers, her eyes watching Squab so intently that Squab shifted on her feet and was getting ready to walk away. Removing the finger from her mouth, she said, "That's really noble. You hope for all that from such an ungrateful and ratty mob of people, who are so stupid they started yelling at you and demanding things."

"I'm not noble. I'm practical. I've seen a lot of things. I know people and I know how they behave when they are afraid. Give them some structure, some basic rules and something to do, and they'll be all right in the end. I remember overhearing Brill talk to Danton once when they first met. He talked about people trying to survive and how that made them do things they normally wouldn't. He was right about that. Give them time to settle, give them time to experience safety."

"What if there is no time?" Miraka asked.

Squab tried to smile, but was startled when Miraka took her hand, smiled and then rested her head on Squab's shoulder. Squab suppressed the urge to pull away. The young Hiem girl didn't deserve to be stuck here with someone like her. She drew comfort from the warmth of the girl's hand and the fact that Miraka seemed to like her, even though she was old, definitely ugly and very squat. "If there is no time, then it doesn't matter. What matters is what we do with the time we have left. I decided to do something useful with my time. I want my life to matter, even if there is no one to talk about me and my deeds. I know what I did, and I think I'll take that with me."

Looking around her and seeing they were alone, Miraka pulled away and tugged on her elbow. "Come and eat with us. The future parents of the human race are settling quietly into their selected abodes. Tomorrow is another day and there will be more problems then."

"I'd like that. What's on the menu?"

"Fungi soup and flat bread."

That was standard fare these days. Squab rubbed her middle. It was a filling meal and having a full belly meant she could sleep.

Chapter Nine
SMOKE AND SPIRITS

Brill surveyed the group, four of them down. Above, the sky was a boiling cauldron of ash and cloud. Smoke and dust laced the air. Brill considered Danton. He had at least stopped twitching, but he was still out cold. He called out to Eneit. "Salinda?" Eneit shook her head.

Brill called to Karol to ask about Nils. "Anything?"

"He lives, but his mind is in turmoil." He pointed to the sky. "Like that."

"Can you read minds?" Brill asked Karol, slowly and carefully.

Karol tilted his head. "Sometimes, if I am close. If the person projects their thoughts."

Brill's skin went cold, uncomfortable with the knowledge that his mind could be read; he needed to ensure he kept his thoughts low-key around the Hiem child in the future. He muttered to himself that at least Nils was alive and had a mind. They were depending on him, after all. Their eggs were all in one basket, so to speak. Unless Brill went ahead and tried to use the machine himself.

"Laidan?" he called. Garan was stretched out before her.

Laidan looked up. "I think he moaned. That's something, right?"

"Maybe...call out if there is more or if you think he's coming to."

Brill felt like an idiot standing there surveying four unconscious people and just fretting.

A boom sounded and his head jerked up. A bright meteor scoured the sky, seeming to ignite clouds. It looked like it was heading for the Stoli continent. He shook his head. How much more punishment could the planet take? There was a haze surrounding them, and more smoke probably meant some of them, if not all, would develop breathing problems. Unconsciously, he took a deep breath and held it. The air seemed quite breathable still.

"His eyelids are flickering," Laidan called out. Brill looked down at Danton, surmising he was doing all right, that the Ufak Monta wouldn't kill its new host. Brill sped over to where Garan lay sprawled in the dirt, his eyes jerking back and forth rapidly under his eyelids.

"Garan?" Brill shook his shoulder. "Garan! Wake up."

Garan sucked in a breath. His violet-colored eyes were bright and bewildered when he opened them, gradually focusing on his companions. "Laidan? Brill?"

Laidan held Garan's hand to her chest and studied him earnestly. Brill blinked and narrowed his eyes. *Oh*, he thought. *She cares for Garan. You knew that. She forgot Garan and she forgot you...now she remembers.* Brill nodded to himself and helped Garan to sit up. "Are you hurt? Can you move?"

Garan tested his limbs and then put a hand to the back of his head. "My head hurts." He tried to stand only to flop back, even though Laidan and Brill tried to steady him. "The thing?" Garan peered at his friend's prone form, recent events slotting back into place. "Poor Danton."

Brill shot a look in the direction of the rebel leader, but Eneit shook her head worriedly when he caught her eye. Brill focused on Garan, thinking that at least one of them was alive, reasonably intact and talking.

"Laidan?" Garan said, nodding to his hand where she still gripped it tightly.

Blushing, Laidan released it. "Sorry. I've been so scared for you."

"Thank you," Garan said softly.

Laidan met his gaze, pleasure obvious in her smile.

"What can you tell us?" Brill said. "You no longer have the Ufak whatsit or the cadre. How are you?" Brill really wanted to know if he could count on Garan still having his own amazing power. He had once been very good in a fight.

With help, Garan climbed to his feet and staggered over to the supply glide. Laidan walked behind him, sometimes reaching out to steady him. Garan uncovered some equipment he had stashed there: a square box and a small sack. He reached into the sack and flicked over the edge of it to reveal a crystal a large as his fist. "Let me see if I still have it," he said, closing his eyes. The pale amethyst crystal sat inert as he touched it. Then, after a few moments of watching Garan's face tense and contort, Brill saw the center of the crystal warm and glow. Garan drew his hand back with a gasp. "That was harder than before..." He waved a hand at Brill. "Before the cadre, I mean. I think with practice I can get up to my old strength."

"How do you feel, Garan?" Laidan inquired. "After the...uh..."

He turned to her, lips pressed into a thin line. He gave a shaky jerk of his head. "Different."

"Different how?" she asked.

"It changed me. The cadre and the spirit thing."

"Changed for good or bad?" she asked, nervously twisting her fingers.

"I do not know," he replied and then folded his arms across his chest. "Neither, I suspect. Just different. I have no inclination to harm anyone or anything like that, if that's worrying you. I just sense that there is a before me and an after me. I cannot explain it better."

Laidan surged forward and put her hands on his folded arms. "I do know what you mean, really I do."

They heard Eneit call out urgently. Brill strode over, sliding to his knees next to Salinda. She was coming around, a bit fuzzy and groggy, unable to say anything intelligible. He looked at Eneit. "The baby?"

"I don't know, but everything seems okay for now."

A moan escaped Salinda and Eneit raised her eyebrows. "Or maybe not."

Brill frowned down at Salinda, at a loss as to what to do.

"Can you bring water and a cloth?" Eneit asked.

Brill shook himself. Why hadn't he thought of that? "On it," he said and darted away to the supply glide to find a cloth and a flask of watered wine.

"It's watered wine, will that do?" he asked Eneit.

Eneit took the stopper out of the flask and tilted it to her mouth. "It will do," she said, then took a drink and wiped the moisture from her lips. She put her arm under Salinda's head. "Drink some. It will help."

Salinda understood enough to open her mouth and swallow. Brill cast a look over at Nils and Danton. Those two weren't coming around yet. "Wing dust!"

Salinda continued to revive, although she couldn't quite stay sitting up. She asked. "Nils?"

When Brill didn't answer, she asked, "Did it work?", and opened her eyes.

Brill blanched at the sight of her. Her eyes were puffy and bloodshot, so bloodshot that the whites were completely red. Parting from the cadre must have hurt badly.

"How do you feel?" he asked her softly.

"Like freshly squished dragon dung."

"That's not too bad," he quipped back. "I understand dragon dung has a lot of uses."

"*Phaw!*" she retorted. "Stop delaying and tell me. How is Nils?"

He let out a big breath and lowered himself to a sitting position on the ground next to her. He cast his gaze over to where Karol tended the inert Nils. "He is alive, although non-responsive."

Salinda sniffed against the heel of her hand as she held it to her nose and forehead. "*Argh*...and Danton?"

The wind picked up, channeling dust and smoke-tinged air their way. Brill wiped his nose. The dust was annoying him as it was Salinda. Eneit's eyes were watering too. The air was filling with dust and other irritants and they needed to find somewhere...but there was nowhere. They had to keep going along this path. "The same."

Salinda pinned him with a hard stare. "The same?"

Brill shrugged. "May as well be. Both are senseless. Danton was fitting earlier."

Salinda lowered her head. "That's not good. Source preserve us. We need to move on." She looked up and rubbed at her neck as she surveyed the group. "Garan?"

"He's awake and feeling a bit worse for wear. Laidan is looking after him. I think he'll be well enough to move. Moving the other two, I don't know about."

Salinda studied the two inert forms, biting at her lips and worrying a long strand of hair that had come loose from her braid. She had dirt and creases on the side of her face that had been lying on the ground. Her face crumpled and she began to sob. Shaking her head, she said, "The cadre. I'm nothing without it."

Eneit rubbed her back and stared meaningfully at Brill. Brill squinted in return and then understood the silent message. "It must be hard losing something you have carried so long," he said, launching in. "You have a lot to offer. You are still our leader."

Salinda scrubbed her face free of tears. "I'm sorry. I'm just so empty inside. I lost focus for a moment or two. We must press on…"

She moaned and rubbed at her belly and then she tried to shift positions as the pain increased. Eneit grabbed her hand and Salinda squeezed.

"Getting worse?" Brill asked in a heavy voice. He expected the worst. What else was going to go wrong?

Salinda nodded, acknowledging her discomfort openly. "I'm sorry."

"Salinda," Brill said in a low-pitched voice, hoping that Salinda alone would hear, but he noticed Eneit's attention shift to him so he guessed she would hear, too.

"Should I go on ahead and try to work the machine?"

Salinda, suddenly alert, jerked her head up. "What? No! You don't know what needs to be done."

"Do you?" he replied.

Moisture bloomed in Salinda's eyes. Her voice broke when she answered, "No."

"So, what are your orders?" Brill asked her, not without some sarcasm.

"Let's give it a little more time. Nils might be out of it for a while. I'm hoping Danton can fight his way back sooner."

"Then what?" he asked briskly.

"We put Nils on the supply glide and keep going."

Brill considered this and thought it a good plan, provided Danton cooperated. The light darkened as clouds obscured the sun. By his estimation, they had wasted the whole morning. They should have been there by now. They should have blasted those pieces of moon. They should be celebrating their success, not anticipating their doom.

They weren't dead yet, so there was still hope, he supposed. "I'll go and see if I can rouse Danton. Do we have any pure dragon wine? The watered stuff isn't sufficient for what I need."

Salinda's face creased. "I think so. I packed some that I brought back from the observatory."

Brill climbed to his feet. Salinda put out a hand to stay him. "Be careful. He has that Ufak Monta spirit inside him and I'm not sure how that will work. Garan is different to Danton."

"Less violent, you mean," Brill said with a chuckle.

Salinda tilted her head and nodded. "Yes, that's exactly what I mean."

Danton could lash out, so Brill should be prepared.

Brill tried to wake Danton for ages, with no response. The sky was a spectacle of vivid red, black, and purple. It portended doom, Brill thought as he looked back down at Danton's still face.

"Come on, Danton. Come back to me, buddy. I need you."

Danton sucked in a sudden, deep breath and Brill started, nearly pissing himself it was so unexpected.

"Danton?" Brill ventured. He nursed the flask of dragon wine, letting it dangle from his fingers.

Danton's head turned in Brill's direction. "Is that dragon wine you have there?"

Brill lifted the bottle, nodded and handed it over. Danton propped himself up on his elbow and took a long draft. Brill watched for the tell-tale blue glow in Danton's dark eyes, but he could see no sign of it.

"Is that thing in there with you?" Brill said hesitantly, hoping that Danton had dodged that fate.

Danton took another deep swallow of the wine and stoppered the flask. He turned to face Brill. "It sure is. Weirdest experience ever."

Brill thought Danton was in control for now. "Can you sit up?" He had to get Danton on his feet as that would leave only Nils, and Nils could be strapped to the glide.

Danton winced. "*Ow!*" he exclaimed and then rubbed his head.

"What?" Brill asked.

"Massive headache. I may have to stay down here for a bit. How is everyone else? Did they manage to transfer the cadre?"

Brill looked around. Garan was groggy, Salinda woozy, and Nils out cold. "The situation is improving on what it was a few minutes ago. They did transfer the cadre. Salinda and Garan were blanked out, but are awake now. Nils is non-responsive, unconscious still, and Salinda thinks he may be like that for a while. Between you and me, I think Salinda is the worst off. Not only has she lost the cadre, something that was long part of her, she's in labor. Really in labor."

Danton lay back and closed his eyes. His skin tone had paled and he squeezed the bridge of his nose with his good hand. "I think I'm going to be sick."

Brill stepped back just in time for Danton to roll and vomit the wine he had consumed into the dirt. Brill looked at the dark, spreading stain. It had been meant to help Danton...it hadn't.

As he lay back down, panting and coated in a sheen of sweat, Brill detected a pale-blue glow to the whites of Danton's eyes. So, the daemon thing didn't like dragon wine.

"I'll be right back," he said and darted off to get water and a cloth. When he returned Danton drank the water and let Brill place the cool, damp cloth on his forehead. Very soon, Danton was asleep. That was better than unconscious, except not helpful in getting them mobile.

Brill had to keep his frustration in check as he rallied the group to move on to their next destination—the great machine.

Garan was able to assist Brill in strapping Nils's inert form to the supply glide. Among the stricken members of the group, Garan had come out of it the best. He was subdued and at least functional. Fortunately, Salinda had her own personal glide, enabling her to keep up. Danton staggered to his feet when roused and followed them slowly.

The ground rose up gently and when he crested the hill, he was able to see the land out in front of him. To the left was a bay, pale-green waters lapping at the shore. And towering over that was a ridge running along a peninsula, covered with rust-colored rock and dotted with gray-green foliage. Light glinted off a building halfway up and along the ridge. It had to be the machine.

As Brill stood there, taking in the landscape, Salinda came up beside him. "We are here," she said. "So close now. Look, is that a building reflecting the light?"

"Yes, I think so. The machine?"

Salinda nodded. "We did it."

Brill's throat tightened. "Nearly done."

Her gaze ranged over the view and then she sucked in a breath. "What is that?"

Brill squinted. "What? Where?"

Salinda pointed. "Can't you see it? There, in the bay. A ship."

Brill focused and spotted the wooden vessel. "Wing dust! Someone else is already here." He turned to Salinda, eyebrows arrowed together. "Who could it be?"

Salinda's expression darkened and her mouth twisted in thought. "It could be someone who lives here in Arvoli. Or it could be someone else seeking…what?" She shrugged, throwing her hands up expansively. "All I know is we're going to find out. Soon."

Brill swallowed, a sick feeling growing in his gut. He cast his eyes up to the sky and shook his head slowly. It was growing late.

"Let's get to the machine. Maybe they don't know it's there and have no interest in it. Maybe we can get by them without being noticed."

Salinda shared a look with him and nodded slowly. "I hope so, with all my heart. At least Danton appears to be improving."

ᏜᏜᏜᏜᏜ

After waking in Barrahiem from his prison of sleep, Nils had not wanted to live. While he did live, he had not wanted to mix with others. He reveled in his solitude and misery. He had lost everything. It was curiosity that had got the better of him, had led him out into the world of Margra. It had led him to Salinda. And now she had led him to this.

Caught in a maelstrom of light and confusion, Nils floundered. This cadre had exploded into his mind and burnt new pathways to memories he had never known existed. The universe expanded and rolled through him. He felt on the cusp of oblivion. He was but a small speck lost in the murky clouds of a primordial soup with no cohesion, no form, nothing. He may as well have been dead. Yet, he wasn't.

Once again death was denied him. He had lived through the destruction of the world, the obliteration of his people, of his family, of everything that ever meant anything to him, and now he had unwillingly taken on this cadre, this alien thing—a product of a technology that he didn't know or understand.

Images flashed across his mind, consuming his intellect; thoughts and feelings foreign to him filled up his flesh—a multitude of heartbeats throbbed in his chest; a chorus of disharmonious voices filled his ears. The weight of the cadre pushed down on him. He was barely clinging on by a fingernail, to reality, to his life. A voice called to him in the dark place. It was like a hand reaching down to pull him out. Salinda...

The part of her that had been joined with the cadre floated out of the turbulence. Her emotions, her loves, her hates were laid open to him like a banquet on a table. Seeing himself through her eyes astounded him. Was he really that pathetic? Was he really that emotionally and physically fragile? He saw into the heart of her: strength so full and forceful inside her. She would never give up, never ever give up on him. She was never going to let him give less than his full effort.

Nils grabbed onto her hand and let her pull him up. He was still surrounded by burning light and a raging storm of personalities. They

80

warred with each other, fought over their place in his mind. Nils had had no time to prepare for this onslaught. Salinda had given him the merest technique to attach the cadre to him. No one had ever had to accommodate a large, complex cadre, with its lives upon lives, minds upon minds combined into one organism. It had been split early in its existence, a simple thing then. Now that it was unified, it lacked cohesion. Nils had to tame it, had to provide a structure for it.

Lightning bolts of power pierced into him, sending his limbs jerking, making his flesh spasm and his mind gibber like a loon. Images from the past lurched to the forefront of his mind, and then sped away. There were Hiem, and Sundwellers of old. There were memories of vast cities, of the great works of the people of Margra. There was Ruel Moon high in the sky, ready to split, the red bands of power throbbing and oozing like a wound.

Nils found it hard to keep a sense of himself. Yet he clung to the kernel of his identity. He was Nils of Barr. His grandsire, Trell of Barr, was in here. It was the memory of Trell that Nils had used to draw the cadre into himself. They had shared a special bond. Nils needed to find his grandsire, because he needed help to make sense of this, and he needed help to find his way out so he could communicate with those around him. If his sacrifice was to mean anything, if he was to achieve anything with this cadre and help Margra survive, he needed to master it.

"Trell? Trell, help me."

So many faces came roaring out of his mind's storm of thoughts and images. None were people he knew. He held to the essence of Salinda within the cadre. Just a hint of her helped to calm his panic, keep him focused. Thus anchored, Nils extended himself into the cadre, seeking his grandsire. Buffeted, he had to fight to stay in there until at last he touched Trell's essence.

Immediately, the storm disappeared and he was walking along the corridors of Barrahiem, the Barrahiem of his past. Intellectually, he knew he wasn't actually there, but it seemed quite real. His kin walked along beside him, some raising their hands in gestures of greeting. He was home again in the Hall of Elders, where a group of Hiem stood in respectful silence. The sacred flame surged up with bright tendrils. "Trell?" he called out, though none turned to him.

Trell had been solidly built for a Hiem, a towering figure with a full, deep voice and a distinctive personality. It made him unsuited to Hiem politics, yet allowed him to mix with Sundwellers and study the skies. It was probably Trell's inability to compromise with his fellow Hiem that made him leave Barrahiem for good. Trell's words of warning about the imminent destruction of Ruel Moon were ignored and Nils could understand his grandsire's frustration.

Suddenly, before him flared the eternal flame and around him were the murals and the designs that decorated the Hall of Elders. Trell had to be here. Feeling frantic, Nils looked for him. As he searched, dodging the people standing around, it grew even more crowded. There were too many people in the Hall of Elders, too many Hiem talking at the one time, all demanding answers. It was as if he had stepped into a hall of dead souls, rather than the collection of memories that made up the cadre. It was too much.

Nils hunkered down, curled himself into a ball and let the thousands of words wash over him. It was like being at the base of a waterfall, the water hitting, kicking, punching, pushing him down, compacting him into a solid core of life.

It grew quiet in the Hall of Elders. The silence made him lift his head, had him on his feet turning full circle. He saw, standing beside the golden flames, the single figure of Trell of Barr, his grandsire. His manifestation was much like Nils remembered him.

"Trell," Nils said as he moved forward.

"Nils!" Trell exclaimed, surging forward with hands extended. They clasped one another, and to Nils it felt so real, so like the times that his grandsire had held him in the past, that tears filled his eyes.

Muscle moved under Nils's fingers. "How can this be? This is not real," he said in a voice clogged with emotion. Fear had fled and now there was only a burning curiosity, the need to understand what was happening.

"Ah, Nils, the same as always." Trell stepped back, holding Nils by the shoulder, and studied him, his large, round silver eyes taking in everything. "It has been hard on you, I see. You live in the flesh as well as in the mind and spirit. I see that much time has passed. You slept long, longer than anyone imagined you could or would."

Trell shot a glance around the Hall of Elders. "It must have been hard for you, waking alone. I wish I had been there. I am so sorry for what you have suffered, Nils."

Nils stammered. "How...how can this be happening? You are dead."

Nils resisted believing what he was seeing. Trell wasn't really there, despite the seeming reality. Nils's heart keened for what he had lost.

Trell chuckled, a rumbling sound in his barrel chest. "Part of me is dead and part of me is alive, and at this present moment we are sharing space. Impossible as that sounds, it is true." He moved his hand forward and back again between them. "We are communicating in real time." Trell looked around, his face full of wonder. "Who knew it would be so long? The cadre endured far beyond expectations."

Nils damped down his incredulity. He had to suspend his disbelief, or he would go crazy. "I read your book, Trell. It did not mention this phenomenon." Nils spread his arms to indicate the simulacrum of Barrahiem they were inhabiting. "It did not discuss the cadre."

Trell laughed. He looked askance at Nils and laughed some more. "We didn't know," he said. "Something went wrong. Something went right. I don't know. All I know is that my colleagues were inside my head at the end. I walked out of that machine, and the essence, the seed that became the cadre, was in me."

Nils frowned in puzzlement. "But how? Even if that happened, how did you know to pass it on, and how did they then know to pass it on to the next person? How did you even know what this is?"

Trell's face became serious, the lines of merriment disappearing into his simulated flesh. "I didn't. It happened spontaneously when I passed from this life. It wasn't until this had happened many times over that I got a sense of myself within the greater expanse of what has become the cadre. It is only because you sought me out that I was able to appear here with you as I am, as I've come to be. I am Trell, but not in the same way that you are Nils. You still exist in the material world. You can interact. You can make a difference. I cannot."

Nils let out a pent-up breath. "That is why I'm here. That is why I sought you out."

"Good, you'd best get on with it."

While speaking to Trell, the chaos of the cadre had settled in his mind. The city of Barrahiem now became a mass of archways and corridors, and Nils knew instinctively that along each one was a pathway to the experiences and knowledge of each of the holders of the cadre. It was like a library, containing information that it could take his whole lifetime and more to explore. At the same time, he knew it was part of him and he was part of it. Forever. And he smiled. He had one thing to do. And when he'd done that he could be one with this.

He reached out to Trell and grasped his hand. "Show me," he said.

They were no longer in Barrahiem, they were in the machine. Trell's voice droned in his ears, explaining the components, explaining what had to be done. Nils took it all in. He now had to get to the machine.

It was then that Nils grew aware of his physical body. He was moving, but he was lying down. He wasn't walking. A bit confusing at first. He heard the sounds of people talking around him. Salinda's voice was close to his ears. "Something is happening," she said. "I think he's coming around."

The back of Nils's head ached, and his elbow throbbed as if he had banged it somehow. His mouth was dry and he tried to move his lips, to speak. Only a croak came out.

"Stop!" Salinda cried out.

Nils's eyes snapped open to ominous sky, black, portending death.

The movement stopped. Brill was there, undoing the straps that held Nils down.

Nils allowed himself to be helped to sit up and have a flask pressed to his lips. He gulped down water, then pushed the flask away when he was done.

The world swirled around him and his head was light, like it was about to float away from his body.

"Um, maybe you should lie down again," Brill said. "We will be stopping soon. I'm going to scout ahead."

Nils agreed to this and lay back down. "How long?" he asked Salinda when she took his hand in hers.

"A couple of hours. There is trouble ahead. Someone else is here. There's a boat in the bay."

"Bay? What bay?" Nils screwed up his face. "Oh, so that little indent was a bay." He would have to adjust the map. They continued on, Garan and Danton shuffling slowly, while Eneit and Laidan kept alert. Nils struggled to remember...he had been out of it, and so must have been Garan and Danton.

"There's a bay to the left of us, a sea beyond," she said.

"The machine?"

Salinda gave him a small smile. "It's there. We saw it."

"You are sure? Is it intact?"

Salinda turned her head to face forward. "We won't know that until we get inside."

She squeezed his hand and he saw that she was afflicted by a birthing pang. Nils shivered in spite of himself. He did not know about childbirth. It was very much a women's thing, unless a male was invited. He had never had cause to be.

"Is it bad?" he asked.

Her flushed face turned back to him. Her jaw slowly unclenched. "I think so. Though Eneit assures me it will get worse."

Brill came running up to them, face full of alarm. "There is an armed force ahead and I think they might have seen us. They seem to be looking for something."

"What? No!" Salinda said.

"Yes," Brill replied. Danton and Garan straightened up, alert.

"We need to take cover quickly," Salinda said. "Hurry."

Chapter Ten
MAN MEAT

They were currently in scrubland and, although the height of the foliage wasn't very tall, it was sufficient to afford them some cover if they were careful.

Brill leaned close and whispered, "Keep low."

Salinda stopped worrying at her bottom lip and lowered her glide so that it skimmed close to the ground.

Danton lifted a finger to his lips and nodded ahead. Then he signaled for them to go around. Thank the source, Danton had revived enough to be helpful. Garan, too, was almost his old self.

Salinda tugged on Danton's sleeve and he leaned down to listen. "We need to break up into smaller groups so we can more easily hide."

Danton paused and waved the others over.

Eneit was there next to Salinda suddenly. "I'd better go with you." She had the tether to the supply glide in her hand. Nils had climbed out and she had placed her stave there.

Brill moved quietly into view. "I can take Laidan and Karol."

"No," Danton replied in a low voice, "Garan should go with you. He is pretty good in a fight. I'll take Laidan and Karol. We should be able to manage. Nils and Eneit will go with Salinda. Fan out, but stay fairly close. I'll keep in contact."

"Right, then," Salinda said. "Let's go."

Salinda skimmed along the ground, with Eneit on one side pulling the supplies, and Nils crouched and jogging on the other side. The foliage grew thick and they had to travel in single file. Salinda weaved around plants.

When Nils caught up with her, she realized he had panicked at having lost sight of her. The cadre was still new to him and she had to be mindful of that and not upset him unnecessarily.

Salinda slowed to a stop, listening, then signaled the others to do the same with a lift of her hand.

The noise came again and her skin grew cold. "What's happening?" Nils hiss-whispered in her ear.

"Burden beasts," she whispered back.

Nils grew still. The sound did not immediately repeat. Then the snuffle-grunt that was so indicative of a burden beast sounded ahead and to the left of them. Who were these people? What were they looking for? It didn't matter. They were a danger, in any case. Salinda flicked her wrist to indicate they should move to the right. Not long after they came into a clearing.

She turned to the others. "I think we will need to leave the glide behind. It's too big. We can't hide or run easily."

"We will need the supplies," Eneit said.

"I know. The others took some into their packs to make room for Nils. See if you need to add more to yours," Salinda said in a whisper.

Eneit rummaged around and stuffed her pack with more food. She passed another pack to Nils and one to Salinda. This latter was the pack they had prepared together for the journey, which included things they would need for the birthing. Salinda put her arms through the straps and tied it under her breasts to anchor it.

"Only the heavy stuff remains. We need to disguise it, quickly." Salinda looked around the small clearing, her eyes passing over a large, half-rotted tree trunk. "There." Eneit crouched over as she tugged the glide into place.

Salinda started snapping young, green branches off the bushes nearby. Nils grabbed a few and threw them onto the glide.

"I'll help," Nils said. He helped Eneit lower it so it hovered just above the ground.

Salinda got to her feet, supporting her swollen belly as she tossed branches. She leaned against the fallen tree as another pain ripped through her and she tried her best not to make a sound.

Eneit's eyes grew round as Salinda battled through it. Eneit drew close and touched Salinda on the shoulder. In a low voice, she said, "They are getting stronger. Should I check to see if I can see the baby's head?"

They stood in silence, listening for any intruders. When there were no sounds of approach, Salinda gave her silent agreement. There were tears in her eyes. Nils picked up her hand and squeezed. That show of support made Salinda want to weep. Eneit gestured for Nils to help Salinda lie down. Eneit then peered between Salinda's legs. In a quiet voice she said, "I can see it. It's not far down, but it's visible."

"May I?" Nils asked. Salinda shrugged and he got on all fours to inspect the birth canal. "Oh my, that's our child." Tears stood out on Nils's cheeks. "I did not think I would feel this way."

Salinda needed to focus and could not let herself be distracted by Nils's show of emotion. If they didn't succeed there would be no child. Damn, she wished there was a way to avoid this. Later would be so much more convenient.

Eneit helped Salinda to adjust her robe and Nils helped her stand. Salinda hugged him, hard and long, resisting the urge to weep. The sound of a burden beast sent chills up her spine. Without speaking, they hurried to get out of the clearing. Salinda sat on her glide and engaged it. Eneit and Nils stood either side of her. "Over there," Salinda whispered. "It has denser foliage."

They moved out of the clearing and hunkered down out of sight. "Let's hope they don't find the glide," Salinda whispered.

They had just ducked down into the bushes when the crashing of a burden beast grew louder and it, and its rider, blundered into the clearing. Salinda peered through the bracken and had a view of part of the clearing including the fallen tree where the glide was positioned. Another burden beast burst through the branches nearby.

Two men on foot strode in beside the two on burden beasts. They were well armed with swords and had bows and quivers of arrows slung across their backs. They reminded her very much of the armed men stationed at the Eternity project. The baron's men. A chill filled her gut. Not possible. Not him. Not where the machine was.

Even though Salinda no longer had the cadre, she could put clues together. The boat, the men, were from Stoli, not native to Arvoli. Somehow they knew about the machine. It was also possible these men knew Salinda's group were there and were bent on stopping them. *No, it can't be.* How would they know? She and Nils had had to decipher Trell's book. It was the only means...but maybe it wasn't the only documentation of Trell and his fellow scientists' experiment. Karol's people? Perhaps they'd known, perhaps they'd told.

Salinda tried to control her panic. If she gave in, she would destroy the fragile hope of the others in her group. As ragged and depressed as she was from losing the cadre, from being in labor, she couldn't do it to her companions.

The armed party stepped around the small clearing where only the tips of the bracken swayed in the light breeze. One of them sat on the fallen tree trunk and took out a flask. He upended it. "I'm out of wine. You got any, Brex?"

The mounted man shook his head. "Nah, finished mine yesterday. Here's hoping the boss has got more."

"'Ave you got any food?" the seated one said.

Brex searched his pocket and drew out a small morsel. "Just this." He flung it at the seated man. "A bit of human sausage."

The seated man laughed as he caught it and then fell backward, straight onto the glide.

"Dragon shit." He sat up. "I hit my head on something metal."

The mounted man swung his leg over the saddle and dropped to the ground "What is that?"

He edged around the tree in a large circle and came at the glide from the other side. Salinda's heart hammered in her chest. She did not have a weapon. She could not summon the cadre. If only Nils could.

Salinda put her hand on his arm and Nils turned to her. She shook her head. *Do nothing.* They could do nothing.

Twigs and branches went flying as the two armed strangers uncovered the glide. "Look," said the one who had fallen on it. "It moves if you push it." He ducked his head down. "No wheels or nuffin'."

Brex looked up and surveyed the clearing. His gaze passed over Salinda, Nils and Eneit crouched in the bracken and disguised by shrubs. "Well, Nissie, looks like you've got something to do with your hands. We better report back to the boss."

"Ay, Brex."

Brex remounted his burden beast. The other two came over to inspect the prize. One had his bow out, arrow nocked, aiming it over the surrounding vegetation. He probably suspected the owners of the glide were nearby, Salinda mused. The group of men made a lot of noise as they left the clearing, chatting together while the burden beasts growled and scuffed the soil. They had no fear of being surprised. They were either doing it deliberately to lure people to them, or they didn't care about discovery.

Salinda rolled onto her back and lifted her knees. Another pain had come. Eneit took her hand. "Squeeze," she whispered, "it helps."

Nils took Salinda's free hand and gasped as she wrung it hard, near twisting the life out of it. She did not squeeze Eneit's hand as hard, knowing Nils could bear it better. When the pain passed she let him go.

"Thank you," she whispered.

Nils massaged his fingers. "That was interesting," he commented when the sound of the armed party died away. "Did you hear how much noise they made when they left?"

Salinda bit her lip and nodded. "They knew we were here, I think. Or suspected it. They wanted to let us know they were leaving."

"They took the glide!" Eneit said. "What are we going to do? My stave is on it. And the rest of the supplies and equipment."

"We have food supplies," Salinda said quietly, rubbing at her middle. "We can make do."

"The glide has that box thing Garan found, remember? And it has the big crystal. He will need them."

Salinda's jaw dropped and she hit the heel of her hand to her head. "How stupid of me. Of course. Damn this brain." To Salinda's own surprise, she burst into tears. Eneit immediately hugged her and Nils looked on perplexed. This was not normal for her. Suddenly, she was overwhelmed.

Nils tried to say something, but Eneit caught his eye and shook her head. He grimaced and stared back out into the clearing. "We have to warn the others," Nils said.

Salinda just wept some more. Eneit waved her hand to get Nils's attention. Then Eneit mouthed some words at him. Distracted, Salinda hiccupped.

"It's the cadre?" Nils repeated, confused.

Eneit rolled her eyes and gave him a barely perceptible shake of her head.

"Oh? I can sense you in here," Nils said, rubbing Salinda's shoulder.

Salinda huddled away from him, tears rolling down her face. His words made her hurt more. Just as suddenly as she had loosed her emotions, she straightened and took control. There was no time for this, she had things she must do. She sucked in a loud breath and wiped her eyes. "I'm sorry about that. I am not feeling myself and, yes, losing the cadre has shaken me. I thought I knew who I was and where I was going and all of a sudden I am not so sure anymore. I'm so distracted. We need to decide what to do. Do we find Danton and Brill? Do we follow those men who took the glide?"

Nils tilted his head. "It could be dangerous. They mentioned a boss."

Salinda wrung her hands. "Yes, very dangerous, so do we pursue, or push on? If they are taking the glide back to their boss, maybe we have a window to slip around them and reach the machine."

The sounds of a fight rippled over the trees. Grunts and swords clashing. Salinda sat up. "Oh, no, no." Life just got more complicated.

Nils got up. He peeled off his outer robe and stuffed it in his pack. "We need to make up our minds. Go to the machine, follow the glide, or help the others."

Salinda's eyes darted from side to side. "I can't decide. You have to, Nils. You have the cadre."

"I do not think the cadre works in the way you think it does," Nils said in a curt voice.

Salinda blinked at the implied rebuke. "I don't have time to hear this now, Nils. That could be Brill or Garan or Laidan getting killed."

Eneit stood up, fists clenched. "We are going to help." She pointed in the direction of the noise. "That way, I think."

Eneit darted out of sight before Salinda had even engaged the glide. Nils was up and following. Salinda skimmed along the ground and caught up with Eneit. Nils brought up the rear, his tunic catching on the branches and gathering green smears. Branches bent under his arm and flicked back into position. Salinda decided she was lucky she was not behind him.

Eneit came to a halt. Salinda veered sideways to avoid colliding with her. Nils caught up with them.

"What's wrong, Eneit?" Salinda said.

"We have no weapons."

Salinda furrowed her brow.

"My stave is on the glide. I forgot."

"The cadre?" Salinda asked, turning to Nils. The cadre was not defenseless.

Nils stared at her blankly.

"Thurdon had that little fireball thing. Try asking for it."

Nils closed his eyes. "Thurdon, this is Nils of Barr. I need assistance right now. Apparently you have a fireball."

Nils's faced clenched as if he was in pain.

Salinda head angled down, regarding him. "Did you find him?" she asked.

"I must have," Nils replied, shaking his hand.

She demonstrated with her hand. "You try it like that."

"Now, Salinda—"

"Just do it," she insisted.

He tried what she showed him. Nothing happened. A vee grew between her eyebrows as she watched. "Try again."

Nils rolled his eyes and tried again. Nothing happened. The sounds of the fight intruded.

"Just go," Salinda said with a heavy sigh, "before we are too late."

Salinda led the way, adjusting their path to where the sounds were coming from. Wary of blundering in, she slowed her pace.

Nils bumped into her. "Sorry," he mouthed at her.

They continued on, though the sounds had now ceased. Salinda thought they were close to whatever was happening and paused for a moment until she heard distinctive grunts that indicated effort of some kind.

Salinda parted two palm fronds and peered out. It was another clearing, slightly larger than the previous one. It looked deserted. Carefully, she looked around and drew back.

"I think this is the spot," she whispered.

Nils moved in front of her and stepped into the clearing. Salinda followed close behind with Eneit bringing up the rear. The space was longer than wide, and curved like a bean. That meant they could not see everything. A splash of red on some dead leaves gave Nils a start. Salinda hovered next to him and peered into the shrubbery beyond them. Eneit squeaked in surprise and Nils and Salinda swung around. Eneit was backing up. Moving over, she saw what had startled the girl. A wounded man lay on the ground, his head at a strange angle and one leg bleeding with blood pooling underneath him from the wound in his side.

Salinda licked her lips after staring at the man for a few minutes. "It's not one of the ones who took the glide. That means there are more of them."

She thought back to the ship and hoped it wasn't full of armed men, but the chance of that was slipping away.

"A large group of armed men," Nils speculated.

A gasp slipped out of her mouth and she clapped her hand over it. If they could hear a fight through these woods, then someone could hear her cry out.

"Eneit," Salinda said in hushed tones, "can you see who was here? Danton? Laidan? Brill?"

Eneit checked in the bushes and looked around at the ground. She came back. "I think it was Laidan or Karol. Smallish footprints." She peered into the foliage then dived into it. Nils started, then relaxed when she emerged with a stave in her hand. "This was Laidan's."

Salinda looked at her, her expression full of concern. "We don't know who won. If Laidan lost her stave, then maybe…"

Eneit brandished Laidan's stave. "We should follow the trail. Maybe we can overtake them."

Salinda scratched her head. "Nils?" she asked him.

He shook his head. "You decide. You know what is best."

"But…"

"The cadre defers to you in this," Nils explained.

A stab in the heart, that comment. Confusing, too. She had once looked to the cadre for guidance and Nils's response annoyed her.

"It is true," he said, seeing her expression. "You are a fighter. You have instinct. The cadre cannot match that."

Salinda had to accept that. She licked her lips and said, "We will follow at a distance and look for opportunity."

Salinda looked ahead, then lifted her eyebrows at Eneit. "Yes, that way," Eneit confirmed. "I'll lead."

That left Nils to bring up the rear. They left the severely injured man behind in the clearing. They did not have the time to attempt assistance, and not much inclination either. Salinda was too worried about the others and they also had to get to the machine. Silently, she wished that Nils would access the cadre more. Her confidence in the decision to make him the bearer of the unified cadre was a little shaken.

Her frustration grew, knowing this was a diversion from their true purpose. She hazarded an assessment of the skies: did they have one more day? She did not think so. Time was running out and these armed men thwarting their plans were not just an annoyance, they were an outrage. Salinda found her hands clenching and a raw, burning feeling filled her chest. She wanted to hit something. Pure anger seemed to flow through her veins.

"Salinda," Nils whispered, "are you all right?"

"Shhh! Something up ahead."

ᔧᔧᔧᔧᔧ

Eneit threw herself to the ground and slithered forward. Salinda stopped her glide and hid behind a bush. Eneit pushed a piece of bracken out of her face, then let it gently rock back into place as she licked her lips, worried. It wasn't any of their party. It was two armed men, just like the others they had seen. These two were young and lean, one with a trim beard on his chin, the other clean-shaven. Both sat on a rock drinking out of a flask and chatting, seemingly oblivious that there might be hostiles in the scrub around them. Or that they might be observed. "Fresh meat," one said. "Can't wait."

His offsider peered farther down the clearing. "You're just thinking of yer stomach. There's fun to be had there."

Something wasn't quite right. Eneit peered through the bracken again. She decided to roll away to the left and crawl quietly through the undergrowth until she could see better. As she made her way forward again, she gripped the stave tight in her hand. When she peered through the foliage, she saw a booted foot. There was someone else there, someone lying on the ground, just opposite the men. She watched a bit longer. The foot didn't move. It looked like Laidan's footwear.

Before she could even blink, a crash sounded from the other side of the clearing. Eneit sucked in a breath and peeped through the leaves and branches to see Danton coming in wild for an attack. Without thinking, Eneit was up, stave at the ready. She burst through on the other side, just as the two men leaped up, swords swinging to meet Danton, unaware that Eneit was behind them. She didn't care about a fair fight and jabbed the bearded one in the back, hard. He fell to his knees on top of Laidan. Laidan screamed and tried to shuffle away using her bottom and her elbows. When her tangled legs were free, she kicked the downed man in the face. He was out cold, nose a mashed bloody pulp. Eneit was reminded not to engage in hand-to-hand combat with Laidan.

Danton was squaring up against the other man, deflecting slashes of the

95

blade with deft ones of his own. Eneit kept her gaze on the surrounding bushes, then did a sweep with her stave to trip Danton's assailant. Danton stabbed down with his sword, finishing the man off. Laidan was now on her feet, fists clenched, a trickle of blood marring the white perfection of her hair. "That stave is mine," Laidan said coolly, putting out her hand. "Thank you for bringing it."

Eneit passed it over, giving it a regretful look. She was about to ask Danton to make her another one when Salinda came zipping in on her glide. One look showed her that Salinda's complexion was gray, sweat beading her face. Salinda panted hard and pushed at her belly. In the midst of a labor pain, she was here checking on them all. If she didn't stop, she was going to kill herself and the baby. Eneit didn't understand such directed and constant focus. Nils came at a trot, looking around as if someone or something was going to jump out at them.

Danton frowned after he had cleaned the sword. "Where's the supply glide?"

Salinda couldn't speak, waving a hand for Nils to step up. "We stumbled onto some armed men. We hid it and then took cover. Unfortunately, they found it and took it away. We were chasing them when we saw the man you had downed and found Laidan's stave. We came to help."

Danton grinned. "Actually, Laidan was faking it. We were trying to draw more of them out. There must be fifty men in these woods with us."

Salinda panted and then her breathing steadied. "Fifty? Magol's tits! If we can't go around them we have to go through."

Danton was nodding at her, eyebrows drawn together. "You look like dragon shit, Salinda."

"Thank you for your concern. I was hoping to reach the machine before the baby comes. Unfortunately, with all these..." She shook her head and tears welled in her eyes. "I don't know what to do. Where is it safe to give birth? I don't even know when, except it will be sooner rather than later."

Nils stepped closer to Salinda, but it was Danton who took her hand and smoothed her hair. "We are here now. I think we should stick together. We can protect you if anything happens."

Salinda wiped her tears with the edge of her robe. "I'm sorry. I'm not normally so fragile."

Danton shook his head. "Oh, Salinda, there is nothing fragile about you." He turned around and squinted into the mass of gray-green foliage moving gently in a breeze. "I wish Garan was here. I can't get my bearings."

Nils pulled his map ball thing out of his pocket. He looked at it, then pointed. "That way."

"To the machine?" Danton asked.

"Yes, although we have to skirt the bay first."

"What about the glide?" Salinda asked.

"Let me worry about that," Danton said. "Although if these men are from the ship, that's probably where the glide will end up."

Salinda looked down, her hands knotting together. "Yes, that ship worries me. Why are they here? What are they looking for? If the glide gets back to the 'boss', then they will know we are here. We should stop the glide from getting there and kill the men who took it."

Danton shifted his weight into a more casual position, one leg bent forward. He pulled out a charming smile, one that Eneit had seen him use, but not often on Salinda. "Salinda...when the men we killed or incapacitated don't report in, they are going to know something is up, that something is out here. As there are no dragons raking these woods with fire and eating random strangers, I think our cover is blown already."

Salinda's shoulders slumped. "You are right, I suppose. It's just that Garan put some important items on that glide. We might need them. I have a feeling we definitely will."

Danton's dark eyes shifted skyward before meeting Salinda's gaze, his charming smile gone. "Wing bloody dust!"

"My thoughts exactly," she replied and then doubled up in pain. Eneit ran over to her. The birth was getting closer and Salinda was no good to them like this. She needed to be somewhere safe, so she could relax and give birth.

Eneit winced as Salinda squeezed her hand.

"Follow me," Danton said. "Laidan, you range out on that side. Be quiet and careful." Danton looked to Eneit and chewed the inside of his cheek. "You'd better stay with Salinda. Do you have a knife?"

Eneit patted her belt.

"Good," he said.

"Nils, you'd better stick close to Salinda. You're too important to lose."

Salinda nodded her head in agreement while she breathed through her labor pangs.

"What about the others? Where's Karol?" Nils asked.

Chapter Eleven

TALENT

Karol liked the one-eyed human and was glad he had been picked to go with the rebel.

Once they were attacked, Karol had slunk away. Danton and Laidan knew what they were doing and Karol would be in the way. It was said his people had a knack for not being seen. Karol thought he had that trait, too. He merged with shadows and no one noticed.

Danton called for him afterward, but Karol thought it best to be on his own. It was safer. He could be quiet on his own and he could watch, listen and learn. That was his talent.

He slipped from shadow to shadow, sinking into himself when he came upon the intruders. That is what he thought of them. They didn't belong in these woods. They didn't belong on the continent. They were strangers, just as he was.

Tendrils of body odor lingered in the air and dust tickled Karol's nose. He listened to the armed humans as the four of them sat around eating.

"Don' know how, but this salty smoked meat tastes good."

"'Tis probably your old neighbor," replied a younger man next to him. They looked similar to each other so perhaps they were close kin.

That quip made Karol's stomach twist. They were eating other humans.

One of them wasn't eating. Instead, he was drinking from a flask.

"Want some meat, Ked? You can't exist on watered wine."

The man, Ked, shook his head. "The thought of it makes me sick."

"You'll die, mate. What a waste when there is plenty of protein here to keep you alive."

Ked sat back, put the lid on his flask and slipped it into the loop on his belt. He faced the man who had spoken to him. "You going to eat me too, Lyal?"

Lyal stood up, shoulders hunched, knees bent. "I oughta punch your pretty face for saying that. We don't eat mates."

Ked jerked his chin up. "How do you know that that piece of meat didn't come from someone you know?"

Lyal spat and launched himself, fists flying. He knocked Ked off his perch and landed two punches to the other man's face. Ked didn't fight back.

Lyal pushed off the downed man, turned and kicked him in the side. "You're bloody weak. You deserve to die."

Ked lay there, looking up at the sky. "We're all dead. I may as well be killed by you...my so-called friend."

Karol licked his lips. He wasn't learning anything from these four men. He needed to get closer to the ship in the harbor if that was where these people came from.

"What's that?" Ked said.

Karol turned, paused and looked over his shoulder. Ked's pale eyes met Karol's startled gaze.

"What?" Lyal said with a grunt. "Stupid git. What's got into ya?"

Ked lowered his head slightly, a nod of acknowledgment. Then he turned to his friends. "Nothing. That punch in the face made my eyes funny, I reckon."

Karol slunk back into the shadows and breathed a sigh of relief. That man could have betrayed him and while Karol was fast, he wasn't sure he could have escaped them.

He had to be careful.

The shore of the bay was too open for Karol to explore without risking exposure, so he lay down flat and covered himself in sand, using his ability to hide as a way of not being seen. *They don't see me.*

The wooden craft rocked gently in the bay. It had a long keel in the center which became visible when a wave lifted it. The boat was fitted with masts for two sails and had housing for oars.

Farther along the shore, Karol saw smaller boats pulled up. He turned his attention back to the ship. Was anyone left on board?

Nothing happened for a long time and Karol began to tire. It had been a hard journey so far. He withdrew a piece of bread and nibbled on it, the sand from his fingers crunching against his teeth.

He swallowed a mouthful hurriedly when three men came running along the beach as if pursued. Karol scanned the area, but there was no one else. Two jumped into a little boat and the other gave it a shove and climbed in as it floated away. Soon they were frantically rowing to the larger vessel.

As they neared the ship, someone came out on deck. Karol stared. Whoever it was looked monstrous and had a tail, the voice hoarse and rough like his throat had been burned. Karol heard him clearly as he roared orders.

Could this be the Gercomo that the others had talked about? Karol lowered his face to the sand. He had to warn his friends, yet had to wait for these men to go inside the ship or leave again. His heart thudded.

Gercomo was known to consort with real dragons and Karol was afraid to look up in case one was skimming the breeze looking for a meal. He could trick humans into not seeing him, not dragons. Salinda had said the dragons in Arvoli had died. Did she mean all of them? Could he risk it?

More activity burst to life on the deck of the ship as more men spilled out. Three more small boats were launched and Karol counted a good twenty armed men lowering themselves into them on ropes. Where would they go?

He watched, breath held as they reached land and started up the ridge. His heart sank. They were heading toward the machine. If they were there to use it, why were they armed? Had they come to strip the place of its equipment? Was it some kind of trap?

With a heavy heart he saw them make a barrier to blockade the path up the ridge. The beast man stood on the deck talking to a shorter man next to him. It was a pity Karol's stealth skills did not include distance lip reading. He could hear the distorted echo of their voices across the water, but not what they were saying. He had to get word to the others. He put his head down and rested while he waited. He didn't sleep, but allowed his body to rest, a trick he'd learned when young, something his father had taught him.

Tears burned in Karol's eyes. Why did he have to think of his father now? His whole family was dead. The only person who was like kin was Nils, and the last time he had seen the Hiem he had looked like death. Those others had harmed him, but Nils trusted the humans, particularly Salinda.

Karol trusted her, too. She needed to know.

Something changed. A booming sound. His head jerked up. Lights streaked across the sky. The beast and the other man were gone from the deck. Karol used this opportunity to slink away, hastening to the easy shadows of the woods, the comforting camouflage of the foliage.

Once hidden he let out a pent-up breath, checked that he hadn't been followed and darted away. He didn't know where Salinda was. At one time, he had been able to sense Nils, to call out to him. Perhaps he could use that talent to find him.

৩৩৩৩৩

Garan's brooding silence, while convenient, was annoying Brill. A lack of concentration could be lethal in this situation. So what if he'd been possessed, had had to give up the cadre? Right now was what was important.

Brill lifted up a hand for Garan to stop. Garan blundered into him and they both fell to the ground. Garan shook off his pack, trying to disentangle his limbs from Brill.

They wrestled for a bit and separated. "Will you pay attention?" Brill snapped, dropping his own pack at his feet. His voice was hushed, but still sharp.

Garan's violet eyes widened. "Sorry."

Brill grabbed the neck of Garan's tunic and drew him close. "Just pull yourself together. I'm not going to save your sorry ass if you keep going on like this. The world is not over yet. We still have important stuff to do."

Garan's head jerked back as if Brill had struck him. The hurt expression in his eyes made Brill relent a bit. He released Garan's tunic, eased him back and patted him on the shoulder. "I'm sorry, the stress is getting to me. I don't like not knowing what's going to happen, and we don't know what's going to happen, do we?"

Garan pursed his lips. "We will win. I know—"

Garan's sentence was cut off with a gasp and he threw himself sideways. A spear thrust into the space where Garan had been. Brill winced as he threw himself flat and rolled in an effort to avoid being skewered, but he couldn't get out of the way in time. Thrusting again, the spear found flesh. Pain, hot and sharp, filled Brill's upper arm.

He automatically kicked out, breaking the shaft of the spear. The metal tip dropped to the ground beside him. He grabbed the pointed end with his

102

left hand, and then brought his foot back to kick his startled attacker in the groin as hard as he could. The man came down. With his left hand, Brill struck with the spearhead, cutting his hand in the process. The man grunted once then was still.

Brill climbed groggily to his feet. More men were there. Crouching, Garan was circling, angling his body to keep the three attackers in view.

"Blast them," Brill said, struggling to stand. He wavered, clutching his upper arm and tried to ignore the blood trickling down. One of the three men going for Garan turned his way. Garan clenched his jaw. His attackers had knives; swords swung from their belts.

Brill focused on the one coming close to him. Wounded, Brill's options were limited. It wasn't bad, except he was growing light-headed, shock beginning to set in. He could trust his balance enough to use his feet, but his left hand was not the best one for throwing knives. His attacker didn't know that so Brill pulled out his knife from the right side of his belt and lowered into a fighting stance. It was going to be ninety percent bluff and ten percent luck.

He smiled, thinking about Danton. Danton would like those odds.

The man thrust and Brill ducked. The man had brown, narrow eyes. His head was shaved and he stank. The man could probably knock him down with his stench.

Brill's face wrinkled. The man tilted his head, sheathed his knife and drew out his sword. Brill's eyes widened. "Great! Bring it on," he said with false bravado.

The man had his legs apart and lifted the sword backward to hack at him. Brill had his gaze riveted on the man's movements, ready to move quickly if he had to. Nothing like a sword raised to clear your mind of shock and blood loss.

A *bang* shot through the air and a pained scream had Brill's ears ringing. His attacker started, and began to turn to see what the commotion was. Brill ran at him, punched him in the side of the throat with his good hand, and then stepped around him to bring his hand down on the choking man's sword hand and around again to knee him in the nose. The satisfying crunch made Brill grin. He really had been hanging around Danton too much. He didn't like to maim and kill, but when his own life was at risk and their goal was close at hand, he had to put everything into defending himself and his companions.

103

A grunt from Garan and he looked over to see that Garan was grappling with the last man standing.

Brill went up and readied himself. They needed to question one of them. Brill kicked the man in the back of his knees and he collapsed. Garan landed on top of him, hands crushing the man's throat.

"Easy, Garan. We need him to answer questions." Garan was bleeding from his mouth and nose. He glared at Brill, a mutinous look that was foreign to the gentle Skywatcher lad. "Ease your hold a little."

Garan did so. The man's face had purpled and he sucked in a breath, and another. "Where are you from?" Brill asked.

The man shook his head. "Squeeze harder," Brill told Garan. The blood from Brill's wound now blanketed his arm. The pain radiated down his arm to his hand and up his shoulder into his jaw. He checked it briefly and it seemed to be a flesh wound. *Teach me to get distracted.*

"Okay," Brill said, and Garan released his hold.

"Where are you from?" Brill asked. The man coughed and writhed, gasping for breath. His throat was probably starting to swell.

"Sar...tell," he said, sucking in huge breaths.

Brill's heart skipped a beat. "You came in that ship?"

The man nodded and Garan didn't squeeze.

"Who is leading you?"

The man wailed and shook his head. Garan closed his hands around the man's throat. Brill put his good hand on Garan's and the pressure eased. "Talk and we will let you live."

The man shook his head. Closing his eyes, he shoved sideways, dislodging Garan. It was enough, the man had his knife out. Before they could stop him, he shoved the blade into his own neck. Blood fountained up. Brill backed up. Garan cried out.

"Aw, wing dust!" Brill exclaimed, wiping blood off his face.

"We'd better find the others. I don't like the look of this. Who is leading them that this—" he kicked the dying body "—would take his own life to protect them? Either it's his mother or someone really scary. Right now, I can only think of one person and I thought he died in Eternity."

Garan's eyes widened. "The baron? The one that Salinda tried to kill?"

Brill nodded and rubbed his chin. "We'd better move."

"Wait," Garan said. "Your wound. We need to bind it."

Garan lifted his tunic and started ripping at his undershirt. Brill unlooped his flask, took a sip and then tipped some on the wound and winced.

Garan came over and peered at the rent flesh. Blood oozed down. Garan sniffed and grimaced. Brill narrowed his gaze. "What's wrong?" Brill asked. "You hurt?"

Garan shook his head and started to wind the bandage around Brill's upper arm. "I need to make it tighter and find something to soak up the blood."

Brill felt around in his pocket. Danton had given him the clean handkerchief as a joke when they set out. When Danton had lost his eye, Brill had only had a small piece of mostly clean rag. So to honor that moment Danton had given him a freshly laundered cloth. "Here, use this."

Garan took the proffered cloth. His shoulders sagged and his mouth was turned down so much it looked like it was going to fall off his face. Brill held down the cloth while Garan got the dressing in place. Brill winced at the tightness of the bandage. "What's eating you?" he said to Garan.

"'Tis my fault you are injured. You told me to pay attention and I..."

Brill shook his head, half-dismayed, half-annoyed. "You can't blame yourself. I should have been paying attention." He looked away to the surrounding vegetation and back to Garan. "I can't even begin to understand what you've been through lately. I really can't. Just thinking about it makes me quake."

Garan sniffed again and wiped his nose, then finished tying off the bandage. "How is that?" Garan inquired.

Brill moved his arm and sucked in a pain-filled breath. "It will do for now. We need to find the others and quickly. We can check it later."

Their eyes met. "Can you walk?" Garan asked, and then he noticed the fallen men and a smile lit his features. "I know you can fight."

"Yeah, let's get out of here. Do you know the way to the machine? If we are all heading the same way then we should converge."

Garan shuffled his feet as he looked around him. "I am a bit turned around. The shrubs here are too high to see the ridge." He stared at a nearby tree. "Give me a minute."

Garan ran at the tree, jumping up to grab a branch. It wasn't a big tree by any means, but it was solid and would provide a vantage point. It seemed Garan's sense of direction was better under the ground than on it.

Brill sighed and put his left hand on his injured arm. It throbbed. The skin of his forearm was streaked in red and patches of darker blood were caked on the inside of his elbows and in the webbing between his fingers. His shirt was splattered with dirt and blood, not all his own, and his pants had rips in them as well as long trails of bloodstains. The others were going to fall into hysterics when they saw him like this. "Anything?" Brill called up to Garan.

Garan turned around, stood on tiptoes, the branch creaking warningly beneath him. Garan pointed. "That way."

Brill slapped the tree trunk. "Come down. Let's get going."

Garan scrambled down and jumped the last bit, wiping bark fragments off his trousers.

Brill scanned the ground for their backpacks, then pointed. "Can you pass me my pack, please?"

Garan loped over to where their packs were and shouldered his way into his own. He didn't pass Brill's to him when he walked up.

"I can take that," Brill said, putting out a hand.

"'Tis all right for the moment. I will return it when I get tired."

Brill couldn't think of a sensible comeback. He studied Garan, thinking about how Garan only had a knife as a weapon. He didn't carry a sword. "Why don't you grab a sword from one of those..." Brill waved at the corpses.

"I don't know how to use one."

"Doesn't matter. Just having one in your hand can make someone think twice before attacking you."

Garan hunched over and retrieved the closest one. "I am ready," he said, sword hilt pushed through his belt.

"All right." Brill put a hand out to stop Garan walking off. "Why did you take so long to blast them with that power of yours?"

Garan's eyes widened and he stepped back a step. "I do not...I cannot...I should not use it to kill people."

"Even if they are going to kill you?"

"Yes. No," Garan replied. Garan shook his head, his expression showing how much the thought of killing upset him. "There's another reason."

"Oh?"

"I did not know if it would work, not after everything that's happened. It was only when I thought I was going to die that I tried."

"Well, it does work and very well." Brill chewed on his lip. "Salinda said you have your own power. I can only envy you that. She said it was very strong and she doesn't know the extent of it. I don't think you do either. Maybe having the cadre mixed things up and some of the power you think came from the cadre might have come from you. If I were you I'd do whatever you think you might be capable of, and only change tack if it doesn't work."

Garan looked to the ground and nodded once, mouth in a thin line.

Brill shifted on his feet and cast a look around the clearing. They'd better move. If someone found the bodies of these men, they'd start looking for those who killed them, so the sooner they caught up with the others the better. A *boom* overhead signaled more meteors. Margra couldn't take much more of this. Garan surveyed the sky, his eyes reflecting the light in a way that made it look like his violet-colored eyes held an inner glow.

"Remember, we need you, Garan. We need you ready."

Garan watched the sky until the meteors had screamed across it and landed in a distant place. Brill noticed that the air seemed to be more visible: dust and haze. Just the thought made his throat tickle.

Suddenly, Garan sighed loudly. "We should go."

Garan stepped into the woods, pushing branches out of the way and making sure Brill was safely through before letting go. It was a bit awkward because Garan held Brill's pack. Being effectively one-handed meant that Brill needed to keep his hand free so he shut his mouth and accepted Garan's help.

Brill had a massive headache and his throat was dry, not surprising given his injury and blood loss. They couldn't afford for him to be out of action. "You don't happen to have any dragon wine, do you?" he asked in a quiet voice.

Garan shook his head. "It's on the supply glide."

"We'd better hurry up and find Salinda and Nils and the glide then. I think I need some if I want to be ready for what is to come."

"What *is* to come?" Garan asked in a hushed voice. He turned his head, peered about, listened and then took a step.

Brill thought about the boat, the men, and it didn't take him long to come up with an answer. "Trouble, Garan. Trouble."

Garan bent down to push a branch out of the way and then leaned in, sniffed and pulled his head back.

"Trouble has been this way."

Brill scoffed and then stopped himself. "You can smell them, too?"

Garan glanced back at him. "'Tis what they are eating that gives them that stink."

Brill frowned. He had an awful feeling he knew what it was.

Garan sniffed and wiped the edge of his nose with the back of his hand. "You know?"

The dust was beginning to irritate Brill, too. He nodded and replied, "People."

"No," Garan exclaimed, a look of horror on his features.

Brill's heart twisted in grief, but he knew it was true. He nodded solemnly. When they'd rescued the children in Sartell, they had all smelled the horrible stench of death and blood and guts that permeated the city. They were eating human meat. Brill found it hard to hold onto hope. Really, what hope was there for humankind on Margra if they were stooping so low as to eat each other?

Garan pushed through the foliage and, for a moment, Brill lost sight of him amongst the green and mauve leaves. Then he followed to find Garan standing over some dead men.

"Looks like Danton has been here before us," Garan commented and inclined his head toward the downed men.

Brill clutched his throbbing arm and scanned the scrub around them. "I am worried about this. It seems to me that these men are creating a cordon, preventing access to the machine." He shook his head in dismay. "How did they even know about the machine in the first place?"

Garan eyes narrowed, an absent expression on his face. "Perhaps that Hiem, Nakel, the one that Nils encountered, had told them more than we expected. Karol said there were others taken from his people who never came back."

Brill swallowed, a hard lump in his throat. Danton didn't like to elaborate, but from having nursed his rebel friend, and listening to his harrowing cries when he was in a feverish state, Brill understood that the baron was an expert torturer. He glowered at the ground, at the dead men. "Then we have to expect they know everything we do."

Garan threw up his hands. "What can he gain from preventing us? If we succeed, he lives too."

Brill agreed. "Maybe he doesn't know about us. Maybe he thinks it is some prize." He shrugged. "We just better be prepared for the worst. We are likely to encounter more of these men when we close in on the machine."

⋐⋑⋐⋑⋐⋑

Going through the process of giving birth while trying to save the world put one in a vulnerable position. On top of that, the woods held a mysterious force of armed men, who grew in number the closer they got to the machine.

With her labor progressing strongly, Salinda hardly had any time to adjust to living without the cadre. And so many different emotions kept rising to the surface. As well as feeling bereft at the loss of the cadre's presence, there was the loss of power, and the effect of this on her own views of her status and role. She was no longer the person who would use the cadre to save Margra. She shook her head, still bewildered by that reality, and she wondered if it always had been meant to be this way. Or was it just the result of circumstances in which Nils knew more about the machine…was it always meant to be him? Try as she might, she couldn't decisively answer any of these questions.

Her role had been important; she had to believe that. There might also be a role for her to play in these last hours.

Danton leaned over. "Are you thinking? Is that why you are so quiet?"

"Guilty," she replied. "Worried."

Danton scanned their surroundings. "I'm worried too, about a lot of things." He paused as if struck by a sudden thought. "Why guilty?"

"It's complicated. I thought I would have more of a part in…"

Danton's dark eyes met hers, his facial scars pink in the light. "You mean the cadre, don't you?"

"Yes," she replied, shifting uncomfortably. Another pain was coming on and she didn't want Danton watching her writhe about. They were getting harder and harder to bear.

"You have a role still. You forget I knew you before you had the cadre. You were strong and clever then. You led a rebel force. You—" he tapped the side of his head with a finger and Salinda swallowed, seeing the mutilated stumps "—have knowledge of strategy," he finished.

Her breath hissed in and she couldn't help crying out. Danton started. "Eneit? Something is happening."

Eneit came over to put her hand on Salinda's mid-section. Salinda closed her eyes. "I need to stand. I need to walk."

109

Danton nodded. He reached over and used the control to lower the glide, then helped her to stand. She hunched over, holding her belly, not believing how much it hurt. It was like her whole body was seized by pain. It ran down her legs, gripped her lower back, her middle, her lungs.

Eneit supported her while she took a few steps.

Danton went over to Nils. "How far along are we?"

Nils inhaled. "The bay is just ahead. I think we will clear the woods soon."

"Right. I'm going to scout ahead. Wait here. Look after Salinda."

Nils shifted his gaze to Salinda. She met his terrified look with a grimace and nodded.

"Let's keep going," Salinda managed to get out. She didn't want to sit still, or sit on the glide, or lie down. And she didn't want to hold anyone up. It was bad enough that her birthing was on its own trajectory. If only she had given birth earlier she could have left the child in Barrahiem; if only this child would come later. Because right now, in the middle of the whole damn mess, was so inconvenient. She was so damn useless, she wanted to scream and punch something.

Laidan walked in the lead, stave at the ready. The bushes around them rustled and Salinda went to tap the cadre for power, but it wasn't there. Nils let out a loud yelp. Eneit had a knife in her hand.

Garan burst through, followed by Brill. Salinda could barely talk, her heart was beating so fast, and she could barely take a breath in. What a scare they'd had.

"Where is Karol?" Nils asked immediately.

"I've not seem him," Brill replied. "He went with Danton."

"That child is out there all alone. Why?"

Laidan piped up. "He slipped away when we were first attacked. At first I thought he had gone off to hide, but he didn't come back and we couldn't find him."

Salinda relaxed as the pain subsided. "Danton has gone ahead. We are following."

"Can I lend you my arm?" Garan said, coming up beside her.

"Thank you." She slid her arm into his and she kept walking to ease her back pain.

Nils still muttered just behind her and she understood his fear. Karol was a Hiem and young, but they had to believe he was all right.

Flimsy trees were interspersed through the scrub as they came along the flatter stretch of land to the right of the bay. Reeds grew in clumps and the ground was spongy and black in places. Dried peat, perhaps. Ahead the peninsula rose up, and from not too far ahead Salinda could hear the gentle waves of the sea as it washed ashore in the bay. Pity there were so many obstacles in the way of their goal.

Danton surprised them, coming at them at a run. "Trouble. We have to prepare a place to fight. Now."

"What?" Brill said.

"There is a line of men blocking our way and they look prepared for a fight. Behind them is a pathway that looks like it heads to the machine. I had a quick look and from this distance any other trail looks impassable. They're guarding the trail that looks to be our only way in."

"They know we are here," Salinda said.

Danton gave her a quick nod. "Yes, looks like it."

"How many?" she asked.

"Twenty...twenty-five."

"Weapons?"

"Standard. Bows and arrows. Swords. A portable catapult. I would hazard some explosives. They are constructing a bunker. We need to do the same."

"They have our glide," Eneit pointed out.

Danton patted her on the shoulder. "I know." He slung off his backpack and untied a chopping blade to give to Eneit. "Go cut yourself a stave." He turned to Laidan. "Go look for dried peat." He pointed to the black patches on the ground. "It looks like that. There's more over through there. We could use it." He put his hand on her arm. "Be careful."

Salinda breathed and unclenched her hands. She looked around at her companions, grateful for them, yet she was frustrated that their appointed task was not as easy as they had hoped.

At the corner of her eye, she caught movement, a flash of white and blue. Her grin was spontaneous. "Karol?"

They turned as one to see the Hiem lad emerge from the scrub. "I apologize for making you worry," he said. "I have news. It is not good."

"What is it?" Salinda asked.

"The boat has lots of men on it. The dragon beast man is here with them."

111

Salinda stilled and swallowed the bile rising in her throat. Gercomo here. Gercomo here and her so vulnerable.

"Who else is with him," Danton asked.

"A small man," Karol said, and mimicked a bulging stomach. "Slightly round here."

"The baron," Danton said, as the air fled his lungs. He dropped to the ground and hung his head. "Why did it have to be him?"

Salinda glared at Danton. Where would they be if the thought of their worst enemy was enough to defeat them?

"Danton, get up. Pull yourself together. We can't plan if we are wallowing in self-pity and gnawing on fear like a rat on stale bread. There is no time for it. None! We have to move forward. Start thinking up ways around the problem."

Danton's head had jerked up when Salinda let rip at him. His mouth dropped open and his remaining eye grew larger. Then he bit his lip and his cheeks grew pink, making his scars look very white and angry. He pushed to his feet. "Sorry."

He turned to the rest of them as Eneit returned, dragging a branch. "Let's get thinking. Any food? We may as well refresh ourselves while we get ready." He stared at the scrub in front of them. "I'll be right back. I need to look for a place we can make a stand."

Laidan came back and forth, each time carrying an armload of something black that she placed in a pile. Then, after wiping her hands on her trouser legs, she picked up her stave and stayed on alert, keeping a watch on their surroundings.

Meanwhile, Eneit went to fetch food out of Salinda's and her own pack. Garan helped lay it out, placing his cloak down. It wasn't his Skywatcher cloak, but a plain one he'd removed from his pack, along with a flask of water. Brill kept an eye out for intruders, walking the perimeter of the clearing, while Nils had a hushed conversation with Karol, checking him out for injuries.

Salinda climbed on her glide, needing a rest after all her walking. Casting her gaze around, she realized this could be the place where she would give birth.

Danton slid back into the clearing and gave her a nod. He had found a strong position for them to fight. Eneit passed her some flat bread, but Salinda shook her head. "Just a bit of water," she responded, unable to think of eating.

Danton was pacing like he was ready for anything, drinking water and eating the bread that Eneit had passed over.

"We need to take out the boat somehow," Danton said, straight up. "That will make them afraid. They might even head back to it to try to save it."

"How do we do that?" Brill asked. "We aren't exactly flush with explosives."

Danton looked pointedly at the pile of peat. "That stuff's flammable. We could use that but I have other plans for it. I was thinking that Nils or Garan or both could use their power to blast the ship."

Brill's head shot round to stare at Garan. Something had happened between them and Salinda could guess what...Garan didn't like to use his power to kill. Now he was free of the cadre and the Moon Binder daemon, Garan was back to seeing the world on his own terms.

"I can blast the ship," Garan said. "Most of the passengers are ashore, I expect. The rest can save themselves if they want. The ship is a thing. I have no problem destroying things."

Danton nodded. "Great. What about igniting peat bombs while they are in the air? I was thinking we could lob them at the bunker and if you can set them afire, we have the advantage of surprise."

Garan sat down, knees drawn up to his chest. He stared at his hands and Salinda could see the struggle. "I'm not sure. If they were stationary, I think I could."

A ferocious look came over Danton's face, yet he said nothing, and turned to Nils. "What about you, Nils? Can you use that flame-throwing trick that Salinda had?"

Nils's eyes widened. "I...er...yes, I hope so. What do you want me to do?"

"Apart from setting fire to peat bombs to destroy the barricades that shield our attackers? Why, burning down the ship."

"I think I can manage that." Nils didn't sound too confident.

Danton paced again. "We are vulnerable, don't get me wrong. However, we do have a few tricks up our sleeves and we need to keep the hand-to-hand fighting to a minimum. Remember, Gercomo is out there. We don't know if he can call his dragons."

Salinda closed her eyes. A contraction was coming. If she was quick, she could reach out...and nothing. She gasped.

"What?" Danton asked.

"I...um...tried to sense if there were any dragons around. I can't feel anything. I forgot." She shrugged. "No cadre."

"Can you feel Gercomo?" Danton asked her.

Salinda wanted to scream just thinking about that. The pain was growing, so she had to be quick. She reached out as she had in the past. There was something there...a presence. It grew suddenly in her mind and she fled. Panting hard, she stifled a moan as her pains came on again. Through clenched teeth, she said, "I sensed him."

Danton's eyebrows shot up. "Then your affinity with the dragons was not related to the cadre."

"He gave me tainted essence. I think it was that, and the cadre made it easier."

Warm liquid leaked from her at the end of that contraction and she thrust her hands down, thinking she had wet herself. Eneit's head shot up. "Your waters have broken. It won't be long now."

"We'll fix you a shelter while we build our bunker," Danton said, talking to everyone. "You will be hidden, Salinda. Safe. Eneit, are you all right? Can you protect her...help her?"

"Yes," Eneit's voice wavered.

"Do you need one of us to help you? Do you need anything from us, because later we will be busy fighting."

Eneit shrugged. "I don't know...I can't think."

Danton softened his voice. "You will have to time to think of things while we make this hideout. All right?"

"Yes, I suppose so," Eneit replied.

"Well then," Danton said, slapping his hands together. "Who has finished eating?" A few hands shot up. "Good, we have work to do. We need something to dig with." Brill dug a small spade out of his pack. It was for digging latrines and better than bare hands.

Eneit lifted the chopping blade she had used to cut her stave, which lay unfinished at one end of the clearing. "Good. Eneit, I'd like you to cut more branches. Make them bendable ones." Eneit ducked off into the woods.

"Brill, I need you to collect branches and palm leaves to use as a roof and for camouflage."

Brill gave him a salute with his good arm. "On it."

114

"Laidan, you start digging. The ground is soft. I'll be back to collect the dirt. If you can think of a way to bring it to me, that'd be good."

"Garan, Nils. I think you two could help me." Danton beckoned them to follow as he darted out of the clearing.

Karol was the only one left. He walked up to Salinda. "Can I get you anything?"

"Some more water would be good, thank you," Salinda said.

Karol nodded and went to fetch more water. Then he packed the food away in the backpacks and had them lined up for people to either collect or leave. He went to give Laidan a rest from digging, so she found a blanket and piled dirt into it, tying it like a sling around her shoulders. "I'm off to take this dirt to Danton," she told Karol.

There was definitely a change in the air—one of anticipation, excitement and positive thoughts. That had been quick. As Salinda was going to be out of it for the battle, she had to let Danton run the show. It was time she focused on the birth. It was not going to be fun, she supposed, but she was going to have a child, a baby, very soon. A half-Hiem and human baby. Nils's baby. She wanted it to go well.

Tears welled in her eyes. She didn't want to be frightened, yet she knew childbirth was dangerous. She had a young girl to help her. Although Eneit was not a midwife or an expert, she had some experience. Salinda swallowed a lump in her throat and hurriedly wiped her tears in case anyone saw. She was essentially on her own. It required strength, forbearance, sheer willpower, and a whole lot of luck. Another pain hit and her abdomen was like wood, hard and unyielding. She writhed on the glide, biting down on her yell of outrage and pain.

"Hurry up and come, damn you," she said to the child. As the pain eased off, she remembered that Karol was there. Her eyelids flicked up and she bit her lip when she saw Karol looking at her. "I'm sorry about that," she said.

He shook his head. "No need. I wish you well, Salinda." He dug another spadeful of dirt out. Laidan came back and refilled her blanket sling.

"How is it going?" Salinda asked Laidan.

"Good. They are digging and using wood to build a bunker." She tapped the now full sling. "This dirt is useful."

Then she was gone. Eneit came back with more branches and changed

115

places with Karol. After checking with Salinda, he went off with the blade to cut more branches.

Three more labor pains had come in quick succession before Brill and Laidan returned. "Danton is coming back." Brill checked the space that Eneit and Karol had dug, making sure it was easy to access for Salinda. "That's looking good. We should start the hide."

Laidan picked up a long, trimmed branch and bent it experimentally, nodding in satisfaction.

They proceeded to anchor the branches in the dirt, then bend and tie them together. Karol jumped up to lay leafy branches over the structure and her birthing place started to take shape.

Salinda lowered the glide and rolled off it to a spot on the ground. Tiredness filled up Salinda's legs and arms. She curled up on her side and drifted off until she was rudely awoken by an intensely strong contraction. It was if some giant had taken hold of her body and squeezed.

Danton darted into the clearing. "Nearly ready. Let's get you set up." Jogging up to her, he grabbed the glide, helped her sit on it and drew it after him. "Not long now. You can hunker down, be safe. All right?" he said, voice soft and reassuring.

Salinda screwed up her face, trying to hold back tears. Brill was busy tying down the branches that Eneit had found. As they worked, Brill put the finishing touches on the foliage. "Down you go." Danton turned to Karol. "Can you bring our packs? They may as well go in here too."

Karol darted back as Salinda stepped off the glide. Danton grabbed her hand, steadying her. "Careful. Take it easy. There's no rush." Salinda wanted to laugh. She was in a rush. She wanted this baby out. The end of the world was pending.

Eneit rolled up a blanket and placed some of the packs Karol had brought so that Salinda had something to lean back on. Danton braced himself to lower her down. Her body was fat and awkward and too much time on the glide had made her legs stiff and clumsy. "I'm going to get Nils now," Danton said and leaned in to kiss her forehead. He clasped her hand and squeezed. "You can do this. In normal circumstances, I'd be here for you. Nils would too...but..."

"I know," she whispered back. "It's not normal. Take care of yourselves. We have to win."

"Losing is not an option. I understand." Danton tapped his head. "My

Moon Binder buddy has a few ideas." He dug into his pocket and carefully tugged out a handkerchief. It contained something and was tied at each end. "Take this."

"What is it?" Salinda asked. The cloth was grubby. She managed to peer inside. It was full of fine gray dirt.

"Moon dust."

"Moon dust? What am I to do with it?"

"The Ufak Monta says that dragons find it deadly."

"All the dragons are dead." She tilted her head. "Mostly." Salinda decided not to question anymore. She put the handkerchief with the moon dust in it by her side. "Thank the Moon Binder for me."

Danton grinned, squeezed her hand and departed.

A minute later, Nils slid himself into the hole. The roof covering was almost done.

"Nils," she said and reached out to him. "Be strong. Relax and don't fear. The cadre doesn't like fear. Understand? It will be most helpful to you if you relax and completely trust it to help you."

Nils nodded, his gaze tracking down her body, his hand reaching for her baby mound. "I hope I live to see our child. I hope I live to see you again."

"You will," Salinda said, trying to keep her voice calm and unclogged with emotion. "I know you will."

Nils took his robe in his hand so he could climb to his feet. "His name should be Elan of Barr, after my father."

"What if it is a girl?" she asked, swallowing her emotions like so much hot tea.

"Elan can be a girl's name. It's rather pretty."

"What does it mean?" Salinda asked. Nils was at the crawlspace that was all that remained of the opening. He turned back to her. "It means 'flame that burns warmly'."

And then he was gone.

Eneit shuffled over and filled up the doorway with her reserve of branches and leaves.

"Now," she said, turning to Salinda, "I think we should get you out of those clothes."

Part 2

Dragon wine tastes divine. It is like victory, with a sweeter bouquet.

Chapter Twelve
CRUNCH TIME

"**We** need that dried peat," Danton said. "Can you bring it?"

Laidan nodded. "I might need help."

Danton shifted his gaze to Brill and the lad nodded.

"Good. Nils, you and Garan head to the bay and deal with that ship. We need it out of action. Then come back as quick as you can."

Nils put out his hand to halt Danton as he was striding quickly ahead. "What about Salinda?"

Danton turned. "I've done the best I can for Salinda. The best we can do now is for us to deal with this situation as soon as possible, and get up to that machine. Otherwise," he shrugged, "what is the point?"

Nils backed up, dropping his hand, and nodded. "I will do as you ask," he said.

Garan loomed behind him, expression somber. Garan gave Danton a slow nod of acknowledgment, his lips compressed together as if his mouth was full of regret. "Be careful," Danton told the lad.

Apart from the occasional suggestion appearing like a random thought, the Ufak Monta was a silent dark wall in Danton's mind. It did nothing to interfere with him, yet there was a sense of waiting about it, of it being ready to pounce, that scared Danton. He might be carrying this alien being around with him, but he had yet to experience the full force of the creature. Just the thought of losing control of himself made him shudder. He glanced back to Salinda's rough hideout, and tried to put the worry he had for her to the back of his mind. If he didn't succeed, the child would have a very short life.

"What's our priority?" Brill asked.

Danton hesitated as he thought through the options. "You and Laidan get that dry peat into sizable lumps. We're going to have a competition to see who can get the most peat balls to hit their barricades and defenses."

"That's not going to do too much damage to them," Brill commented. He turned to Laidan and jerked his head. "We should make the peat balls here and bring them to the battle lines."

Laidan screwed up her face. "That stuff smells funny and looks like...dung."

Brill flashed her a grin. "I bet I can throw with my left hand better than you can with your right."

Laidan just scoffed at that boast. "As you are one-handed, I think a slingbag would be best. I'll make us one each." Taking her knife, she cut the blanket used to cart dirt into smaller sections. These she tied at the ends to make slingbags.

"Good plan," Brill said after seeing what she was doing. "I'll go start making the balls. Meet you there."

Danton noticed Karol standing around, looking lost now that everyone else had a task. "Come along, Karol. You get to help me and be my runner."

The lad's face brightened and he grinned suddenly. "I can run fast and I can make people not see me," he said enthusiastically.

"That's really good, because I want you to be careful and keep an eye out for me and if you see anything, and I mean anything, tell me."

"I will," Karol replied and fell in behind Danton as he walked to the bunker they had set up. Then Karol snuck out into the woods to see what he could learn.

A short time later, Karol appeared at the bunker, startling Danton. "Something is happening." Just then an arrow shot over Danton's head and he ducked instinctively.

"So, Karol, tell me," Danton said, crouching down to keep the bunker between him and the arrows.

"They have brought up more supplies. I saw a pile of weapons. They are getting ready to attack."

"Good work," Danton said. He eased his head up to get a quick look to confirm what Karol had told him.

It looked as if they only had a few hours of daylight left and since poor visibility would not help Danton detect attackers sneaking up on them in the dark, he needed to get the show going.

He turned toward the bay and listened, waiting for the tell-tale sound of an exploding ship. What were Nils and Garan up to?

ꙮꙮꙮꙮꙮ

On the walk down to the bay, they had to take a few detours after encountering enemies on the trail who were carting supplies from the shore to the barricade. As Garan and Nils crouched in the dry reeds and peered through the stalks, they could see no sign of the small boats that were used to ferry people from the ship to shore. Something about that bothered Garan. Before he could put his finger on what that problem was, Nils grabbed hold of his hand and squeezed.

"I need your help," Nils whispered. "You have experience with this...cadre."

Garan stared at him and then shook his head. Nils was serious. Garan had thought Nils was used to some degree of power, but that did not appear to be the case. There had been an expectation among the group that Nils would have immediate access to unspeakable power. Garan sighed, realizing that had been a lot of pressure to put someone under. "'Tis okay, Nils. We can do this. I can help you."

Nils leaned in closer. "Thank you."

"Have you used the flame before? I thought that you..."

Nils nodded vigorously. "Yes, I did not do it well. I was fearful...I had no control."

Garan understood how frightening that could be. On learning that the power he wielded did not, as he believed, come from the crystals he'd been using all his life, but from inside him, he had recoiled in fear. Such a realization makes one question oneself—whether they're a danger to other people. Garan knew that he could be. He had killed Turnet, hadn't he?

"Control comes in time," he told Nils. "I know we don't have a lot of that right now. Salinda did tell me that if you are calm and centered you should be able to touch the power of the cadre and also wield it. Now, if you touch the skin on my arm can you sense the power within me, as Salinda was able to do?"

Nils reached out a hand, tentatively splayed his fingers and rested them gently on Garan's forearm. He closed his eyes and exhaled, his nostrils flaring slightly. Nils's touch felt cool and light, as Garan tried to reach for the power he had used to shoot down meteors as a Skywatcher and had used to help defend the observatory against Gercomo and his army. A

121

switch in his mind and he found what he was looking for. A kernel of light flickered inside him. As his power ignited, Nils sucked in a breath and snatched his hand away.

Garan guessed that response answered his question. "Good. Put your hand back on my arm and this time try to touch the cadre at the same time. This is essential if we are to work together." Garan glanced at the ship. "I think I could deliver a big blast. If you throw flame at the same time, then the job will be done."

Nils's strange eyes shifted from studying Garan to stare at the ship. "I do not think I can reach that far on my own. I'd best work with you."

Garan pursed his lips briefly, then his mouth curved into a smile. "Yes, right then. We'd best get started and make it count. If this does not work the first time, they will come after us."

"No, really?"

"Yes, so be ready to run and hide, because we have to sink that ship one way or another. Best we do it first go."

☙☙☙☙

Salinda's ears were filled with the sound of panting. It worried her that she was hearing her own breathing. Eneit cooled her forehead with a damp cloth. Salinda was naked except for the cloak she'd wrapped around herself, which made it easier on her clothes. Already, she had made a mess when her waters broke and Eneit had put her clothes aside to dry out.

"I don't think it will be long now," Eneit said. "I can see the baby's head quite clearly."

Salinda nodded in acknowledgment as it was difficult to talk. Another long contraction and Salinda was too exhausted even to cry out. She just moaned a little.

"Almost there, Salinda. Just try to rest a little. The next part's much more physical."

Salinda wished she could unhear that. This whole pregnancy had been exhausting and had been getting in the way of doing normal things, and was really uncomfortable as well. Right now she was stuck in a ditch, pushing a baby out, when she should be helping. What had she been thinking of, getting pregnant? If they didn't get to the machine soon, there wouldn't be a place for the baby to live anyway.

She shouldn't be thinking like this. At least she had Eneit to help her. But if things were to go wrong with the birth, having a mid-wife wouldn't

122

be much help. They had lost too much knowledge and technology after Ruel Moon split, so babies and birthing mothers died all the time. Tears started in her eyes. What if she died? What if she died and didn't get say goodbye to Nils...or...Danton?

Squashing the heels of her hands against her forehead, she tried to squeeze these negative thoughts out. She couldn't afford to get into a panic right now. She couldn't afford to be afraid. She had been through worse and survived. She was going to live through this. She was going to live to see the world saved.

"What's happening?" Salinda said with a gasp, feeling a change inside her body.

Eneit leaned over, felt her stomach and sat back. "Do you feel like you need to push?"

In answer, Salinda strained upward and pushed.

"Source!" Salinda said, falling back. "Did it come out?"

Eneit peered up at Salinda. "No. You need to do more pushing. I'll just check the baby's progress."

Donna Maree Hanson

Chapter Thirteen
FLAMES AND POWER

Laidan's shoulders ached. They really did. As fast as physically possible, she had rolled at least fifty balls of dried peat, bundled them up into the sling and run toward the bunker. Then she had run back again to roll more. It wasn't that she was in competition with Brill. It was because he was injured that she worked harder and faster. Their lives depended on it.

Danton told her there had been three more arrow attacks while he had been lookout on his own.

"Where is Karol?" she asked, wiping her hands clean of peat residue on the top of her trousers as she squatted in the shelter of the bunker.

"I sent him to see how Salinda is doing. He should be back soon."

Laidan gave a thin smile, nodding slightly to give the impression she understood. Everyone cared for Salinda as they did for each other, of course, but Danton's concern was more than that. Laidan was confused, because Salinda was sort of married to Nils, wasn't she? And the baby was definitely Nils's. She let out a loud sigh, shook her head, and then sprinted back to fetch more peat balls. Suddenly, rolling peat was easier than trying to understand the intricate relationships within their group.

Laidan did her best not to think about relationships, or the opposite sex. She blushed to think about the things that she had done in that regard. What the old her had done. It was much easier to pretend that men didn't exist. It would change, she knew that. This aversion was a reaction to knowing that she had had a relationship with Brill, while at the same time caring about Garan. It beggared belief that she could care about someone and hate them at the same time.

"I think that's enough," Brill said as she approached. Beside him was a mound of peat balls.

She dropped to her knees. "That's good. Are you sure you can throw with that arm?"

"We will see," Brill said, helping her load his peat balls into the sling to be carried back to the bunker.

She climbed to her feet. "Race you back."

She jogged down the path, the sling weighing her down. Brill was stuck behind her due to the narrow path. She grinned as she listened to him panting heavily in an effort to keep up.

"Glad to see you back," Danton said as they dropped to the ground beside him. "I think they're getting ready to charge."

Brill popped his head up carefully and then dropped down again. "We should do something about that and change their minds."

Brill picked up one of the peat balls and lobbed it over the lip of the bunker.

Danton snuck a quick peek and ducked down again. "Came up a bit short."

He picked up his bow and readied an arrow on the string. "I'll fire off a few deterrents. That should give you time to better your aim. Laidan?"

She had a ball in hand, ready to leap up and toss it. She gave him a sharp nod in salute. "Ready." Danton got four arrows off, but before they could stand up and take better aim, they had to dart for cover under a rain of enemy arrows.

"Now," Brill said, standing, taking a moment to aim before tossing a peat ball. Laidan bobbed up next, but her throw also fell short.

They tried again and this time both Brill and Laidan hit their targets. They set about firing off the rest of their many peaty missiles. The arrow storm halted. Perhaps the enemy thought they were throwing bombs.

"Good," Danton said. "At the moment they are still blocking our way, but I wouldn't put it past them to sneak around behind us. Brill, I need your eyes out there on the perimeter, keeping us safe."

Brill's mouth twisted as he took in their situation. "We are seriously short of people here."

"Garan and Nils should be back soon. They will be a help." He reached out and squeezed Brill's shoulder. "We have to keep Salinda and her child safe. So, if you do come across a situation, give me the signal and I'll lead them away from her. Understand?" Danton flashed a grin. "Karol is my runner. I'll send word when we need you. When we've won here."

"Yes," Brill said, his tone of voice suddenly rough. He turned to Laidan. "Take care of yourself, Laidan. Keep your head down."

"I will," Laidan replied and then caught him up in a hug. "You be careful. Don't be a hero."

Brill blinked a few times, perhaps because he had tears in his eyes. He gave them one last look and, in the next breath, he was gone. Danton handed her a bow. "I know this isn't your best weapon, but I could use you. We don't have an unlimited supply of arrows so use them well."

Laidan looked at the arrows that had been shot into their bunker. "What about those?" She grinned at him.

"You can certainly send them back where they came from."

Both Danton and Laidan ducked and rolled up against their bunker wall as arrows pierced the ground in quick succession. The last one landed oddly and skittered into the bush.

"Blasted dung beetle crap!" Laidan cursed. She had an arrow in her bow and shot it up at an angle. There was a satisfying yelp.

The enemy hadn't been expecting that.

👁👁👁👁👁

Karol backed away from Salinda's makeshift hut.

Eneit had whispered that Salinda was doing well and the baby was on its way. Karol suggested they try to keep the noise down in case there were any stray armed men around.

Eneit assured him that Salinda understood the danger and they would do their best. Karol chuckled when Eneit suggested they exchange places.

"I'm faster than you," Eneit said with a grin.

"In your dreams," Karol said. "I have a few tricks up my sleeve."

By way of practice, Karol kept to the shadows and did his best not to be seen. Brill came along the track and Karol greeted him. Brill leaped into the air and drew his knife. "Oh, source preserve me! I nearly stuck you. What are doing sneaking around like that? I didn't see or hear you."

"I'm sorry," Karol said. "I was just practicing. What are you doing?"

"Keeping the perimeter safe. Do you know our signal?" Brill asked.

Karol did a version of it and Brill nodded. "Next time, use the signal. I will find you if you have a message. Are you heading back now?"

"Yes. I've just seen Salinda...she's doing well. No baby, but very soon."

"It feels strange not having Salinda bossing us about," Brill whispered.

"I'd better go now." Karol smiled and waved.

He had only taken a few steps when a thought jumped into his head: he could use his skills to spy on the other side. A bit of intelligence wouldn't go astray. It would be invaluable. Although he was pretty sure Danton would disagree, because of the risk. Danton didn't know how good Karol was, though.

Karol blended with the shadows and made his way through the line. There were men in twos walking up a section of land either side of the main defense force. He couldn't call them attackers because officially they hadn't charged or engaged with them in any meaningful way. He stayed in the shadows and listened.

At first, he could only make out grunts and one-word comments and commands. Then someone obligingly shared their opinion. "I 'eard there're at least fifty men in those woods."

The man he spoke to spat over the barrier. "Nah, can't be that many. Probably only half that."

"It's why we can't attack. They will kill us all."

"Nah," his offsider responded. "We haven't had the order yet. Then we'll mince 'em and crush 'em under o' boots."

"Do you think they will pass out rations soon? My stomach is achin' like a damn—"

"Stop yer whinin'. You'll get fed soon enough."

An officer walked into their small enclosure. "Send another volley to keep them busy."

Five men stood, nocked their arrows and sent them to the bunker.

"Good," the officer said. "Any word from our patrol?"

"Nah...nuttin' yet."

The officer peered into the distance. "They'll get a big surprise when we sneak up behind them."

Karol jolted in fear. He had to get back and warn the others. Brill was patrolling on his own. Karol slunk away, moving from shadow to shadow.

"What was that?" he heard the officer say.

"What?" a man said. "Nuttin'."

"I saw something...someone moving. Aim over there, into the woods. Quickly."

Karol cursed himself for being clumsy. He was so shocked he lost his concentration and sped up. Arrows whizzed through the air, one fluttering his hair. That was too close. He decided to run for it.

"After him!" the officer bellowed.

༄༄༄༄༄

Nils and Garan changed positions a number of times, but still had not attacked. Garan wanted to make sure they made a clean strike and that they had a place to hide afterward. He did not want to think about people dying, so he figured if anyone was left able to fight, they would come looking for him.

Garan didn't know much about ships and neither did Nils. "We should blow a hole in the side, just where it meets the water," Garan suggested. "Then water will flood in and it will sink." He peered at the ship, trying to pinpoint the exact spot.

"We should burn it, too, so it cannot be repaired," Nils said.

Garan pondered this. "All right, then. You can throw flame and set fire to it."

Nils's eyes widened and he did not look confident.

"It will work better if we do it together. I blow a hole, you set it afire."

While the ship was at anchor, its sails had been rolled up and were tied to the crossbars. It rocked gently to and fro in the light breeze and Garan could hear its ropes creaking. Such a beautiful thing. It was a shame to destroy it.

"It is a bit far, but I will try," Nils said.

Garan studied Nils and then the ship. "So…after a count of three."

Garan hummed to himself, the thrill of power rising quickly to his summons. He had thought, after everything he had been through, that the power would be damaged in some way, but it was clear, violet and pure. Garan bent his knees to brace himself and to better aim. He put out a hand, keeping the exact impact point between his thumb and forefinger. "One. Two. Three."

His power lanced out, cutting through the air straight into the side of the ship. A loud bang echoed around the bay. Screams and shouts erupted. Garan turned to Nils. "Flames?"

"I could not get it to travel that far." Nils had not managed to link with Garan as Salinda had done sometimes.

Garan smelled smoke and, to his dismay, he saw dead reeds burning a few feet in front of them.

"We have to move. They will see us."

"The fire," Nils said.

Someone was pointing at them from the rail of the ship. Water was gushing into the breach and the ship was starting to tilt. Garan could see boards being passed hand to hand; the crew were going to repair it. They had to act.

"Nils," he called out as Nils started to scurry away. "Link with me. I will help your aim."

"Very well." Nils came forward and placed his hand on Garan's forearm.

"On the count of three. One. Two. Three."

This time, Garan detected the cadre's link and Nils's clumsy grasp on the power. Garan fed the flame and aimed it.

An almighty explosion threw them backward into the reeds. Stunned, Garan shook his head and elbowed his way into a sitting position. Where the ship had been was a blackened, sinking mass of wood. The bay was littered with debris. Plants, boxes, bodies and other things. Garan's stomach churned.

A shout from farther around the bay alerted him that they had attracted unwelcome attention. "Come on, Nils," he said, leaning down to give the Hiem a hand up. "Time to run."

Nils's white-blond hair rippled as Nils tried to get his bearings. He put a finger in his ear. Garan sympathized. His ears, too, had taken a bit of a pounding.

Still dazed, Nils did not resist when Garan dragged him away. They had one hiding spot in the woods, which was not going to last long since they had been seen. They needed to move fast and circle back to Danton.

The whistle of an arrow alerted him to an attack. He pushed Nils to the ground and landed on top of him.

Garan rolled off and Nils ranted at him. "Be careful! I am not a mattress."

"I was trying to save you."

And then they were up and running in a crouch.

Nils leaned on the back of a tree trunk, panting. He said, "I cannot believe you did that." He angled his head in the direction of the destroyed ship.

"We did that."

Nils shook himself. "You people will be the death of me."

"I hope not. Come on. We need to move."

The preparation they had done, paid off. They had a number of spots to hide and observe as they slowly but surely made their way back to Danton and his bunker.

There was an awful lot of bodies in the water and Garan had the feeling that he was not the one who had killed them. The thought came unbidden that they had been in storage below decks. His stomach flip-flopped as the smell wafted over the water in their direction. It reminded him of the armed men's food…

All of a sudden, the thought was too much. Garan stopped, bent over and vomited into the grass. He could not get the smell out of his nostrils. He could not get the thought out of his brain: they were eating humans. Intellectually, he could understand…however, faced with the direct evidence in this way was too much.

The sky overhead grew darker. Moonfall. He wiped his mouth and put on speed, not waiting for Nils. They needed to get rid of these men and get to the machine.

♋♋♋♋♋

The boom vibrated in Karol's chest and rocked him back on his heels. Nils and Garan had done it.

The men chasing him stopped and gaped at the plume of smoke pushing its way into the sky. Karol didn't have time to gloat, instead taking the opportunity to slip away unnoticed, grateful to Nils and Garan for saving him. Not that they knew that. No one knew he was here.

Not long after, Karol stepped into the bunker. Danton was peering over the top and he seemed excited. He grinned at Karol. "You're back. What kept you? We were beginning to get worried."

Karol slid his gaze to Laidan. Her crystal-blue eyes stared at him. "What's wrong?" she asked.

"I went to their camp. They think we have fifty men here."

"You did what?" Danton near bellowed, hushing himself quickly. "You risked yourself?" he continued in a low voice. "You're just a little kid. No, you can't have done that."

"I did. I'm not a little kid. I'm a man. I'm clever. I can sneak around like the Hiem used to do…remember, Nils must have told you. They didn't see me."

"Are you sure?" Danton said, forehead stormy with creases.

"Well, mostly. Just at the end, I lost my concentration and I think they

131

saw me. Then they were distracted by the boat blowing up and I got away clean."

Danton shook his head. He lifted his hand, the forefinger in a point. "Don't you ever do that again without asking first." He emphasized his words by jabbing his finger at Karol.

"Sure. I'll check with you next time."

"How was Salinda?" Danton asked.

"Doing all right according to Eneit. No baby yet."

Danton bit his bottom lip and looked down.

"I saw Brill. He told me his signal so I wouldn't surprise him or give him a fright."

"Right, then. I'm expecting Nils and Garan back soon. Then this party begins," Danton said.

Karol raised his hand.

"Anything else?" Danton asked.

"They have sent a patrol to the rear and Brill is on his own."

"Source preserve me!" Danton cursed as he looked around the bunker.

"I'll go," Laidan said.

Danton nodded once. "Be careful. Warn Brill. We will try to get this over with as soon as we can."

Chapter Fourteen
WITH A CRY

Salinda couldn't stop herself pushing. "More," Eneit encouraged her.

The baby didn't want to move, no matter how hard Salinda pushed.

There was blood on Eneit's hands. "Is that normal?" Salinda asked, hysteria in her voice.

"Yes," Eneit said and wiped her hands on her tunic.

"How much longer?"

"Not long. Push," Eneit said.

Salinda leaned forward and grabbed her knees. She pushed and grunted and pushed, and then she couldn't stop pushing.

"Wait. Stop pushing," Eneit said. "It's coming!"

"I need to…to…" Salinda pushed, unable to stop, and she screamed as she bore down.

She quickly covered her mouth with her hand, her eyes bugging out as she muffled her screams. She did not want armed men bursting in.

"Okay, here is the head. Take it slow." Eneit put her hands out. "Slow. Slow. Easy."

Salinda now did as Eneit instructed. Excruciating pain seized hold, like she was going to split open and shit a giant melon. A stifled roar left her mouth.

"The head is out. Just one more gentle push."

Her vagina burned like a hot poker was inside. Warm fluid rushed out and Eneit was wiping the baby's mouth and placing it gently on Salinda's belly.

The baby didn't move. Salinda caught her breath, fascinated and scared. The cord connecting her child to her body throbbed, but the baby's skin was dark purple. A little cry escaped its mouth and its color changed. Its body and limbs grew pinker with each breath. It lived.

Salinda didn't know what she would have done without Eneit. What a comfort—what a calm head. So much responsibility for one so young. "Another little push, Salinda," Eneit said.

Salinda did as she was bade. She put her hand on the baby's head. "What is it?" she asked.

"A girl. A baby girl."

A sob escaped Salinda. She didn't know why she cried. Eneit picked up the baby with bloodied hands and lifted her to Salinda's chest.

"Let her try to suckle while I clean you up."

Salinda didn't reply, just gazed at the baby's closed eyes and tight little fists. The tiny being cried and whimpered. "There, there, little one. It's all right now."

Then the sound of an explosion reached them. Salinda gasped, the baby jerked and Eneit's head shot up. "The boat?" she speculated.

Salinda lay back and closed her eyes. She was so tired. The leaves and branches forming the roof of the hide rippled in the breeze. Danton's little, safe hut. Salinda didn't think she could have given birth out there, surrounded by enemies and with fighting in progress. If she got the chance, she would thank Danton for having had this built.

The baby's skin was pale, the pinkness fading. She studied her child's face—it looked like Nils. Salinda smiled and truly realized it was a girl. *Elan.* A pretty name.

Eneit wiped her hands. Salinda reached out to her and Eneit took hold. "Thank you, Eneit. Thank you so much."

Eneit blushed and looked to the ground. "You did all the hard work."

Salinda smiled serenely. "I could not have done it without you." She frowned. "There is bleeding. Is that normal?"

"Yes, pretty normal. The placenta looked good. You have a small tear where the baby came out, but that should heal. For a while it will hurt when you walk and go to the toilet."

Salinda nodded. "We brought some rags for the bleeding."

Eneit went through their things, locating the rags and passing them over.

"I'd like to get dressed now."

"Try feeding the baby, first, while I bury this placenta."

Eneit moved away from where Salinda sat and started scooping up gray earth, which looked to be soft, thankfully. She looked to the side of the hole they were in and saw that it was sliding in from outside. Was it pulverized moon, the dust that the Ufak Monta said harmed dragons? It was everywhere around them.

After finishing that task, Eneit helped her put clean clothes on. Elan lay on a blanket. Then Eneit cuddled the baby while Salinda completed her toilet. Using a damp cloth, Salinda wiped the sweat from her face. In her pack, she found clothing for the baby, consisting of a blanket and some wraps they could use as nappies.

Salinda gazed at the child, waiting for some overwhelming feeling of love. She sighed heavily. Closing her eyes, she remained calm. There was so much going on. It would take time.

୭ଓ୭ଓ୭

Garan stopped to let Nils catch up with him. The use of power had exhausted the Hiem and Garan had sympathy for him. That blast had been magnificent. Although it was unusual for Garan to take any joy in destruction, he stared at the machine perched on the ridge, glinting in the sun lowering toward the horizon, and he knew it was necessary.

The blast had stirred up things on land. Twice they had to avoid the patrols heading for the bay at a fast pace. Finally, they reached the bunker and Danton leaped up from where he sat whittling a thin length of wood, giving it a sharp point to form a spear.

"What kept you so long?" Danton asked, hair looking like he had been pulling it every which way. He put the spear aside and stuck the knife in his belt.

"Patrols. What do you want us to do?" Garan asked.

Nils lifted his gaze from where he had been staring into space sightlessly. "Salinda!" he cried.

Danton sucked in a breath. "Is she all right?"

"The baby has come. She is well. Both of them are well."

Danton nodded. "I'll send Karol when he comes back to check up on them. He took Laidan to give Brill some assistance. There's a patrol coming around to the rear of our position. I need you to set fire to those balls of peat, then ready yourselves for an attack, because the ship blowing up will have them fired up and mad for revenge. Hopefully, we can thin out the numbers some more. Then we can go help Brill."

Garan took a peek over the bunker wall, ducking as an arrow shot over his head. Danton pounced on it, stuck it in his bow and shot it right back.

"Can you do it?" Danton asked. "Because if you can't, we can shoot flaming arrows instead. Not as good though, because they can pull them out and the effect would not be as dramatic."

Garan pursed his lips and drummed his fingers on his thigh. "Just fire? Nils would be best for that."

Danton nodded, eyes hooded as he considered this idea. "Yes. I don't need to advertise all our strength just yet. Can you still do that fancy shield thing that Salinda talked about?"

"I am not sure. I think so," Garan replied, face serious.

"Well, I suppose we'll find out." Danton cocked his head. "Nils, can you fire the barricade?"

Nils looked between Danton and Garan. "Yes, if Garan can help guide me."

Danton scampered over to where a pile of weapons was heaped. He picked up a sword and passed it to Garan. "Just in case..." Garan slid it in his belt. He'd left the other one back at the clearing with Salinda. He already had a knife in his boot.

"Can I give you anything?" Danton asked Nils. Nils backed up and shook his head.

Danton stood in a half-crouch and gestured with his arm. "Let's do this."

Garan and Nils edged closer to the lip of the bunker. Garan eased up to assess his target. Peat balls were scattered in front of the barrier the enemy had set up, but some were in a small pile that leaned against the barrier. That was where they needed to send the flame.

"Nils, touch your flame."

Nils did as Garan asked. This time the connection was easier, faster. Nils threw his arm and Garan directed the Hiem's power. A *whoosh* of flame ate up the air, then a sharp wind blew and the air around the enemy line erupted in fire. Screams filled the air. Garan chanced a look and winced. A man ran with his clothes alight, no one able to go to his aid. Garan ducked down and then up again, looking to the other side. Bodies littered the ground, seemingly still aflame. The barrier itself was alight. Behind this fire, shadowy shapes loomed. They had killed a number of their foes, but the rest were readying to charge. Danton had pricked them and now they wanted to make their tormentors bleed.

Danton shot three arrows in quick succession.

Garan stood by Danton, sword in hand. Nils stayed behind the bunker. At close range, he could send globs of flame. It would have to do. Garan was surprised that there were so few coming in for the attack. A measly seven men. Surely they hadn't killed so many in the peat fire.

Then there was no more time to think. Garan deflected a sword and followed it up with a kick. His opposite recovered and came in for the kill. Garan was quick to make a side slice as the man held his sword high, ready to stab. He didn't see Garan's blow coming. Perhaps he had thought Garan too scared to think, or maybe it was he who was scared and hesitant. He roared as Garan's blade bit into his flesh, a surprised, angry look on his face.

Another attacker took that one's place. Garan was slow to disengage his sword from the fallen man and lifted an arm in defense. Not much use, but instinctive. Then a glob of flame engulfed the attacker, sending him flying backward to land bottom first on the ground. Nils had saved him. Danton hacked, kicked and punched at his assailant.

The last three men backed up, as if summoned to retreat. Garan heard nothing. He listened harder, breathing too fast and loud. A growl that curled his innards filled the air.

Ahead loomed a man-sized creature with stumpy wings, eyes blazing. Gercomo!

ꙮꙮꙮꙮꙮ

Karol was running along the track, thinking speed to be more important than stealth, when he heard the sound of battle coming from Brill's direction. He'd passed Laidan, taking a shorter path. He slowed, slipped into a shadow and waited. Laidan would be too late to help. He stopped her as she came up behind him. "There is fighting," he whispered. "Men in the woods."

Laidan acknowledged him silently, her hand going to her knife. "I'll be careful," she whispered.

Karol weighed up whether he should run back to Danton or go on to see how Salinda fared. From what he could tell, they would find it hard to get to Brill. Salinda was probably in more immediate danger.

A baby's cry drifted through the trees. It almost sounded like a bird call, until it repeated itself. Salinda! That decided it for him. Laidan gave a nod of agreement and followed behind him. Karol hurried, slipping from shadow to shadow, halting and not breathing when he heard something foreign.

Movement through the woods; the clink of metal; harsh breathing not his own.

Sounds of battle came from Danton's direction, so there was likely nothing Danton could do for Brill either.

When Karol reached the hut, he bent over double and panted. He had been tense with worry and to find everything all right, at least from the outside, was a relief. Laidan took up a guard position, eyes on the foliage around them, as he ducked inside.

He pushed away the sticks that covered the opening. When he pushed through to the other side, he caught sight of Eneit, stave at the ready. She relaxed when she saw him.

"We heard the blast. What's happening?" Eneit asked.

"There are men in the woods. There is fighting all around."

Salinda leaned forward, the baby on her lap. "How is it going?" Her face was flushed, though she looked fit enough.

"Danton and the others are fighting at the bunker. Brill is close by guarding the rear, but some may have got past him."

"We should stay put then," Salinda said.

"I heard the baby. They may have, too, and come looking." Karol moved forward, peering into Salinda's lap. "How is the baby? I came to check and take back word."

Salinda let him look. "If we can't stay here, we'd best move. Just give us a minute or two to get organized."

Karol backed up, casting Eneit a quick smile. "I'll come back. I have to check on Brill. I think he might be under attack. Laidan and I will go to him, then come back to take you to Danton."

"We heard explosions," Salinda said.

"Nils and Garan blew up the ship, then the barricade."

Salinda grinned. "Off you go."

Karol turned and climbed out of the hide. He replaced the branches and then whispered to Laidan. "To Brill. Be careful."

Laidan firmed her grip on her knife and her stave and they ran off in Brill's direction.

ᖤᖤᖤᖤᖤ

The Moon Binder beast, which had been so calm and unobtrusive, burst through Danton's consciousness with the subtlety of an axe biting into soft flesh. Danton staggered.

He had to fight to stay in control of his body.

"Abomination!" he rasped out. Danton agreed with this sentiment and that was probably his undoing. The Moon Binder rode that thought and Danton was pushed under by the Moon Binder's hatred.

"Abomination!" The voice left his mouth like molten lava.

"Danton," Garan said, grabbing his shoulder.

Danton swung around, a growl leaving his lips. Garan recoiled. "The monster?"

Danton's arms swung around in an arc, catching Garan on the jaw. The lad toppled.

Danton clung to consciousness by the barest thread. He was piggybacking in his own body while the Moon Binder ripped free. Something about Gercomo as the beast, tore at the beast in Garan. The Moon Binder hated dragons with every fiber of his being. With strength he never knew he possessed, Danton leaped, clearing the enemy's bunker with plenty to spare. His feet hit the ground running, heading in a straight line to Gercomo, a sound erupting from his own mouth that made Danton cower in fear. He no longer sounded human.

Gercomo had other plans than to fight. Focused on his goal, he didn't even flinch, but darted away. The Ufak Monta gave chase.

৩০৩০৩

Eneit knelt and hastily packed their gear into one pack. "We have to be quick."

Salinda was dressed now, rags firmly secured between her legs. She hadn't tried to stand or walk since the birth. She would just have to manage. A knife lay next to her.

"I need a way to carry the child, so that I can fight."

Eneit nodded. "I can make you a sling from this blanket."

The blanket was a smallish one, thin and well worn. Eneit came over and helped Salinda to stand. Salinda wavered and she felt a hot flow of blood leaked into the rags. She shifted her legs and sharp pain shot into her lower abdomen. She hissed in a breath. "A bit painful?" Eneit asked.

Salinda glanced her way. "A bit."

"Hold the blanket open here," Eneit said and knelt to pick up the baby.

Between them they nestled Elan against her breast and Eneit tied the blanket firmly so that the baby was bound against her chest.

"Make sure it can breathe," Eneit said, on tiptoes to check.

Salinda looked down at the warm bundle of flesh. Elan squealed and then settled after Salinda cooed to her.

Eneit froze. Salinda jolted her head up. Someone was pushing through the branches.

Holding her arm over the baby protectively, Salinda bent to pick up her knife. Eneit had her knife ready when a burly man thrust into the hut with a roar.

Elan cried at the sudden sound. Eneit turned and in one fluid motion threw her knife. The man caught it in the gut and bent over, rolling forward to huddle on the ground, whimpering and moaning. The man behind him backed up as Salinda threw her knife and just missed.

"Quickly," she said to Eneit.

Eneit bent to swing the pack over her shoulders, picked up her stave and went to retrieve the knives.

The smell of smoke tickled Salinda's nostrils. A crackling sound of fire reached her ears. She turned to see smoke coming from the back of the hut. It had been set alight.

"Bastards!" Salinda growled out.

Eneit hopped from one foot to another. "We know there is at least one."

Salinda agreed. "We wait a bit longer."

Eneit growled out. "Shouldn't we rush them?"

"Maybe...I have the baby to worry about. We need help."

There was a growl that sent chills down Salinda's back and clutched at her heart.

"Eneit—take Elan. Quickly."

Eneit looked up. "What is it?"

"Gercomo." Salinda had sensed him earlier. Obviously, Gercomo had detected her too. To be alone and vulnerable like this was more than she could bear, but bear it she must. With no cadre to help, Salinda had a hard time containing her panic.

Eneit tied Elan to her chest.

"Keep her close, Eneit. I will protect you best I can. If you see a chance to run, go. Understand? Just go."

Eneit sniffed and nodded. Smoke was filling up the hide. The green leaves weren't burning fast, but the white smoke was pungent. Eneit lowered herself to the ground to keep under the cloud.

The front of the hide, their only exit, disintegrated with a howl as Gercomo ripped it apart. "Sssalindasth."

Salinda's heart thumped erratically. She had two lives to protect besides her own. Salinda stepped forward. Fear, anger and the need to protect her child filled her blood. She growled low, body tense. She was going to rip him apart or die trying.

"Iss will eatsth youth." Gercomo stepped back, kicking at the branches that were hampering his movement.

Salinda gripped her knife and charged. Gercomo wasn't expecting an attack apparently. Her blade met flesh before he threw her off, sending her flying sideways out of the hide. She clutched at the gray soil to halt her slide and climb upright. Her blade stuck out of his upper chest, near the shoulder. Not a fatal wound, unfortunately, and it didn't seem to bother him. Salinda scrambled away from the hide, hoping Gercomo would follow. Eneit needed to get clear before she suffocated or got burnt alive. Her ploy worked. Gercomo followed her. He was big, ugly and clumsy. Salinda was euphoric, feeling no pain, and she had strength. She charged, aiming for the knife. Gercomo rocked back when she hit against him. She still had her dragon wine strength.

Claws raked her skin as Gercomo swiped at her, lifting her up and away to land in a heap. Her head throbbed and her jaw ached from the blow. Her hands gripping the soil tingled...she looked at the dark, gray soil covering them. The dust from Shatterwing. Gercomo drew close, coming in for the kill. His mouth opened and his jagged, broken tooth dripped saliva. His claws dug into her thighs and his overlarge penis hove into view. She blocked the memory of the attack on Laidan, the horrific injuries. She had to focus. She would die to save her child. There was no getting out of this. His fetid breath washed over her. "Diesth!"

The jaw opened wider, the jagged tooth kissed her cheek. She shoved a handful of gray moon dust in his face, and another. The dirt went into his mouth and eyes and rained down on his shoulders. A great roar of pain deafened her. Writhing, he backed up, clawing at his face, trying to dislodge the offending dirt. The moon dust sizzled his flesh. He stumbled about, screeching, flailing, while a faint purple haze drifted skyward from where his flesh disintegrated.

"Abomination!" a deep, booming voice yelled. Salinda turned at the sound.

Danton stood there, eyes glowing blue.

☙☙☙☙☙

Laidan ran, but had trouble locating Brill. Karol had disappeared into the woods. An urgent whistle carried on the wind. She blinked, sucked in a breath and listened again. She heard the signal.

"Brill!" she said urgently.

A narrow path led her to where Brill's signal had come from. His whistle was louder now. She drew closer and then it was cut off.

The clash of blades and grunts reached her. She pulled out an arrow, glancing down as she brought up her bow and rounded the bend. Three on one. Bad odds.

Laidan stopped, took aim and her shot went wide as Brill moved. "Dragon tits!"

Brill cast a quick look in her direction and backed up, giving her space for a clear shot.

She took out another arrow, nocked it and let fly. *Wump!* It was sunk into one of the attackers. The other two didn't give the downed man a look. One thrust low and the other high. Brill parried the high blow, but not the second. The blade chewed into Brill's abdomen.

"No!" Laidan cried, coming at a run. Brill dropped to the ground like a dead weight. Laidan threw her knife. It caught his attacker in the throat. The remaining one had evil intent in his eye and posture and Laidan wished she had her stave. Then the attacker looked up, filthy face smeared with dirt to hide his skin. He ran off into the woods.

With a cry, Laidan skidded to a stop and landed on her knees next to Brill. "Oh, no."

Chapter Fifteen
ABOMINATION
GAME

Nils reached Garan in time to help him up. "Are you all right?"

Garan was dazed, slowly rubbing at his chin. "The Ufak Monta has control of Danton."

Nils inclined his head on an angle, peering at Garan. "He has been possessed by the Ufak Monta since we transferred it from you. What has changed?"

Garan staggered a little, still rubbing his chin, which was red and swollen. "Well, yes, Danton said he could tell it was there and it was letting him do what needed to be done."

A loud growl from Gercomo had them both staring in the direction Danton had taken. "It doesn't like dragons, calls them vermin," Garan said. "But it had a very weird reaction to Gercomo, calling him an abomination. Could it be that a hybrid is beyond its limits to tolerate, more than it can countenance?"

Nils's eyes glowed with warm light, letting Garan know he was consulting with the cadre. A scream pierced the air. It was getting darker now as the sun dropped below the horizon. Only a few blotches of blood red stained the sky. Garan wished he could tell if this was to be their last night alive. Surely, the end was near.

He glanced up at the black shadow looming in the distance—the machine, higher up the ridge. It was so close and yet it might as well have been on the other side of the planet.

Garan lowered his gaze and Nils spoke to him. "The cadre does not understand the Ufak Monta. Not even Trell."

A sound of feet running alerted Garan to the attacker. He swung, sending a burst of power out. It caught the intruder mid-section and flung him back, hitting the man coming along behind.

Nils cried out, lifted his arms in defense over his head and bled fire. Garan ducked and rolled out of its way, a ball of flame passing over him. The screams told him that Nils had not missed his target.

An unearthly shriek issued from the dark and Garan guessed it could only have come out of Danton's throat. Garan shivered in spite of himself. He had carried the Ufak Monta. The stain of its occupation lingered still. Garan did not think he would ever see the world in quite the same way again. He had lost the cadre because of the strange creature.

Nils straightened and there were tears in his eyes. "Salinda."

Garan swung around. "Danger?"

"Yes. Come."

Nils pushed in front of him and ran. Garan caught up to him, frustrated that he could not pass the Hiem, then recollected that Salinda was Nils's mate and it was his child in danger.

The hut they had made for Salinda was alight. Bodies, dressed like the attackers, littered the ground at the opening.

"Salinda!" Nils called desperately.

Coughing sounded and Garan spun. Salinda moved slowly, a blanket draped and tied around her, and she was supporting Eneit who had a cut to her arm.

Nils raced over to her. Garan swung about, eyes peeled for more attackers. The flames might draw them. He stepped away as the heat grew intense.

Nils helped Eneit to the ground. He tore off some of his robe and wound it around her arm. Salinda pulled down the blanket and there, nestled at her breast, was a small, white-skinned baby.

Nils turned to peer at his child. A look of wonder crossed his features and a thin finger edged into the blanket and stroked the baby's head.

Garan looked away, scanning the woods for more attackers. Surely they had come to the end of them. "Are you well, Eneit?" Garan asked softly.

Eneit coughed and winced. "Yes. It throbs, but I'm all right. The other guy is dead."

Garan blanched at her words. Eneit had seen too much, done too much, to ever go back to being the child she should be. Yet, she had wanted to fight, to do her bit. No one could have denied her that. If they survived, maybe one day she could have children of her own and they would live without this bloodshed.

Garan sniffed and withdrew his gaze from her. Too many painful thoughts of what could have been, what may never be. People did not choose their time. Garan was born at a time when Margra could be destroyed and he had done all he could to stop that happening. In the end, it was out of his hands.

The scream of the Ufak Monta reached them. He thought he heard an answering cry from Gercomo.

"Gercomo...he came...and then Danton," Salinda said, tucking the child back where it was safe. Nils helped her to stand.

Garan saw the lines cut into her flesh, the bruising on the jaw. "You fought Gercomo?"

Salinda lifted her head. "Yes." She rubbed at her jaw. "I might have won, because the moon dust is deadly to dragons." She shook her head slightly. "The Ufak Monta is finishing the job. He seems to be enjoying himself."

Nils put his hand on her shoulder. "The Ufak Monta is powerful. It drew Garan through the Ways to a sealed room. I do not think Danton is defenseless while the Ufak Monta is in control."

Salinda looked close to tears. She hugged the child to her. "Where are Brill and Karol?" She glanced around. "And Laidan?"

Garan oriented himself. "That way. Laidan went to help Brill when the attack started. Karol came here?"

"Yes, then he left to find Brill," Salinda said. "Can you lead us?"

Garan studied her and shifted on his feet. "I can, though it is better if you seek safety."

"There is no safety, only survival. Nils must get to that machine."

"Stick close," Garan said, resigned.

As far as Garan could tell there were no other people in the woods. That didn't mean there weren't any, so he wanted to make as little noise as possible and keep them in tight formation.

Before long, he heard weeping. It sounded like Laidan. "Hurry," he said and quickened his pace.

Karol appeared in front of him, suddenly emerging out of shadows. "This way," he said.

Garan and the others followed Karol closely, until they came to a small clearing. Laidan looked unharmed, but she was sobbing. Garan's gaze dropped to the bloody heap on the ground. He darted over, exclaiming, "Brill!"

Eneit ran up beside him and dropped to her knees. She ran her hands down Brill's body. "Stomach wound," she said through gritted teeth. "Head wound. A leg wound."

Straight away she slung off her pack and drew out some bandages. She passed one to Laidan. "Quick. Use that on his head. There's some wadding in the bag, too."

Garan's stomach churned. Eneit wrapped the leg wound, also studying the angry, bloody slash to Brill's gut, which looked the worst injury. It was so deep that Garan did not think dragon wine would help, even if they'd had some. It was an injury that needed the healing tray.

Eneit picked up Brill's hand and he opened his eyes. "Make a fist," she said and Brill did. She placed it on his wound. "Press down."

Garan gulped as Brill shuddered in pain. Brill lived, thank the source. How on earth were they going to move him with injuries so severe?

"The glide?" he whispered to himself.

"Yes, the supply glide," Salinda said. "We need to fetch it." Her personal one was tied to her pack.

Garan glanced around. There didn't seem to be any attackers in the vicinity, no tell-tale noises. A few distant shrieks that Garan thought were caused by the rampant Ufak Monta. "I will get it."

Laidan's clothes were blood-soaked and she pulled them away from her skin as she stood. She picked up Eneit's stave. "We will protect them. Hurry back."

Garan nodded, then swiveled on his heel. "Wait!" Karol called after him. "I'm coming with you. You might need me."

Garan didn't argue. Karol had already proved himself talented and capable and Garan figured that Karol could help out in a tricky spot. Nils could probably incinerate any attacker alone, especially now that he had his child to protect.

Garan led the way back to the bunker, from where they could go across to the barricade. Garan hoped the glide was still there so they could transport Brill. Otherwise they would have to make a sling, and it would take at least two people to carry him. Besides, there were important items on the glide. Garan wasn't certain, but he had a conviction that the square box was a power source and that the machine would benefit from it. He might not know his history very well, but he understood machines and they needed to be powered by something. The healing tray in Barrahiem was a machine powered by a source deep within the ancient city, unlike the lights, which had their own power sources similar to crystals.

The large crystal he'd brought from the observatory could also be useful. He just hoped he had enough power inside him to ignite the crystal.

Innate caution slowed his steps as they approached the bunker. Across the divide, the peat still smoldered, golden-yellow and black, and the scent of it filled his nostrils. Scanning for Danton, Garan could only pick up faint cries, as if someone was fighting and killing people.

Karol stood at his elbow. "Do you want me to go over there and scout around? I can do it without being seen. I did it before."

Garan's head snapped around. "You were on the other side of the barricade?"

"Yes," Karol said, his silver eyes eerie in the darkness.

"Did you see the supply glide?" Garan asked.

"I wasn't looking for it. I was listening, you understand, trying to get a sense of what they knew." Karol's eyes briefly took on a faraway look, then he shook his head. "I'm sorry, I can't picture it. It wasn't my focus. I'm sorry."

Garan nodded and chewed the inside of his cheek. "Okay. We will cross over to the barricade. Be on your guard. If you see it, let me know."

"I will," Karol said. "I will go my own way. Meet you there."

Garan turned around and Karol was gone. "What the..."

Karol was a tricky one. He was more Hiem than Nils sometimes. Garan climbed over the wall of the bunker and trod over to the barricade, careful to avoid the glowing embers of peat. Bodies lay sprawled and there were burnt corpses propped up, stuck to the fabric of the barricade. Garan shook his head. What a way to go. Why did these people do this? What was there to gain from preventing others access to the machine?

Stepping carefully, Garan peered beyond the bodies. A stack of supplies had spilled over and he recognized one of the packs that had been strapped to their glide. He saw Eneit's stave, which he scooped up. Better not to leave it, even though she had a new one.

A pile of cloaks lay ahead of him. He used the end of the stave to delve into it, flicking cloaks away but finding nothing under them. He backtracked along their supply trail, then paused and reversed his tracks. This had been their base of operations so here was where the glide ought to be. He chewed on his bottom lip as he peered into the gloom. The peat fire gave off some faint illumination, disturbing the shadows such that Garan was unable to keep his attention on one spot. His gaze would jerk to where light glinted and reflected, constantly expecting someone or something to charge out at him. He went behind piled boxes that were stacked high, where a blanket was spread out and anchored to make a tent-like structure.

"Karol?" he whispered, hoping the young Hiem had stayed close and had not gone wandering off.

"Yes," came the reply, seemingly from nowhere.

Garan turned and squinted. "Can you see if the glide is in there?" he asked, pulling the sword from his belt.

"Sure. Give me a few minutes," Karol said, his voice trailing off as he went to investigate. Garan followed, keeping his distance and his sword ready. His heart beat like a drum and Garan felt he could sense bugs burrowing in the sand and insects flying through the air, though he could not see any. Life went on, regardless of the bloodshed.

A yell from inside the tent nearly made him drop the sword. He went to charge in, just as someone charged out. It was one of the enemy, a Sartell man. He pulled up short in front of Garan. "Don't kill me," the man said. "They made us, they made us come here."

Garan kept his grip on the sword. They were not set up for prisoners. Hope leaped into the man's eyes at Garan's hesitation. The man crouched and sidestepped, hoping to get around Garan, who also crouched ready to respond to attack.

A movement behind the man distracted Garan and the man went for a knife in his boot. Garan could only dive to the ground to dodge out of the way. A little *thunk* sounded. The man crumpled, face screwed up in agony. Behind him stood Karol. "The tent is clear now."

"Thank you."

"No problem. I'll keep watch while you search."

Garan went into the dark tent. He felt around for a crystal shard and ignited it. On the ground, he saw what looked to be some of their equipment. He opened a bag, which was full of flat bread. It was theirs, all right. He squinted and pulled down a box, then another. A glint of metal drew his attention and he shoved boxes out of the way, not having time to be tidy. One of the boxes in turn tipped over a barrel and a terrible stench spilled out. He gagged at what he saw: arms and legs in brine. The soldiers' food. Garan lost control and vomited on the sandy floor. Wiping his mouth, he took another box down and chucked it into the corner so its contents covered the severed limbs. Cannibals.

Hurriedly, he uncovered the glide. It had been turned on its end and carefully hidden behind the stores. Where was his power source and his crystal? He rummaged around, panicking, then he saw them, obscured by some weapons. "Got you."

"Hurry," Karol hissed through the opening. "There are more men coming.

Garan wrestled the power source and the bag with the crystal onto the glide and engaged the power. He chucked on supplies that he thought were theirs and put the stave on it. Then he took the tether and bolted from the tent. Karol ran along beside him.

"Found it?" Karol asked.

Garan nodded. "We need to get back to Brill."

A thud from two big bodies coming together echoed in the night. Karol looked around, mouth open. "Is that…?"

"Danton and Gercomo, I think."

Karol winced. "That's likely to crush Danton."

Garan shut his mouth. He had to hope the rebel leader was all right. Danton did not know that Brill had been injured. Not that that would make a difference to the Ufak Monta. Given the strength of that alien mind and the power that resided in it, Danton had to be all right. The monster would protect him.

They reached Nils, Salinda, Laidan and Eneit without further incident. Eneit and Laidan both hovered over Brill, who looked to be unconscious.

"Let me put him on the glide. We need to move."

"What about Danton?" Salinda asked, putting her hand on Garan's forearm.

Garan pursed his lips. "Still fighting Gercomo. The Ufak Monta is strong, Salinda. I think while he possesses Danton, Danton will be protected."

As if to punctuate his remark, a loud growl roared through the night. Salinda's eyes widened, then her gaze dropped to Brill and she removed her hand. "Hurry, then. We'd best see if we can get through to the machine."

Eneit retrieved her stave and laid it on the ground while Laidan removed the packs that Garan had retrieved. Eneit and Laidan took one of Brill's legs each while Garan took his shoulders and they lifted him onto the glide. Salinda kept Brill's fist in place. The bleeding had slowed somewhat.

"Is there any dragon wine in those packs?" Salinda asked.

Garan was busy rearranging Brill on the glide, covering him with his cloak and tying him in place. "Not sure. There's some bread."

Salinda dove onto the packs. She handed out bread to each of them, except Brill who was asleep. She went through the other two packs and, with a cry of victory, pulled out a small flask. "This is it. Pure dragon wine."

"Can it help him?" Garan asked. The more he looked, the more he saw death in Brill's gray skin, in his white lips and dark-circled eyes.

"It can't hurt for him to drink some. I don't think putting it on his wound will do much except kill him with pain."

That was Garan's opinion, too. Salinda knelt by Brill and lifted his head. "Brill. Brill? Can you drink some of this?"

Groggily, Brill opened his eyes. He did not look awake as such, but Salinda managed to hold the flask to his lips and dribble some wine into his mouth. Brill coughed and a trail of dark wine spilled out of both sides of his mouth. Garan was relieved to see him swallow some. Satisfied, Salinda handed the flask to Laidan, who stoppered it, and Salinda eased Brill's head back.

"Brill, we have you now. Hang on. You are on the slide and we will try to make you comfortable."

Brill groaned faintly. It would have to do. Garan packed their supplies around him and tied them in place. They would help cushion Brill against movement and keep him from too much rocking. With a nod to the others, he took up the tether and moved off. Eneit and Laidan jogged alongside the glide and Salinda and Nils brought up the rear. Karol ran ahead of them, ready to signal danger.

They traveled without encountering anyone else until they reached the ruins of the barricade. Nils was alert and tense. The child Salinda carried cried and gave Garan a fright. What if someone heard? What if Gercomo found them? Then he remembered who Gercomo worked for and his stomach sank. He wondered if Salinda had drawn the same conclusion.

A bolt of lightning lit up the sky and a wall of wind slammed into them, nearly knocking him down. Garan lifted his head up to the sky. The clouds were backlit with flame as a vortex developed and grew, a roiling cloudy mass of dust and water vapor, igniting as the moon fragments began their fall.

"Garan!" Salinda said as she followed the direction of his gaze. "We need to move."

Donna Maree Hanson

Chapter Sixteen
RAGE

Danton could not believe how fast he could run. It was impossibly fast. The Ufak Monta had taken over and filled him up and it was exhilarating.

The downside was the Ufak Monta's seething hatred of Gercomo, of what he stood for, a forbidden hybrid. "Abomination!" the Ufak said in words that burned Danton's throat. An armed man lurched out of the gloom. The Ufak Monta put out Danton's fist and downed him in a single blow. Danton did not feel a thing as his fist glowed blue. *Power.* He was infused with the Moon Binder daemon's power—well, Danton wanted to kill Gercomo, too, so they certainly had a unity of purpose. Gercomo's path was erratic. Danton thought he would transform back into a dragon and fly away, but he hadn't. Maybe he couldn't.

Danton growled, "Face me!"

Gercomo cast a glance over his shoulder as he charged away, putting on more sped. The Ufak Monta took over Danton's body. His legs pumped, his feet pummeled the ground and he gained on the fleeing beast.

Two armed men stepped in his path. With a scream of rage, the Ufak punched the air between them and swept them away. They lay like litter in the dirt by the track.

"Face me, coward!" Danton screamed at Gercomo. Whether it was him or the Ufak Monta, he didn't know anymore. It was a continuum of rage, of all-consuming hate.

For a moment, he glimpsed something of his possessor's life. Its role had been to round up the beasts to kill them, to capture and imprison them. The being enjoyed it. Its whole life revolved around killing dragons, except he called them vermin; they were its kin, but kin who did not evolve and who were, therefore, despised.

All at once, Danton gained on Gercomo as the latter flagged after the prolonged pursuit.

Gercomo hissed, warning him away.

Danton slowed, carefully positioning himself until he was only five yards away. He could smell the rot on Gercomo. He'd been eating the dead and the taint was high. Moon dust was eating at him, too, making his skin fester, eating at him from the inside. Already there was a hole in his throat. The Ufak Monta wanted to end him by the quickest means possible.

Gercomo darted forward, a growl accompanying the snapping of his jaw. Danton just lifted his fist and punched.

Gercomo staggered from the blow, shaking his head as he tried to get a fix on Danton.

"Vermin. Unclean," Danton hissed in the Ufak Monta's voice. "You must be destroyed."

Gercomo let out a hot, wet hiss. He was trying to blow fire and couldn't. He wasn't a real dragon. He was an abomination, a confusion of power too strong for a human to withstand.

The Ufak leaped, bringing Danton's fist down on Gercomo's head. Gercomo's jaw lifted and he bit...air. The Ufak Monta had maneuvered Danton's body with inhuman speed. Danton darted in again, his fist a ball full of power. Gercomo's flesh gave, ribs cracked. His tail flicked up and caught Danton in the chest. He fell back, staggered and landed on the dirt with only one hand holding him up. The Ufak Monta launched him upward again, so that in one movement he was diving forward to make his fist connect with the hybrid abomination. Gercomo shook his head as teeth flew.

"You don't have your friends now, do you?" Danton said. "Not so powerful without them."

The inhuman sound of terror and pain issuing from Gercomo's mouth twisted Danton's gut.

The Ufak continued to taunt him. "Just one touch of Ruel Moon will break them down to their essential elements, will return their essence to the planet. I know. I cast the spell that imprisoned them. So many have died from just a touch of the dust that is already corroding you from the inside. I will take what is left of your doomed life."

Danton had had enough of this. *Just kill him*, he thought at the Ufak Monta.

Not yet, it replied. It launched Danton's body so that Danton sat astride Gercomo's back. The beast whipped its head around and shook it back and forth, trying to dislodge Danton, trying to bite and buck.

The Ufak made Danton's hand into a blade and drove it into Gercomo's back. Danton could not break free as Gercomo went wild, desperate to save himself. Danton leaned down and the Ufak spoke into Gercomo's ear. "I'm going to rip your heart out."

It drove the hand farther in, until Danton was up to his elbow. He felt the hot inner tissues give as his finger sought the large, beating heart: his hand opened, surrounded and grasped.

The scream that came out of Gercomo's mouth struck terror into Danton's heart. The Ufak was unmoved. "You should not exist. I will unmake you."

Then he grabbed the heart and wrenched it out, dragging it out through the back, through hide and broken ribs.

Blood burnt his skin as the Ufak Monta squeezed. The heart burst and Gercomo collapsed in the dirt, face now half-eaten. Dead eyes stared at nothing. Danton rolled clear and by the time he climbed to his feet, the dragon beast was gone. There beside him was Gercomo, human again, dead, heart ripped through the bloody remains of his back.

The Ufak spoke to Danton. "Thank you for giving me the satisfaction of killing the abomination. Moonfall should eradicate the rest of the vermin, most of them at least."

Someone moved ahead of him. A small man flanked by two taller men holding torches.

"Baron," Danton's voice rang out.

"You want to kill this one," the Ufak Monta said. "It is only fair that I let you do that on your own. His mark is on you. It is your right to vanquish his touch from your flesh."

For a moment, Danton didn't want the Moon Binder spirit to leave. He wanted it to crush the baron, but it was right. This was Danton's duty.

"Thank you," he said to the Ufak.

He got the impression the daemon smiled before blue light was no longer inside but outside of him. It formed a ball, hovered for a moment, and then shot into the sky.

Danton breathed deeply, excited to be in his own flesh again. He may not have superhuman strength, but he had enough to end the baron.

"Well, well," the baron said as he drew nearer. "Danton, my tasty little rebel. Have you come back for more? Greedy little man."

The growl that escaped Danton made the baron take a step back, obviously having seen what had happened to Gercomo. What did the baron know? Let him fear Danton. However, the baron surprised him with a show of bravado. The baron thought to put the fear back into Danton. "Tell me, is Salinda here?"

Danton screamed and crossed his arms, diving his hands into his belt and drawing out two knives, flinging them at the baron's lackeys. One caught a knife in the throat and the other in the chest. They dropped to the ground, choking and writhing. Danton grinned at the baron who looked from his fallen men to Danton. His eyes glinted with light from the guttering torches.

ॐॐॐॐ

The last of the refugees on garden duty made their way out of the corridor and headed back to their abodes. Squab sighed, not disguising how tired she was. These people managed to really get her back up. They were privileged, entitled and totally out of touch with the real world, although the Vanden folk were better than the observatory people. They had themselves been touched by the violence of the world. Squab shook her head, thinking there were a few choice things she would say to Danton when she saw him again. She'd rather be killing people than being nice to this lot. Dragon fire was starting to seem nice and friendly.

Miraka stood by her side. "You really hate doing this, don't you?"

Squab tried not to smile. She didn't want to scare the girl. "Is it that obvious?"

"Yes, and it is a pleasure to see."

Squab drew in her chin while she pondered that answer. Miraka's quick wit appealed to Squab and it was a battle to keep her at a distance. "I don't understand you sometimes. Why aren't you off playing with your Hiem buddies?"

Miraka turned her stunning gaze on Squab. Her eyes weren't as silver as Nils's or Karol's, having dark patches in the silver iris. Squab thought Miraka had beautiful eyes and the flaws in the irises were part of that. "My Hiem buddies? Are you deliberately trying to be insulting?"

They started to walk back to the upper level now that the garden was empty. Nils didn't want these people in the Hall of Elders and other key areas of the city, so Squab had deputized a number of the Hiem to be watchers and minders. Miraka was her runner. In reality, Miraka seemed to be always at her side and, sometimes, Squab deluded herself into thinking that Miraka liked her, although that thought was usually screwed up into a ball of dung and tossed with enough force to leave Squab reeling.

Miraka was a beautiful young thing and it could never be. Squab was ugly and big. Miraka was just a girl, way too young.

At the moment, Miraka's face was frozen in anger and Squab smiled. She liked seeing Miraka angry, as it took away some of the gloss and the smugness the girl often portrayed.

"We were the last of a community, so close to being eradicated before Nils and Karol found us that I thought I would be dead in a few hours. They aren't my buddies, although we do have a bond, since most of them are close kin. You don't have to insult me, you know, because they make you feel uncomfortable."

"They don't make me feel uncomfortable. Look, I was trying to piss you off. I don't understand why you hang around so much. You're just a kid. You need to hang with kids your own age."

Miraka got ahead of her and swung round to block Squab's passage. She could have gotten the girl out of her face easily, but didn't. "You really have no idea about me, do you? We've been working together. Working well. And now you push me away. How old do you think I am?"

Squab shrugged. She guessed maybe sixteen or something like that. "I don't really know."

"If my age bothers you so much, why don't you ask instead of assuming, instead of insulting me?"

Squab squeezed her hands into fists and rubbed them against her trouser legs. "Don't push me, okay? It's none of my business how old you are. Get out of my way."

Miraka took a step closer and put a hand on Squab's chest. "You don't get off that easy. Ask me."

Squab growled and her face was so heated she knew it would be suffused with red, making her scar glow white. She hated that Miraka challenged her, confronted her and made her face her insecurities. Thank the source they were alone. Didn't Miraka realize that Squab wasn't normal, wasn't nice? Didn't she realize she should stay away from her? That she was dangerous?

Squab's body was tense, a compact ball of tight muscle, and she had to struggle not to physically push Miraka away. "How. Old. Are. You?" Squab ground out, as if the words had been dragged up out of her gut and torn out of her mouth.

"I'm twenty-five," Miraka said deadpan. Her startling, beautiful eyes watched Squab. "So don't call me a kid unless you are freaking one hundred years old."

Squab's eyes widened. The kid...no, scratch that...Miraka had a point. "I'm sorry. I won't do it again, Miraka."

Miraka's eyelids flickered and Squab knew the woman was evaluating her. Miraka took a breath and stepped back. She turned sideways and swept her arm through the air in an "after you" gesture. "Apology accepted."

Squab released the tension in her muscles, although she wasn't relaxed by any means. *Miraka is twenty-five years old. Old enough to know her own mind.* Squab had no defense now. She couldn't keep Miraka at bay, not for the reasons she had supposed. Miraka made her head spin, threw her so often out of her depth that Squab spent sleepless nights worrying over it.

"My place or yours?" Miraka asked.

Squab shrugged. "You are welcome to share my meal."

"Thank you for your gracious invitation. We have some talking to do."

Squab rubbed her chin and ducked her head as she puzzled over that statement. "We have nothing to talk about." She turned on Miraka, sticking her face so close the young woman stepped back. "You don't have to eat with me if you don't want to. It's no never mind to me."

Miraka blew her a kiss. "I love it when you're angry."

Squab scoffed and barreled ahead, using her weight to give her a powerful momentum. She hoped no one was in her way because she didn't feel like stopping for anyone. She had had a gutful of people. Their questions, their demands, their disrespect. Now Miraka, who she trusted, wanted to play mind games. Miraka had climbed out of the box that she had put her in, had challenged her, and that was scary territory for Squab. Miraka knew Squab was attracted to her, she was sure. Now Miraka wanted to torment her, make her pay for her audacity.

Squab mashed her teeth together to stop herself from roaring out her anger and fear. If Danton were here she could talk to him. He knew how to talk her down, he knew how to focus her. It had been a mistake to leave her in charge. She had too much freedom and there were too many people who didn't understand her. These weren't the rebels that she had trained. These weren't people who respected and responded to her. Now Miraka, the delightful child she had admired in a perfectly honorable way, had turned the tables on her. Squab was drowning in feelings. And so much fear. A sob escaped her.

Squab came to a halt. A sob? Squab and sobbing didn't mix. This had to be wrong. Another sob escaped. *No. No. Nononononono!*

Squab put on a burst of speed. This could not be happening to her. She ran up the stairs two at a time, making for her abode. Squab couldn't look behind her, couldn't look to see if Miraka was following. The air was so tight in her lungs. Squab squeezed through the door of her abode, dove straight for her bedroom and slammed the door. Resting her back against it, she struggled for control. There were actual tears in her eyes. *You're losing it.*

Squab sobbed. Real, wet tears ran down her cheeks. A deep crack had developed in her hard exterior. Her control was crumbling. She shook her head in denial. This can't be. *Oh, Danton, where the fuck are you? I can't do this.*

"Squab?" Miraka called from the living area. "You there?"

Chapter Seventeen
TACTICAL MOVES

Squab paced, her palms sweaty. She didn't want to have this conversation.

"Come out, Squab." Miraka was at her door, not quite invading her space, yet giving notice of intent.

Squab ran her wet palms down the front of her mud-brown shirt and trousers. They still felt damp. She cleared her throat and eased the tension out of her neck and shoulders, hearing a satisfying click.

This is ridiculous. What am I afraid of? I like her.

Squab came out. Miraka was sitting on the sofa. Squab just had stone slabs for her sofa. No cushions or anything. She didn't sit there and didn't have visitors.

Miraka made the stone sofa appear comfortable. She sort of lay on it as if she was enjoying the experience. "Were you always called Squab?" Miraka asked.

Squab stood there, shifting from foot to foot, not sure whether to sit down or stay standing, or run out the door, for that matter.

"No."

Miraka grinned. "So what was your name?"

"Lou," Squab replied. "Short for Louella."

Miraka nodded. "The Lou suits you." She wrinkled her nose. "The Louella not so much." Her face became gentle, if serious. "Squab's not a real nice name."

"I'm not a nice person."

"Not true."

Squab lost control of her temper. Who was this girl to challenge her? To probe into things that weren't her business? "What do you know? You hardly know me. You don't know shit about me...about what I've done."

Miraka remained cool. "The same could be said about you understanding me."

Squab stalked to the door and jerked her head toward the exterior. "Just get out."

"No." Miraka stood. "I like you, Squab. I like you a lot."

This threw Squab. People didn't like her, normally. Her appearance put people off. Her manner did the rest. Danton had been the only one to reach out and dust her off and see her for who she was and what she could do. He'd been there when she had killed her father. She wasn't used to admiration. It had to be a trick, a game of some kind.

"There's nothing to like. You know that. I know that."

"I don't know that. I know you're smart. You're clever. You're strong. I'm attracted to that."

Squab narrowed her gaze. "I'm ugly." She lifted her hand to her face, to her scar. The scar that twisted everything.

Miraka stepped close to her. Squab held her breath, waiting for the insult, the punchline. Hesitantly, Miraka lifted her hand, her eyes staring deep into Squab's. The black fleck in her eyes loomed large in Squab's mind, captivating her. A soft fingertip traced the line of her scar. "This is a symbol of your strength. It is part of your story. Your past, not necessarily your future. I see beyond this. I see into you."

"That's dragon shit. A great smelly pile of it." Squab stepped back and Miraka blinked and lowered her hand.

"Well, then...do you like me?" and before Squab could reply, Miraka picked up the hem of her tunic and drew it up and over her head, letting it puddle on the floor at her feet.

Her skin was flawless and so white that it seemed to glow in the shuwai light filtering in through the door. Squab's mouth was dry. She couldn't look away. Miraka was so divine, so pure, her long white-blonde hair fanning out down her back. Miraka turned slowly, showing Squab her taut buttocks and smooth-skinned back. Squab didn't think she'd seen a woman so beautiful before and never had she had one display herself this way.

"Now you. Show me who you really are."

"I...I..." Squab couldn't say the words. She could not take off her clothes. Would not. Yet she was helpless. She couldn't refuse this vision of loveliness. Maybe it was because Miraka was an alien, one of the Hiem, that she didn't understand how truly repulsive Squab was to look at. A whimper escaped her lips. She wasn't used to being indecisive.

"Well, then, let me help."

Miraka walked forward. She ran her hand down Squab's arm, like she was gentling a wild burden beast. "Now relax. This won't hurt a bit."

And she helped Squab undress. Squab hated every moment of it, shook with terror, afraid to look at Miraka's expression. When she finally did, she saw acceptance there and wiped the tears from her cheeks.

෨෨෨෨෨

Salinda threaded her way through the remains of the barricade. Garan and Laidan kept watch, weapons at the ready. Eneit had the tether to the glide that carried Brill. Nils brought up the rear. The baby squirmed against her breast and she peeked into the fold of cloth to make sure the baby was able to breathe. Elan looked up at her and Salinda's heart flipped over. "Hello, little one," she whispered. "Stay safe in there."

All around were bodies. Some had arrows protruding. Salinda lifted an eyebrow as she passed them. She gave Laidan a side glance. "Is this your work?"

Laidan tilted her head. "Some." There was a grin in her look. The barricade up still smoldered so they had given it a wide berth. Salinda's gaze ranged about, seeing nothing untoward. She heard something, though.

"Is that…?" Salinda asked.

Nils came up beside her. "Someone's fighting."

Salinda pursed her lips. Could it be Danton? There was no time to find out as they had to make their run for the machine now. Danton could take care of himself.

"Is our way ahead clear?"

Nils's gaze ranged out and she caught the tell-tale light in his eyes, meaning the cadre was starting to synch with him. She let out a breath and her shoulders relaxed. She hadn't realized until then how tense she had been, how worried about Nils and the cadre. Its comforting warmth was gone from her and she still felt the loss. She had wondered if Nils was fighting against it, having given no outward sign that he carried it.

It was Garan who responded: "'Tis clear for the moment. We should hurry."

And so it was that they left the field of battle and made for the ridge. Two men came running out of the dark and instantly Laidan had an arrow through one before Salinda could even react. Garan deflected a sword strike, then Eneit was there with her stave, striking the attacker mid-section, then sending a sideswipe to his head.

Salinda had been taken by surprise because she hadn't heard them approaching and had been lulled into thinking they were alone, unopposed. She decided to pay more attention.

The sky roared above their heads and Salinda fretted. *Please,* she thought, *please give us more time.*

The narrow track was steep. "Leave Brill at the base of the ridge," Salinda told Eneit.

"We can't leave him," Eneit said.

"You should stay with him."

"Are you sure?" Eneit asked.

"Yes, Brill needs someone who can care for him and protect him."

The girl sent her gaze to where Brill lay and she bit her lip. "I'll stay. Do you want to leave Elan with me?"

Salinda caressed the outline of the baby on her chest. "No, Elan will come with me. We may be gone a while and she'll need nursing." She turned to Garan. "Can you carry the power source?" It was on the supply glide and that was needed for Brill.

Garan nodded. "Give me a minute." Garan lifted the power source off the glide and rearranged Brill, who had lapsed into unconsciousness. He was deathly pale and his chest hardly moved up and down. Salinda didn't like the look of him, but there was nothing she could do. Not now.

Garan knelt, upending his pack to spill food and other stuff on the ground. He scooped up the crystal and stuffed it back into the pack. Eneit knelt down and packed supplies into her own pack. "We can't waste it," she said when she noticed everyone looking.

"How will you carry the power source?" Salinda asked Garan. "It's too heavy to lug up there."

Garan cocked his head. "Can you spare your personal glide?"

"Yes." She was feeling all right, if a bit exhausted after taking on Gercomo. Still well enough to walk.

Garan undid the ties holding the personal glide to her pack. He placed the power source on the glide and secured it in place.

"I'll take the tether," Laidan said, moving forward with hand outstretched. Garan hesitated briefly before giving it to her.

Salinda put her hand on Laidan's arm. "If we find it's all clear to the machine, Laidan, you can come back here and take care of Eneit and Brill."

Salinda turned to Eneit. "If you see Danton, let him know where we are."

"I will do that," Eneit said.

Salinda kissed her on the forehead. "If we don't come back..." Salinda trailed off. What could she say? *Leave? Stay safe?*

Eneit's eyes filled with tears and she nodded, licking her lips as if wanting to speak.

Salinda stepped back. With a quick look at the sky, she spun around and started leading them up the track. The going was tough almost immediately. A rock rolled under her foot and she stumbled. Nils dodged the disturbed rock as it tumbled downhill and Garan stepped right over it.

It was dark, too, and difficult to make out the trail. Salinda didn't want to risk using light, not if there was someone up there waiting for them. Her heart thudded when she thought of the baron. Was he up there waiting? Had he set a trap for them? Her mind ran through the possibilities: that the baron had dismantled the machine, that he had destroyed the machine, that he had booby-trapped the machine. Why would he? And had he arrived that far ahead of Salinda and her party? She thought not. Surely there hadn't been time.

Her pace quickened. The path disappeared suddenly as she stepped into rocks and loose earth. Garan grabbed her.

"I can't see the path," she said.

Garan looked around him. "We have to risk a light."

"But...what if..."

"If we are dead or lost on this ridge, then it doesn't matter."

"All right then. A small one." Salinda carefully moved behind Garan, holding onto him as they changed places.

A small, mauve-tinged light grew in Garan's hands. Garan lifted it and looked around. "There," he said, pointing behind them. "The path divides there."

They backtracked and Garan took the lead. He lifted his light and sighted up the trail, then extinguished the light. "The path is fairly straightforward. Hold on to me."

Salinda took a handful of the back of his tunic. Nils came along behind and steadied her. Laidan was behind him, bringing the glide.

Salinda's legs began to cramp before they were halfway up the hill. She wished it was daylight so she could see where the machine was and know that they were not in danger of going past it.

Tree branches jumped in front of her and she jerked back, then edged around them. Soft earth filled her shoes then leaked away under her feet. "Careful," she warned the others behind.

Then loose rocks slid under her feet and she fell to her knees. "Salinda," Nils said, "take care."

"Sorry." The child was unharmed, though Salinda had skinned her knees slightly.

"It didn't seem that far away when we saw it across the bay," Laidan commented as they continued their climb. The track had dwindled to nothing and large boulders now had to be clambered over.

Garan took out his crystal and lit it. He studied the way ahead and groaned. "What is it?" Salinda asked.

"This next part is a sheer climb. Risky in the dark, without ropes."

"Do we need to backtrack? Surely there is another way."

Garan ummed and ahhed. "'Tis possible we missed a turnoff. I can go back and check."

"Do you think we can climb this?" Salinda asked and licked her lips. She had just given birth and that was a steep incline. Maybe she should have left Elan behind with Eneit. One slip could mean neither of them had much chance of surviving. She would also have to sling the babe on her back, otherwise she'd be crushed between Salinda's body and the rock face.

"We should backtrack. We must have missed a turnoff. You will have to keep your light on, Garan." Salinda peered to where his bulk loomed. "We have to take the risk."

"I agree," Nils said.

"Laidan," Salinda said.

"Yes," Laidan replied.

"Be ready. If there are any of the baron's men left out there, they will be able to pick us out."

She heard rustling and caught the outline of Laidan unslinging her bow and nocking an arrow. While she was impressed with Laidan's aim and ability, she was also surprised at how calm the girl was. The memory of Laidan whimpering and whining surfaced, and there was just no comparison with this confident girl willing to risk her life for others. Salinda shook her head. She hadn't thought Laidan had it in her and yet she had been wrong. Laidan remembered her past and had reconciled herself to it.

It was deathly quiet. They backtracked and then Garan ignited his crystal. His flesh glowed pink and mauve as the light passed through it. Garan moved the light around, searching the ground, walking back and forth. "Here," he called. He illuminated the path to where he was standing. "Sorry, the vegetation disguised it."

The hurried along, taking care where they put their feet. The disheveled state of the track they were on fueled the hope in Salinda's heart that the machine was intact and there wasn't a garrison waiting for them.

In silence they walked and then the baby jerked, kicking her feet and pushing back her head. A baby cry filled the silence around them. Salinda froze and so did everyone else. Then, as one, they turned to her. Salinda made a shushing noise, which was totally ineffective in quieting Elan.

"I think I have to feed and change her."

Nils came up behind her and helped untie the blanket. Salinda cradled Elan carefully and then looked around to find a place to rest. She didn't think she could manage standing up.

Nils took off his outer robe and placed it on a flat patch of ground, then he helped her to sit. His long finger stroked the crying baby, whose head turned, mouth opening, Elan's instinctive need for food coming into play. "My pack has some cloths."

Nils drew out the cloths while Salinda changed the child. She was soaking wet. Eneit had told her that if the child pissed and passed motions that its plumbing was fine. Once the baby had been changed, Salinda lifted her to her breast. Laidan and Garan had their backs turned, hopefully to watch for attackers rather than privacy concerns. Salinda flinched when the child latched onto the nipple. Nils soothed Salinda's hair. "Thank you," he said.

She looked into his silvery eyes, puzzled. "Thank you for what? Leading you into danger?"

He shook his head, a gesture he'd learnt from her. "No, not that. Although it does follow you around." He brushed a finger across Elan's cheek while the baby suckled. "I did not realize my lack. I leave a child behind me. Part of me remains here on Margra. I understand so much now about my mother and my father and even Trell. It was important to them...I was important to them. I was the part of them they left behind. The better them, you could say." He smiled one of his rare smiles and Salinda's heart wrenched at the sadness in it. "If not for you, I would not have this. If not for you, I would not even be here now, in this moment, contemplating saving Margra for my child."

Salinda touched his hand and said softly, "You will live in this world when we avert moonfall. It won't be easy...I know...there is so much damage already and you prefer solitude, but there's hope and you gave us that hope."

Garan's crystal light made Nils's hair glow mauve. He looked so beautiful to her at that moment, like some kind of mystical creature that one day people would tell their children about.

"I think Elan has gone to sleep," Nils murmured. "May I take a moment to hold her? Once we get to the machine, I fear there will be no time."

Salinda's eyes lifted to the sky. Time seemed too short, but she had to give Nils this moment. She had to. She carefully transferred Elan to his arms. His lips lifted in a delighted grin and Salinda put that vision of him into her mind, locked it there. Tears trickled down her cheeks.

"While you hold her, I must see to my own needs. Garan, can you give me light?"

Garan lifted the light to show her a safe place to tread. "Thank you." Garan adjusted the light so she could still see and have privacy. Her blooding cloth was soaked through. In the faint light it looked black. After changing to a fresh one, she buried the used one. It was too disgusting to carry around. The air cooled the light sweat on her skin as she peered up to where the machine lay. So many of her hopes were bound up in that thing.

Don't worry about what you can't control. If the machine is destroyed, then there is nothing you can do. You will die.

Salinda thanked herself for the optimistic spin, muttering, "We aren't going to die."

Nils's head shot up when she came back to the path. "What did you say?"

"Let's go."

Nils stood up and this time it was Laidan who helped secure the baby in the blanket. "Thank you, Laidan."

Laidan kissed Elan's forehead before she helped slip her into place. "She's lovely."

Salinda's eyes began to burn again and tears welled. "Thank...you," she could barely say back.

Garan led the way and Salinda's feet were growing heavier and heavier with each step. It wasn't morning and yet there was a glow to the sky that revealed the landscape. Ahead was a blocky shape. "Is that the machine?" Salinda asked excitedly.

Garan's words floated down to her. "It could be."

The pace increased as the party drew closer to their goal. "What's happening to the sky?" Laidan asked.

Garan harrumphed. "Nothing good. It's not daybreak."

"Oh!"

The path came to an abrupt end.

The machine building rose up in hard, sharp lines and, at the top, was a dome made of some metallic substance that glowed softly. It was that, Salinda supposed, that was responsible for the light visible from afar.

The land before the machine was smooth, dark rock, seemingly polished. Over it was a light spray of dirt.

"Eyes keen," Salinda said. "Check for signs of life before we go in."

Salinda's gaze tracked over the layer of dust, looking for footprints. It seemed to her that the coating was fresh, and as the wind picked up it swept the coating away, so it wasn't going to help them determine if the baron had already been here.

Garan disappeared behind the machine and came back around the other side after a short time. He shook his head. "No sign of anyone being here."

"Still," Salinda said, "I don't trust that. Why was he here if not for this?"

Salinda's gaze traveled over the building, a darker gray against the night. Patches of yellow light backlit the sky. "What's happening up there, do you think?"

Garan pursed his lips. "I think that's the outer atmosphere reacting with the falling pieces of Shatterwing. I think a lot of it is coming down over the Stoli continent."

Salinda's heart thudded. "Not much time then."

Garan nodded, mouth set in a grim line. "We should enter."

"Wait!" Salinda tried to recall the vision she had had when she explored the cadre's origins: seven people entered a building similar to this. She wondered why there was no pulse of familiarity in seeing the building. She hazarded a guess it was because it was not the original building, but a

169

duplicate. Despite giving up the cadre, her memory was good. This building had a solid-looking door of metal and she moved closer to examine it. Garan shadowed her. Salinda was tempted to reach out and touch the door as she did a minute visual inspection of the door seam where it met the wall. Then she walked along the bottom line of it a good thirty paces. Garan stiffened.

"What?" she asked him, not daring to move another step.

"A wire," he breathed softly. "Step back, Salinda."

They both retreated to the edge of the podium, the base that the building sat on, and took shelter. Laidan and Nils had been exploring the rear and now came running back, having caught sight of Salinda and Garan retreating.

"You were right," Garan said. "They were here. The door is rigged with explosives."

Salinda bit her bottom lip thoughtfully. "Maybe not sabotage. Maybe they were trying to get in. Did any of you see how we would open the door?"

Nils returned her gaze. Laidan shook her head. Garan breathed out a long sigh.

"Why is there no obvious means of unlocking the door?" Salinda said, not able to hide her frustration. The baby wriggled at her tone of voice, and she soothed its back with her hand.

No one answered her rhetorical question. Salinda frowned...suddenly, an idea blossomed. "Nils!"

"Yes, Salinda."

"Can you explore the cadre? We need you to ask the cadre, search it..." She shrugged. "Whatever you need to do. We need to know if there is another way in."

Nils met her gaze and gave her an almost imperceptible nod.

"What about the explosives?" Garan said. "They are still a danger. They could go off while we are inside."

"Can you disable them?" Salinda asked.

Laidan stroked Garan's forehead and shook her head. "Don't do it."

Salinda's eyes widened at the show of affection.

Garan's eyes brightened and then he turned to Salinda. "I'm no Brill or Danton when it comes to explosives, though I learned a bit when I helped mine the gems in the caves beneath Trithorn Peak. And you know I helped at Gateshead. I am the best you have."

Salinda nodded. They had to let him try. One look at the sky and she knew there was no choice.

"All right then. Do it. By the source, be careful."

He stood, stretched his arms over his head and cracked his knuckles. His forehead was already a network of concern. "You all need to take shelter. If anything happens, I am not sure how big the blast might be."

Nils lifted his head. "We will move back to the path. I will try to meditate there. I know about the machine itself, but not the building."

Salinda got to her feet and brushed off imaginary dirt. "Right then, let's move."

Garan stood on the perimeter of the podium and watched them. Salinda turned once and waved. Laidan had her head down, shaking it now and then. As soon as Garan was out of sight, Salinda turned her attention to finding a place that would shelter them. Off the path was a rocky outcrop that would provide some degree of safety. "Over there. See?"

Nils turned his head in the direction her finger was pointing. "Good. That looks promising."

Laidan stood on the path after Salinda and Nils had stepped off it, heading for the outcrop. Salinda half-turned. "Laidan?"

"You can't let him do it on his own."

Salinda's mouth turned down. "I don't want to, but we have no choice."

"I'm not important in the scheme of things. Let me help him. Please."

Salinda shook her head. "You'd be a distraction. You know that. Besides, Garan would never put you in danger. Look at the bloody sky, Laidan. We don't have time for this."

"For feelings? For sentiment?" she asked.

"We always have time for feelings and sentiment." Salinda patted her chest. "In here, where we can treasure them."

"But I..."

Salinda let out a heavy sigh. "You haven't told him how you feel, have you?"

Laidan met her gaze. "No."

Salinda put out her hand to the girl. "Come on. Have faith that you can tell him what you feel later."

Laidan sniffed, nodded and placed her foot off the path.

⊃ᴄ⊃ᴄ⊃ᴄ⊃ᴄ⊃

Out on the plain dotted with clumps of spiky grass, Danton caught up with the evil baron who had made a run for it, but now stood there confronting Danton with confidence in his stance and perversion in his eyes. With each breath, Danton felt the loss of the Moon Binder spirit's strength, speed, and magical ability. It had left behind an empty shell. His muscles twitched, his hunger burned and his heart thudded.

Danton narrowed his eyes to slits, the rage and anger from what the baron had done filling him up. Danton didn't fight it. He was going to need every iota of his strength and focus to win this.

"Is Salinda here?" the baron asked calmly.

Danton only grunted in reply.

"I see that you survived my handiwork." The baron eyed him in the torchlight. "Your canvas still has space for another scene to be etched into it."

Knees bent, Danton stayed steady. Let the baron goad him. There was nothing the man could do or say that could harm him now. The baron had had his go in Eternity; Danton had survived everything.

"What, nothing to say? How disappointing?" the baron said in a calm voice. He stepped back and Danton watched, wishing he had a hurling blade to take him out. But that would be too quick, too easy. He wanted the baron to suffer like he had suffered. Danton wanted to repay just a small portion of the harm meted out to the innocent and the unprotected.

The baron lifted a hand palm up, then bent his fingers in a beckoning gesture. "Come on, Danton. Why are you holding back? Someone got your balls?"

Danton shuddered, stopped himself. He couldn't let the baron bait him. He had to see what the baron hid. He was bound to have a blade, poison, explosives…something.

Danton let his gaze rake the gloom behind the baron. Maybe he had backup, though Gercomo was gone and most of the men he had brought with him. A thin blade cut through the air. Expecting it, Danton sidestepped. The wind of its passing ruffled his hair.

"That's one less knife," Danton quipped.

The baron's lips were a thin line of disgust. The baron bent his knees, taking a step to the right. His hands were held in a fighting posture.

Danton was taller and broader than the baron, who was older, a little rounded in the middle, but Danton knew he couldn't underestimate the man. Even with his age, and without his lackeys, the baron was deadly. He had to be, otherwise, how had he got to be so powerful?

The baron ran at him. Danton was late in reacting and saw the blade sticking out of the baron's sleeve too late. It cut through his arm.

Danton punched with his other hand, catching the baron on the side of the head. They both pulled back from each other and the baron smiled. It was a nasty sight.

Blood dripped from Danton's arm, which now throbbed, but it wasn't a mortal wound. Danton took out his own blade. He wasn't going to throw it. He was too shaky now for that.

The baron shook his head. "I think we are evenly matched."

Danton shook his head. "I'm a better fighter. You're an old, indolent man, too reliant on others to do your dirty work."

The baron's lips lifted in a grin. "Go ahead and think that by all means."

They were circling each other, like wrestlers getting ready to grapple. The baron kicked out and Danton dodged the foot, catching the glint of the blade too late. It was a close one. It sliced the top of his thigh. Not a deep cut, though it had a mild sting.

The baron was more agile than he'd expected. The man dove in again, landing a jab to Danton's ribs, the spot where the ribs were missing because the baron had hacked them out. Danton dropped, winded. The baron turned quickly and kicked him twice. Once in the thigh and once in the stomach. The boot blade ate flesh and Danton roared with pain. He tried to roll away. The baron was coming at him with a downward strike, arm blade out and ready. Danton kicked and then rolled, escaping what was possibly a death blow.

Danton didn't get a chance to breathe before the baron was on him again. The baron struck again and again. Danton was deflecting as best he could and landing punches on the baron's face. He could find no gap to get his own blade in.

Danton's arm was shredded from blocking the blade. The baron's face leaked blood at nose and mouth and one ear.

Danton scrambled to his feet, the pointy end of his blade facing the baron.

"Don't get too confident, Danton. My wounds are superficial. You're bleeding like a freshly slaughtered burden beast."

"You will find that I don't give in easily. I have a lot of hate inside of me. It's thicker than blood."

"Ah, how self-deceiving you are. You gave in to me. You sucked my cock. You orgasmed with my cock inside you. You have nothing left."

Each word from the baron's mouth was like a blow, bringing up the suppressed images of his torture. *Don't let him get into your mind.* Danton shook his head, flinging blood out of his eyes. He had warm liquid dripping down his face. He kept ready, though.

"Ah...so you want me to possess you again...is that why you are toying with me?"

Danton launched himself. Instead of just barreling into the baron, he flicked the knife underhand to catch the baron in the gut. The baron sucked in a breath as his whole body lifted up. He fell back a step and stared down at the blade sticking out of his stomach. Slowly, he extracted the blade and blood pulsed out in its wake.

Pain registered in the baron's eyes. He reached down to his belt and appeared to fumble.

Pain dulled Danton's senses.

"You got lucky," the baron said in a thready voice. His hand shot out and Danton caught the hurling blade in the chest. It hit with a *thunk*. Danton fell back and landed heavily.

He reached up and pulled out the blade with a cry dragged from his very soul. The baron lurched over to him. "Die, Danton. Die, so I can pull Salinda apart limb by limb. I want her beating heart to stop in my hands."

Danton threw the hurling blade back. The baron chopped it out of the air. Then the baron dived on him. Danton punched and bit as the baron stuck him with a little knife.

Stab. Stab. To his face. His neck. It was a short blade, more like a tool. Danton punched the baron in the gut, feeling the flesh give way from the force of his blow, the hot innards spilling out. He pulled back his fist and punched again. The baron's little knife like a snake biting, nipping. Slowing...

Danton's hands grabbed the baron's neck. The baron thrashed and then rammed his head against Danton's. They rolled. Danton on top, crushing the other man's windpipe.

"You will kill no more," Danton said, in what he thought was a calm voice. The ringing in his ears told him he was shouting.

The baron hit out and Danton didn't feel it. He had the baron in a death grip. "Die, you gutless little prick."

The baron's struggles lessened. Danton held on. He was bleeding badly from so many wounds. He would probably bleed out. He didn't care.

He had rid the world of the Baron of Sartell.

Chapter Eighteen
A BLOODY CANVAS

Danton fell into the dirt beside the baron's body. His head spun and his face was slick with blood where the baron's knife had cut. He patted his leg and cringed, feeling the wound. Blood pumped out of him. He needed to bind it.

Rolling onto his side, he tore a strip from the baron's shirt. Grunting with the effort, Danton made a makeshift bandage, tying it tight. The pain was unbearable and he almost fainted. His breathing was ragged, and he wanted to vomit.

A roar in the sky overhead and Danton fell back against the baron's cooling body, a pool of blood beneath him.

This had to be the end. Danton's eye fluttered closed and all the cuts and all the bruising sang him down to unconsciousness. He couldn't bear to die anywhere near the baron. He fought himself awake, and, not really aware of where he was heading, dragged himself away. On instinct, he put more and more distance between himself and the baron.

As the sky convulsed around him, he thought of Salinda. He wouldn't be alive to witness moonfall…but Salinda? His eyes flickered open. What about Salinda? She needed him. He tried to keep moving, but his strength failed, his body stiffening in pain, coated in drying blood.

⊙⊙⊙⊙⊙

Garan knelt by the wiring carefully. The light was not good, but there was no time to wait until sunrise. There might not be a sunrise. He dared not risk the crystal light, in case it triggered the explosives. With the tips of his fingers, he dusted away the loose dirt to reveal the fuse, the many wire strands twisted together and snaking along the rim of the door. He knelt and looked along the edge; either they had been intent on blowing a hole in the door or wanted to destroy the whole building. Shuffling along, Garan

177

followed the fuse wires, which kept on going to the edge of the building proper. He backtracked and followed them to the other side. The light surrounding him brightened somewhat and in the distance he heard thunder and rumbling growing louder.

Source, let it not be now. He stood up and peered into the crack where the large, rectangular door met the stone of the building. He ran his hands down the stone. It was, or at least had been, smooth and straight. Not stone, then. Some sort of mortar. Impossibly strong, having lasted these thousands of years.

A fine wire had been pushed into the crack. Garan tested whether his fingers could fit into the tight space to pull it out. No good. He needed tools. Something he didn't have.

He carefully trod to the other side of the door and it was the same. The complexity of the rigging was beyond his knowledge.

He stepped backward until he had the whole door in his line of sight and tried to put himself into the minds of the saboteurs. Rubbing his chin while he studied the place, he gave a grunt of disgust. He would have to check the whole outside of the building. If it was the nasty baron, then there was no saying what that mad mind might have intended. For safety's sake, he had to look.

೫೫೫೫೫

Brill started awake and let out a low moan. Eneit was there in an instant, grabbing hold of his hand. "I'm here," she said in a whisper. Her gaze flicked around. There didn't appear to be anyone close, but she couldn't be sure. Her job was to look after Brill, to protect him. She would never forget what he had done for her when he saved her from those who had killed her mother.

Brill's help had been like sunlight, bright and optimistic when she herself existed in darkness. She had known what was coming. She had hoped her mother would save her, but that hope had waned in proportion to the distance she'd been borne from her home. She'd seen things she never wanted to see again, things she didn't want anyone else to see or experience. She didn't, couldn't, talk about it much. If she spoke of it, the dam holding back the pain and memories would burst and she'd vomit it all out. There was enough evil in their lives without her adding to it.

Her eyes dropped to Brill's face and he was looking at her, puzzling over something if the little vee between his eyebrows was any indication.

"How are you?" she asked, trying not to betray how badly wounded he was.

"Light-headed. Hungry. Thirsty."

Eneit nodded. "Wait a minute," she said, before ducking out of sight to fetch the flask. She didn't think giving him something to drink would make any difference to his condition. His whole torso was black with dried blood and the wound was still seeping through the bandages. His skin was pale and sweat beaded along his hairline.

She supported his head as he drank, taking only one mouthful before turning his face away, and she helped lower his head. Water dripped over his chin and down his neck. Eneit took out a cloth to wipe it away.

"Did you want food? I have some of Garan's flat bread."

Brill nodded, his mouth clenching in a spasm of pain. Eneit turned away, not wanting to cry in front of him. It was better he didn't know. Not now, anyway.

"Here you go," she said, turning back with a small piece of bread between her fingers. She held it close to his mouth and he took the tiniest bite.

"Thank...you..." he whispered. He swallowed that tiny morsel and tried to talk. Eneit couldn't understand him. She leaned closer to his mouth.

"T...others..."

"You want to know where they are?" she asked.

"Yes," he said so quietly she could barely hear him. Fever glistened in his eyes.

"They have gone to the great machine. I haven't heard anything more."

"D...D...ton?"

Eneit shook her head. "I haven't seen him, not since before we found you." Eneit's gaze traveled over the place where they were hiding. "He must have killed Gercomo and the others...it's very quiet now. Not a soul moving about."

Brill's eyes glittered. "Be...be care..."

"I will. Don't worry, I'll look after you."

Brill didn't quite manage a smile before he lost consciousness. Eneit let her tears roll now there was no one to see. She was so acquainted with misery she found it welcomed her like a well-worn cloak. If she believed in Magol, she might have prayed to him. Magol had deserted her when he allowed her to be taken from Vanden and Magol had abandoned her when

Lenk killed the prince and when Gercomo and the rebels came. So many times Magol had had the opportunity to intervene and hadn't. She was happy to believe there was no divine Magol. Her heart broke as she wept over Brill.

ᏪᏪᏪᏪ

Nils followed Salinda's instructions to the letter. He had to believe she knew what she was doing. Yet, he did not have the luxury of time that she had had to delve into the cadre's origins. There was no way he could go off alone for days. He had to make short work of it.

In his mind, the cadre was arranged like an amphitheater adorned with archways and corridors and dark, mysterious spaces. In the center was light. Nils dived into the light. It was the quickest way to find what he sought. The avenues of information behind the arches were there to distract him, to make him gorge on the others' lives. If there were years to do so, he would love it. Right now he needed one small piece of information.

"Trell?" he said, trying not to believe he was being consumed by the fire at the center of the cadre. "I need to know how to get into the machine. The main door is blocked."

Trell proved to be elusive. "Come on, Trell. Otherwise, I have to seek out your friends. You know me. You have touched my mind. Show me."

Still, there was silence, and a cool blue light bathed Nils. That was strange. The blue light grew brighter and Nils fell into it, falling as if there was no end.

There was a door and Nils tried to pull back to see where it was. The door was on the side, close to the rear of the building, and disguised.

"Why disguised?" Nils asked, then considered the current situation. If it had been easy to find, the baron would have got inside.

"What would the baron want?" he asked himself.

Trell loomed large, blocking the blue light. "He wanted whatever he could get. Mostly he wanted to thwart Salinda. He does not think Margra can be saved. You know it can, just as Salinda does."

"Thank you," Nils said. "I'll need more. How do I use the cadre with the machine? I am carrying it, so it must be for a purpose."

Trell's eyes grew into balls of fire and they slammed into him. Nils awoke choking. Salinda came running over. "Nils. Nils!"

She propped him up. "There's another door," he gasped.

"Good. Garan has nearly finished disarming the main one. Best not to

180

have it there to threaten us once inside."

Nils drew breath again and peered at the sky. He coughed, a hacking cough, like he had before. Dust in the air, an irritant, something that would shorten all their lives.

"Help me up."

Salinda braced herself and allowed Nils to use her arm to pull himself up. He adjusted his robe.

Out of nowhere, a wind blew, strong, sharp. Then the roar hit his ears and he made out a scream.

Salinda was screaming Garan's name. "Hurry!" she said. "Garan is hurt."

Nils hurried after Salinda. Laidan was already there, staring down at Garan's body.

"Oh, no, no," Salinda said.

Garan lay still, then his eyes snapped open and his breath hitched and he hauled air into his lungs.

Salinda fell to her knees and started slapping at Garan's clothes, putting out smoldering sections. Garan huffed and puffed as if he could not get enough air.

Laidan wailed and felt along Garan's arms and then tested his legs. "Broken!" she said.

Garan's leg was at a strange angle and he moved it up and down in his distress. Nils's stomach churned at the sight.

"Anything else?" Salinda said clinically.

"His head, I think," Laidan said. "He hit it pretty hard. Small burns. Abrasions."

"He's not in danger of dying. We should bind his wounds."

Nils peered through the smoke that lingered after the explosion. He couldn't tell if the door was open now, whether the explosion had made them a way in. He breathed and coughed as the smoke joined the dust, scouring his throat.

A puff of wind cleared a path to the door. It was intact. From the looks of it, Garan had almost finished clearing the door of its wiring when a section exploded. He had been incredibly lucky that the whole lot had not ignited. It was likely that would have destroyed the machine and their chance of averting moonfall.

He chanced a look at Garan's tearstained face and supposed that Garan was not considering himself lucky. Nils thought of their other casualties. Poor Brill. There was not much that could be done for the boy. There was no healing tray at hand.

"Nils, can you find the door while we make Garan comfortable?" Salinda asked. She had to shout twice to get his attention.

"Yes, I will start on the door. Some excavation will be required. Dirt would have accumulated over the years."

But Salinda no longer listened. She was busy talking soothingly to Garan and instructing Laidan to fetch bandages and a flask of dragon wine.

"I'll need your stave too, Laidan," she said. "It's about the right size for a splint."

"Sure," Laidan said, laying the stave down before she ran to where their supplies were.

Nils plunged into the night, looking for the elusive door. The light grew brighter and he glanced overhead. The clouds were white and thinning, as if they were being consumed. The wind had picked up and he thought it would only get stronger and stronger.

Soon the sounds of Laidan and Salinda had faded and there was nothing in his ears but his own heartbeat and the sound of the wind.

༄༅༄༅༄

Laidan grabbed the pack with the bandages in it and searched the others for the small flask of dragon wine. The bag with the bandages was half empty. They had used a lot on Brill. She thought of Brill lying there deathly-white and sorrow filled her. The sight of Garan mangled panicked her in a way she hadn't expected. She had come to care for him deeply, and now she knew she wouldn't want to live on without him. By the looks of the wind and the sky and the rumble under her feet, she didn't think she would have much choice in it anyway. They were all going to die, which made her angry. She had wasted so much time being stupid, idle and vain. Now she was useful, time was too short. She had no time to prove her worth. *At least*, she thought, *I can face Thurdon with pride. I may have once been ignorant and stupid. I learned to do better.*

Garan faded in and out of consciousness. Salinda assessed the broken leg. "It's not as bad as it looks. Not broken through the skin. Looks like the smaller bone in the lower leg. I think I can set this. I'll need your stave though."

Laidan handed it over and Salinda broke it across her knee in almost equal parts.

Salinda asked Laidan to help, tugging and holding the leg taut while Salinda bound it, using the two halves of the stave to immobilize the leg and keep the bone aligned. Garan came awake with a throaty yell, although he had wits enough not to fight them.

Salinda made him drink pure dragon wine and his eyes rolled up in his head and he fainted.

"We can drop the power source by the rear door and I think Garan can then use my glide to get around. What do you think?"

Laidan bit her lower lip. "That is a good idea. I was wondering what we were going to do with him. Brill's on the other glide."

"Yes, and we don't have time to go fetch it and, besides, I think the supply glide is too big to maneuver in there. My glide is the best for that. Garan needs to help Nils with the coordinates, and installing the power source if it's needed."

"Right. I'll go fetch the glide with the power supply and bring it here."

The baby squirmed and Salinda sighed. "I'll have to tend the baby right now, but I'll keep watch on Garan while you are gone."

Laidan jogged back to where they had stashed their gear. The power supply was strapped to the glide and Laidan also slung the pack over her shoulder, remembering the crystal Garan had stuffed in it. Slowly, she made her way to the rear of the building and placed the power supply and the pack close to where Nils was studying the building. Then she hurried back to Garan, the empty glide in tow.

☾☾☾☾

The cadre had given Nils an idea where the door was situated, but the passage of time had changed the surroundings. Soil had built up, eroded, impacted. It was not easy to find.

He used some light that the cadre had gifted him, a small flame that did not burn his palm. He held it high, finding the top part of the door, and sat on the ground to consider his options. Now that he was more acquainted with the cadre, it was easier to rummage around and find what he needed. The cadre was united, the two halves of knowledge now one. He was very tempted to sink into the dark places beyond the arches and see the times that had passed while he slept. He held back, though. Margra needed him to stay focused.

He sifted through many of the gifts the cadre offered up and then found one. He tested it and was satisfied with what it could do. A channel appeared in the clogged earth before him, funneled out as if by a large drill. The shape of the door grew more distinct. It was a normal rectangular shape, a secret way in.

Salinda had sacrificed so much, he could not let her down. She had surrendered the cadre to him and there was enough of Salinda left in it for him to understand what that had cost her. She had imagined it was she who would wield the cadre and save Margra. Now it would be Nils, a lone Hiem who had had nothing to live for until Salinda had given him a reason— more than one, in fact: knowledge of dragons at first, then their bonding, and then their child. Maybe it had been a subtle plan of the cadre's, but if so, he did not mind. It recognized who and what he was—the potential he offered.

Hunkering down to the level of the door, Nils tried to open it. At first it was stuck, though he could tell it was not locked. He jiggled the handle, persevered, and it finally creaked open, the door swinging inward. It opened up to a wall of black. He breathed out slowly. He had to get the others.

He returned to where Garan lay sprawled on the ground. His damaged leg was bandaged and Salinda sat with him, hunched over and feeding Elan.

"I found the door. It is unlocked," Nils said.

Salinda's head shot up. "Really?"

"You sound surprised," Nils commented, reaching out and lightly brushing a forefinger along Elan's brow.

Salinda glanced at the sky and then back at him. "Everything has gone against us. I expected...well, I expected more trouble."

Garan groaned and lifted a hand to his head.

"Is Garan in any condition to help?" Nils asked.

"I hope so. We are depending on his help. I don't know enough about moons and astronomy to be of assistance. Neither does Laidan."

"It is time," Nils said, lurching to his feet again. "We must go now. Garan?"

"He needs a few moments." Garan had been out cold, and Salinda was hoping the dragon wine would help. She tried slapping Garan's cheeks gently and pinching his arm. Nils loomed over her and gave an exasperated sound.

"Can you do something?" she asked.

Nils dropped to one knee and put his palm on Garan's forehead. His eyes glowed for a second or two and he removed his hand. Garan sat up so fast, Salinda nearly fell on her rear. Garan gasped as if he had been startled, then looked down at his leg. "I thought...I thought..." He looked at them helplessly. "I thought I died."

Salinda winced. "You broke your leg. Your other injuries are less extreme. I think you will hurt worse later."

Garan fixed his attention on Nils, then lifted his head to the machine. "The door is still shut."

"We have a back way in," Nils explained. "We are surely running out of time, though."

Salinda tugged the glide over. "We thought you could use this. Laidan stashed the power pack and crystal at the back door earlier. She'll carry them inside and put them where you think they should go."

Garan's jaw dropped and then he shut it quickly with a click. He shook his head and banged at his temple. "Right. Yes."

Salinda and Laidan helped Garan to sit himself on the glide. He couldn't cross his legs so he had to hold onto the sides in order not to tip himself out. His splinted leg jutted out awkwardly. He did a test and managed to move the glide in a circle.

Nils stood by the building, waiting impatiently. He dared not look at the sky. The impending doom pressing down on them was likely waiting for that one last look.

Garan went on ahead with his leg sticking out. Fortunately, he kept his balance on the glide. Salinda put a protective arm around Elan and walked alongside Nils, Laidan just ahead of them.

They headed for the door with Nils holding his breath.

Chapter Nineteen
The Great Machine

The back door to the machine was an ordinary looking door. Salinda bit her lip. In plain sight, it was. Yet when she looked about her, she saw the freshly removed earth and rocks. "You did this?" Salinda asked Nils.

He inclined his head. "Indeed. The cadre is a most useful tool in a time of need."

Garan passed ahead, holding a light. His gaze was all for Laidan, who was picking up his equipment. He called out instructions, warning her to be careful.

Salinda couldn't quite hear Laidan's response, but smiled at the tone.

"What's it like, the complete cadre?" she asked, a note of wonder in her voice.

"Beyond my imagining. Full of knowledge and lives past. A kernel of power that can be directed at will. I see you in here, also," Nils said.

Salinda's eyes widened. "I see." She understood that although she wasn't wholly inside the cadre, as she wasn't dead, a part of her could exist there.

Nils pushed open the door and disappeared into the dark. Salinda hesitated on the threshold.

"Nils, can you make light, please?" she called into the dark. A small bluish glow emanated from within. It was enough to let her see where to place her feet and, once inside, she saw Nils's face lit from beneath. His eyes were dark holes; his hair glowed bluish-white.

Entering into the building that housed the machine was like entering a tomb of some unknown figure, buried for thousands of years. The stories it would tell, the knowledge it would bring. Salinda hoped it would be the answer. They had risked everything to reach this machine.

Garan came alongside with a glowing crystal so Laidan could see her way in. Nils had moved away from the door and they could see a corridor with smooth walls, a layer of dust coating them. Salinda ran her hand along the wall, experiencing a similar sense of awe to when she first woke up in Barrahiem. This building, this machine, was made so long ago, when humans were great and numerous. They had cities and learning and peace. Now there were few who remained and no great cities, no learning, no peace. Humans were like dust on the surface of the planet, the residue of a great culture. She was so breath-taken she could hardly speak.

"Get out of the way," Laidan scolded Garan.

"Sorry," he said, and then bumped into the wall and fell off the glide with a grunt of pain. Salinda's awed mood dissipated, and then she realized that Nils was gone. Panic seized her until she noticed the door. Laidan fumbled, helping Garan to get back on the glide while at the same time trying to shift the power pack inside.

Salinda shook her head and went after Nils, who was lost in the gloom. A small light flickered ahead. "Nils?" she called out. She dared not enter any farther, having no idea where her feet would land. With the baby held tight against her, she called out again.

There was a sound, a *zoomp*, and many lights came on. Salinda crouched, hand over her eyes to shield them from the brightness. As her eyes slowly adjusted to the light, she stared, astonished by her surroundings. At first, her mind couldn't comprehend what it was seeing. The dome above was transparent and the angry sky looked ready to burst through. A hum filled the air, reminding her of the sound of the healing tray. It was the machine; it was turned on now. Panels of lights filled the walls and then in the center, she saw it. The machine. The one she had seen in her vision. The one the seven people went into. Nils stood by it, rubbing his head as he studied it.

Salinda looked down and saw that the machine extended beneath her feet. A transparent floor allowed her to see tubes and flickering lights continuing way beyond where she could see. She took a tentative step. Walking on the transparent flooring made her knees shake and her heart do flip-flops. Closing her eyes, she punched down her fear so it became a knot in her stomach, something easily ignored, and looked straight ahead as she walked toward Nils. The constant hum in the air gave her hope that the machine was still functional after all this time.

CARCARCAR

The blackness that had overtaken Garan during the explosion threatened to come back. He only had to turn his head too quickly to feel it rushing at him. Falling off the glide to the sound of Laidan's laughter was a mixture of dark and light. Her laughter was soft and light and merry, not derisive. He knew her derisive laugh, having heard it often enough. This was different. He shook his head, trying to dislodge the thought that she cared for him.

He hopped about on his good leg, trying to get the glide to stay still so he could plant himself on it. At the same time, he was apologizing to Laidan because she had to lug the heavy gear.

"Shut up, already," she said. "Just get your butt in that thing and get over to Nils. He needs you."

He inclined his head, the best bow he could manage now he had succeeded in sitting on the glide. He wished he had practiced with it more when he had repaired it for Salinda's use. He was ashamed of his own clumsiness. His broken leg throbbed something awful and falling off the glide hadn't helped. Yet his veins throbbed with life and vigor courtesy of the hefty dose of dragon wine Salinda had poured into him.

The straight lines of the corridor traveled along the edges of his perception. He could honestly say he had not seen a construction like it. The observatory's corridors were not so straight. He put out a hand and ran his finger along the smooth surface. Dust painted his finger and he wiped it away. It was old, but it seemed so new.

Once out of the corridor, he came alongside Salinda, who looked shocked, mesmerized and bespelled. He shifted his eyes from the walls to the floor below and let out a shout. He could see way down into Margra's depths. Peering up, he could see the roiling cauldron of the sky. His gaze flew to Nils, who stood before a panel where lights winked on and off. Beyond that was a double-walled room with chairs. Although the two walls were clear, they were easy to detect because a faint mist circled within.

Garan pressed the glide control and raced over to Nils to look at the panels. Their function was not apparent and Garan no longer had the cadre to explain things. He could work with Hiem technology, but this appeared to be something else.

Nils acknowledged his arrival and started talking. "These green lights indicate that the system is functioning." He lowered his hand and hovered over the red lights. "These indicate issues with alignment, and the other power supply."

"That it has any power is amazing. Where does it come from?" Garan asked.

Nils cocked his head and met his gaze, then dropped his eyes to the controls. "This machine taps into the power of Margra's core." He moved his hand back to the red controls. "There has been some breakdown in the power supply. Some is getting through, though not enough. There has been no one maintaining this facility for a long time." Nils lifted his head to stare above him. "Indeed, I am amazed it stands at all. I can see that Hiem technology has been used in its making. They owed this to Trell and, perhaps, some of Trell's Hiem supporters."

Nils pointed to the double-walled room. "That is the control station. In a similar room, the cadre was created."

"Created. Deliberately?" Garan asked.

"No. An accident. Seven people walked in there and only one walked out. Trell."

"Ah," Garan said.

Nils studied the double-walled room. "It seems that the Hiem mind was better able to cope with the power the machine unleashed. Yet that power is not enough and we need to channel even greater power into this machine."

Garan nodded. "The power pack?"

"Yes, and your crystal, although you will need to adapt it to this technology somehow. I will work on repairs to the power generator."

Garan frowned. "How can you do that?"

Nils tapped the side of his head. "It is all in the cadre. Those who formed the cadre built this machine. They know better than anyone how to repair it and operate it. They know why they failed last time."

"Failed?" Garan queried at the same time as Salinda, who had come up to them while they talked.

"Yes, their success was only partial. They had planned on obliterating Ruel Moon so that none of it fell onto the surface. First they changed the weight and size of the fragments, then they meant to reduce those smaller fragments to their essential elements. They did not complete the process."

"I see," Garan said, feeling his stomach drop to the ground and bounce back up again. "I will start on the power pack."

"You will need to charge it."

Garan smiled. "I have been, bit by bit, as we traveled. It will only need a top-up."

Garan assessed the walls, looking for where the power reserves were stationed.

He undid a panel, saw the inlets and shut it—not the right one. He went back to the main panel and opened it, looking for the direction of the conduits. It was strange technology, not as intuitive as Hiem tech. The Hiem lights had simple parts and a charge unit. Garan did not have time to map these conduits, so he summoned his power, channeled it to his hands and touched the conduit. His arm went numb and he could feel where his power went, could taste where his power did not go. Then he closed his eyes and drew a mind map of where everything was. First, he had to attach the power pack. He called to Laidan and went to the far wall. There was a ladder going underneath the transparent floor. "We need to take the power pack down here," he said to her.

She looked at him, face red and sweaty, and grimaced. "Right."

Garan could not descend the stairs on the glide as his leg jutted out awkwardly and the hole in the floor that held the ladder just would not let him through. He tried to figure out what to do, and there was no way other than getting off the slide and climbing down unaided. It meant sliding between rungs and jumping with his good foot. Risky. One wrong move and he would be clinging on for his life and struggling against the pain. He needed Laidan to lower the power pack on the glide, he could not ask her to help him down, too. Besides, he weighed too much and if he slipped, he could cause Laidan to fall.

Garan lowered the glide to the ground as close to the stair as possible. He pulled himself upright so he was near the lip of the opening in the floor. He put his splinted leg into the hole, placing his arms on the top rung. Then he hopped down, aiming his good leg for the second rung. He lost his grip, his fingers slipping. He quickly hugged the metal stair. His broken leg banged against the metal pole that supported the stair and the blackness threatened to return.

"Garan!" Salinda called.

Garan breathed and fought for consciousness. He really could not afford to faint right now.

When next he looked up, he saw Salinda's face. "Garan? Wing dust! What a predicament? Can you climb back up?"

The back of Garan's neck was wet with sweat. He shook his head and looked down. Suddenly it looked a lot farther away than it had previously. Sadly, there wasn't any rope to help lower him.

He took a few breaths. "I'm going to try to go down one rung at a time."

Garan changed his grip, bringing one hand and then the other to the stair rail. It really was no better than a metal ladder.

The pain in his broken leg subsided to a throb. He could no longer feel his toes and he hoped that was a good thing. Holding fast with both hands, Garan kicked out and down. It jerked his bad leg, which made him cry out, but he had succeeded in going down a rung. He slid his hands down the rail and tried it again. His leg was on fire and pain shot up his back. He laid his head against the rung in front of his face and panted until it lessened. "This...may...take time."

He glanced up at Salinda's worried face. She shook her head and looked away, probably at Laidan. She came back again.

"You're not thinking of taking that power pack down there, too?"

"Yes. We can tie it to the glide and bring it down using the tether."

"Fine," Salinda said, sounding less than happy. He understood her frustration. They should have been able to come in here, turn the machine on and zap the moon fragments before the world ended. At this rate, they would still be trying to get the machine to work when they all ceased to exist.

Garan grasped the rail again and shot his foot out and onto the next rung. He did it again and again. He stopped three more times to get over the intensity of the pain in his leg. The knee was none too happy at being bashed against the rungs either. If the splint had been on the lower leg only it might have worked out better.

Garan slid down to the floor, missing the last rung. He caught the heel of his bad leg on the floor, jolting him hard. He cried out, fell the last bit and landed flat on his back. He might have passed out because he heard Laidan calling him urgently.

"What?" he yelled up.

Laidan's head, surrounded by her blonde hair, appeared. "You all right there?"

"Yes," he called up to her. He groaned when trying to right himself. "Can you bring the power pack down here? You will need to tie it to the glide and bring it down with the tether."

Laidan ducked out of sight and came back. "I will have to go back for the ties as I left them where I took the power pack off so we could get the glide to you. Why don't you look around while I'm gone to work out where this stuff goes, instead of lying there like a lump."

Garan pressed his lips together, biting back a retort. Even though Laidan had mellowed, she could be annoying at times.

Garan gripped the ladder to help him climb back on his feet. The room he was in stretched out in many directions and it was much wider than the room above. It was under the podium, the stone base that the machine building was perched on.

Without the glide, moving around was going to be interesting. He tried hopping and that doubled him over in pain. The jolting caused by his weight coming down was too much for him. He would have to try sliding sideways. He didn't want to be found in the same place when either Salinda or Laidan came down.

Even using the ladder rail to brace himself, it took careful maneuvering to lower himself to the ground. He screamed when the pain became unbearable and flipped himself over, so his buttocks were resting on the ground. When he caught his breath, he realized that he would have to pull and drag himself backward to a panel against the wall. He tried it and, while his leg throbbed and threatened to overwhelm him, it worked best when he dragged his legs along behind him.

Slide by slide, he neared the first of the panels winking at him. The red lights drew him near, for they signified the power failure. He yanked open the first panel and saw where the leads delved down deep into the bowels of the building. He made it to the next panel and the next, until he found something useful. It was an auxiliary power outlet. He thought that term might have come from the cadre, some remnant of memory. He did not really care about the terminology, but it did look like it had a compatible coupling.

Garan rested there while studying the insides of this part of the machine. He could not try anything until Laidan returned with the ties and brought the power pack down.

"Garan," Laidan said with a grunt, "I have the power pack thing tied to the glide. How am I supposed to bring it down?"

Garan shifted position and tried to decide what should go first. "I think if you climb onto the ladder, then use the tether to fill the hole with the power pack and gently tug it down."

"Why did I know you were going to say that?" Laidan said, not trying to disguise her disgust. "Come closer, and I'll pass your pack over to you—the one with the crystal."

Garan shuffled under the opening. Laidan climbed down with the backpack across her back. When she was a couple of rungs from the bottom, she slid it off and dropped it in Garan's waiting hands. He caught it, almost tipping over. Laidan obviously thought the crystal within was impervious to harm. Garan opened the flap and inspected it.

When he looked up again, Laidan's head hovered over the opening. "I'm coming down now."

The tether cord was wrapped around her hand twice. She lowered herself down a little, then a dark shadow blocked off the light from above and she pulled at the glide, helping it with her hands as much as possible. Garan stopped breathing. She was balanced against the rungs, both feet on one rung and knees resting on the one above. Very carefully she succeeded in getting the power pack through the opening. As she took steps downward, the power pack followed on the glide. She must have thought it through initially, because she managed to bring it down easily. Garan frowned, as he had thought of doing it another way. Laidan's method, though, meant less risk to the power pack.

Garan edged away so that Laidan's way was clear. She jumped down, skipping the last rungs, grabbing the edge of the glide to steady it, and stared around at the machinery. "Wow! This is something. How can you make head 'n' tail of it?"

Garan followed the direction of her gaze. Row upon row of machines. He would probably never know what they all did. He jerked his thumb behind him. "This machine appears to be the power controller. That's where the power pack goes."

She withdrew her reluctant gaze from the array of machines. "Right then." Laidan headed for the machine he had pointed out and the cover he had opened. Garan bum-shuffled over.

"Can you place it there?" he asked, gesturing to the spot.

"Do you know how heavy this is?" she asked, starting on the ties.

"Actually, I do," he replied.

"Yes, now you're just being a smart-ass. Show me exactly where you want it placed."

Garan's face flushed. "I am going to help you."

She had finished undoing the ties and Garan levered his fingers under one side, Laidan the other. "After three," he said.

Laidan nodded, screwing up her face with effort.

"One. Two. Three."

They lifted the power pack free of the glide. Laidan nudged the glide out of the way with her hip and it moved a short distance away before stopping. With a big groan of effort, Laidan helped him place the heavy pack.

"You all right?" he asked.

"Sure, I'm fine. You like the look of the sky, do you?"

Garan did not need to look up to see it. He knew what was happening. "No, I...let's work on this."

He studied the power pack and found a flap that jutted open with a little shove. There were several types of outlets there, a place to fit cables. He studied them and then lifted the cable attached to the machine. "It looks compatible to this one."

Laidan narrowed her gaze. "How can you be sure?"

"Only one way to find out," he said. He picked up one of the cables and moved it to the power pack.

Laidan sucked in a huge breath.

"Do you want to go back up to a safe place?"

"No. There is no safe place," she said.

"You sound like Salinda." Garan tilted his head. "Here goes."

As soon as he brought the end of the cable closer, the power arced between them. Garan nearly let go. He was unharmed so he rammed the ends together and the cable locked in place.

Laidan studied the machine above his head. "About half the lights went green."

Salinda called down to Garan. "That's it, Garan. Hurry."

Laidan dragged over the pack and when he drew out the crystal, she asked, "How are you going to use that?"

Garan assessed it. "I am not sure."

The crystal did not look to be compatible, yet he picked up another cable and studied the ends.

"I am going to charge the crystal. Maybe you should go."

"No," Laidan said, "my job is to get you out of here."

Garan stared at her, but had no time to argue. He put his hands on the crystal, summoning its power. Or, if he believed Salinda, he put *his* power in the crystal. It glowed faintly and it took a lot of effort to concentrate on such a large stone. He focused on the middle, on the core of the crystal; he found humming helped him focus his power and soon the crystal was pink and glowing.

He picked up the cable. "Be ready."

Laidan gave a slow nod and backed away to the base of the stairs.

Power arced between the crystal and the cable. As the cable meshed with the crystal, the concussion threw Garan backward and dark stars shot out of his eyes, or so he thought. Laidan screamed and Garan knew sadness, thinking he might have hurt her.

When he shuffled back to inspect the machine panel, all the lights were blinking green. The cable end was stuck to the crystal, which was pulsing intermittently.

Laidan lay inert not far from him. He drew his body over to her and cradled her against his good thigh. He brushed the hair from her face and noted the big red bruise forming on her cheekbone. "Laidan?"

Salinda's voice echoed around them. "Nils says the power is good. You need to get out of there."

"Coming! Laidan is hurt."

"What?" Salinda called. Garan sighed and gave up trying to communicate. Salinda's voice reached them, but his did not reach her, apparently. He nudged Laidan, patted her cheek, but she was out cold. He reached for the glide, snaffling the tether. He would need it once he was up the ladder. He wondered whether he could heave Laidan onto it and get her up the ladder. That was wrong on many levels, not least because the opening to the stair was too small to fit her prone body.

"Laidan!" he yelled at her. Her eyelids flickered and he let out a breath he had not realized he had been holding. He patted her cheek gently now while saying her name. He tried to heft her upright in his arms. "Come on," he said, urgently, "you need to get up. We have to get out of here."

A groan issued from her mouth and her head flopped forward. Garan tensed until she moved her head. "What happened?" she said, slurring her words.

"I will answer you later. Right now, we need to get to those stairs."

Laidan studied her surroundings. "You did it?"

Garan flashed her a grin. "Yes, with your help. Are you well enough to climb the ladder?"

Laidan turned in his arms and lifted her gaze to him. "Yes, I can climb the ladder. What about you?"

"You go first."

Laidan grimaced. "Really? I should go after you in case you lose your footing or hold."

Garan shook his head. "I will feel so much better when you are out of here safely. Salinda said we had to get out."

"I don't want to leave you behind."

"You are not. I am following, so move." He gave her a nudge and she climbed to her feet, swaying slightly. Laidan was not one hundred percent, but she moved to the ladder and he followed, dragging the glide with him. "Can you tie this to your belt?" he asked.

Without answering, she took the tether and attached it. Then she turned and put her foot on the first rung. "If you don't follow me, I'm coming back down."

Garan was touched by her concern. "Thank you. I'll be right behind you."

As soon as she cleared the fourth rung and was not likely to kick him in the face, Garan put both hands on the rails and pulled himself up, first into a kneeling position on his good leg. He stifled the yell. It hurt to move his bad leg. The splint pressed into his groin and he could do nothing to fight off the blackness threatening his sight.

He grabbed the next rung and then thrust his good leg into place, keeping his bad one away from the ladder. His bad leg bounced a little. He slid his arms up and repeated the move. Sweat poured off him and the muscles of his arms and shoulders screamed in protest. Halfway up, his hands slipped because of his sweaty palms and his leg *thunked* against the rung below. Garan hugged the ladder as he slid down and then got his good foot on a rung to stop his fall. He began the process again. His knee ached, feeling terribly bruised.

"What's taking you so long?" Laidan called from above.

Garan conserved his energy by not replying and continued to pull himself slowly, inexorably up the ladder. Both Laidan and Salinda were there to pull him through the opening at the top.

Garan screamed out because the tip of the stave stuck into him again with the jerky movements to drag him free.

Laidan asked him what was wrong and he explained. She cast her gaze at Salinda.

"Get him on the glide and out of here," Salinda said.

"I need to help Nils," Garan protested. "There were seven minds that drove the machine, remember."

"I do...but they are inside Nils now. He says we all must leave. The danger is too great."

"But Nils...he..." Laidan said, her expression not disguising the horror she felt leaving her Hiem guardian behind.

"He says that if Trell survived, then he has the same chance. Plus, he has extra power, both from the cadre and from you, Garan. When you hooked up the crystal, all the gauges went crazy."

Laidan helped Garan to sit on the glide and he engaged the device. He was ill way down in his stomach. He did not think it right that they risked Nils. "I should stay. I could help."

Salinda shook her head. "Get outside and take cover. Nils's orders." As if to punctuate her meaning, the sky screamed. "Hurry," she said.

Garan took the tether from Laidan's hand. "I will go over the coordinates with Nils and join you outside."

Salinda tightened her mouth and then shook her head. "You are brave, Garan. For that I thank you."

Salinda and Laidan headed out of the building. Garan saw Nils checking the machine and saw more and more lights go green.

⚬⚬⚬⚬⚬

Nils ran through the checklist he had memorized from Trell's book. When Garan had installed the power, the indicator went to the top of the scale. Trell had said that insufficient power had been one of the causes of failure; now they had the maximum possible.

Nils understood now why he had not known about the power cell and what it was for, because it was not of Hiem manufacture. It looked more like a hybrid component that had been carried back to Barrahiem, so it made sense, he supposed, that he had found no record of it. And Trell's book had been left deep in the ruins of the old observatory. Nils had not been able to read all of it yet. There was no time now to interrogate the remnant of Trell that existed in his head and gain more instructions.

"Nils?" Garan said from behind him.

Nils swung around. "What are you doing here? I said you should all leave."

"I can help you with the coordinates."

"I have them," Nils said, through clenched teeth. "I do not want to be responsible for your life. Already you are injured."

"Where did you get the coordinates? From the cadre? From what I left in there?" Garan asked.

Nils shook his head. "No, they were written in Trell's book."

Garan slid forward on the glide. "They are wrong. Out of date," Garan said urgently. "I have the up-to-date ones from the observatory. They had been testing different blasting patterns to push the moon fragments out of orbit, to nudge them sideways."

Nils listened impatiently. They did not have time to tinker with this machine, but he knew things had gone wrong with the first attempt. Some of the matter they had intended to weaken had not been affected, probably due to the moon having properties that defied the science of the time. What Nils theorized as being Moon Binder magic—the power used to bind the moon and bind the dragons there, those creatures they called vermin—was the missing link.

As there was no real science, it was impossible to make calculations to adjust the beam to account for the Moon Binder magic. The machine was now set for maximum blast. Given the sheer number of moon fragments that had fallen to Margra's surface, Nils theorized the magic that had once infested Ruel Moon had mostly dispersed into the debris field. Hadn't Salinda said the dragons died when touched by the pieces of Shatterwing?

"Over there," Nils said finally, and pointed to a screen. "The coordinates are there. Please check them. Then leave."

Garan glided to the monitor and leaned over, grasping the console with his hand as he peered at it. Nils saw the lad's lips move as he repeated the coordinates. Garan looked up. "Can I change these?"

"Yes, but, well, just do it carefully."

Garan adjusted the settings and they registered in the machine. Nils keyed open the dome. The clouds were a mixture of gold, blood red and black, a roiling mass of sky lava. The moon fragments they were aiming for were not visible to the naked eye, but their effect on the atmosphere could be observed. Guided by the cadre, Nils switched on a console and screen that had sat dormant.

Garan came to look over his shoulder. "'Tis the sky beyond the clouds." Garan's voice was full of wonder. If the situation was not so critical, Nils could have admired the technology, too.

"Does visual confirm the coordinates?" Nils asked.

Garan studied the screen. "Yes, these are the two big ones, Ruelette and Rueline. A lot of little stuff has been pushed ahead of them, as we have been witnessing of late." He lifted his violet gaze to Nils.

"Garan. Leave now. Protect Salinda and Laidan. With so much extra power, I cannot predict what the wave might do to the surroundings."

"The wave?" Garan asked.

"Yes, there is a wave setting within the blast, which cannot be removed. It is what changes the composition of the moon debris. It may affect this site in some unknown way. Take Salinda and Laidan off the ridge and find shelter."

"What about you?" Garan asked.

"There is safety for me inside." He rapped on the transparent wall. "This is shielding. In the other machine, it protected Trell. When I am done and have achieved what we set out to do, I will come down and meet you. Keep an eye out for me."

Garan sniffed and wiped the tip of his nose with the back of his hand. "You take great risk."

"I know." Nils's brow furrowed. "It is my birthright to do this. I have the cadre within me, minds bound into a cohesive whole. It exists to do this one thing and it needs me. You understand, Garan? The cadre needs me."

Garan reached up and squeezed Nils's shoulder and Nils returned the gesture of affection. Garan had a pure soul and a power that, even with the cadre, Nils found difficult to comprehend. If he had more time he would like to explore Garan's gifts.

"Go now," Nils said gently.

Garan nodded, his mouth drawing into a straight line that held back unspoken words and deep emotion. Nils turned away. He could not bear to see it.

When he turned back, Garan had gone.

ᏬᏬᏬᏬᏬ

In the command center, seven chairs stood empty. Each chair had a helmet contraption designed to go over the head of the person in the chair. This time, there was only Nils. Despite having the cadre awake, its power in full

200

flood inside him, Nils shivered in trepidation. Nevertheless, he strode into the center of the ring of chairs and examined each one. Layers of dust besmirched the chairs and lay thickest on the seats. Nils had to choose one of them to sit in.

The great machine hummed beneath his feet, its pulse building to a peak, a peak that was moments away. It really did not matter which chair he sat in, but one looked the most comfortable to him, one that seemed less ravaged by time. He turned and sat down. The chair creaked, tilted to one side, and he shifted his weight until it came upright. Then he reached up and gently lowered the waiting helmet over his head.

Trell's voice was strong, giving words of comfort, of support, although the pride in the voice may have been Nils's imagination.

Nils wished he had held Elan one more time and said a proper farewell to Salinda, just in case things did not go to plan. But they had risked everything to get here and Nils could not let fear of the unknown stop him. "You are doing it for them," he said aloud. His words were quickly absorbed by the rising hum of the machine. He could only hope Salinda, his child, and the others were now far enough away.

Nils keyed the switch. The connection between the cadre, himself and the machine snapped into existence. He clutched the chair arm in a death grip, his teeth clenched so tight he imagined they would break under the pressure. Pain seared into him from the top of his head to the tips of his toes.

His vision went white like the cadre. The command center disappeared.

"Is he in place?" a voice said.

"Yes," another replied.

"Power levels?" a woman's voice said.

"Exceeding expectations," another woman replied.

"The coordinates are different," a man said.

Nils breathed and breathed. He needed to answer that one. "Updated coordinates," he said into his mind.

"Ah...yes...it has been so long."

"Trell?" Nils asked. He opened his eyes—not his worldly ones, but the eyes of his mind.

"Yes, Nils," Trell's voice replied. There in front of him was his grandsire and Nils smiled. Six Sundwellers joined him. "We are all here."

Behind them, Nils discerned other people who had added to the cadre, their lives and knowledge culminating in this moment.

Tears fell down Nils's cheeks. "We have to give my people more time to get away from the machine," he said.

Trell loomed large. "I am sorry, Nils. There is no more time. Engage!" he commanded.

The noise in Nils's ears peaked. It was as if he was being undone and rebuilt by sound waves alone. The vibrations around him shook the chair. Nils was once again as aware of his body as he was of the cadre in his mind. The room was hot, glowing so blue it was almost violet. Then his awareness separated and he could see the ravaged, wounded planet below; his spirit flew fast through valleys and over plains as tears fell from his eyes. Dragon carcasses lay rotting on the ground, their bodies dissolving in the dust of Ruel Moon, its magic destroying them and returning their essences to the land. He moved again, like an arrow, upward. Two large chunks of moon were in his sights. He was Nils of Barr and he was the machine: he was power and he was light.

The collision came with a sickening judder and his chair shook him hard. The cadre was aflame now, the individuals merged into one, into Nils. The power ripped through him, ripped through the moon rock. It split and sped away at such a high speed that Nils would have missed it had he not been watching.

His spirit grew thin but he clung on. He had to see it through. He called on his reserves and they were vast. Power shot through him, dissolving him, the rock giving way. Fragments burst into flame and became fine dust. Another big hunk of moon blew apart with just the focus of Nils's mind trained upon it.

And yet there was more. Nils was hungry for rock, for stone, for dust, for power. He went on and on, blasting and eating and growing thinner with each breath.

Nils knew he had gone beyond, past saving, past redemption. He saw in his mind's eye that he could make Margra a better place, if he only kept on sweeping through Shatterwing, clearing it away.

Heat surrounded his body. Once again, he was there in that chair inside the machine, and everything was melting. Heat rolled over him, his skin seemed to stick to the chair. He closed his eyes, threw himself back into the cadre and forced himself to go on. Around the world he went, higher and higher, lower and lower, either eating the debris or sweeping it out on a trajectory to Margra's sun.

Nils was as fine as a thread, exhausted, aware of impending doom. The machine, forced beyond its capacities, was going to blow. He said goodbye to Salinda and Elan. He said goodbye to Karol and the other Hiem. He said goodbye to Garan and to Brill and Laidan and Danton. There, waiting for him, was Trell of Barr, hand outstretched.

"Welcome home, Nils."

Nils went toward the light. To Trell, who had waited for him. Then, with an almighty roar, the machine exploded.

Nils ended.

ຄາຄາຄາຄາ

Salinda held back in her flight to wait for Garan and sent Laidan on ahead. He came speeding out of the side door, yelling, "Move! Run!"

Salinda didn't need a second warning. She ran, holding the baby to her breast and praying she did not fall.

Behind Garan a whining sound grew louder and louder. Salinda could feel the vibrations through her teeth and her ears thumped once, letting her know that she was hearing, but not quite hearing.

Garan caught up with her. "What about Nils?" she cried.

"He said he was fine," Garan said breathlessly. "Said to seek safety."

Salinda slowed and looked back to the machine. "But if it isn't safe for us, it isn't safe for him."

Garan's jaw clenched. "I know. Hurry." He grabbed her elbow and urged her on.

Tears fell as she ran, and she turned her attention to the treacherous path. Fear and grief intermingled in her chest. *Oh Nils. I'm sorry.* Underneath it all, she wasn't sorry: she was grateful. She held Elan to her chest and ran for their lives. Nils had given them a chance. A small chance for them, a bigger chance for Margra.

The horizon looked like flaming peaches, even as the sky was a cauldron of doom. She ran as fast as she could, given that her reserves were at their limits, her body protesting the stress she was putting it under.

As they made their way down the ridge, a single beam of blue-mauve light cut through the sky. Startled, Salinda halted and turned back to look. Garan had done the same. As they watched, the beam broadened, became more like a fist than a needle.

"Keep going," Garan said. "We have to get off the ridge."

"The whole ridge?" Salinda asked, thinking it an impossible task. The machine was running, its energy focused. Tears began to streak her face. *Nils, you knew. Knew, or expected the worst.*

"The energy feeding the machine comes from beneath us. There are weaknesses there that the machine exploits. We may not survive what is to come. Just run."

Clutching the baby tight, Salinda turned and ran. Garan nearly lost his footing when a concussive wave hit them and they took shelter behind a boulder, panting hard.

"We need to move," Salinda said. "I can feel the earth trembling."

Garan nodded. "Yes, keep going. I will follow."

They caught sight of Laidan ahead of them and yelled for her to run faster. "What about Eneit, Karol and Brill?" Salinda asked.

"We have to hope they can run, too."

ᗢᗢᗢᗢᗢ

Miraka had taken up residence on Squab's sofa and Squab grew used to having her around. She didn't want to grow used to it, but the Hiem woman rebuffed any attempt to move her on. So what if Miraka said she liked Squab's intellect. It still wouldn't be long before some young, beautiful thing attracted the woman and she moved on. Squab was not going to fall for that. She was not going to fall in love and have her heart broken.

There had been many thunderous sounds echoing through Barrahiem in the past week. This morning, or what she thought was morning, Squab was going to the lakeshore to see if any of the rumblings were due to N'Barek subsiding.

Miraka was out of her blankets quick smart when she realized Squab was going out. "I'm coming with you," Miraka said, pulling her robe over her head after giving Squab a really good view of her naked body.

Squab begged the source for patience and strength, then set a cracking pace down the stairs and along the balconies until she found the path to the lakeshore. Immediately, she knew something was different. The water churned and moved in a way she had not seen before, although, admittedly, she was a fairly new resident of the city. As she moved closer to the shore, she saw that the waterline was different...the lake had risen a good yard, maybe two.

"This can't be good," Squab thought she said to herself. Unfortunately, she had said it out loud.

"What can't be good?" Miraka asked, catching up, and she looked at the lakeshore. "Oh, I see. That can't be good."

She looked to Squab and Squab just gave a helpless shrug of her shoulders. She didn't know what it meant. She didn't know if they would have to evacuate, or even if they could.

"Let's look over to N'Barek." Squab shifted to a better position. The light wasn't good and she couldn't get more than an impression that, maybe, part of N'Barek had sunk.

"Let me stand there and look," Miraka said. "I have superior eyesight."

Squab stepped back and Miraka stood very still as she peered across the lake. "Hmm...some serious subsidence. Not enough to account for the state of the lake." Miraka turned and surveyed the lake as far as she could see.

"Well," Squab asked, "what do you think it is?"

Miraka squinted. "Some outside disturbance, I think. More water is flowing into the lake than normal." She pointed to a cascade of water spurting from a fissure in the wall of the cavern that housed them all. It was flowing at about twice the strength it used to. "We should get people to boil their water before drinking, just in case."

Squab agreed with that suggestion. Her face creased in concern. "Do you think it will get much higher?"

Miraka finger-combed her hair. "Are you worried it will flood Barrahiem?"

Squab looked skeptical. "It would need a lot of water to fill this space, I suppose." She turned and surveyed the city that curved around them. "I'm worried the water might undermine the city's foundations, the structure of the rock. I need to have something concrete to tell the people here when they notice it. You understand?"

Miraka smiled grimly. "You don't want them to panic like before?"

"Exactly." Squab began to smile, then quickly checked herself, as usual.

"Why don't we check the archive tunnels, then? If water is getting in, we will be able to tell. We could relocate any stored items down there, if it seems necessary."

Squab moved uneasily from foot to foot. Nils had instructed her not to let anyone into the precious archive space and related storage depots. They were allowed to access the garden, their food storage area, and the cloth manufacturing sections only. The Hall of Elders was also forbidden, except for the Hiem youngsters, because of its cultural and spiritual significance to them. But what would be worse: Nils never forgiving her for violating his instructions, or the destruction of the archives?

"Let's do it now then, before more people wake up."

Squab had been down below once and she had hated the stink then. It smelled of a place that had never seen the sun, of stale soil and mold. It had not improved. If she had the ability, she would close her nostrils and block it out. She also didn't like the small, closed-in spaces. Barrahiem was bearable because it was a huge vaulted cavern. Intellectually, she knew she was underground, but as there was so much space, she was able to sublimate her fear. Down here, no amount of sublimation was going to keep the fear at bay. Her control was good, though. She didn't run out as she yearned to do, but squared her shoulders and continued on. Miraka led the way, being much more at home in this space than Squab ever could be and definitely didn't want to be.

Squab held a light at low power, just so she didn't trip. Ahead, Miraka turned around, her silver-bright eyes taking Squab's breath away. "This is the main section that abuts the wall closest to the lake."

"Let's take a look around."

Squab peered under shelving housing weird metal discs and around shelving containing something resembling paper or parchment. She ran her fingers along the shelves to see if there was any tell-tale signs of moisture. They checked inside a number of rooms and with a deep sigh of relief, Squab said, "I think we're good."

Miraka grinned. "Yes, for now. Perhaps we should monitor the lake and these storage areas daily."

Squab nodded and scratched an itch on the back of her neck. "We could get your Hiem family to do that. What do you think?"

"Sounds good. I'll assign them to do regular checks. I'll give you the timetable so you know where they are at all times...you know, in case."

Squab nodded. "Yeah, in case."

Turning one-eighty degrees, Squab faced the way they came. "Let's get back and we can send a message to people to boil their water. I bet they'll be screaming at me by the end of the day."

A soft laugh escaped Miraka. "I don't know why you tolerate that shit from them. You are looking out for them, protecting them. I don't understand why they don't get it. I really don't."

Squab started walking along the corridor. "I don't know why, either. I've never really understood normal folk. I have trained rebels and commanded them. Mostly, they did what I said. They were there voluntarily, and they wanted to learn and to fight. In that situation, you grow to trust your comrades. These people are different. They are holding on by a thread."

"So why do you bother helping them?" Miraka asked as she walked behind her.

"Because I was fighting for them. They were what mattered."

"How difficult it must be to see them at their worst."

Squab let out a sigh. "It is indeed."

Sometime later that day, a great boom reverberated through the earth and a ripping, crunching sound shook Squab in her bed. She ran to the outdoor common area. Miraka came tumbling after. The sound continued and Squab's skin prickled and her hair stood on end. A loud, alarming *crack!* had them looking above to see a gap opening in the roof of the cavern. Another ponderous *boom* loosened rocks that fell like rain. Screams rose up around her, and one was lodged tightly in her throat. Was this the end?

"Take cover," Squab bellowed. "In your houses."

The stone under her feet vibrated and Squab bent over double to vomit. She had not expected this doom, not in Barrahiem, deep in the earth. Did this mean that the mission had failed? That moonfall was here?

A huge boulder dropped out of the crack, which now had nearly reached the other side. From where she stood she heard the rock plunge into the lake and heard the resultant upwelling of water. A wave washed over the rim of the lake.

Squab breathed and closed her eyes as chaos erupted around her. Humans crying out in fear…calls for assistance…shouts that someone had died, crushed by falling rock. She listened and listened. Then came the realization that the ground had grown quiet again. The crack stopped growing, the rocks ceased their fall. They were alive among the mess that was now Barrahiem. Balconies had collapsed, broken stairs blocked access to the inner city and more water fell into the lake through new cracks in the cavern walls.

She waited for those around her to notice. Miraka came up, took her hand and squeezed it lightly.

The fear subsided and there were no screams. Now it was an occasional grief-filled wail that tore through the city. When nearly an hour was done and there were no more tremors or threat of destruction, they picked up the pieces.

To Miraka she said, "See who is injured. See who is dead. Send your Hiem friends to check the Hall of Elders and the archives below. We need to know the full extent of the damage."

Miraka's eyes were wide. "Was that moonfall?" she asked.

"I don't know. I thought moonfall would be much worse."

Miraka nodded once, a swift jerk of her head. "I'll go."

ᏊᏊᏊᏊᏊ

Karol darted out of the darkness, taking Eneit by surprise. "I'm sorry," he said. "We need to move."

"What about Brill?" Eneit demanded.

"We move him, too. He's on the glide. It won't hurt him."

A thin bright light shot up into the air and carved a path through the roiling clouds.

"The machine," Eneit said.

"Yes, and it is not safe. We must take cover."

"How do you know?"

"I hide. I see things. I hear them, too."

"What about the others?" Eneit asked, checking the ties that held Brill in place. Brill's face was pale, his lips, too. His forehead was wet with sweat. She knew the gut wound had gone bad.

Eneit grabbed the tether and put the packs at the base of the glide. Karol picked up a pack and slid it on his back. She did the same.

"Where do we run?" Eneit asked, surveying the gloom. The sun looked to be coming up, but it didn't help them much.

"Just away. Distance is what we need. If we could make Danton's bunker, that would be good."

Eneit ran, as smoothly as she could, pulling the glide and regularly checking over her shoulder that Brill was stable and not being flung about. Karol ran behind them, his right hand lightly resting on the other end of the glide.

Eneit turned her eyes front and kept an eye on the path. She did not need to trip or take a tumble. Too much depended on getting where they were meant to be in one piece.

They ran down a slope and Karol called out to her. "Stop here."

Eneit slowed her steps and stopped, leaning over to catch her breath. Her heartbeat was like someone playing a crazy drum rhythm.

The light from the machine widened perceptibly and grew more intense. A wind picked up. Eneit found herself wrestled to the ground by Karol. The blast wave went over their heads.

"What was that?" Eneit asked.

Karol shook his head. "Just the beginning, I think. Stay down."

"Will we be all right here?" she asked.

"I think so. I hope the others get clear in time."

The clouds overhead were now backlit by fire. "Do you think the machine is working?" she whispered huskily.

Karol flipped over so he lay on his back and he peered at the sky. Eneit did the same. "I don't know. Something momentous is happening. I can feel it in my skin."

"Oh, that must be strange."

A rumble built under them and they held hands. "I'm scared," Eneit said.

Karol gave her hand a squeeze. "Me too."

Eneit turned her head and smiled at him.

"Think of it this way. It can't be any worse than it was or was going to be."

Eneit's eyes widened. "Then we could still die."

"We are all going to die sometime. But," he paused to look at the sky, his forehead clouded, "I think we won't die tonight. Not from that." The clouds had shrunk, revealing the stars and the black of night.

The ground shook and the wind blew at them, snatching their breath. The scrub around them flew into the air, great swathes of bracken ripping from the ground. They hunkered down, holding each other tight as they slid across the ground in the force of the blast. Eneit had the tether to the glide and held on as the wind tore at it, trying to blow it away. Then it grew quiet and the rain of dirt and leaves stopped.

"They did it," Eneit gasped, wiping dirt from her face. "They saved Margra." Tears spurted and she cried, sobbing into her hands.

"Eneit." It was Brill's voice, thin and weak. "What is happening?"

Eneit scrubbed at her face with her hands and flashed Karol a sideways look. She wished she was elsewhere at this moment. Brill was her friend and she cared for him deeply.

Crawling over to where he lay on the glide, she squeezed his hand. "I'm here," she said.

Slowly he turned his head, squinting as if he needed to focus on her. "Did we win?" he asked.

"Yes, Brill, we did. You're a hero, don't you know? You helped...no, you saved the world."

Brill's eyes widened and a ghost of a smile played around his pale lips. "Hero?" His eyebrows drew together. "I always wanted to be a hero." He sought her eyes again. "Will the world be a better place?"

Eneit nodded, not caring about the tears running down her cheeks and dripping off her chin. "Yes," she said, giving him a smile. "The world is a better place. We will be better humans."

"You promise?" Brill asked, his voice now so thin she had to lean close to his mouth.

"Yes," she replied almost crushing his hand. "Yes, I promise."

"Tell Danton that...I'm sorry," Brill said. He just stopped and, a moment later, all the air sighed out of his lungs.

"Brill? Brill!" she shouted and grabbed his bloody tunic, rocking him. "Brill."

She had known it was coming. It still hadn't prepared her. "No...no..." She bent over him, crying into his chest. "Brill. No..."

Karol came up beside her and rubbed her back, trying to tell her it would be all right, he was in a better place now...some such crap. Eneit turned to him. "It's not fair. He deserved to live. To see the world safe. He gave his life for that. Why? Why is it so? Why is it so unfair?"

"I don't know," Karol said. "I lost my whole family, my whole clan. It wasn't fair. None of it was. It is what we do with our lives and our opportunities that counts. I believe in the source of all things. I don't think it directs us. The part of the source within gives each of us the spark that lets us choose, lets us see opportunities to do good or ill and act on them. Brill is safe now, back with the source."

Eneit found it hard to talk over the sobs. The pain made her angry. "Why? Why does it hurt so much?" Choking on sobs, she gave full vent to her grief.

"I don't know, Eneit," he said softly, and sniffed. "It's the price we pay for loving another."

Eneit threw herself at Karol, gripped his robe hard and cried into his thin shoulder. She didn't think her tears would end. Never end. Never, never end.

Sometime later she awoke, still clinging to Karol, but now huddled on the ground. "Eneit?" he said.

"Yes," she said, pushing away from him and wiping at her gluey eyes where dust and tears had mixed.

"We should make a fire so the others can find us."

Eneit sniffed. "Do you think they are still alive?" She scanned the terrain. The air was full of dust and haze, but the sunlight that filtered through was warm. Her gaze fell on Brill and she covered her mouth. He ought to look peaceful, she thought, so she leaned over and closed his eyes. When she pulled back her hand, she thought he rested easier.

"Yes, some of them at least."

"I'll go to fetch some wood. Will you stay here and guard him?"

Karol nodded. "No more than ten minutes. Then come back with what you have. Then I'll go. We take equal turns."

Eneit nodded. Her limbs were sore from sleeping in an awkward position. She felt her gait was off-center as she walked off the stiffness and she paused to rub at her calves. The wind had blown debris everywhere, so there were plenty of sticks and brush to be found, blown from the woods, from the ridge. She started gathering and had deposited two armloads in the ten minutes allocated. Karol went off to do the same.

Bugs were coming out of the wood and brush and Eneit dug around for a blanket to put over Brill's body, though she didn't want to cover him up. It was hard to let him go. Having him there was like a part of him was still with her.

The sun shone bright and warm and Eneit knew she should be happy for the dawn of this new day. The joy was bittersweet, tinged with sadness and grief. Karol appeared as if from nowhere and dropped a bundle of sticks.

Eneit shaded her eyes with a hand. "How big is this fire going to be?"

"Big. If it was dark we wouldn't need so much. We need smoke to attract their attention. I'm bringing branches with leaves next. You should start laying the fire, get the flame going. We don't want to miss the others."

Eneit knelt and started with the kindling. She didn't have anything to start the flame, but Brill did. With a heavy heart she started rifling through his pack.

Chapter Twenty
THE AFTERMATH

The sound of a baby's cry woke Salinda. Stones poked into her back. Her arms and legs were spread out. Lifting her head made her vision go dark. Where was that noise coming from?

The crying was increasing in volume and Salinda's mind started working. Elan? She put her hand to her chest. The warm bundle of flesh was gone.

Opening her eyes, she blinked away dust, licked her dry lips and saw a blurred shape not far from her. She rolled onto her side. "Garan? Laidan?"

As her vision cleared, she saw the baby and tried to understand why she was over there. Elan's fists punched the air. Her swaddling clothes were spread like a puddle under her. Salinda dragged herself over, fighting the dark patches that threatened to overwhelm her vision.

Running her hands over the baby, she saw there was no visible damage. Dragging herself up against a boulder, she took the distressed baby into her arms and started to feed her. Salinda noticed her clothes were ripped and her skin had a grayish cast. She was covered in dust.

As the baby suckled, she laid her head back and events came rushing in. Nils dying. She sensed it, lived it through their bond, seeing with his eyes. Tears rolled unbidden down her face. "Oh, Nils!" she cried to the air above, to the dust of his existence. There was a faint taste of him at the other end of her bond. She blinked and lifted her head up to take in the wasteland around her. That sense of Nils she had, was it wishful thinking? Would he always be there, just inside her heart, keeping her warm, soothing her and reminding her of what he did for Margra? At the end, she had sensed his happiness. He had not been afraid to die.

A smile shone through her tears. Nils had done it. The cadre she had protected with her life had made it possible. The vindication of her life was as joyous as surviving. She looked down at her child feeding hungrily and wept.

She did not know how long she sat there. She knew her tears had dried. Her muscles felt like they had been bent into shapes they were not made for and her head ached something fierce.

Patting around herself, she found no trace of the pack with the baby's cloths in it. She and her daughter would have to make do. Elan would just have to wait before she was changed again. At least she was no longer hungry. Salinda propped the baby up on her shoulder and patted her back, soothing the wind pains. Elan was her miracle. Salinda's gaze kept going back to the spot where Elan had lain. She must have been violently torn from Salinda in the storm generated by the machine exploding. The blanket that was used to hold her was in shreds. How had Elan survived that without breaking?

Salinda held the baby to her chest and half-crawled and half-staggered to peep around the boulder she sheltered behind. "Wing dust!" Her eyes grew round as she took in the damage. The building was no longer there and half the ridge was blown away. Beneath where the machine had been was a deep depression in the landscape.

The sun's rays were having trouble penetrating the dusty haze. Dust from the surface, dust from Shatterwing, and dust from ancient, magic-infused Ruel Moon. Yet, the light that did penetrate was warm.

"Garan?" she called out and then coughed, the dust making her conscious of how dry her throat was. "Laidan?"

There was no sign of them. They had been together. Perhaps they were still unconscious. She refused to believe they were dead. Salinda hauled herself backward with her hands, shuffling until she leaned against the boulder.

Closing her eyes, she let her weary body rest and let those last thoughts of Nils surface. He'd swept Margra clear of Shatterwing. No more would it dominate the lives of those on the surface below. No more beauty and peril to shape the future of governments. *Is anyone left?*

Through Nils's eyes, she saw the surface of the world. It was sorely wounded. Could it heal itself? The vision of the dragons brought wonder to her heart; their magic was from their Moon Binder prison. She screwed up her face trying to work it out. She didn't understand why, but the Moon Binders had bound the dragons in Ruel Moon, in rock that contained their power, their magic. Once they were touched with a potent portion of the dust of Ruel Moon, it destroyed or changed them, and it gave the dragon's magic back to Margra. It was a very long bow to draw, but it was the only theory she had. Salinda was thinking that people had a chance to live normally now. They no longer needed dragon wine, because the magic had dispersed. It was everywhere: in the air, in the ground, and eventually it would be in the food and the water.

She must have dropped off to sleep, because she was woken by a hand shaking her. "Salinda," Garan said.

The relief in his eyes when she opened hers was palpable. The baby started awake from sleeping peacefully on her lap. Elan fretted and grizzled to herself.

Garan dropped a pack next to her. "Where is Laidan?" she asked him.

"She's fetching up our gear. Some of it got blown away."

Salinda's head still felt like it was being mined for some important mineral. The stabbing pains hacked and hacked at her. She closed her eyes.

Garan opened the pack and started foraging. When she opened her eyes again, he held out a folded cloth. She nodded her thanks and changed the baby. Then she fed Elan and remembered Eneit saying that as long as the baby was eating and pooping, it was doing all right. "What about the others?"

Garan leaned over and roughly scrubbed the dust out of his curls. The cloud he created made Salinda swat the extra dust away from her face.

He lifted his head. "We do not know about the others. We have to search."

Footsteps announced the arrival of Laidan. She had a scrape across her forehead that looked like it had taken off some of her scalp. Dried blood and congealed dust left a black and white trail in her hair.

Tear trails left braided paths down her cheeks. "Oh," she said, "you're all right."

She came to her knees and threw her arms around Salinda. Her sobbing was silent and Salinda just held her. She drew back from Salinda, blinking away dust and tears and asked, "Nils, is he…"

Salinda shook her head. "He saved us. He knew he was going to die; he never let on. He spun me some dragon dung about Trell surviving and I bought it. He suspected the extra power would immolate him."

"He's a hero," Laidan whispered, sounding awed. "He always was, you know. He saved me. He risked his life to do that."

"Yes," Salinda said, closing her eyes. "Nils would have it that it was against his nature to sacrifice himself for others. He had a lifetime of being different in the old world before Ruel Moon split, and he had seen what this world was like and he didn't like any of it. Deep inside he needed to connect to others."

Garan pulled up a bit of ground and sat down next to her. "Do you regret not being the one?"

Salinda bit her bottom lip as she puzzled over his question. "I never saw the future clearly, Garan. I hoped that I would be the one to deliver the cadre so that it could save us." She glanced at him. "I wasn't the one to wield it, but I think I did a pretty good job of safeguarding it and delivering it. You both did your part."

Laidan shook her head vigorously. "No, I did nothing but cause trouble."

Salinda reached out with a trembling hand. She was still weak from shock and everything else. Laidan looked at her hand, then met her gaze and, with a nod, she took it. Salinda patted it with her other hand. "If you had not been there when Thurdon died, the cadre would have been lost. We would not have this." She gestured at the sky. "We would not be here."

"But—" Laidan tried to interrupt.

"You were a child then, Laidan. Now you are a woman grown. You have made what you could of yourself without the cadre. To you, it was not a crutch. I relied on the cadre a little too much. I was jealous of Nils, you know." She shook her head. "I wanted to be the important one. The one who would see the cadre save the world. Now I have had time to consider and understand the right of it. I didn't know the cadres needed to be combined, I was limited in my viewpoint. Caught up in what I could do with the power." She turned her head meaningfully in Garan's direction and Laidan joined her in that scrutiny. "Garan had power. He was humble with it. The cadre was safe with him for the interim. Do you miss it, Garan?"

Garan shook his head. "No, I was glad to be rid of it. Always glowing in my mind, making strange, cryptic remarks and otherwise behaving like a headache that would not leave." Garan shrugged. "Sorry. It did not mean as much to me as it did to you. Then again, I only had it for a short time. I did not need it to survive, not as you did."

"Well," Salinda said with a grimace, "that doesn't say much about me, does it?"

Garan flustered. "I did not mean...I meant no disrespect to you..."

Salinda laughed, a little sadly. It helped to wipe away the cobwebs in her mind. "I was only teasing you, Garan. You are a wonder with or without a cadre. Tell me, can you still ignite crystals?"

Garan dug around in his pocket, pulled out a shard and had it glowing before he even held it up.

"Oh, excellent," Salinda said as she studied the landscape. "I wonder where the others are? Danton. I don't recall seeing him before we went up the ridge."

"He went after Gercomo..." Laidan said.

Salinda's eyes widened. "Then the baron?"

Laidan shrugged. "Danton must be out there."

Salinda's gaze tracked around her. There was no sign of life and her aches and pains were really making themselves felt. "If they are there, we will find them. We won't leave until we do."

Garan nodded and Laidan grinned.

"First, let's have a short rest, and then go find the others."

Elan was already fast asleep in Salinda's lap. Laidan snuggled up next to her and Salinda rested her head on the rock behind. She was half-asleep before she touched it.

The wind caressed her skin. Insects hummed and the sun warmed her flesh. It was strange not having to worry about the end of the world anymore. It had already ended. There was a new world to be made. There were people protected from the surface damage, the people she had made sure were in Barrahiem. It wasn't everyone. That would have been impossible. They'd saved a core of people to continue on. She recalled the images that Nils had shared with her across their bond. He showed her what some of the world used to look like. Tall buildings, wonderful machines and the laughing, smiling faces of the Sundwellers. He'd sent her that to give her hope. Salinda sighed slowly and then drifted away on a good dream.

▢▢▢▢

"I smell smoke," Garan said, and then pulled the glide closer and sat on it. He turned it on, and it rose to standing height. The sun was high in the sky, not quite noon. They had only been resting for an hour or two. He sheltered his eyes with his right hand and scanned the surroundings. Some way off he spotted the smoke.

"What is it?" Salinda said, coming around woozily. The baby was asleep and made sucking noises with her lips. Laidan came to stand by him.

"I see smoke from a fire. 'Tis a signal, I think."

"It could be Eneit, Brill, Danton and Karol," Laidan said, flicking her gaze from the view in the distance to him. "It has to be one of them."

He angled his head down. "We should check it out."

"Of course we must," Laidan said. She dropped to her knees and scooped up the baby who was coming awake now, stretching its arms and legs. "We must go and see who lit the fire." She rocked the baby in her arms as Elan began to cry.

Salinda blinked away sleep and accepted the baby back into her embrace. Garan looked away when she started feeding. He knew it was natural and all that, but he blushed as he did not want to be seen looking too closely.

There was not much sign of life out there, but he did not wish to be complacent about the baron's armed men either. He thought they had been dealt with. Hoped they were.

Laidan packed up their supplies and tossed him some flat bread. The big batch he had made had lasted well. It was no longer soft, but it filled the stomach. He munched on it. "Can you pass me my pack?"

Laidan checked the flap was closed tight and hefted it up to him. He lowered the glide back to the ground and slipped the straps over his shoulders. Salinda needed the glide, he thought. She was done in. Fatigue, injury, grief were all starting to take their toll. If not for his broken leg he would have given it to her in a moment. Salinda checked their makeshift camp and was nodding her head in approval. They had not left anything important behind.

To Garan's surprise, Laidan still had a bow and a few arrows in a quiver. "Does it still work?" he asked her.

She shrugged. "It should. The string is intact. The arrows are a bit beat up, but they make a good bluff if we meet someone who isn't nice."

"Remind me never to play a game of bluff with you."

She chortled and it was such a joyous sound that Garan grinned from ear to ear. It was good to smile again, to experience joy. Yet it was grief-tinged for him, too. So many people had died. He had watched the towers of the observatory fall. He had had that thing inside him. He frowned, thinking about the Moon Binder. The taint of its presence would never leave him. The Moon Binder spirit had changed him. Time would tell if that change was for the better.

The bleakness of the landscape depressed him. Before the blast, there had been green woods, trees and bracken, and now it looked gray and dead. *It will grow back*, he told himself. *Everything will flourish again. Do not lose hope.* His frown deepened. Was that him trying to cheer himself up or was it a residue of something else? Whatever it was, it slipped away just as he tried to focus on it.

As they drew closer, they saw the flames leaping up. Farther on, they heard a shout.

"Eneit," Laidan said and she burst into a sprint.

"Be careful..." Garan shouted and then shook his head because she just ignored him.

"Thank the source," Salinda said as she trudged up behind him, hardly able to lift her feet.

"Would you like me to take Elan?" Garan asked. Salinda looked up at him.

"That would be lovely. The blanket we used to tie her to me is in shreds and after a while this wee thing feels like a big rock."

Carefully, Garan took the baby into his arms and nestled her in his lap. "Do you want to rest?"

Salinda shook her head. "When we get there." She jerked her head in the direction of the fire.

By then Laidan had met Eneit, who had come running out to her. They embraced and Laidan swung Eneit around in the air. Moving closer, Garan made out Karol. The stoop of the lad's shoulders warned him there was bad news waiting.

He cast a quick look at Salinda and worried for her. She did not look ready for more grief. Garan gazed at the sleeping baby in his lap. A new life for a new future. He stroked the baby's forehead. A treasure in this field of desolation.

Eneit talked hurriedly to Laidan and Garan watched her stance change from one of joy to one of sorrow. Salinda must have noticed, too, because she glanced at him sideways and sped up. Laidan ran to where the fire was and Garan heard her wail.

By the time his glide settled in the camp that Eneit and Karol had made, Laidan's weeping filled his ears. "Oh, no," Salinda said when she saw Brill. Laidan had lifted off a blanket and was cupping Brill's pale cheeks.

Salinda squeezed Garan's arms and went over to the larger glide. "Oh, Brill," she said.

Laidan's weeping increased, echoing in the empty landscape that had recently seen so much violence. Garan should have been prepared for this. Brill's wound had been severe and no amount of dragon wine was going to repair a stomach wound like that.

Eneit stood off to the side, wiping tears. The fire made her skin turn red.

Salinda looked up from touching Brill's forehead and squinted at her surroundings. "Where is Danton?"

Karol moved toward her. "He went after the baron. I have not seen him since."

"Do you mean he is out there, dead or dying?" Salinda was nearly shouting.

Karol flinched. "We don't know that. He might have lost us."

Salinda walked to the edge of the camp, away from the heat of the flames. "No, he's out there all alone. We have to find him."

"I'll go," Garan said.

Karol chimed in with the same words. "What should we do about Brill?" the Hiem lad asked.

Salinda swung around. "We should bury him in the ground so that he can be one with Margra."

Laidan's eyes flashed. "You know he believed in burning."

Salinda lifted her chin. "I do, but he had come around to our way of thinking, I believe."

Eneit nodded. "I'll start digging his grave then."

Laidan wiped her tears. "I will help you."

"I want to look for Danton." Salinda's eyes rested on her baby in Garan's lap and her mouth twisted and she began to cry.

Garan put his arm around her. "We will find him and bring him back."

It took a few tries for Salinda to speak. "Thank you. Bring him back. Bring him back no matter what." She took Elan from him and held her to her shoulder. "We will meet you at the Way Gate."

"All right. I'll take the supply glide," Garan said.

Karol nodded and asked Eneit to help him place Brill's body on the ground.

Garan swallowed a lump in his throat, not mistaking Salinda's meaning. She wanted him to bring the body back. It was not in Danton's nature to stay away. After Brill was laid on the ground, Karol came to stand beside Garan. "Where do you think we should start?" he asked Karol.

Karol pursed his lips as he looked around them. Nothing but flattened vegetation and bare earth. "If we can work out where Danton's bunker is, we might be able to follow his path from there."

As there was little else to go on, Garan agreed. "Do you think you can find it?" he asked Karol. Garan's head was a tad muddled and he did not wish to waste time getting lost. For some reason, he could find his way better underground than above.

"This way," the lad said. "If you look at the bay, what's left of the bay, you can see where the waterline used to be and then track back around forty-five degrees. That's approximately where the bunker was."

As they went along, Garan on his glide and Karol jogging next to him, tugging the empty supply glide, they saw the remains of some armed men. Karol checked them to make sure none was Danton. Garan held his breath each time.

Flattened bracken stretched out ahead of them. Trees had been torn out and flung far away and only dark stains and holes in the ground remained to testify to their existence. If Danton had been out here during the blast, there would be no telling where he would have ended up. Garan tried not to fret. The last thing he wanted to do was return to Salinda empty-handed.

"Wait," Karol said, "look!"

Garan studied the ground where Karol was walking and pointing. "What?"

"I think there was a fight here. Gercomo the beast man and Danton."

"What makes you think that?"

Karol bent down and brushed dust and sand away.

Garan eased his glide over and examined what was revealed. "It looks like a tail made an impression here." Garan had to accept that it was Gercomo's. "Let's look around in widening circles."

They did this, Garan on the glide, Karol on foot. There was nothing else to give them a sign where Danton could be. All trace of footprints had been erased.

"We should split up," Garan said.

Karol agreed. "Yes, it will be faster. We don't need to go to the bunker just yet. I don't think he would have backtracked to there. Not if he thought we had gone to the ridge."

"If he found the baron, he would have chased him."

"Do you think the Moon Binder spirit took him away?" Garan asked.

Karol shook his head. "No, I think the Moon Binder spirit would have gone away after it killed Gercomo. Danton took off from the bunker. It looked as if the Ufak Monta was in control and it kept saying 'abomination'."

Garan found a kernel of memory expanding. A little gift from the Ufak Monta. It thought dragons were vermin. It had used those words in Garan's mouth. And a man that was half-dragon was an abomination to it.

"I agree. The Ufak Monta had no interest in the baron. So you think the Ufak Monta just left of its own accord?"

"Yes, it could tell as well as we could that the planet was on the verge of death. It had killed its abomination. It had imparted a few words of advice. It was free."

Garan oriented himself. "I'll take this half and you take that half. We travel slowly and look for signs. He could be buried under dust or blown far off our path. Check everything."

Karol gave him a salute, one such as Danton used to give. Garan's eyes watered and he turned the glide away.

A few items of debris lay on the ground: a broken bucket, planks of wood, possibly from the ship; a flask with the lid missing, a severed hand. Garan near tipped out of his glide at the sight of human body parts. He remembered what the ship had contained and what the people had been eating. He couldn't smell the stench of people who fed on the dead anymore. The blast had scoured that from the air, burnt it away. Garan wished the memory was as easily dealt with. Unfortunately, he would take those memories to the grave.

Garan tracked methodically, as systematic as a Farsighter searching for an asteroid, while he steered the glide up and down. The ground was so uniform in appearance at times his vision blurred, or he lost focus and had to go back over the same ground. He was on one of these backtracks when he spotted an odd shape out of the corner of his eye. He sped the glide over to it and hovered while he studied the mound. It was a body, he thought.

Lowering the glide, he reached out to scoop the accumulated dust from what he thought were the head and shoulders.

The man was on his back, one arm bent over his face and the other outstretched, the fingers bent like a claw. There were black stains on his clothing, showing wounds to his torso. With so much dust and damage, he had to be sure.

Garan gulped as he moved the arm to see the face. He let out a low breath of relief. It was not Danton, definitely not Danton. It looked like the baron, judging by the size and the rounded gut. Garan's gaze tracked over the body to make sure, to fix the details in his mind. He backed away from the baron and looked around, eyes set to find any other lump.

Danton had fought the baron. It looked like he had won. The concussive wave from the explosion of the machine could have thrown the body here. But it was, at least, a new point of origin for their search.

"Karol!" Garan called, his hands cupped around his mouth. He turned the glide slightly and called again. "Karol!"

He waited, sniffing and finding the taste of death in the back of his throat. While he waited for Karol, he mentally divided the land into two sections. One for him and one for Karol.

Running footsteps alerted him to Karol's approach. "Is that the man Danton fought?" Karol asked when he came up, barely panting. Garan envied him his stamina and the ability to run. Garan's glide could go fast if he wanted, except he then ran the risk of overturning himself. He had to take care with his leg sticking out at an angle.

"Yes, that's the baron. He was the one that was in charge of Gateshead. That's where I saw him."

Karol growled low and Garan started. He had never heard such a sound from Karol before. Next, the boy started kicking at the carcass and screaming, the kicks growing more and more savage until the body made gooey crushing sounds.

"Karol," Garan said, sickly fascinated and appalled. "Karol!"

Tears streamed down the boy's face. He stopped kicking and stood there sobbing. "It was him. He took them. He killed them. My father. My mother. All my kin."

Garan nodded and swallowed a lump in his throat. He empathized with Karol's grief. "I am sorry. He was a very bad man. He did many, many terrible things."

Karol looked to be trying to control himself. He used the sleeve of his robe to wipe his face. "I'm better now. Can we move away from him?" The boy stepped back and rubbed gore off his shoes while pretending not to.

Garan nodded and moved ten paces away, waiting for Karol to join him once he had calmed down.

Karol turned his pale eyes in his direction. "What now?"

"I think Danton must be near here. If they fought, Danton might be wounded."

"Or dead, too," Karol intoned morosely. The breeze lifted his hair and fanned it around his face. With a hand, he wiped it out of his eyes as they examined the surrounding terrain. Karol lifted his face and met Garan's inquisitive stare. "He is most likely dead, otherwise he would have come to us."

A shiver passed over Garan and he had to bite back a denial, even though he knew Karol spoke true. Garan had to prepare himself to lose another friend. "Either way," he said at last, his voice soft like a sigh, "we need to find him. It's important to Salinda, to all of us."

Karol nodded. "Yes, you're right. I'll take this side." He moved his arm in a cutting motion and then moved it left.

"That's what I was thinking." Garan patted him on the back. "Good luck."

Karol moved off, tugging the supply glide along behind him.

Garan bit his bottom lip and looked back at the messy corpse. The stench was starting to rise and insects swarmed. He engaged the glide and moved away and then slowed down. He did not want to miss any signs.

Garan's thigh pained him where the splints dug into his flesh. There had been no time to fix them before he had gone in search of Danton and the constant ache was starting to weary him. A sudden gust of wind threw dust into his unprotected eyes. Vision impaired, he could not halt the glide and, as he tried to adjust the splint, he was slightly off-balance. Lack of sight and balance meant he was dumped unceremoniously onto the ground. Winded, in pain, he struggled for air and his irritated eyes streamed with tears. The glide halted close by once it had lost his weight.

Careful of his broken leg, he managed to sit in the dirt and find something to clean his eyes. As he sat there, cursing to himself, he heard a moan.

His head jerked up. All he could see was a smear and the pain in his eyes had them blinking madly to clear his vision.

Maybe he had imagined that sound. He calmed his breathing and his cursing and listened. The wind blew around his ears, rustling his hair, making a noise. He slowed his breathing and there it was again. A low, pain-filled moan.

"Danton!" Garan called out. "Danton!" He hoped Danton would moan again so Garan could figure out in which direction he lay. It didn't come again. There was no answer to his call.

Finally, his eyesight cleared. He saw Karol, running, as if his feet did not touch the ground, kicking up dust and leaving it billowing behind, the supply glide following smoothly. "You found him?" Karol asked, not even panting after such a run.

"Not exactly. I think I heard him. He is close."

ᘒᘒᘒᘒᘒ

Karol joined Garan to help him get back on his glide and to pinpoint where Danton might be.

"So which direction?" Karol asked.

"That way," Garan said pointing. "At least I think it was. The breeze may have distorted the moan I heard."

Karol's eyes narrowed. "We go together. You look that way and I'll look this way."

Garan engaged the personal glide and started moving. Karol kept pace with him as they went slowly, studying the ground in front of them and to either side.

They had not gone far when Karol's hand shot up and he pointed. "There."

Garan followed the direction Karol indicated. There was a low mound of dust, with darker patches visible. "Yes, go."

Karol sprinted ahead and Garan increased the speed of the glide. Karol fell to his knees and started to brush at the dust gently. A moan escaped from the mound.

They had found Danton. Garan lowered his glide, turning it so he could get his broken leg out of the way.

"Danton," Garan said urgently. "Can you hear me?"

A moan was his only response. Danton moved slightly in response to Karol removing the dust from his face and hair. Garan looked down at his friend's body. There was a gaping wound in his chest and lacerations all over him, as if he had been used as a pincushion. His skin was pale and his breathing was shallow.

Karol glanced up at him. "Can we get him onto the glide?"

Garan's eyes watered again and it was not the dust irritating them. "We must." Garan could barely repress the sob that was stuck in his throat. First Nils, then Brill, and now Danton's life hung in the balance.

Danton lay, barely breathing. Garan peered at the wound. It was not as severe as Brill's. It had not ruptured anything. If Danton had lasted this long untended, then he might last until they returned to Barrahiem. They had lost two of their number and they could not afford to lose another. Garan shook slightly as he wiped dust from Danton's legs and kept finding more wounds. He let his tears fall as he counted and assessed the injured man's wounds. It was a miracle that Danton was still alive. He had obviously lost a lot of blood. From the looks of it, the explosion had thrown or rolled him a great distance. Perhaps being unconscious had enabled him to survive—all floppy arms and legs.

Karol lowered the supply glide and used a partially filled pack to make a pillow for Danton's head.

Wiping tears from his chin, Garan spoke to Danton, even though Danton was not able to respond. "We have you now, Danton. We did it. Margra is saved. Nils used the machine, which blew up. I am afraid that Nils died in saving us.

"Salinda and the baby, Elan, are doing well. Eneit is with Laidan. Those two brave souls have fought hard and fought well. You taught them that. You gave them that."

Karol spoke to Danton. "Now I am going to move your leg. It may hurt and I am sorry for that." A moan greeted this moving of his wounded limb, but Danton needed to be straightened out so he could be transferred to the glide.

"Karol is a good lad, you know," Danton said. "He's quick, and he can hide like he is one with the shadows. Just like Nils used to do."

Danton moved an arm, just a little bit. It gave Garan hope, brought a smile to his face. "Soon we will put you on the glide and take you home to Barrahiem. We will look after you. You are safe now."

Garan considered the cuts to Danton's face and neck. One cut looked particularly nasty, and very close to a major blood vessel. Had the baron done this to him? What kind of hate had been inside that man? "We found the baron dead. You will make Salinda happy, you know. She wanted to kill him at Gateshead."

Another moan from Danton as he threw his head from side to side, like he had a fever. Fresh blood leaked from his cuts, but Garan did not try to stop the bleeding. It would carry the dust away and clean the wounds.

"Now the hard part," Garan said. "We need to lift him. You take the feet. I will take his head and shoulders."

Karol took position while Garan positioned the glide close to Danton's head. "On three." He counted and they lifted Danton onto the glide. The moan Danton emitted was more like a cry. Garan winced, wishing he had not hurt him. It was difficult for Garan to lift from a sitting position. With a grunt, he managed to get enough height to help slide Danton onto the waiting glide.

He spoke softly. "That is the worst part over. Smooth sailing now. We are taking you home, Danton."

He shared a look with Karol. "You all right to pull the glide?"

Karol's grin was lopsided. "Definitely."

The set off at a brisk pace to intercept Salinda and the others. Karol ran and Garan put his glide at a faster speed. He was aching to get back to Barrahiem, too. He wanted this splint cut off. Maybe some of the observatory refugees knew a bit of physicking. The afternoon sky was gray and the wind came in rough spurts. A storm was coming and Garan did not want to be out in it. They may have saved Margra from moonfall, but it was going to be a while before the planet healed and maybe longer before they could all leave Barrahiem.

Donna Maree Hanson

Chapter Twenty-one
HOMECOMING

Salinda had Elan strapped to her chest as she paced near the entry to the Way Gate. She had been strong for so long that feeling weak was galling to her. She had had to surrender the cadre, then she had had to give birth when the fighting was at its worse.

Brill was dead because of her, because of her weakness.

Eneit and Laidan leaned against the rock face watching her, faces tight with grief, eyes red from weeping. They had dug Brill's grave and Salinda had said a few words, words that had to fight their way out of her throat. If it wasn't for her he'd be alive.

Logic fought this emotional slant, this obsessive cast to her mind. She grieved, she suffered. She'd lost the cadre, lost Nils and Brill. And Danton? She had no idea if he lived. Had she lost him too?

Her arms clasped the warm mound of flesh snuggled inside the new sling Eneit had made. Elan was the only living proof that Nils had lived. She would grow up with other Hiem around her, only because of Nils. He had found the Hiem youths, the last remaining members of a dying clan. He had saved Margra for them and for Elan. For her.

Try as she might she couldn't conceive of life without Nils. He had saved her, he had made her whole and, as prickly as he was, she had seen into the core of him and nurtured it. She had come alive then because of him, and was alive now because of him.

The gray sky seemed to grieve, mimicking her heart. *Stop. Stop thinking this way. Giving birth has made you crazy. Just like being pregnant made you stupid in the end.*

She caught sight of Garan first. His tall frame sitting on that glide, his leg at an angle. It should have made her laugh, but her heart was too heavy for laughter. When the longer glide hove into view with its wounded burden, she clenched her jaw. She wanted to scream and rage and beat her fists in the air. It was so unfair.

Danton had killed the baron…must have. She had dreamed of doing that for so long. Yet Danton had just cause, too. She knew what the baron had done to him. Slowly, the tight bindings on her heart loosened. Danton had killed the baron for himself, and for her.

In the blink of an eye, Karol was beside her, appearing out of the shadows and making her jump. "Karol!"

He grinned at her. "Danton is still alive. If we hurry, we can get him back to Barrahiem to the healing tray. Shall I open the gate?"

"Yes, please." Salinda didn't watch Karol move to the Travel Way entrance and it was only in passing she heard him exchange words with Eneit and Laidan. Her gaze was transfixed by the glide. Garan held the tether in his fist and the harsh lines of his face spelled out his misery. Salinda leaned to the side and gasped when she saw the unmoving body. If Karol hadn't told her Danton lived she would have taken him for a corpse.

She ran up to grip the side of the glide and stared hungrily down at Danton. Then she recoiled. His face was cut and looked like someone had poked at a steak with a knife too many times. Blood covered his face and neck and hands. His empty eye socket was bare and it seeped blood.

Holding a sob in check, her gaze traveled down the rest of him. A gaping wound in his chest. Lacerations down his thighs. It was a wonder he breathed at all. When she called his name, he didn't give any sign he was conscious.

Salinda swallowed and lifted her gaze to Garan. She couldn't form words.

His violet-colored eyes were bright and red-rimmed, either from tears of grief or the irritating dust.

"How can he have lived through that?" she asked.

Garan had a ghost of a grin about his mouth, though his eyes were haunted. "He's tough."

Salinda nodded, folding her arms around herself. Eneit called to her and Salinda looked back to see the Way Gate open. She glanced to Garan, her jaw set determinedly. "This time…if he makes it back to Barrahiem alive, he goes directly into the healing tray."

Garan let out a breath. "Praise the source you said that. I thought I might have to argue with you."

Her eyes widened, wounded by his words. She had made a choice before, a necessary choice. It had almost cost her her sanity. It had certainly torn at her heart every time she looked at Danton after Gateshead, knowing how mutilated he was, how he had been tortured because of her. Each time Brill and Garan had reproached her, it had cut deeper. This time there was no choice to be made by her. It was a matter of fate. Danton had lingered long enough to be rescued and he had to endure for a while longer if he was going to be saved.

Salinda reached out a hand and ran her fingers very gently through Danton's tangled hair and the memory of making that same movement before, long ago at the prison vineyard, surfaced. So much had happened since. Salinda wanted to feel vindicated, but she wasn't quite there. It was a concept that had yet to be understood.

She followed the glide into the Way, trailing behind Garan as if all the cares in the world still held her bound.

Danton lingered in life during their passage through the Ways and outside when they took a detour around the collapsed section. The water was less now, leaving a muddy plain, but they made good time. Salinda kept focused on Danton. On the home stretch, she talked to him and murmured things and when they stopped, she fed Elan and ate her ration of flat bread and watered wine next to his glide. Eneit tried to get Danton to drink some wine. It was futile because she couldn't rouse him.

For a group of people who had saved Margra, they were a sorry-looking lot. All of them grieving for dear lost ones. Salinda realized that living in a wounded world in reality was harder than expected. They hadn't talked in any detail about the future, but it was obvious they should stay in Barrahiem for many years. The air needed to clear, the climate needed to settle, and the land needed to heal.

They trudged along, Salinda rubbing her baby's back absently. "We're here," Karol said.

Salinda's ears pricked up and her heart beat faster. Barrahiem! She had come to love the place, though without Nils, it would be very different.

They exited into the city and straight away Salinda noticed the difference. She gasped. Garan paused beside her. "What is it?"

"Look," Salinda said, her gaze raking the tall ceiling of the cavern. A jagged rip cut it nearly in half. Panic welled up. "Hurry!"

"Wait!" Laidan cried out. "Danton...he's stopped breathing."

Salinda swung around. "Quickly, lower the glide."

She untied Elan and handed her to Eneit. Salinda gripped Danton's nose and breathed into his mouth. She did that a few times and then listened for his heartbeat. It limped along weakly. There was still time.

"Karol? Can you get Danton to the Hall of Elders and into the healing tray as quick as you can?"

Karol nodded, took the tether and sprinted. The glide shot after him. It was fortunate that Danton was tied to the glide or he would have been flung out. "Can I go after him?" Laidan asked.

Salinda agreed. "Thank you. I must see how things stand in the city."

With Garan and Eneit, Salinda increased her pace, suddenly concerned with things other than how bad she felt.

"Let me take Elan, so you can go on ahead," Eneit suggested.

Salinda handed her daughter over as she walked, impatient to see how things stood with the city.

Signs of damage became apparent immediately. Abodes directly under the crack had roofs caved in by fallen stone. A layer of dust, reminding her of the surface of Margra, covered everything. There were no people to be seen, and fear throbbed in her chest, making it difficult to breathe. *Don't panic.*

Eneit's eyes were round as she looked about her, Elan resting on her shoulder. Garan's eyes were flat and his mouth tight. He was as worried as she was. The Stoli continent had received a bigger battering than Arvoli, where they had traveled to find the machine. Salinda prayed to the source that she had not led all those refugees to their doom...

A lone figure came down the stairs from the Barr family node. Squab...she stood there, fists clenched and face in a snarl. Even from this distance, the woman's tension was evident. Squab was alive and apparently unharmed. That gave hope that the others were also. Salinda increased her pace. Squab started walking down toward her.

"Salinda!" Squab's demeanor softened a little as she surveyed the group. "Where's Danton? Brill?"

Salinda's lips tightened and she lowered her gaze as they each took the last steps that brought them face-to-face. "Brill died of his wounds. We were ambushed by Sartell men in Arvoli, by the baron and Gercomo."

Squab's complexion paled. "Danton?"

Salinda let a small smile come on her face. "Karol has taken him to the healing tray. He's barely alive, but once inside that he will be healed."

"I've heard about that particular miracle. And Nils?" Squab asked, her gaze shifting between her and Garan.

Salinda couldn't stop the tears that welled in her eyes. "Gone," she said in a voice that was barely there. "He saved us. He saved Margra."

Squab wiped at her own eyes. "Your mission was a success then?"

Salinda managed to get out a watery, choking, "Yes!"

Squab surged forward and gathered Salinda into a hug, holding her tight in her arms. "Thank the dragon's holy ass." She eased Salinda out of her embrace and held her by the shoulders. "I don't think I could have borne another moment in charge of this lot of cantankerous refugees. When can we get them out of here?"

Salinda wiped at her eyes, laughing and crying at the same time. "Years."

Squab swore.

"How is everyone?" Salinda asked, sending her gaze overhead.

"That was a bit of a surprise," Squab replied. "A few injuries. A couple of deaths."

"You mentioned cantankerous?"

Squab shrugged. "I'm not good with people and they were pretty ratty at first. Miraka has been a great help, moral support and all that. We have things running pretty smoothly now."

Squab shifted her attention to Garan and pointed. "If you make your way up there, you'll see a green sign. That's the infirmary. They should be able to help with your leg and any other injuries you have."

Her gaze dropped to Eneit. "Is that the baby?" She laughed. "Of course it is. May I?"

Eneit received a nod from Salinda and Squab took Elan into her arms. "Name?"

"Elan. It was Nils's father's name. Apparently the name is not gender-based."

Squab nodded. "Miraka mentioned that. Some Hiem names are, but most aren't." She rocked Elan and then smiled. "She is very beautiful. Born at the end of the world that didn't end." She squinted and then ran a finger over Elan's forehead. "I see Nils in that face of hers."

Elan squealed loudly and suddenly. Squab blanched. "What did I do?" she said as she hurriedly handed the baby back.

"Nothing. She's hungry and needs changing. I take it I still have an abode?"

"Yes, all ready and waiting." Squab stood aside so Salinda could pass by. "By the way, later we shall be celebrating your victory and remembering those who passed."

Salinda nodded. "Sounds like a good idea. I think I could sleep for a week, but alas, the baby feeds every few hours. Don't expect me to be perky."

Squab nodded. "It will get better. It will."

"I'll come with you," Eneit said. "I can help with Elan."

Salinda's eyes burned as she felt tears coming again. She was so over the weeping. She had to accept that she was going to feel sad, even though they lived. Technically, she had nothing to worry about—other than the state of the city, the refugees, Elan and trying not to think about Danton. At least he was alive.

Nils was gone. Barrahiem had never felt so alien and unwelcoming. The memory of Nils was everywhere, like a breath exhaled again and again.

⬬⬬⬬⬬⬬

Garan sat by the lake, musing about how high and choppy the water was, theorizing that the fissure had been opened up by changes in Margra's crust, allowing more water to enter. The waterfall was flowing hard and fast from the wall of the cavern and crashing noisily into the lake. As the population had grown, their need of water almost matched the new rate of fill. The gaping fissure in the ceiling of the cavern, though, looked far more dangerous. These last two weeks, since he had come back, it had been stable. As the causes of the seismic activity had been dealt with, he was confident that the danger had passed. At some stage, he would have to figure out how to explore the cleft in the bedrock above their heads to make certain. Now that there were no meteors to blow out of the sky, Garan had a chance to think about the future. One that did not involve being a Skywatcher.

He reclined on the shore, resting on his side, propped up on an elbow, a smile lingering on his face. There was plenty of technology to explore. His previous restraint had been at Nils's behest, but now Nils was gone the forbidden nature of the exploration of the storage areas had passed. Garan had spoken to the other Hiem and they were happy for him to see what there was in the warehouse. In fact, they wanted to explore as well. It was their heritage more so than his, anyway.

Dreams of a future filled his mind with delight. Perhaps, one day, they would return to their former glory. Thankfully, the Hiem had agreed to investigate and report on the contents of the archives, in as much as the information contained within pertained to the Sundwellers of old at least. Karol had learned the archive language from Nils and was more proficient than Salinda.

Salinda, unfortunately, had not recovered her full strength. Not yet. Those last weeks before Elan was born had been hard for her. Now there was not much for her to do and a sort of depression hung over her. Squab still ran the place and ran it well. Eneit helped Salinda care for the baby, who had grown so much in such a short time.

A chink of grit being ground underfoot had him angling his head to see who was coming. It was Laidan, a bright smile on her face. Her long hair was now cut short to curve around her face, making her eyes look larger and brighter. It suited her.

"Laidan. Is anything wrong?" Garan sat up, resting his elbow on a cocked knee, half-turned to her and half to the lake.

"No. Does there have to be? Can't I come and talk to you without there being a problem for you to solve?"

Her gaze was intent, her face tight. Not with anger, he thought. Fear, perhaps. "No, of course not." He gestured with his hand at the ground nearby, welcoming her to sit.

Garan had been by the lake for a few hours. As there was nothing to do he did not feel bad about wasting time or relaxing. His leg could bear weight now, even though it was strapped up tight. The intensity of Laidan's gaze had him worried. Had he forgotten something? Had he done something wrong?

He waited for Laidan to seat herself, then met her look with an embarrassed grin. Despite everything they had been through, Laidan had the power to make him feel like a foolish boy. While he waited a bit longer, his face creased in bewilderment. She said nothing, just put her head on her knee and stared at her feet. He let out a steady breath, and waited a bit longer still.

This went on for five minutes or so. "Well, aren't you going to say something?" Laidan said, eyebrows raised over intense crystal-blue eyes. As always, they had the power to seize his heart.

"Nice day," he said, then coughed to hide his blush. Even he knew that was stupid.

He chanced a look at her. She was sitting there, forehead furrowed and her head cocked at an angle as if she was trying to puzzle something out. Probably how many degrees of an idiot he was.

"The days are the same in Barrahiem. Do you mean you are having a nice day while you sit down here, brooding over the lake?"

"I am not brooding. I am studying the lake. I do not think we have to worry about the rise in the lake level. I was going to report that to Squab and Salinda tonight when we have dinner."

She nodded slowly. "So that's all the news you want to give them?"

Garan screwed up his face while trying hard to think. Had he missed something? "Is it your birthday?"

Laidan snorted, then slapped her thigh and laughed out loud. She rolled onto her back and held her shaking belly. Garan found it funny, too, because it was good to see Laidan laugh. He had always loved her laugh.

She calmed eventually and then rolled onto her side and gazed up at him. "Oh, sky eyes, you are wonderful."

Garan's breath caught in his throat. "I am?" This was news to him. He had been so careful with her during her recovery. He had stayed out of the way when Brill was alive in case she and Brill found each other again. With Brill gone...he did not...

Laidan reached out her hand to him. On automatic, he clasped it in his own. "I have been a fool, Garan. I know I have hurt you as I have hurt others. I have seen clearly now for many months. Brill was a good friend. I respected him, cared for him and loved him as well. I mourn his passing and I will miss him always.

"Garan, you are the one I want to spend my life with."

Garan's mouth fell open and his heart thudded so hard he thought he heard wrong. "You want to spend your life with me?"

Laidan's smile was radiant. "Yes."

A sob rose up and near choked him. He was so shocked and stunned that emotion hit like one of the bolts of power from a crystal hitting a meteor. His defenses were blown. He was open, bleeding, laughing, in love.

Taking pity on him, she threw herself at him, hugging around his neck.

She cried, too. "I'm so sorry for hurting you. Please say you will forgive me."

Garan shook his head, reaching for speech. "Oh, Laidan, there is nothing to forgive. Will you forgive me, more like?"

She put her hands on his shoulders and pushed back so she could see his face. "There is nothing to forgive." With that, she leaned in and pressed her mouth to his. Warmth and desire flooded into him as he returned the kiss.

Life in Barrahiem moved from satisfactory to wonderful in that moment.

♋♋♋♋♋

Squab stood next to the healing tray. She couldn't see Danton, but had to be there; she had to know that he was close by. He was the reason she was here. He was the reason she was alive.

Garan had related the list of injuries that Danton had sustained and who he had fought. Tears rolled warmly down her cheeks. She didn't like being in this room. She didn't like the Hall of Elders with its flickering flame and strange decorations. It reminded her of aliens, of a people she didn't really understand. Not that she had anything against the Hiem. Miraka had become close to her and she was a pale creature who walked and talked and was real. The scenes in the murals and the grandeur of the Hall of Elders reminded her that the world had been different, even more strange than the one she lived in.

Salinda believed in the power of dragon wine. She believed that those dangerous feral dragons had magic. Squab didn't believe such things, as she was too practical, but she didn't argue about it. Sure, Garan could make machines start working by touching them and he was rumored to have shot down meteors for a living. She had seen the beams of power in the distance when she was fighting for her life and dragon wine and Brill had said it was Garan and Salinda. As she'd been too occupied with surviving, she hadn't thought about it.

Yet, there was Danton covered in a transparent lid and obscured by mist. He wasn't dead, he was going to be fixed. Squab tried to smile. She would believe that when she saw it. Wiping her face with her forearm, she turned away from the place where he lay and returned to the city proper. As she walked along the corridors, she didn't fail to notice that these important parts of the city were in the rock itself. They weren't vulnerable in the same

237

way the abodes had been when the cavern split.

The archives, too, were safe. Miraka and the other Hiem had taken her down there when they were assessing the damage to the city. Those records had been untouched.

The quality of the light changed as she saw the balcony up ahead. Miraka was there, leaning over the balustrade, waiting. Squab's heart beat a little faster. It was impossible not to be taken by the girl, or woman, rather, as Miraka had very pointedly stressed. She was an adult and could do what she wanted. She had moved into Squab's abode and taken up residence on the sofa.

Little by little, Miraka was beating down Squab's defenses. Squab hated feeling vulnerable. Miraka had the power to peel open her chest and expose her heart to the elements for dragons to feed on. The risk that Miraka posed to her emotional safety both thrilled and terrified her.

As she walked up, fists clenched, Miraka turned and smiled. "Finished?" she asked.

Squab nodded, not trusting herself to speak. There was no Danton to seek counsel from. She was on her own. Despite Salinda being back, Squab was still running things and this suited both of them. Salinda because she was tired and heartsore. Squab because she needed a purpose or she would run mad.

Squab was stuck here until the world healed.

They walked up the hill together in silence. Occasionally, Miraka would look at her and smile. Squab kept her gaze front and center. She could almost taste the ending. Miraka was going to leave. She was tired of being Squab's friend. The crisis was over and now she was more settled in Barrahiem it was time for her to move on. Squab didn't know what to do or say. She couldn't bear to ask.

How was it that she could face men with a sword, and fight, but couldn't ask someone she cared about what they were thinking and planning? *Are you leaving me, now?*

It was so unfair. Miraka had practically forced her friendship on Squab, had made Squab accept her presence and made Squab dependent on her.

Once inside the abode, Miraka dropped the curtain down that closed off the door.

"Can we talk?" Miraka said.

Squab, still facing away, focused on the wall. "Of course," she replied.

Miraka sat on the sofa, her Hiem robe gracefully arranged around her. "Won't you sit?"

Squab pursed her lips, and then sat down. She couldn't quite look at Miraka. One look and Squab's need would be naked to her eyes. Squab needed a friend. She needed Miraka in her life.

Miraka let out a breath. "So, things have sort of settled into a routine now that Salinda and the others are back. Did you hear that Garan and Laidan have made a match of it?"

Squab nodded, biting her lip. Apparently, it had been Laidan who forced the issue. Squab admired her bravery, for going after what she wanted. Garan was a good lad. Sweet, too.

Miraka cast a sideways look at her. "Are you all right? You seem tense."

Squab sat forward, elbows on knees, and clenched her hands together. "I'm fine."

"I think," Miraka began, "that we need to talk about us."

"Us!" Squab barked out. Then her eyes widened and she fell back against her chair. "What about us?"

"That's the problem, isn't it?" Miraka said, a glint in her silver-colored eyes. "There is no us."

"Oh," Squab said, and it was an expression of despair. She thought they had a thing.

Miraka stood up, leaned over Squab. "Is that all you can say? *Oh!* Don't you want there to be an us? I want more than a casual thing. I want to share my life with you."

Squab quailed. Not quite understanding. "You want a relationship with me?"

"Yes, a full and committed relationship. I love you, Squab."

Squab shook her head. "No, you can't. I'm ugly and I'm..." She gestured to her stocky body.

"What? You're clever and strong and I like how you treat me...except for the not desiring me. Is it because I'm different. Do you find me ugly?"

Squab pushed to her feet and Miraka stepped back. "No. No! You are beautiful. Too beautiful for someone like me."

Miraka shook her head. "Give me the benefit of the doubt. Accept that I know what I want and what I like and that's you."

A kernel of hope sprang up in Squab's chest. Dare she believe, dare she accept? "Miraka," Squab said in a tear-laden voice.

It was enough. Miraka bent and lifted the hem of her long Hiem tunic and pulled it over her head. She stood there with her beautiful body. "I want you, Squab. Don't turn me away."

Later, when they held each other, Miraka snuggled into the hollow of Squab's shoulder. "Thank you, Lou," Miraka said.

Squab leaned her head so that her chin touched Miraka's head. "Squab."

"No," Miraka said and giggled. "To me, you're Lou. It's much nicer than Squab. Why don't you use it?"

"My father gave that name to me, so I left it behind." As they had previously discussed the terrible things her father had done to her, there was no point in discussing it further.

"Well, what would you have chosen to call yourself? What name do you desire?"

"You want to call me something other than Squab, is that it?"

"Yes, it's a horrible nickname. Given to you by rebels who were obviously men. Come on," Miraka said, propping herself up on her elbow to look down into her face.

"Well, I've always been partial to the name Lily." Squab kept her eyes fixed on the wall in case Miraka laughed.

"Lily is a beautiful name. From now on, everyone must call you Lily. Including Danton, when he's better."

"All right then. Can we sleep now?" Squab asked with a grin.

"Only if you really want to." Miraka leaned down and kissed Lily on the lips.

☾☾☾☾

Karol found Eneit sitting in the common area of the Barr family node. She had Elan on her lap. The baby was asleep and Eneit had a faraway look on her face, as if she was daydreaming and the dream was something pleasant.

Standing still, he watched her and then bit by bit she noticed him and started. "Oh, what are you doing?"

She lowered her head to study the baby in her lap and ran a finger lovingly along its cheek. The baby was half-Salinda and half-Nils. Karol thought the baby took more after Salinda. So far Elan had slate-gray eyes and her skin was pale cream. Not the clear white of a Hiem.

Eneit looked up at him. "She's beautiful. I think I want to have babies. Lots of them."

240

Karol came forward. "Why do you think that?"

Eneit looked at him, really looked at him. "To replace what I've lost. A brother, a mother, friends…"

Karol pointed to the bench beside her. "May I?"

"Sure," she replied.

Karol sat down and sighed. "We have lost so much." He turned to her, took her hand in his. "We still have that which we cherish."

Eneit's eyes rounded, her lips curling, then her teeth showing in her broad smile. "You like me." She didn't ask, she told him.

"Yes, I do."

Eneit laughed. "Well, that's good because I like you too."

Karol smiled and put his arm around her, peering over his shoulder at the baby. "So how many babies did you say you wanted?"

"Lots. When we are ready."

Karol grinned at her. "Yes, when we are ready."

Donna Maree Hanson

Epilogue

Salinda sat at her little table, turning the Pardu tea in the pot, waiting for it to be ready to pour. She made the tea in this way because it brought the memory of Nils closer to her.

Garan hailed her from outside. "Come in," she responded, and leaned over to the shelf for another cup.

Garan grunted as he squeezed through the door. His face was alight with joy and had been since Laidan had cornered him and told him what she wanted.

Good on Laidan, Salinda thought. Garan would never have gotten up the courage. Not after what happened. Not after his words had hurt her, made her run away, made her walk into Gercomo's beastly clutches. Laidan had come into her own and Salinda was gladdened because of it. Laidan had exceeded all their expectations. Thurdon would have been proud of her.

"Tea?" she asked, lifting the cup in his direction.

"Thank you, yes." He took a seat opposite her and together they turned the cup in the way Nils had shown them. Salinda smiled sadly and looked away until she had herself under control.

They had been back a month and Salinda had not stirred much from her abode. Eneit helped her with Elan and just today Salinda thought that she should start exercising, maybe take a walk down to the lake and back.

"How are things?" Salinda asked Garan. They spoke more than once a day so she didn't expect much to have happened since the morning.

"The fine webs are starting to clear," Garan said.

Salinda froze, then lowered the cup. "You can see him?"

Garan nodded. "Yes, he looks...well, like Danton."

Salinda touched her eye with a trembling hand and he nodded.

"Yes, he has both eyes."

Salinda stared at Garan and then burst into tears. Chest heaving with sobs that she hadn't known were inside her.

Garan came to her side of the table and put his arm around her. "Yes, he is coming out of the tray. Tonight, maybe tomorrow morning. Do you want us with you?"

Salinda calmed down. Her tears still ran freely, but she was no longer sobbing. It was as if she had been holding her breath for a month and it was suddenly expelled and drawn in.

"I will feed Elan tonight and go up to wait."

"We will look after Elan."

"Thank you!" Salinda buried her face in Garan's shoulder and wept.

Patiently, gently, Garan just held her and soothed her.

಄಄಄಄಄

The golden light from the eternal flame lit her way across the floor. Majestic murals danced along the path with her as she trod to the healing tray. She was dressed in a clean robe, cinched at the waist. Clad in sandals, her feet whispered across the floor. Her long, dark hair hung down her back, washed and brushed. As she walked up to the tray, she saw Danton there. No webs to hide his nakedness.

She rejoiced in the newness of his skin. Scars had been wiped clean. Two eyelids closed over the balls of his eyes. His face was whole, his hair dark and wavy, his fingertips new and pinkish. Her eyes drifted to where the baron had maimed him and he was whole. Everything where it should be.

The memory of tending his wounds came afresh. She batted them away. Yes, Danton had suffered. She had suffered. They had all suffered.

Suffering was part of life. Yet, now Margra had hope. A smile lit her face and then she saw that Danton was awake. The tray opened.

"Salinda?" Danton said as he sat up. He looked down at his body in wonder. "How did I get here?"

He touched his face, grabbed his crotch and jerked in surprise. "The healing tray?"

He sat up and slid his legs over the side. "I thought I was dead."

Salinda shook her head. "Not you. No."

It was the hint she needed to let him know who they had lost.

"Who?" His dark eyes had a sad expression in them.

Salinda bit her bottom lip and then said, "Nils. He died in the machine saving Margra."

Danton's eyes widened. He glanced down at her belly and raised an eyebrow.

"Elan is well. She's nearly five weeks old."

"Who else?" Danton asked, and she saw the tension in his eyes and in the tightening of his jaw.

"Brill," she said in a whisper, fearing to say his name too loud.

"No!" Danton buried his head in his hands. "Not the kid, no."

"He died of his wounds. He died a hero."

244

Danton's head jerked up. There were tears on his cheeks. "Fuck being a hero. I wish he was here, now."

"Me too."

"And?"

"The rest of us made it back. Karol is a wonder. A youthful, courageous version of Nils, I think. By the way, Squab is now called Lily. So best you remember that."

"Lily. I will remember that." He grinned, eyes gleaming in the reflected light.

Salinda chuckled as joy filled her up.

Danton smiled and wiped at the tears that had started to track down his cheeks. "Did you bring me any clothes or am I going to exhibit to everyone in Barrahiem?"

She leaned over to where she had stacked some clean clothes for him and placed them in his lap. "I'll wait for you over there."

She turned away and he reached for her hand. "Salinda?"

She faced him. "Yes."

"I know it's really soon after losing Nils." He raked his fingers through his hair. A smile lit his face and then was chased away by a frown. "But...ah, wing dust! I'm just going to come straight out and say it. My feelings for you have never changed. I love you. I'm yours if you want me."

Salinda smiled through her tears. "I want you, Danton."

Danton slid off the edge of the tray, grabbing him to her. Light exploded inside her—a warm, luscious light. Danton was back. He was whole. And he still cared for her, after everything that had passed between them.

Sometime later, they headed back to the city. "I should warn you that there might be a celebration waiting for you."

"Not Laidan's cooking?" he said in mock horror.

"No. Garan's...and I should say he and Laidan...well, they sorted themselves out."

"Thank the source for that. First you better introduce me to Elan. I think we are going to be very good friends."

"Sure thing."

"Any dragon wine?"

"I might have some somewhere, but there won't be any more after it has been drunk."

His eyebrows arrowed together. "The dragons are gone?"

"Most of them. Maybe all. We won't know until we can go back to the surface."

Danton drew her to him, put his arm around her waist and together they walked up the stairs to the Barr family node.

Already they could hear the chatter of gathered friends.

She was home.

The job was done.

The End

A note from the author

This is a sad moment. I say goodbye to these characters and their challenging story of survival. I've journeyed into the dark heart of humankind and I've seen the beast within. I have found the core of truth, of goodness and love. It wasn't always easy writing Dragon Wine. It was hard to balance the dark and the light, to find humor amid the savagery of Margra's world. Thank you to those of you who have journeyed with me. Thank you to those who have encouraged me to keep writing until the series was done.

This series has had a hard road. The publisher closed shop. Not enough books sold. The series languished and then I decided I needed to get it out there. I needed to complete the story and find my way to the end. I hope you enjoyed it. I hope you were on the edge of your seat until the last.

A series doesn't come together on its own. Nor does it appear overnight. I wrote the first lines of this series back in 2003, while I was living in a small vineyard. While I checked the grapes for disease, pruned them, sprayed them, put nets on them and finally harvested them, the prison vineyard came to life. Now, fifteen years later I am writing the last words of the story.

In those early days, I received encouragement from Peter Bishop at Varuna, the Writers' House, as part of their manuscript development program, at the time run in partnership with HarperCollins. Early versions of Dragon Wine made the long list and finally the short list. Alas, Dragon Wine was not chosen by HarperCollins.

I kept working and polishing. Feedback from Stephanie Smith, then an associate publisher at HarperCollins, and Deonie Fiford, editor at Hachette, served to keep me going. Rejection feedback from Marc Gascoigne at Angry Robot Books also fueled the creativity. A big thank you to you all.

The publishing market changed and I continued on, writing and polishing and cutting back. I had rejections and setbacks. Finally, a bit of good luck. Haley Nash requested the manuscript. She was working at Pan Macmillan at the time. She made an offer for the book for their digital imprint, Momentum. Never had an editor read a submission from me so fast. Usually, it was a year-long wait. Haley only took a couple of weeks. It was wonderful to hear that she loved it. The rest, as they say, is history. Momentum split the book into two parts and I had to think of new titles.

Shatterwing did not sell well. Dark fantasy, my publisher said, was a hard sell. I didn't believe that. There were lovers of dark fantasy out there, I just had to find them. After Momentum closed, the book languished at Pan Macmillan. After a year or so, a bunch of Momentum authors asked after their books and found they were not being promoted, so they asked that the rights be reverted to them. I got mine back.

There you have it. The complete series done now. Dark, dragon-themed covers. I hope you enjoyed it.

I have to give thanks to my writing retreat buddies. Thank you to Kylie Seluka, Russell Kirkpatrick, Trudi Canavan, Nicole Murphy, Cat Sparks, Rob Hood, Matthew Farrer. Also, Ian McHugh, Alan Baxter, Joanne Anderton and Gillian Polack. I'm lucky to have some amazing writer friends such as Shauna O'Meara, Leife Shallcross, Kimberley Gaal, Lily Mulholland and Val Toh. They helped me by just being there.

In the beginning, I received some very helpful feedback on early drafts. Thank you to Kaaron Warren, horror writer extraordinaire, Glenda Larke, awesome fantasy writer, Kylie Seluka (again) for just being really good at feedback and patient as all hell, and Gillian Polack, who endured a very extreme early draft and survived. Trudi Canavan also provided some feedback that helped with the overall story of *Shatterwing* and *Skywatcher*. Phil Berrie also deserves thanks for a continuity edit early on and some advice on moons.

Another writer who has been amazingly supportive is Craig Cormick. He's read some of the books and given me comments. He launched *Deathwings* and *Bloodstorm*. He's a busy man and an award-winning writer, but still had time for little old me. Nicole Murphy, writer buddy, who gave me such wonderful compliments on the books, will be launching the last two books at Conflux in Canberra in September, 2018.

Two other writing/editing buddies are Kaaren Sutcliffe and Maxine McArthur, who provided support and advice throughout these last fifteen years. Thank you both.

Of late, thanks go to Liz Munro of Canada for amazing reviews on her website of the first books and then the later ones. She made a great beta reader of the last two books.

Being a member of the Canberra Speculative Fiction Guild has been very useful and rewarding from the early days. A big thank you to them.

To my partner, Matthew Farrer, thank you for understanding the writing game and just being amazing. I hope you get time to read the Dragon Wine series one day. Maybe when you have a break from novel writing yourself.

Lastly, my thanks to you, the readers. I would not have made it here, to the end, without your enthusiasm.

With love
Donna Maree Hanson

And if you have a mind for more. Here is an epic fantasy series.

Preview of Argenterra, The Silverlands Book One—a portal fantasy

Sophy is not looking for a talisman: she is the talisman!

Chapter One

Lost

The low roof loomed over Sophy's head as she ducked to enter the next lot of tunnels beneath Castle Crioch. "God, it stinks in here."

"You're the one who wanted to go on a ghost tour. Stop complaining." Aria lifted her lantern and leant in closer to the stone wall, her nose wrinkling. "The quilts and flowers would have smelled nicer, but no, you had to do something more adventurous."

Sophy peered over Aria's shoulder to see what her best friend, now foster sister, was looking at. "You could've said no."

In the cracks between the stones, mortar had bubbled and oozed, leaving a rust-coloured trail of froth. Aria screwed up her face. "Gross. I can't believe I let you talk me into this. These old dungeons and tunnels are disgusting and creepy."

"I seem to recall that I have to suffer the quilts and flowers once we get out of here. That was the deal, right?" Sophy said.

"Yes, and you're not getting out of it." Aria sent her a piercing glance clearly discernible in the gloom. "You owe me. I haven't recovered from that awful story of murder and ghosts the guide told us."

Ahead, the guide in question's voice echoed off the walls and the rest of the tour group were lost in the shadows. "Don't stress, it's only a tour," Sophy said, waving her hand to dispel the dank stench. "It'll be over soon." She shrugged. "They just make up the stories anyway. Besides, I'm here to protect you if anything really monstrous comes clumping towards us."

Aria scoffed and resumed walking. "You'll have to. My phone doesn't have a signal down here. I can't even call for help."

The hair on the back of Sophy's neck rose and she swung around. Something was there—a man-like shape in the darkness, with red, glowing eyes. Sucking in a breath, she blinked instinctively, but when she looked again there was nothing. Unsettled, she said nothing to Aria who was already creeped out.

In a few minutes they had caught up with the stragglers from the tour group. Brady, their tour guide, had a broad Scottish accent, rolling his 'r' and mumbling half the rest. Light from lanterns flickered and jerked as people moved. Sophy listened a bit harder as the story Brady related took a nasty turn. "An' the Laird returned to find the heads of all his loved ones hanging from the walls..."

Her gut twisted. Betrayal, murder, ghosts lamenting. Were people really that nasty? As she listened a bit longer, she decided they could be.

"How much longer?" Aria asked. "Mum and Jeff will be waiting for us." The tour rounded a corner.

Sophy drew out her phone to check the clock display. "Another half an hour, I think. I'm sure Maralain and Jeff will figure out the tour is running late. Don't worry about it."

"I want to go back right now." Aria hissed the words in her ear with a decided edge of panic

"Now?" Sophy turned her astonished gaze to Aria. "But—"

Aria grabbed her upper arm and squeezed with fingers like claws. Aria's eyes were wide, her breaths coming in short pants. "I need to get out of here."

"Like now?"

The light from the lantern quavered in Aria's shaking hand. "Yes!" Aria's voice was hoarse and hard.

"I don't understand."

Aria's fingers dug harder into Sophy's bicep. "Oh god! I think I'm having a panic attack."

"What the? A panic attack?" Sophy gaped at Aria. "But the tour isn't that scary."

Aria covered her mouth, as if holding back a scream.

"I don't understand...why..." Sophy was cut off. The tour moved off again.

"Sophy, please, I'm being squeezed in half. I can't breathe." Aria sobbed. That hit Sophy right in the empathy spot.

"Okay. I'm sorry I didn't realise." Sophy cast around looking for an emergency exit. But this was an old Scottish castle and not an amusement park ride where they could hit an emergency stop button. The tour group had turned a corner. Sophy had a choice: race up there and get Brady to turn back, or they could reverse their steps and go back to the beginning. It would cause less embarrassment to Aria if they just found their own way back. She grabbed Aria's hand. "Come on, we'll head back to the start. We haven't come that far."

Aria kept a tight hold of Sophy's arm. "Thank you," she whimpered.

They turned the corner and walked for a few minutes. A deep groan enveloped them. Aria screamed, bending over and holding her stomach. The floor pitched and rolled. Sophy's heart thumped and her mind went white with terror. She barely kept on her feet. Dust rained down on them. "Quick! The doorway!"

Aria's breathing sounded like a bicycle pump but she didn't move. Sophy snatched at her jacket and dragged her over. "Come on. Hurry up!"

The tremor continued. Aria let out a scream and looked ready to bolt away. "No, wait. Don't run," Sophy said as she fought to keep Aria in the doorway. Weren't doorways the best place during an earthquake?

Aria screamed, panic taking hold. "Noooooo."

Sophy's heart sounded like a heavy disco beat: boom tish, boom tish. She peeled Aria's fingers off the lantern and placed it on the floor. Screams still fled Aria's mouth, creeping Sophy out. "Stop it." Aria didn't listen so Sophy gave her one across the cheek. Aria stopped mid-screech and then cried into Sophy's shoulder.

The earthquake ended, but the ground didn't seem to stop moving. It was as if the foundations of Castle Crioch were reorganising themselves and the dull thuds reverberating under her feet meant the building may not have survived intact. Could the towers have fallen? They had survived the quake but weren't out of trouble. She gulped: there was a big pile of stone above their heads between them and safety.

Sophy couldn't believe their luck. Was Scotland prone to earthquakes? Not that she'd heard. And if it was, why didn't someone say so before they came down here into the bowels of this place? Sure it'd stood for hundreds of years, but if she had known it was seismically unstable she would have thought twice about it. Maybe.

She listened for voices, hoping to hear others from the tour or the guide. It was eerily quiet except for the sound of grit hissing as it fell, timbers creaking overhead and her heart beat.

Aria stiffened, her finger nails pinching Sophy's shoulders. "What's that?" The absolute dread in her voice chilled Sophy. Peeling Aria's fingers from her shoulder, she turned.

"What the hell?"

Before them was a tunnel, one that oozed moisture and smelled weird, like freshly mown grass. Aria grabbed onto the waist of Sophy's jeans. "Don't."

"Don't what?" she replied stepping forward. "It wasn't there before."

"Sophy—"

A glove of cold air enveloped them, snatched them up and dragged them into the tunnel. Sophy screamed and flailed about, her stomach dropping to her toes. Aria's voice was in her ears so she seized onto her and drew her close. They were freefalling. Was it possible to die of fright? Eyes slammed tight, her ears popped with the change in air pressure. She struggled to come to terms with what was happening, yet even in the centre of her fear her brain worked. They were travelling somewhere: how or why she didn't know.

Sophy clung tightly to Aria as wind howled in her ears and snatched her breath away. Her long hair whipped about trying to suffocate and strangle her at the same time. When she dared to open her eyes, nothing but a blur of indecipherable colours surrounded them. The silvery tunnel sucked them down its gullet and become a nothing: a no space, a place of wind and noise and disorientation.

A sudden shift in direction and their bodies dropped, gravity returning abruptly. A force pulled Aria from her grip, her scream falling rapidly away.

No time for panic. A blazing light stunned Sophy just before she thumped to the ground, winded. For a long, uncomfortable moment she couldn't breathe. She tugged at the strap of her shoulder bag wrapped around her neck. Then the world went dark.

Sophy came to. She must have blacked out, but for how long? A second, a minute, an hour? Pushing herself up on her hands, she tried to orient herself, relieved she still had her bag and her precious phone. The light was dim, not dark like the tunnels beneath Castle Crioch.

Wind crashed through dark-leaved trees filling the space around her. An early sun dispelled the shadows cast by their trunks. How did she not get snagged in the branches when she fell? Glancing up, she wasn't sure she had fallen. A sudden pain pierced her forehead. What had happened? She couldn't quite recollect the last few minutes of her life. They were on a ghost tour. Except now she was here. And here wasn't there. "Ohh?" she moaned. Everything hurt—her head, her face, her ears. There wasn't a part of her that didn't feel twisted and bent out of shape.

A shrill scream sounded over the sound of the wind in the trees. Her head jerked up. "Aria?"

Sophy lurched to her feet and staggered at the pain in her head. Aria's next scream impelled her forward; she had to find Aria, had to protect her.

Aria's screams allowed Sophy to gain her bearings. Aria was close by. Sophy's fingers clung to the bark of the nearest tree, but creaking branches made her push away quickly. She didn't want to be squashed if one fell. Around her, light flickered. Dark patches came and went in her peripheral vision. She thought someone was there yet, when she turned, there was no one. Before she reached the shelter of the surrounding woods, a strange wind rocked her, and it felt as if bits of her were ripped away.

"I must have hit my head," she said to herself. "I'm imagining things."

Stepping under a large tree, Sophy called out. "Aria? Aria."

No answer. Sophy kept walking. How had they had become separated? Short shrill screams pierced the wind. Sophy sped up.

♋♋♋♋♋

Aria screamed again. Unhurt, opening her eyes proved too difficult. She was somewhere else. Felt it, knew it in her heart. It was in the air, in the ground and in the trees surrounding her. The taste of this place was on her tongue. She screamed again and then let her panic go.

As her heartbeat slowed, she drew in a breath of clear, sweet air. Instead of scrunching her eyes shut, she opened them. Living things around her exuded golden warmth. She saw life flowing through the trees; saw it in the water burbling in the stream beside her.

Calm, she told herself, be calm.

Crawling on hands and knees, she put her hands on the trunk of the nearest tree and felt the faint pulse of its life. Snatching her hand back, she curled herself into a ball and rocked back and forward. It couldn't be happening, it couldn't, she said like a litany to herself.

Sounds assaulted her ears, making her lift her head and hold her breath. Birds, insects, soft leaves fluttering on a light breeze, all made joyous, vibrant and overwhelming noise. She heard Sophy calling her name. What had happened? How had they ended up in this place, this beautiful place? She could barely remember what she was doing before finding herself here.

ᔕᔕᔕᔕᔕ

Sophy ducked under a low-lying branch and pushed through some undergrowth. With her ginger curls covering part of her face, Aria sat on the ground, next to a pool fed by a small stream. Relief rushed over her: thank goodness.

Sophy knelt next to her. "Are you hurt?"

Aria didn't respond and kept staring wide-eyed at her surroundings. Sophy's head pulsed with pain and her stomach twisted in knots. She leaned over to vomit on the ground. All she wanted to do was lie down and sleep until the weakness faded, yet some instinct made her resist the urge.

"Sophy?" Aria spoke at last. Sophy brushed the hair out of Aria's face, and quickly assessed her for injury. Aria was unharmed, not even a graze on her arm or a smear of dirt on her jeans. Her eyes though were still wide and staring.

"I am here. We're okay."

Aria's green gaze met hers, focusing finally. "We are not...not..."

"No. No. We're okay. We're fine."

Aria shook her head. "This place is different. I can see it, feel it. And look, my phone screen is completely blank. Nothing at all."

Sophy's brows cinched together. "I know something weird happened—"

"We are someplace else. I can feel life here, see it in the trees."

Sophy's mouth fell open. Aria spoke with such conviction that she became uneasy. She cast a glance around her, but all appeared to be normal. "No, we haven't. We're in Scotland—"

"The castle is not there."

Sophy shifted her head, trying to pinpoint the castle, the road, the village and couldn't. She couldn't explain what happened. They were in the tunnel on a ghost tour...She shook her head. Nothing. She couldn't remember. "Well, maybe we're lost." She noticed Aria assessing her. "What?"

"Your eyes...your eyes..." The hint of panic in Aria's voice sent fear crawling up Sophy's spine.

"What?" Sophy pressed her fingers around her eye socket, thinking it quite likely that her landing had caused a black eye.

"The colour has changed from dark blue to...to well...black. And your skin...so pale..."

"Right, I'm calling Maralain. She'll know what to do." Sophy pulled her phone out of her shoulder bag. The display was dead.

"It's not working, is it?" Aria asked.

Sophy shoved the phone back into her bag, with a sigh of resignation. "No. The battery must be dead, though it was fully charged before we went on the tour. Well, if somehow we...er...the castle is not there then there must be a road or a village or a police station around here."

"Do you really think so?" Aria's voice sounded calmer.

"Yes, of course I do." Even though Sophy was rattled by their experience, she needed to be strong for Aria. The sooner they found Maralain the better things would be.

"I doubt if you can walk anywhere," Aria commented her gaze fixed on Sophy's shaking hand and then pushed her hair behind her ears. "You're not well."

Dappled sunlight fell upon the nearby pond, revealing clear water and clean stones along the bottom.

"I think I'm okay. Some water might help." Sophy crawled over to the water's edge and splashed cold water over her face. Turning back to Aria, she asked, "Better?"

Her foster sister stood surveying the trees and the pond. Their gazes met and Aria nodded. Something in her expression led Sophy to believe that her looks had not improved.

☙☙☙☙☙

They walked for a few hours with no sound of traffic or signs of people. Aria had not renewed her unnerving chatter about 'feeling or seeing life' in her surroundings, which allowed Sophy to file it away under hysteria in a moment of crisis. She tried not to let the complete absence of technology or human habitation unnerve her.

They entered a glade. In the centre, Sophy saw a beautiful, silver-barked tree. Sunlight reflected off its prism-like leaves and the air shimmered with colour, shifting and fading as the wind tugged lightly at the branches. Sophy's heart lurched as she tried to get her brain to understand what it was that she was seeing.

Aria gasped. "Look at that!"

"Yes, odd," she agreed. Her gaze roamed about the clearing, trying to put a frame of reference on what they were seeing and experiencing. "Is it real?"

"Beautiful…" Aria said in an awed whisper.

The crystal-clear, almost-silver leaves were vaguely oval shaped with protrusions that made them appear like small, solid stars. They looked as if they could fit into the palm of her hand. Was it a construction of some kind? Was it safe?

Aria reached out and touched one of the leaves.

"Don't!"

Too late. The leaves began to play music. The sound reverberated around the clearing, like little bells tinkling. The melody amplified as it bounced off the forest, flowing back upon itself, deepening the song with multi-layers of notes.

"Listen to that," Aria's expression was full of rapture.

Sophy tried to block out the discordant sound. Even with her ears covered, the nerve-twisting feeling managed to snake up through her jaw into her eyes. Glancing upwards, Sophy spotted two silver leaves floating ever so slowly down. They mesmerised her, fluttering and skipping before her eyes. She couldn't dodge out of their way. One landed on her chest, right below her collarbone. Disappearing through her clothes, it seared her skin. Pulling at the neck of her t-shirt, she tried to get rid of it, but she couldn't see it, only feel it delving into her flesh.

She tried to warn Aria, but pain overwhelmed her and a strange sense of dislocation coursed within her body. Falling backwards into scattered leaf mulch, she heard Aria say, just before she lost consciousness, "Do you hear that? Feel that? Delightful…magic."

Next thing she knew, Aria was leaning over her and shaking her by the shoulder. Sophy's mouth opened, guppy-like, but no sound came out.

"Wake up! Did you faint?" Aria asked, cradling one of the crystal leaves in her hand.

"I'm okay," Sophy finally managed to say in a croaky voice.

"That's good. You know, Sophy, this tree, it's not normal. Now I'm certain that—"

Sophy sat up and saw movement at the edge clearing. "Sssh"

"What is it?" Aria asked. "Do you hurt somewhere?"

"There's someone there." She pointed to the woods behind Aria.

Two archers crept out of the woods behind a man, who slowly approached them. He was young looking, maybe twenty-something, and wore coffee-coloured hose and a brown and green leather jerkin. Sophy was hoping that they were caught up in some kind of medieval re-enactment. Her gaze flicked to the tree, and she quickly squashed that train of thought.

"Lord." Aria gasped and absent-mindedly dropped her leaf.

"Run! Get away," Sophy said, keeping the man in her line of sight.

"It's all right. He means us no harm."

"Are you nuts?" More archers, with arrows nocked, emerged from the cover of the trees. Their chance of escape evaporated.

Aria turned to her. "They glow with a golden light and mean us no harm."

"But they have arrows pointed at us." Sophy climbed to her feet and tried to position herself in front of Aria. Obviously, Aria was affected by their fall.

The stranger approached them, hands held out from his sides. He was tanned and well built. Sophy could also see his clothing in more detail. The collar of his white undershirt, embroidered and elegant, kissed the edge of his clean-shaven, squarish chin. At first he bowed from the waist, left hand sweeping before him and then he looked quizzically at them both. In a smooth and rich voice, he said, "Please move away from the Crystal Tree."

Aria gaped. "I'm not getting that." She turned to Sophy and raised her eyebrows.

Sophy had understood him and that made her frown. "He said to move away from the tree."

Holding on to Sophy's arm, Aria took a step in the direction the man indicated. Aria whispered, "How can you understand him?"

"Don't know, but perhaps we should do as he says before they decide to let those arrows fly." Sophy took another step away from the tree, bringing Aria with her. Angling her head over her shoulder, she checked the position of the archers. Arranged in a rough semi-circle, they had bland expressions, but there was no mistaking the tension in their hands as they held the arrows on the strings.

"What language is he speaking? It sounds familiar, but I can't seem to grasp it," Aria said.

Frowning, the young man kept his gaze on Aria's dropped leaf, glinting in the afternoon sun. He bent to pick it up, took a long step in their direction and placed it gently into Aria's hand. She didn't flinch or edge away and appeared quite comfortable with the stranger getting close to her. The men surrounding them shared looks and murmured. Sophy couldn't quite catch what they were saying.

"The Crystal Tree has gifted you with a leaf, my lady," he said, his gaze lingering on Aria.

"This?" Aria said, holding the delicate crystal leaf. "It's very beautiful." She smiled, then looked over her shoulder at Sophy. "I can understand him now." She lifted the leaf. "I was right. It's magical."

"Sure it is. Why are they pointing arrows at us?" Sophy glowered at the man. When his gaze met hers, his mouth tensed. She tried to fix her hair by hooking the loose strands behind her ears and refrained from scratching her neck. It didn't seem to help.

"Forgive me," he began, facing Aria. "My name is Dellbright. The Crystal Tree Woods are in my care, and the tree itself is sacred to us. It does not give gifts lightly."

"We didn't harm the tree," Aria said, smiling shyly. "I think it sang to us."

He nodded. "We heard. We do not often meet travellers in these woods. Have you travelled far?"

Aria smiled at him again. "Yes...er we don't know, actually."

Sophy moved forward to stand by Aria, ignoring as best she could the six archers with arrows clenched against their bowstrings.

"This is...Sophy and I'm called Aria... Where are we exactly?"

"You are near my home, Valley Keep," he said.

"Do you have a phone? We need to make a call," Sophy asked.

"A phone?" He shook his head. "No. I do not..." He chewed his lower lip, then as if remembering himself, he said, "Forgive me for being so discourteous, but I must ask you to accompany me."

Sophy heard one of the men behind her whisper. "There are two of them..."

When she swung round to look at who was talking, she met blank expressions. Turning back, she saw Dellbright take a gold chain from around his neck. "Please let me," he said, holding out his hand for Aria's leaf. He deftly attached the leaf to the chain. "May I?" he asked and, after Aria's nod, placed the chain around her neck.

"Thank you," Aria said.

His eyes, full of suspicion, moved to Sophy's face. He didn't ask if she had a leaf. Then again, she didn't want to say what happened to hers. She scarce believed it had happened and didn't expect anyone else would either.

"The archers are here because of the Puri raiders. Do not be alarmed."

"Raiders?" Sophy repeated, feeling dizzy. "What are they?"

"Nothing to worry about, I assure you," he said as they followed him out of the glade and into the forest. The archers disappeared into the surrounding trees. Sophy could only see one or two of them at any time, their presence enough to prevent escape.

The party continued walking, for perhaps an hour, when Dellbright stopped.

"Would you like to rest? You appear tired."

"Yes," Sophy said as she dropped to the grass.

"Can I get you some water to drink?" Dellbright asked.

"Thank you," Aria said breathily. "Water would be great, wouldn't it?"

Sophy nodded. Dellbright stared at the ground and took a few steps to the left. He knelt down and spoke.

Sophy's eyebrows shot up, and she looked over to Aria, who smiled as if the goings on around her were perfectly natural. Curious, Sophy climbed to her feet and followed Aria to stand near where Dellbright knelt. Water bubbled up from the ground like a playground tap. What the hell?

Dellbright glanced up, eyes crinkled with a smile. "Come closer and drink. The water is fresh and sweet."

Aria knelt, leaned over and drank deeply. "That's delicious. Thank you."

Sophy leaned over, her lips tracking the water as it slid back into the ground. She pulled up short of the grass and frowned. Dellbright's mouth hung open, and his cheeks grew pink. "I do not understand. I have never seen it act this way before. Please, I will call it again."

And he did, but as soon as she drew closer, it fell away. Her proximity to the water was driving her crazy. The suspicious look Dellbright gave her didn't help. After three more tries, and Dellbright's increasingly sour expression, Aria asked if she could look in Sophy's shoulder bag. Aria took the cap off a deodorant spray and rinsed it before filling it and handing it to her.

Sophy drank deeply, having the cap refilled many times before quenching her thirst. The water receded into the ground, with only a small damp patch of earth to evidence its existence. Fixing her eyes on Dellbright, she asked, "How did you do that?"

"I asked and it was *given*."

"*Given?* What is *given?*" Aria asked.

Dellbright turned toward Aria. "You do not know of the *given?*" His gaze shifted between their blank faces. "Argenterra is famous for its *given*, bounty and craft."

Aria said. "Won't you tell us about them?"

Sophy sat down on the ground and groaned with her head in her hands. Argenterra! A bloody nutter! This was taking the whole ghost tour thing way too far.

"Are you all right?" Aria asked, squatting beside her.

She threw her head back and glared at them both. "I'm fine. What is wrong with you?"

Aria leaned back and replied, "I feel perfectly well." Then turning her attention back to Dellbright, she said, "Please, tell us."

"Very well. The water was *given*. Bounty is for taking and Craft is what we make with our hands."

Aria drew her curls behind her ears. "I'm not sure what you mean, are your clothes *given*, bounty or craft?"

He looked aghast. "My clothes are craft, of course, but of the very basic craft, I assure you." Gesturing to the trees, he stood up. "Fruit on the trees is bounty. It can be plucked. However, if it is not the season for fruit, the *given* will ripen it. Such is the way of a traveller who finds himself without sustenance. If he asks, Argenterra will give it to him."

He stopped for a moment as if thinking of a better way to explain. Then he walked to a bush that was full of green leaves and small closed buds. "The water was *given*, but it was there under the ground. I only asked it to come to the surface, thus not so difficult. This bush has the possibility of a flower." He spoke quietly to the bush and stroked it leaves. The bud grew and opened to a beautiful, green-petalled flower, which he handed to Aria.

When his eyes fell upon Sophy again, the smile in them died. "Let us continue on," he said blandly and marched ahead, stopping to make sure Aria was following.

Sophy kept opening and closing her mouth. The land? Bounty? Was everyone but her crazy? She raced after them. Two archers flanked her, giving each other hand signals.

"So, Dellbright, are you some kind of magician?"

He turned back to her. "All who live in this land may ask and it will be *given*. Wait, I think I know what you are asking. Do you mean am I an adept?"

Sophy nodded, she thought that's what she meant.

"No, alas, I am not an adept. The adepts are recluses who study the mysteries of the land. They have spent many hundreds of years studying them, including the *given*."

He continued walking, eyes constantly straying to Aria. Sophy chewed her lips and tugged on her hair. There was too much to process, too much to deal with. Her heart beat a little faster, and she tried to quiet her anxiety, until a couple of archers leapt out of the trees and startled her.

Argenterra and the rest of the Silverlands are available in ebook and print.

www.ingramcontent.com/pod-product-compliance
Lightning Source LLC
Chambersburg PA
CBHW021419110726
47901CB00008B/2222